SHADOW WORLD

SHADOW WORLD
A Dragon Born Trilogy

www.ellasummers.com/shadow-world

ISBN 978-1-5410-0975-2

Copyright © 2016 by Ella Summers

All rights reserved.

SHADOW WORLD
A Dragon Born Trilogy

Ella Summers

Books by Ella Summers

Dragon Born Shadow World
A Dragon Born Trilogy

Dragon Born Serafina
1. Mercenary Magic
2. Magic Games
3. Magic Nights
4. Rival Magic

Dragon Born Alexandria
1. Magic Edge
2. Blood Magic
3. Magic Kingdom
4. Shadow Magic [2017]

Dragon Born Awakening
1. Fairy Magic
2. Spirit Magic [2017]

Legion of Angels
1. Vampire's Kiss
2. Witch's Cauldron
3. Siren's Song
4. Dragon's Storm

More Books by Ella Summers

Sorcery & Science
Coming soon…

Read more at
www.ellasummers.com

Book 1: Magic Eclipse

PROLOGUE
Prologue / 2

CHAPTER ONE
Dark Days / 13

CHAPTER TWO
Rifts of Magic / 23

CHAPTER THREE
Family / 28

CHAPTER FOUR
The Dragon Commander / 42

CHAPTER FIVE
Date with the Dragon / 50

CHAPTER SIX
War of Magic / 58

CHAPTER SEVEN
Between Realms / 65

CHAPTER EIGHT
The Pier of Tears / 79

CHAPTER NINE
The Spirit Warrior / 89

CHAPTER TEN
The World That Was / 99

CHAPTER ELEVEN
Ghost Town / 110

CHAPTER TWELVE
The Enemy's Fortress / 118

CHAPTER THIRTEEN
The First Day of a New World / 125

CHAPTER FOURTEEN
Here Be Dragons / 132

CHAPTER FIFTEEN
The Winds of Fury / 147

CHAPTER SIXTEEN
A Hell Like No Other / 153

CHAPTER SEVENTEEN
The Forsaken District / 162

CHAPTER EIGHTEEN
Of Beasts and Men / 179

CHAPTER NINETEEN
Memories of a Lost World / 193

CHAPTER TWENTY
Breaking Minds / 200

CHAPTER TWENTY-ONE
Fallen Alliances / 218

CHAPTER TWENTY-TWO
Shifting Magic / 224

CHAPTER TWENTY-THREE
A Storm of Spells / 234

EPILOGUE
Epilogue / 242

Book 2: Midnight Magic

CHAPTER ONE
Wicked Wasteland / 246

CHAPTER TWO
The Demon's Domain / 259

CHAPTER THREE
The Beast / 271

CHAPTER FOUR
Alone / 278

CHAPTER FIVE
Witch Burning / 289

CHAPTER SIX
City of Shadows / 303

CHAPTER SEVEN
When Evil Clashed / 315

CHAPTER EIGHT
The Game / 330

CHAPTER NINE
The Witch Slayer / 340

CHAPTER TEN
The Huntsman / 350

CHAPTER ELEVEN
Secret Garden / 359

CHAPTER TWELVE
Dark Impulses / 372

CHAPTER THIRTEEN
The Seven Deadly Sins / 380

CHAPTER FOURTEEN
Stuck in Time / 390

CHAPTER FIFTEEN
Between Two Worlds / 399

CHAPTER SIXTEEN
Unbreakable / 406

CHAPTER SEVENTEEN
Fortress / 414

CHAPTER EIGHTEEN
Twin Souls / 429

CHAPTER NINETEEN
Midnight Magic / 439

Book 3: Magic Storm

CHAPTER ONE
The Castle / 452

CHAPTER TWO
Battle Dragon / 463

CHAPTER THREE
Allies and Enemies / 470

CHAPTER FOUR
Magic Storm / 479

CHAPTER FIVE
Slayer / 488

CHAPTER SIX
The Shadow Mage / 497

CHAPTER SEVEN
Dinner in the Demon's Den / 507

CHAPTER EIGHT
Mirror, Mirror / 517

CHAPTER NINE
Spirit Magic / 530

CHAPTER TEN
Demon-touched / 544

CHAPTER ELEVEN
The Chamber of Wonders / 556

CHAPTER TWELVE
Sacrifice / 563

CHAPTER THIRTEEN
Love and Poison / 570

CHAPTER FOURTEEN
The Laws of Magic / 575

CHAPTER FIFTEEN
The Gift / 582

CHAPTER SIXTEEN
Dragon Born Legacy / 588

CHAPTER SEVENTEEN
A New Beginning / 596

BOOK ONE
Magic Eclipse

Prologue

THE FAIRY QUEEN was packed that Saturday afternoon, not surprising considering it was the best dress shop in all of San Francisco. The bundle of tiny silver bells over the door jingled, signaling new arrivals: a pair of combat mages, dressed in leather and denim and armed to the teeth with enough steel to make even a former monster-hunting mercenary like Sera gawk at the ostentatiousness of it all. As they stepped inside, she reached automatically for her sword—but she dropped her hand the moment they turned toward the rack of dresses on summer clearance. It appeared they were just regular shoppers after all.

"I'll take the one on the left," Lara told Sera, her head peeking over the rack of white wedding dresses she'd been browsing. "You go for the one on the right. She's giving those sundresses a shifty look."

"Sorry," Sera said. "I thought they might be assassins."

"I don't think anyone is crazy enough to come after the mage who defeated the Grim Reaper."

Maybe Lara was right. In the past few weeks, no one had made a move against Sera, even though the whole world knew by now precisely what she was. Whether they were afraid of her or simply afraid of Kai she didn't know. But she couldn't just let her guard down. The supernatural world considered her an abomination. Sooner or later, someone crazy enough would come along and try to grant her an early grave. There were more than a few members of the Magic Council who were still sour about the fact that they weren't allowed to kill her—at least not if they didn't want her dragon-shifting fiancé to step on them.

"I'll watch the door," Lara said. "You concentrate on your assigned mission." She held up the only scarlet wedding dress amongst a sea of white fabric.

"I don't know. It's a bit ostentatious, don't you think?" Sera fingered the stitching on the dress's high thigh slits. Well, at least she could kick in that skirt.

"My brother shifts into a twenty ton dragon. He *loves* ostentatious." Lara waved the dress in front of Sera. "Try it on. You know you want to."

"I think I stand out enough already."

"Well, you won't be wearing that big sword on your wedding day."

"No sword? I was thinking it would make a great accessory." Sera smirked at her.

"It's a good thing you're not planning the wedding."

"Afraid I'd scandalize your parents?"

Kai and Lara hailed from one of the supernatural

community's oldest and most powerful magic dynasties. The Drachenburgs owned the world's largest magical research company and had a seat on the Magic Council, the organization that ruled the supernatural world. And along with all that power and prestige came a generous helping of age-old traditions. That was just part of being one of the magical elite. If someone had told Sera just a year ago that she would be marrying into one of these dynasties, she'd have laughed in their face.

And yet here she was.

"You're the woman who finally got my brother to settle down, the one who tamed the dragon. The perfect son." Lara rolled her eyes with sisterly affection.

Sera snorted.

"Of course our parents adore you," Lara continued. "They never thought Kai would marry. Like *ever*."

Luckily, the Drachenburgs didn't have a problem with her unusual magic. And they were refusing to let anyone else have a problem with it either. Sera had never had anyone except her own family look out for her like that, but Kai's family was. That meant a lot. There weren't many people who would stick out their neck for a Dragon Born mage.

Long ago, the Dragon Born had been respected, worshipped even. But the supernatural community had turned against them the day they'd learned that the Dragon Born weren't dragons but instead people with a split persona: a mage side and a dragon side. Sera's dragon was a part of her, but during battle she could break away from her, taking corporeal form to fight alongside her.

After the Magic Council had made that little discovery seven centuries ago, they'd labeled the Dragon Born abominations and had hunted them to near extinction. The only Dragon Born mages who'd survived had done so by hiding what they were.

The stupid thing about all of this was the Magic Council considered the other two kinds of dragon magic—mages who could shift into dragons like Kai, and mages who could summon strands of brilliant magic and bind them together into the form of a dragon—as the epitome of all magic. Dragon shifters and dragon summoners were the top of the top, their futures forever secure in the mage hierarchy.

And yet everyone continued to hate the Dragon Born, all because a few of Sera's kind had once decided it would be funny to convince the supernatural community to worship them. It probably hadn't taken much convincing either, likely nothing more than landing in the middle of their village. A full-grown dragon was an impressive sight to behold.

"Are you all right?" Lara asked Sera, her smooth forehead crinkling with concern.

"Fine," Sera assured her with a smile, shaking aside the worried thoughts buzzing around inside of her head. She couldn't spend every waking hour worrying about what the Council would or wouldn't do. She had to live life. "And I think that I will try that dress on."

Lara's mouth lifted into a smile as Sera took the scarlet dress from her and headed for the dressing rooms at the back. Maybe she really should wear red at her wedding. The color looked good on her, and wasn't that what the wedding was all about: her and Kai? Not the bureaucracy. Not the hurdles.

You break down hurdles, her dragon Amara commented inside her head.

Sera chuckled, leaning her sword against the wall. *True.* She set her boots down beside it. *But I think we have to play this song and dance for just a little longer. We have to give the Drachenburgs the wedding they've been waiting for.*

Plus, you want to wear a pretty dress, Amara said.

Pu-lease. I'll have you know that I'm a kick-ass mercenary. She tossed her clothes into the corner.

Former mercenary. You work for Kai now.

I thought you approved of my decision.

I do. The monsters are more interesting, and the pay doesn't suck. Kai isn't an insufferable penny-pincher like your last boss. And there are other benefits.

Like my own armory closet, Sera said, beaming.

And nookie with the boss.

You have the maturity of a twelve-year-old. You know that, right?

I'm a part of you. I'm only as mature as you are, Amara told her.

Sera couldn't argue with that, so she looked at the dress. *Over or under?*

Under, Amara told her, projecting an impish smirk into her head. *You wouldn't want to mess up your hair.*

Before coming to the Fairy Queen, Sera had spent three hours sitting on her rear end at a hair salon. Lara had made the hairdresser try out a dozen different elaborate styles before they'd finally settled on one.

Sera wasn't sure who had suffered more, she or the hairdresser. But of one thing she was absolutely positive: this is why so many people eloped.

She wished she could just bolt out of here and go find Kai. Then the two of them would go back to their apartment to eat pizza and laugh over cheesy action movies as magic flames burned peacefully in the fireplace. From the day they'd met, they'd had to deal with one crisis after the other. But now they had some time to rest, to enjoy things. They should be spending it together. Who knew how long they'd have before the world went to hell again.

Sera had just finished zipping up the dress when her jeans buzzed. She reached down, digging through her pocket until she found her phone. Kai's name shone on the screen, as though he'd read her thoughts. As though he'd known she was thinking about him.

She grinned and answered the call. "Hey."

"Hey."

"So, what's up?" she asked, turning to get a better look at herself in the mirror.

The skirt of the dress kissed the floor, the fabric folds hiding the side slits nicely—but they were still there, just in case monsters crashed the wedding. Geez, what was wrong with her? She shouldn't be thinking about monsters crashing her wedding.

"I just got out of a meeting," Kai said.

"On a Saturday? They don't give you a break."

"The world does not stop because it's the weekend."

Especially, not if you were running a multi-billion dollar company. Or fighting evil supernatural masterminds.

"What was it this time?" she asked. "Researchers fighting over growing plots for their plants? Escaped wildebeests? Kitten with a sprained ankle?"

The phone line buzzed softly with his laughter. "One of these days, that smart mouth is going to get you into trouble."

"Too late. It already attracted your attention."

"Yes, it has," he replied, his words dripping with satisfaction. "I'm finished here. What do you say we go train your magic for a few hours?"

Sera had spent years hiding her magic—a consequence of wanting to stay alive when the punishment for her existence was death—so she was still getting the hang of it. Kai was helping her. Training with him was brutal because he didn't hold back, no matter how much he liked you. She often ended their training sessions with more than a few scrapes and bruises—or even broken bones. But it was making her stronger.

Kai was a firm believer of the 'what doesn't kill you only makes you stronger' philosophy. She'd once had the line printed on one of the muscle t-shirts he liked so much.

"Training, you say?" she replied. "Tempting."

"I'll buy you pizza afterwards."

"Wizard House Pizza?"

"Of course," he said immediately.

It was no wonder he was such a successful businessman. He knew everyone's weakness. And pizza was hers.

"Now you're just making it impossible for me to

refuse," she told him.

"Then don't."

"Kai, I wish I could, but I'm busy for the next…" Week? Month? Who knew how much more wedding stuff Lara had planned for her. "Busy until tonight." If Lara wasn't done with her by then, Sera was abandoning ship.

"What are you doing?" He said it perfectly casually.

"Trying on wedding dresses with Lara at the Fairy Queen."

At that, he laughed out loud. "Try not to sound like you're being tortured."

"It *is* torture. She's making me try on everything. After awhile, the dresses all start to look the same."

"You've defeated demons and Grim Reapers and basically every monster on this earth, Sera," he said. "You can handle my twenty-two-year-old sister."

"It was only *one* demon and *one* Grim Reaper. And your sister is freakishly stubborn." Sera grinned. "She must get that from you."

"Indeed." He chuckled. "I can be there in ten minutes."

"You want to try on dresses?" she teased.

"No, I want to help you try them on. And take them off," he added, his words loaded with suggestion.

"Kai, I'm not making out with you in Nelly's changing room. She would kill me."

"Who said anything about making out?" He clicked his tongue. "You need to get your mind out of the gutter, sweetheart."

"Come say that to my face, dragon," she shot back.

"Thank you for the invitation. I believe that I will."

"Wait, stop," she said quickly, backpedaling out of the hole she'd just dug for herself. "Lara says the dress has to be a surprise. She doesn't want you to come."

"But *you* do. And you just invited me. See you soon." Then he hung up, the devious dragon.

Sighing, Sera stepped out of the dressing room, her skirt swaying gracefully as she crossed the floor. Lara's hazel eyes lit up the moment she saw her.

"Perfect," she told Sera, wiggling her pink-tipped fingernails. The color perfectly matched the flowers on her yellow sundress. "That's the one."

Sera stood inside the circle of mirrors, turning around. The dress was beautiful. There was no denying that.

"So," Sera began as Lara walked around her, brushing down the wrinkles in the dress. "Kai is coming here."

Lara froze. "Damn it, Sera. I told you not to invite him. This is top secret."

"Come on. We're not infiltrating an enemy stronghold. It's a wedding. Shouldn't the groom get to see the dress too?"

"He'll see it when you walk down the aisle," Lara replied stubbornly.

"Well, actually, he'll see it in about ten minutes. Less than that if he ignores the rules of the road." Which he probably would. Kai believed the rules were only for people without supernatural response times and the ability to magically nudge other vehicles out of the way.

As instantly as she'd stopped, Lara was moving

again, shoving Sera back toward the changing room. "Not if I can help it. Hurry. Get changed out of the dress before he gets here."

Sera was about to argue about the utter ridiculousness of this all when dark shadows fell over the shop, like someone had taken out the sun. Sera slipped past Lara, hurrying toward the shop's large glass windows to peer outside at an eclipsed sun.

But it wasn't just any eclipse. The moon in front of it looked strange, like it was doubled. Like one was a shadow of the other.

"This isn't right," Sera commented.

Weird magic was brewing, building up to something. She could feel it in the air. In her blood.

A shrill note sang out, piercing the cold silence. Magic erupted, a wave of unfathomable energy tearing down the street. Buildings shattered, one after the other, the cacophony of magic swallowing the screams of everyone caught in its wake, silencing them.

The shock wave was almost to the Fairy Queen. Sera didn't stop to think. There wasn't time for reason, only action. She tackled Lara to the ground, covering Kai's sister with her body as the shop's windows exploded, raining glass down upon them.

Magic rippled through her, swirling inside her mind. Images flashed through her head, images of herself doing things she'd never done, of a world that never was. She saw her city torn apart by strife. She saw herself and Kai on opposite sides of a war, fighting each other—hating each other.

No!

It's not real, Amara said.

It can't be. Sera pushed against the wave of images flooding her mind, drowning her. One by one, her own memories began to fade out, replaced by a life not her own. She fought against this dark magic.

And she lost.

Kai, I will find you. They can't keep us apart, she promised, her tears mixing with her fading memories as the new, cruel world consumed her.

1. Dark Days

SERA ROSE TO her feet, brushing dry dirt from her leather jacket. The building hadn't been in good shape before she'd gone inside, and that explosion sure hadn't helped with its structural integrity. Thick dust snowed down from the ceiling, replacing the dirt she'd just removed from her clothing.

"Great," she muttered, brushing it off again.

A loud, ominous groan answered her protest. Sera stared up into the rafters. There weren't any monsters up there. She'd done a full magic sweep before entering the building. She hadn't felt anything then, and she didn't feel anything now either. That meant it was just the good old collapsing building scenario.

She'd had to deal with her fair share of those in the six years since the Magic Council had come to San Francisco, bringing their Crusade against the Dragon Born with them. The city had been pleasant before then, peaceful but for a few monsters here and there, nothing Sera and the city's other mercenaries couldn't handle.

Before the dark days had come to her city, Sera had heard about the war, about the Crusaders, but it had all felt so distant. So unreal. Until they were here, they and their campaign of death. Their ultimate goal was the extermination of every Dragon Born mage in the world—and they weren't wasting any time getting to it.

Maybe the Crusaders had been the ones to plant the magic bomb in this building. They'd been setting booby traps like that lately. They knew the Dragon Born came to this area. Maybe they even knew why. Sera looked around for the delivery she'd come to pick up from one of her suppliers—a box of healing medicine—but she didn't see it anywhere. It had probably been buried in the explosion. She'd have to dig through the dust and debris to find it.

The question was where to begin. The place looked awful, even by post-apocalyptic San Francisco standards. The plaster had broken off the walls, exposing the splintered wood beams below. The floor was littered with the remnants of the walls—and whatever had come down from the ceiling. And the magic…yuck. It tasted like someone had mixed hell and earth together inside of a blender and dialed it up to the highest setting—forgetting to put the lid on, so it splashed and spewed in every direction, drenching the world in a cocktail of chaos.

This wasn't like any magic bomb Sera had ever seen. The Crusaders must be developing new ones. As though they didn't already have everything on their side in this war.

Sera continued her sweep of the building, pausing when her gaze snagged on the sight of an unconscious woman on the floor. Her long red hair feathered either side of her pale face. God, she looked young. She couldn't have been much older than twenty. So what was she doing sleeping inside an old building in the city's Forsaken District?

And what was she wearing? A yellow and pink sundress? The dress's colors were too bright, its style too carefree, as though it belonged to a different time. To a more peaceful era. It sure didn't look like it had come from anywhere around here. It was pristine except for a few fresh smudges of dirt, probably made when the explosion had thrown her to the ground.

Sera hadn't worn a dress in years, not since the war had come to San Francisco—and along with it, the monsters. Bright colors were a death sentence here. All the beastly nasties were attracted to their vibrant sheen. And wearing pastels allowed Crusader patrols to pick you off from a distance. To survive, you had to blend into the shadows.

Sera looked from the girl's yellow dress to her own dark outfit. Where had this girl come from? No one had been inside of this building when Sera had probed it with her magic before entering. Before the explosion. This was weird.

Magic shifted outside. Someone was out there. Three someones. They'd done their best to mask their movements, but they couldn't hide the pulse of their magic—or the effect it had on all the magic around them, like ripples on a lake. The ripples always gave them away.

"We know you're in there, Dragon Born," one of them announced. Crisp and clean, the voice belonged to a man who was one-hundred percent soldier.

Sera didn't answer. There was no reason to give her position away.

"Come out with your hands up where we can see them," the Crusader spoke again. "No tricks and no magic, or we'll drop this building on your head."

Sera sighed. Crusader patrols. They'd come here to find her. Apparently, she'd been right about the explosion. It had been a trap.

She didn't want to fight them. Before the war had come here, she'd worked as a monster-hunting mercenary. She'd killed monsters, not people. She didn't enjoy killing people, but she couldn't show these Crusaders that. She couldn't let her facade crack, not even for a moment. They were trained to take advantage of any sign of weakness—and to not feel bad about it. The Crusaders had no qualms about killing her. After all, to them she was an abomination. A monster. According to their mantra, she wasn't even a person.

Sera walked toward the exit, priming her magic.

"Stand down, Dragon Born," the Crusader said. "I can feel you charging up those substantial elemental batteries of yours."

Damn it. They had a Sniffer, a mage who could detect magic like she could. She inhaled the potpourri of magical scents in the air. No, not a Sniffer. A Seer. Which meant that he could not only sense her magic; he also could see her. He could watch every step that she took. She wouldn't be catching them by surprise today.

Surprise was overrated. Sera had raw power on her side. Well, as long as the Crusaders didn't have any bombs or other surprises up their sleeves. From what she could sense of the magic in the air, the three men were equipped with the standard issue accessories carried by all Crusader patrols. A few elemental magic grenades. Whips enchanted with telekinetic magic to fling her at buildings. Damn, she hated those. They stung like hell, and the feeling of her spine being ground against stone wasn't particularly pleasant either.

The only other bottled magic the Crusaders were packing were a few healing potions. Not that they needed them. They had a healer with them. A healer who could also cast defensive spells. Sera would have to take him out first, or he'd protect and heal his two teammates while they pounded her with magic.

Sera had reached the door. As she passed outside, she gave the Crusaders standing there a thorough once-over. Tall, muscular, and appropriately badass in their fitted black battle leather, the three men fit the Crusader mold perfectly. A kill squad. The Magic Council wasn't fooling around.

The Seer, the one who'd been speaking to Sera, stood between the other two. He was the group's clear leader. To his right was an elemental mage, a blond pretty boy. But from the hum of his magic, he wasn't all looks. He was a first tier elemental, which meant it would hurt like hell when his magic hit her. She'd just have to bear the elemental storm long enough to get to the healer. That was the man to the Seer's right. He'd already cast a protective spell between them and her. A one-way spell. Meaning their magic could go through, but hers could not. Now that was just downright rude. And smart.

"Well, look who we've caught today, guys." The Seer grinned at Sera. "Serafina Dering."

He waved to the other two, a subtle motion—but not subtle enough. Sera didn't have to see his hands to feel the motions of his magic. It surged with the force of a conductor. Ice-tipped lightning sizzled on the elemental's fingers, its rhythm as devilish as its caster's smile. The healer stood by, his magic alert.

"My friends call me Sera." She gave them a hard smile, punching her magic through the defensive barrier. It split apart, dissolving into the wind. "You may call me the Mistress of Mayhem." She cast a wall of fire in front of the Seer, blocking him as he tried to pass behind her.

He gave her an irked look.

"Mistress of Mayhem?" The elemental laughed. "Is that name supposed to scare us?" His magic was storming inside of him, building toward an explosive release.

"I don't care how you feel, as long as you put away your magic and surrender," she told him.

Rather than listen to reason, however, the elemental unleashed his spell. A wave of icy lightning tore toward Sera with the force of a winter storm. It raged and roared, its song chilling her to her core.

Sera pulled her fire wall forward to swallow his spell. Magic sizzled and spat. The storm of colliding elements sent out a shock wave that pushed the

Crusaders back.

"I'm only going to ask you once, boys," Sera said. "Surrender."

A fireball flared to life on the elemental's hand. "You're not in any position to make demands. We've got you outnumbered three-to-one, peaches."

Sera puckered up her lips and blew him a kiss. "If you surrender now, I promise to go easy on you."

"She's as crazy as they say she is," the elemental told the Seer, grinning. He launched his fireball at Sera.

At the same time, the Seer swung his sword at her. She lifted her sword, their blades clashing as the fireball rushed toward her. She reached for her ice magic, sending a layer of silver frost down her blade. As her spell spread to his sword, the Seer jumped back, disengaging.

"I might be crazy," Sera said loudly. "But I'm not deaf."

She spun around, catching the stream of fire in her icy grasp. The fireball froze mid-air, then dropped, shattering when it hit the ground.

"And didn't anyone ever tell you how rude it is to speak about someone as though they're not there?" She clicked her tongue with disapproval.

A fist swung at the back of her head. Sera's only warning was the crisp clash of magic cutting through the air. She sidestepped to avoid the healer's punch, twisting his fist behind his back as he surged forward. She gave him a hard kick to the butt to send him along his way.

"Honestly, boys." She shook her head at them. "I'd

expected better manners from Drachenburg's minions, what with how he's always pretending to be civilized and all."

"Minions?" the elemental repeated, his blond brows arching.

The healer righted his tumble before he hit the ground. He swung around, smiling at Sera. "I like her." He waved his hand, casting a protective spell on the Seer's blade. The frost stopped spreading, then shattered. Icy residue crumbled to the ground.

"Don't get too attached, Dal," the Seer said.

He moved in to attack, his blade now protected from her magic. No matter. She'd just do this the old-fashioned way.

"The boss will never let us keep her," the Seer declared as his blade clashed with Sera's. "Even though we *really* could use a monster exterminator to throw at that giant rat infestation in Sector 8." He grimaced. It was a very professional, very polished grimace. This was the sort of gentleman who would knock you hard on your ass, then wish you a pleasant day.

"You're right." The elemental sighed. "The boss would never let us keep her." He lifted his hand, blowing Sera's fire barrier to smithereens. His path clear, he moved behind her. "And if we don't find someone to take care of those rats, you know he's going to make *us* go out there eventually."

Sera had a feeling that they weren't taking this fight seriously. "Do all Crusaders chitchat so much?" she demanded, blocking the Seer's strike as she shot a blast of wind magic over her shoulder.

Unfortunately, the shifty elemental ducked.

The healer smiled at her. "I thought you liked chatting."

"It's your thing," the Seer agreed.

"I don't have a *thing*."

"Sure you do," the elemental countered. "Everyone has a thing. And yours, Serafina Dering, is that smart mouth of yours."

"You wave that big sword around and snark off, distracting your opponents."

"And psyching yourself up for the fight."

"You are surprisingly observant for minions," she growled at them.

The healer flashed his perfect white smile at her. "Well, we aren't just any minions."

"No, I'm beginning to see that you're not. Commandos then."

"Commandos, huh?" the Seer asked. "It has a nice ring to it."

She sent out a shock wave of magic, a hard-hitting spell cast for a single purpose: to break magic. It was called Magic Breaker, and it was an exclusively Dragon Born spell. It tore through the healer's barriers. The impact of clashing magic hurled the Crusaders to the ground.

"Yes, commandos," Sera said, stepping over their spasming bodies. "It really does have a nice ring to it."

She looked down at them. Their spasms had died down to a slight twitch. They were already trying to get to their feet. Unfortunately for them, it wasn't working out all that well. Her spell had broken every strand of magic coursing through their bodies. It took most people more than a few moments to recover from that.

They seemed like nice guys—well, nice for Crusaders anyway. They hadn't brought the building down on her while she'd still been inside. So they had some sense of honor. But they were still Crusaders. It was her duty to kill them. If the Council won this war, every Dragon Born mage would be put to death. An icy fear coiled in her stomach, strengthening her resolve.

Sera lifted her sword. The street was quiet, the eerie stillness chilling. Then a deep howl broke the silence. Sera turned to see a behemoth monster charging down the street—and it was headed right for her.

2. Rifts of Magic

THE BEAST LOOKED like a behemoth wolf—as big as a bus—with spiky silver fur, long raking claws, and paws as large as Sera's head. Red eyes glowed out from the shadows cast over its face. As it bounded forward, the ground shook, and shards of loose pavement split off, shooting in every direction.

"One of your pets?" Sera asked the commandos as they got to their feet.

The Seer shook his head, blinking down hard, trying to shake off the lingering effects of her spell. "No."

"It's not yours?" the elemental asked her.

"No. I prefer scales to fur."

The commandos laughed, and Sera grinned at them. You had to love a man—or three—who could laugh in the face of danger.

The wolf came to a stop a few steps from them. Its unearthly eyes panned across them, settling on Sera. It seemed to be sizing them up, assessing them. The beast snorted, and smoke burst out of its nose. It began to scrape its paws against the ground, like it had decided they weren't above it on the food chain after all. And now it was going to eat them.

When the war had come to San Francisco, it brought monsters with it. They were drawn to conflict, to the rifts of warring magic. And both sides had been so busy fighting each other that they hadn't been able to exterminate the monsters fast enough. The monsters in the city were getting cockier, bolder. Surely, this one must have smelled the dragon magic on her, and it didn't care. It didn't think she was a match for it. Well, she was going to show it just how wrong it was.

Sera glanced sidelong at the Seer, but she didn't take her attention off the beast. "We should take it together before it does more damage to the area—or kills someone."

He nodded. "Agreed."

"Kai won't like it when he hears we worked with the enemy," the elemental said.

"You think Kai would want a monster to go free to kill and terrorize the city?" the healer asked. "To slaughter the innocent. To bathe in their blood and wear their bones as trophies."

"Wow, Dal. Gruesome much? But you do have a point." The elemental looked at Sera. "Ok, how do you want to do this?"

She grinned at them. "You three distract the beast while I kill it."

Then she ran off to the sound of their indignant protests. The beast was already charging forward, the stench of its body flooding her nose, the pulse of its gurgling, crackling, twice-burnt magic smacking against her senses. Swallowing the rising acid in her throat, Sera darted straight at the wolf, rolling under its swiping paw to get up in its face. She blasted it in the eyes with a fire spell. Then, as the beast scratched at its face, she cast a gust of wind to carry her up onto its back. She sank her sword into its neck. The beast roared, trying to buck her off.

Down on the ground, the commandos were hitting the beast hard. The elemental blasted it with a continuous chain of spells, while the healer and the Seer hacked at it mercilessly with their swords. The beast lurched in wild staggering bursts, swiping its massive claws at them. Acid spat out of its mouth, pouring down in glowing green globs. As it stomped about, earthquakes split the ground beneath its paws. The nearby buildings trembled and shook.

Sera dashed across its back, making crisp, efficient cuts with her sword. The beast roared, and the shock wave of sound and magic hurled the commandos clear across the street. Their backs slammed hard into a building. Bricks erupted from the wall, crashing down all around them.

Free of the commandos, the beast was turning its head, its jaw snapping at Sera as its claws tried to knock her away. She kicked off its paw, using its upward swipe to launch herself into the air. Soaring high, she cast fire across her sword. As she came down, she drove her flaming blade right through its head. Bone crunched, fire sizzled, and the monster collapsed to the ground, dead.

Sera jumped off the wolf, landing in front of the commandos. The Seer struggled to his feet, his steps staggered with dizziness. He didn't look so great. His clothes were slashed apart, his skin was marked with acid burns, and his head was oozing blood. The elemental, who didn't look any better, stumbled to his feet too. He limped toward the Seer, supporting the unconscious healer.

Sera met the Seer's eyes. "Go."

She could tell he didn't want to fight her. Their magic was tapped, their bodies falling apart. They wouldn't survive a fight with her in this state, not for two seconds. And he knew it.

"Get yourselves healed," she told him.

He dipped his chin to her.

"We're letting a Dragon Born go?" the elemental asked.

"Actually, she is letting us go. Right now, we're in no position to do anything. And she is in every position to kill us."

"Yeah, I guess you're right." The elemental lifted the healer over his shoulder.

The commandos and Sera exchanged looks, and she saw a spark of respect shining in their eyes. They didn't hate her. They never had. Yet they were still fighting on the other side of this war.

She didn't hate them either. She didn't hate any of them. But she was fighting too. This was all so messed up.

The Seer extended his hand. "I'm Tony." He nodded at the elemental. "That's Callum." He indicated their healer. "And Dal."

She allowed the emerging smirk to touch her lips. "You'll always be commandos to me."

Laughing, they limped off, probably to their nearest safe house.

Sera watched them go, then went back into the bombed building. She didn't think those guys had bombed it. But then who had?

She dug her medicine supply package out of the debris and tucked it into her jacket. Once more, her eyes fell upon the girl in the yellow sundress. She was still lying there, still unconscious.

A chorus of howling monsters sang out in the distance. The sun had set. It would soon be night, and then they'd all come out. They'd flood the Forsaken District, killing anyone trapped inside. She had to get back to base before that. And this girl…she was so young, no older than Sera's brother. Riley should have had a normal life, but this war had ruined any chance of that for him. For all of them, this girl included. Sera couldn't leave her here to be eaten by monsters. She didn't know who she was, but she just couldn't leave her to that fate.

Sera picked her up, swinging her over her shoulder. As she headed back toward the Dragon Born base, shadows shifted all around her, the air thickening. She picked up the pace, trying to outpace the odd fog rolling across the street. Strange magic was brewing. She could feel it with every fiber of her being. The question was what would happen when that magic finally hit.

3. Family

THE SAN FRANCISCO Dragon Born base was located behind the massive wall that surrounded Golden Gate Park, the core of Dragon Born territory. The buildings of the base were scattered throughout the park, housing the Dragon Born mages and their allies. Thousands of supernaturals lived here—but their numbers paled in comparison to the Magic Council's Crusader forces who held the nearby Presidio.

As Sera carried the sundress girl through the main gate, she gave the two Dragon Guard fairies posted there a friendly nod. Then she walked down the overgrown path toward Building 1. Nowadays, they were all too busy to worry about weeds, so the spiky plants had grown out of control, in some places nearly reaching Sera's knees. One of these days, she was going to clear a path with her sword.

Building 1, like the other buildings on base, wasn't

a marvel of architecture. When the Crusaders had come to the city, the Dragon Born forces had scrambled to fortify the park's borders. Most of their efforts had been focused on the wall—and the protective barrier overhead that warded off aerial attacks. The ugly box houses had been built quickly, which certainly showed. They looked more like enormous crates than houses.

"Sera," the Dragon Guard captain said, closing into step beside her as she entered the building. "The patrols on the east side haven't returned."

"How late are they?" she asked.

"About an hour. They called in about some fog they were checking out, and we haven't heard from them since."

"Now that the sun has set for the day, the monsters are starting to come out. It's no time to go chasing after fog."

"They said the fog felt odd. Magical."

Something the Crusaders had made? "I saw it just now too. There's something wrong with that fog. Something unnatural," she agreed, biting her lip. "Send out our best trackers with a full guard. Tell them to track down our missing patrol but stay clear of that fog. Until we know more about it, no one is to go near it."

The Dragon Guard captain nodded, then turned and walked off toward the guard room. Sera made a quick stop at her glorious lodging place, a two-room apartment that she shared with her sister Alex. One room held their beds. The other was her office. The base didn't have much space for indulgences.

Sera handcuffed the sundress girl to her desk—she would have to figure out what to do with her later—then she headed down to the armory. There was a magic side and a mundane side. Her brother Riley stood behind the desk on the magic side, mixing up elemental bombs. This batch was lightning-charged. He dripped a few drops of golden liquid into a vial. It mixed with the liquid inside, swirling like a sky of thunderclouds. Magic crackled across Sera's senses like a bolt of lightning.

"That one's potent," she commented to her brother.

"They have to be potent. Some of the Crusaders are wearing magic-resilient armor," Riley replied, his green eyes looking up at her. His face was bruised, his skin marked by scratches.

Sera frowned at him. "You went treasure hunting again, didn't you?"

He remained silent. Yeah, he'd gone treasure hunting all right. Treasure hunting was his name for going into the Forsaken District to look for supplies inside partially collapsed buildings. There was a lot of treasure to be found in those buildings—medicines, potions, armor, weapons—but it wasn't worth the risk.

"I told you it's too dangerous," Sera said.

She, Alex, and Riley had gone treasure hunting at the beginning, right after the war had come to San Francisco. They'd come away with a few good hauls too—before one of the hunts had ended with a building crashing down on them. After that, Sera had declared an end to their treasure-hunting adventures. But Riley refused to give up. He still went hunting when she wasn't around to stop him.

"I know what you said, and I told you that I don't care," he said. "We need the supplies. I'm not going to let the people I care about die if those supplies might save them."

Sera wasn't sure whether to hug him or punch him. "I love you," she said.

"Love you too."

"But if I hear about you going treasure hunting again, I'm going to chain your foot to the floor here," she promised him. "With a big chain. And an iron ball."

He scowled at her. "You're a bad sister you know."

"No, I'm just a bad person. I happen to be an *excellent* sister who's looking out for her little brother."

She reached into her jacket to pull out the package she'd collected earlier. "We don't need to visit collapsed buildings for supplies. Trust the supply chain, Riley. Here's the latest batch from Cloud."

He glanced down at the package she'd set on his desk. "It's lumpy."

"I had to run across half of the city and fight monsters and Crusader patrols. We're lucky the supplies are still in one piece."

He looked her over with a stern eye, undoubtably picking up on all the blood and dust. "You had quite the adventure yourself. Your method is no safer than mine."

"I don't go digging around inside of collapsed buildings."

"They just always happen to collapse when you're inside," he said.

She sighed. "Yeah, pretty much. That's what happens when you're a target."

"Yes," he said seriously. "It's dangerous out there. You need to watch your back."

"I do."

"You're not just the Prince's second," he continued. "More importantly, you're my sister, and I don't want anything to happen to you."

She ruffled up his dark hair, smirking. "Aww. Do I feel a song coming on?"

He smoothed out his hair with a heavy sigh. "I take that back. Please go annoy the monsters rather than me."

She grinned at him. They'd always stuck together. She and Alex and Riley. The world might be changing, everything might be going to hell, but that would never change. Family first and forever. Otherwise, what was the point of it all?

"As you said, you're a target," Riley said. "You should bring people with you when you go out."

"And you?"

He shrugged. "No one knows who I am."

"The monsters don't care who you are. Only what you taste like," she told him.

"Gross."

"I'd love to take backup, Riley, but our numbers are too small for me to bring a horde with me every time I go out." Especially at the moment. Makani had taken many of their forces along on his visit to meet with the Dragon Born allies in the east. "Our guards have better things to do than babysit me. Besides, I can take care of myself."

Riley looked at the purple and blue monster guts splattered all over her boots and clothes. "Oh, I know you can." He tossed her a vial of silver liquid. "But take care of that gash on your arm before it gets infected. You're not a vampire with super healing, you know. Drink this, and all your wounds will heal."

The Dragon Born didn't possess any healing magic, and neither did most of their allies, so they had to depend on potions and other magical medicines. The few healers they had were already overtaxed, so they only went to them for big issues, not minor scratches and bruises. Riley wasn't wrong that they were in desperate need of supplies. But she *still* wasn't going to let him recklessly risk his life to solve this problem. She'd have to think of another way.

He tossed her a second vial, this one filled with pink liquid.

"What's this?" she asked him. "Something to help my body fight the infection?"

He chuckled. "No. The potion should take care of that. That one's body wash. Go take a shower, Sera. You smell like dead Blight Wolf." He plugged his nose.

Sera stuck her tongue out at him, then wandered off, giving herself a discreet sniff. Damn, he was right. She did stink. Blight Wolf had a potent smell, like wet dog, blood, burning meat, and garbage. Lots of garbage.

She returned to her apartment to find the sundress girl still securely asleep and cuffed to her desk. It was about time Sera tried to figure out who she was—and what to do with her. But first things first. Sera popped the cap of the silver vial and drank it down. A gentle warmth spread slowly across her body, like a warm blanket. The bruises on her skin began to fade out; the cuts knitted together.

"Our brother makes the best potions," Alex commented as she walked through the open door, watching with fascination as Sera's wounds healed.

"He certainly does," Sera agreed, setting the empty vial down on her desk. "Speaking of our dear brother, did you know Riley went treasure hunting again today?"

"No, but I'm not surprised. He has initiative." Alex grinned. "He must get that from me."

"Are you actually *proud* of our brother for recklessly risking his life?"

"Of course I am. Aren't you?"

Sera sighed.

"He's just trying to help. In any way he can," Alex told her.

"I know. I just worry about him, you know? He's our little brother."

"He's twenty-two. He had to grow up sometime," Alex said, taking a bite out of the strange snack in her hand.

"What's that?" Sera asked her.

"Something new from our kitchen wizards."

"Does it taste as bad as it smells?"

Alex held out the hard black lump to her. "Do you want to find out?"

Sera crinkled up her nose. "On second thought, I don't want to know *that* badly."

Alex went back to eating it. "I just pretend it tastes like pizza."

"God, I miss pizza." Sera sighed. "It's been…"

"Too long," Alex finished for her. "Not since the Crusaders came to the city."

Since the war, they'd had to improvise with food—and lower their standards drastically.

"What do you know about the Crusaders who are patrolling the Forsaken District today?" Sera asked her sister.

"Nothing. I was out."

"Still chasing after that assassin?"

"Technically, this time he was chasing *me*."

"Does he ever catch you?"

"Only when I want him to."

Sera couldn't help but laugh.

"Who's the redhead? And why is she tied to your desk?" Alex smirked at her. "Something you want to tell me?"

"I don't know who she is. She's tied to my desk because I had nowhere better to put her. And if I had something to share, you'd be the first to know." Sera smirked back.

Alex punched her affectionately in the arm. Well, what Alex considered affectionate. Damn, the girl hit hard. It was no wonder she enjoyed playing hide-and-go-seek with an assassin.

"I found Little Miss Sunshine here in one of the ruined buildings," Sera continued. "I don't know if she's with the Crusaders, but there's a good chance that she is. She just appeared out of nowhere—right after a magic bomb went off. I didn't feel her in the building, and then she was just there."

Alex was shaking her head. "You really need to

stop picking up strays. Remember what happened to the last one you tried to save."

Sera couldn't forget. She'd pulled a human out of the debris after a particularly nasty fight with a group of Crusaders. It turned out that human's family had died in that same battle. Sera had saved the human, patched him up, but then when he'd woken up and learned who she was, he'd tried to kill them all. He'd stolen supplies and turned himself into a human bomb, trying to take out the Dragon Born with him.

All he'd accomplished was killing himself. No one else was hurt. Fortunately. But the whole thing had reminded Sera of how the humans had paid the price of this war. They were caught in the crossfire, dying because they couldn't defend themselves in a world of magical warfare.

Sera sighed, squatting down to look at the sundress girl. "She's not human. She feels like a mage."

"Even better. She might actually manage to take out some of us with her when she goes."

"It doesn't have to be this way."

Alex hugged her. "Tell that to the Magic Council."

"Alex, this feels wrong," Sera said. "All of it. The supernaturals of the world shouldn't be killing each other. We should be working together. We should be fighting the monsters together. And we will. Someday, somehow. We need to fix this before we're all lost."

"There's no magic in this world that can heal hatred."

"Oh, but there is. Love. Compassion. Empathy." Sera released the girl's cuffs, then laid her on the nearby sofa. "Love is stronger than all of this. We just have to make everyone see that."

"Maybe *you* can make everyone see it. I'll just go kick their asses."

Sera wrapped her arm around her sister, and together they sat on the edge of the desk, looking at the unconscious girl.

"Magic fog. Bizarre explosions. People disappearing—or popping out of nowhere. Weird things have been happening lately," Sera said. "How did she appear? And who is she anyway? Her magic is strong. I thought I knew all the strong players in the city."

"Maybe the Crusaders brought her in from the outside," suggested Alex.

"Then why would she be unconscious in that building? This doesn't make sense."

Alex rose to her feet and walked over to the girl, checking her for any clues of who she might be. Her hands froze and she turned around to face Sera, whistling low. "You, dear sister, have just caught us a Drachenburg."

Sera looked at the mark her sister found on the back of the girl's shoulder: a small dragon tattoo drawn in black ink, magic flaming up from its spread wings. Alex was right. That was the mark of the Drachenburg dynasty.

"I'm not familiar with her face," Alex said. "That family is like a plague, too many of them. Which one is she?"

"Let's find out."

Sera strode forward, lightning sizzling to life on her hands. She hammered her fists down on the girl's chest, shooting her magic through her. The girl jolted awake, her eyes widening with terror when she saw Sera and Alex standing over her. She pushed away from them, retreating to the far end of the sofa.

"Who are you?" Sera asked as the magic faded from her fingertips.

"I…"

"We saw the tattoo," Alex told her. "We know you're a Drachenburg."

"Why were you tracking me? Did you set off that magic bomb?" Sera asked.

"I don't remember any magic bomb." Her voice croaked.

Alex laughed. "Yeah, right. How about you start talking before I need to think up more creative ways to loosen your tongue."

"Why would you do that?" she asked, the air thick with the potent stench of her fear.

She was a powerful mage all right. Even through the cloud of fear, Sera could smell the dragon magic. A dragon shifter. There weren't many of them currently in the world—and not one of them was female. Who was this mage?

"We are at war, little girl. Your people want to see us all dead," Alex spat. "*That* is why I would do that." The room shook with Alex's anger. "Now talk."

"I don't know anything about a bomb or a war. I don't even know who I am."

"Her magic rings true," Sera told her sister.

"Yes," Alex agreed. "But those Drachenburgs are good liars, good at masking their magic. We'll have to break her magic to be sure."

She held her hand out, and Sera took it. Magic streamed across their linked hands, filling Sera with the force of their combined power. A shock wave burst out from them, shattering the barriers around the girl's mind.

As her mind broke, images flooded Sera. She saw herself standing across from the girl, laughing and chatting as they tried on dresses together. A hand closed on Sera's shoulder. As she turned around, magic flashed, blinding her. She was somewhere else. The beach? A man stood opposite her, a storm of elemental magic raging all around him.

The storm cleared, and it was then that Sera saw his face. Kai Drachenburg. Shit. She readied her magic to attack him, but nothing happened. Magic split out of the ground, twisting around her ankles, binding her wrists together behind her back. She couldn't move; she could hardly breathe. The most powerful mage in the world was headed her way, and she couldn't move a muscle.

He stopped in front of her, his blue eyes shining like magic glass, deep and bottomless. He lifted his hand to her face, brushing his lightning-charged fingertips across her jaw. She breathed slowly, trying to push down her rising panic.

"Sera," he said, his voice hard, merciless. "I warned you that you couldn't run from me."

She pushed against the magic bindings, but nothing happened. Where was her magic? He dipped his face to hers, inhaling her terror. A satisfied smile slid across his lips, and then he did something unexpected.

The bastard kissed her.

Alarm gave way to something else—something she couldn't be feeling. Something she *shouldn't* be feeling. The commander of the Magic Council's North American army was kissing her, and she wanted more. The magic bindings wilted from her arms, but instead of hitting him—instead of attacking—she dug her fingers through his hair, pulling him in closer.

Magic split through her like a whip, knocking her over, and the next thing she knew, she was sitting on the floor of her office. Alex sat beside her, her eyes dazed, her hands shaking.

"What did you see?" Sera asked her.

"Logan and I…we were fighting together. The buildings were so grand, like castles. It must have been somewhere in Europe." Alex rubbed her head. "I've never been to Europe. And the world… Sera, it was whole. It wasn't scorched by magic. There was no war. The humans were still here." She took Sera's hand, and they rose to their feet together. "What did you see?"

"It's not important," Sera replied, shaking the images of her kissing Kai Drachenburg from her head. "It wasn't real. It was an illusion." She glared at the Drachenburg girl. "What magic is this? What game are you playing?"

"I don't know what's going on," she said, hugging herself as she rocked erratically.

"I don't believe you," Sera said. Those images she'd seen weren't real. This was dark magic. She turned to Alex. "Have you ever come across someone immune to Mind Breaker?"

"No. We should ask the Prince when he returns."

"Yeah," Sera agreed, then pivoted around.

A Dragon Guard fairy stood in the doorway. As soon as her eyes met his, he quickly dropped his gaze and swept into a bow. Behind Sera, Alex choked down a snort.

"Please, rise," Sera told the fairy. She was in charge while the Prince was away. For the past three days, she'd been telling the Dragon Guard fairies not to bow to her. They'd replied with flowery apologies—then went right back to bowing. It was starting to get really awkward. At least their captain had the sense to look her in the eye.

But not this fairy. He rose but kept his eyes lowered. "We have Kai Drachenburg on the line. He's asking for you."

"Speak of the devil," Sera muttered.

"That's three times this week. He must really like you," Alex commented.

Sera winced, pushing away the memory of him kissing her. No, it wasn't a memory. Because it hadn't happened.

"Kai Drachenburg is a pompous ass," Sera declared. "He can go to hell for all I care."

"Should I tell him that?" the fairy asked uncertainly.

"No," Sera told him. "Duty calls. I can't just ignore the commander of the Magic Council's North American army." She winked at Alex. "He might be calling to surrender."

Then, to the melody of Alex's laughter, Sera picked up the phone to converse with the dragon.

4. The Dragon Commander

"MR. DRACHENBURG, WHAT an unexpected pleasure. I take it you've called to surrender."

Kai could sense the strain in Sera's voice, her fake smile crackling across the phone line. They'd only met a few times in person, but he couldn't forget her magic. It tasted like cinnamon and vanilla, like sunshine and fireworks. It was, quite simply, the most electrifying magic he had ever sensed.

Electrifying in a bad way, of course. That's what he kept telling himself, but he couldn't help but feel intrigued by her magic, a magic so close to his own.

Except it was evil. The Dragon Born had killed countless leaders of the magic dynasties. Their numbers were small, but each one of them was powerful. Especially that Prince of theirs, their hell-hardened leader.

Not that the Dering sisters were to be taken lightly either. Alexandria was constantly taking out his patrols. And Serafina and her team had robbed no fewer than three of his heavily-fortified buildings, stealing weapons and potions. She was too clever. No one robbed from him. No one.

But this wasn't the time to linger on the past. He had a more immediate problem—and she was right at the center of it all.

"Cute," he told her. "But I've called to discuss something far more plausible."

"I won't go out with you," she said, her voice amused. "So don't embarrass yourself by begging. It's unbecoming of a Drachenburg."

Someone in the background was laughing her head off. Probably Sera's sister Alex, the so-called wicked sister.

"One of my patrols went missing tonight," he said, getting them back on track. "You are responsible."

When she spoke this time, her tone was devoid of humor. "One of mine has gone missing too."

"Perhaps they deserted." They must have known their war had already been lost. They simply didn't have the numbers to defeat his army.

"No one deserted," she said, the words burning like a firestorm through the popcorn static. "Except maybe your people. I hear they get weak in the knees when they see our dragons."

Alex laughed again. She was even crazier than her sister.

"A funny thing happened earlier tonight," Sera said. "I found myself in close proximity to a really freaky magic explosion that tried to blow me to bits."

"Freaky?"

"Yes, *freaky*. What dark magic is the Magic Council dabbling in?"

What the hell was she talking about? Kai was about to ask her exactly that when Tony, Dal, and Callum slipped into his office, closing the door softly behind them. The look on Tony's face told Kai that he wanted to hear what his team had to say.

"I'm going to have to put you on hold," Kai told Sera, quickly pressing the hold button. He looked at the guys. "Ok, what's so important that you had to interrupt me while I'm on the phone with the Prince's right hand."

"It's exactly Serafina Dering we wanted to talk about," Tony said.

"Oh?"

"We ran into her tonight while out on patrol," Dal told him.

"Judging by the fact that both you and she are still alive, I take it the confrontation was a stalemate. Or that you didn't engage her." Kai frowned.

Many of the Crusaders were scared of the Dragon Born, but the enemy didn't need to know that. If his patrols turned tail and fled every time they encountered a Dragon Born mage, however, it wouldn't be long before the enemy realized it—and exploited it. Fear was a powerful weapon.

"We *did* engage her," Callum said. "But our fight was interrupted when a Blight Wolf came charging down the street at us."

"We fought together with Sera to kill the beast," Dal added.

"The beast severely injured us. Dal was

unconscious. Callum and I could barely walk," Tony reported.

"Then how did you escape?" Kai asked them.

"We didn't escape," replied Tony. "She let us go."

"She could have slaughtered us with her pinky finger, and she let us go. Why?" Callum wondered.

"She's a good person," Dal observed.

"Now let's not get all warm and mushy. She is still a Dragon Born. They've fooled us before. They always have an ulterior motive," Kai reminded them. He turned to Tony. "What do we actually know about Serafina Dering?"

"Very little. Before the war spread to San Francisco, she was a monster-slaying specialist at Mayhem, a mercenary guild with supernatural and human mercenaries."

Humans. Back then, this city had been a sanctuary for Dragon Born mages and their allies. They'd lived alongside the humans, worked with them. Half of the humans had died during the first few days of war in San Francisco; the rest had perished in the following months as monsters, now unchecked and breeding faster than ever before, overtook larger sections of the city. The Council had expected the Dragon Born forces to fall quickly and quietly. If things had gone to plan, the Crusaders could have contained the monsters before things got out of hand.

Kai had known better than to trust a plan built on hope. Hope was not a strategy; it was a recipe for disaster. The Dragon Born were survivors. The fact that they'd been hunted for centuries and were still here was proof of that. The supernatural world had been underestimating them for seven hundred years. In their arrogance, the Council had refused to believe that the same thing would happen in San Francisco that had happened in every other city in the world that the war had reached.

"Sera is now the second in command after the Dragon Born Prince," Tony continued.

"Well, she is clever," Kai said.

"Yes."

"As well as adept at setting traps for us."

"Yes," Tony said, pausing. "But I don't think she is behind our missing patrol. She saved our lives."

"Going soft, Tony?" Kai asked him.

"Just telling you how I see it. And I could see this in her eyes: she's not a killer."

"She killed that monster nice and dead," Callum said, appreciation shining in his eyes—and bubbling in his magic. "The way she moved. Quick, crisp, without hesitation. It was beautiful."

"Monsters are one thing. People are another," Dal said.

"You don't have to kill a patrol of Crusaders to kidnap them," Callum pointed out.

"Yes," agreed Kai. "The Crusader who got away said the fog swallowed his teammates."

"Swallowed?" Tony asked.

"And when the fog dissipated, the other Crusaders were gone."

"Weird," Dal said.

"Very," agreed Kai.

Disappearing people usually meant spirit magic, and the Dragon Born had a powerful Spirit Warrior on their side. The evidence—what little there was of it—was all pointing in one direction.

Kai was about to press the button to take Sera off hold when a new light blinked to life on his phone. He pressed that button instead. "Whitney?"

"Blackbrooke is on line two for you," his secretary told him.

Sera had been on hold for a while, but Kai couldn't very well keep the Magic Council's Strategic Director waiting.

"Put him through," he said.

Blackbrooke's no-nonsense voice came on the line a moment later. "Missing patrols. Mysterious magic fog that eats our people. What the hell is going on in San Francisco?" The Director sure didn't waste any time—or pleasantries. And just how did he know about all this already? Kai had just found out himself.

"I'm trying to ascertain that now, Duncan," Kai told him. "I'm on the line with Serafina Dering."

"Good. I want you to schedule a meeting with her. Tonight. At Sunset Tower, across from Lake Merced Park."

"Monster Lake?"

Ironically, Monster Lake was one of the only places in the city that the newly invading monsters were afraid to enter—because the creatures living there were even worse. Just going within a hundred meters of the place made Kai's skin feel like he was bathing inside a swarm of fire ants. The magic brewing there was downright vile.

"Yes, I want you to meet her in the old tower. At midnight," Blackbrooke said. "And pretend that you're only *reluctantly* agreeing to meet. She is soft compared to the Prince. She prefers talking to fighting, so she'll come. When you get there, talk to her for a few minutes, then when she drops her guard, apprehend her."

"You want me to lure her out in bad faith," Kai said drily.

"Precisely," Blackbrooke replied, his tone far too enthusiastic. "The Prince's second would make a valuable hostage. The Dragon Born respect and fear Makani, but they all love Serafina Dering. Now get to it. Call me when you have her." Then Blackbrooke hung up.

Kai didn't like this plan. Not the least bit. It wasn't honorable. War, unfortunately, was never honorable. The Council had put him here because he didn't have a problem getting his hands dirty for the greater good. Good people made shitty commanders.

Sighing, Kai hit the button for line one. Surprisingly, Sera was still there.

"Sera."

"Oh, Drachenburg. Alex and I were just talking about you." She chuckled.

Kai didn't think about what they might have said—or that Sera had a beautiful laugh. "We should meet. Alone."

"Aw, I'm flattered. But I'm still not interested."

He ignored her banter. "Somewhere neutral. Sunset Tower. You know it?"

"Should I bring the picnic basket or will you?"

"Ms. Dering—Sera," he said, struggling despite himself not to smile. There was just something disarming about her, even from across the city. "We need to discuss these disappearances. And the fog."

"The fog," she said, suddenly serious. "Right. There's something strange about it tonight. Something…"

"Dark."

"Yes," she agreed. "Something dark."

"It is a common threat," he said. "For one night, we can put our differences aside and work together."

"I can do that," she said, and he felt a surge of guilt in his gut.

Kai didn't want to betray her. "Then I'll see you at midnight," he told her.

"I'll be there."

"Good," he said.

He buried that guilt deep inside, where it wouldn't get in the way of him doing his job. *For the greater good,* he reminded himself as he hung up the phone.

5. Date with the Dragon

WELL, THAT'S AN unexpected turn, Sera thought as she hung up the phone. "Kai Drachenburg wants to meet with me," she told Alex.

"A date with the dragon?" Alex pretended to fan herself. "What ever will you wear?"

"Lots of steel and magic." She glanced at the clock. "I only have a few hours to get ready."

"Excited?"

"Ecstatic," Sera said drily.

"You don't mean to go alone, do you?"

"Of course not. I wasn't born yesterday. The Crusaders can't be trusted. He won't come alone, so neither can I." Sera pulled out her phone, tapping out a quick message to her team to meet her in the garage in half an hour. "Are you coming?"

"You know I'd be offended if you didn't ask." Alex checked the screen of her buzzing phone. "I have to go."

"Hot date?" Sera teased.

Alex laughed. "Something like that. My weapons guy is setting me up with some sweet new blades. But I'll be at Sunset Tower."

"Midnight," Sera told her.

"I'll bring something new and shiny," Alex promised before turning and leaving the room.

Sera looked down at the Drachenburg girl. "All right, come on," she told her. "I can't just leave you alone in here."

And not just because she might try to escape or sabotage the base. For some reason, Sera felt sorry for the girl, even though she was a Drachenburg. She looked so confused, so frightened. What she really needed right now was a friendly face to put her at ease.

"Who's this?" Riley asked as Sera brought her to his desk in the magic armory.

"A girl I found earlier tonight when I picked up our supplies," Sera told him.

"You really did have an interesting adventure."

"And the adventure continues. I'm meeting with the Crusaders' commander in a few hours."

"Kai Drachenburg?" Riley asked.

"The one and only."

"This won't end well."

"Which is why I need you to give me a few healing potions to bring along," she said. "And to watch her while I'm gone." She nodded toward the girl.

Riley's eyes narrowed. "I'll give you the potions, Sera, but I don't have time to watch her."

Sera circled around his desk, wrapping her arm around him as she took him aside. "She doesn't remember who she is, and Alex and I couldn't figure out anything that made sense when we broke her mind," she whispered. "All we know is she's a Drachenburg."

"Sera, this isn't going to end well," he repeated his earlier sentiment.

"This Drachenburg girl is important," she replied. "I don't know how, but I can just feel it. She is the key to ending this war."

"The Council isn't going to give us peace because we're holding one Drachenburg prisoner."

"No, they're not," she agreed. "But there's something more going on. I just wish I knew what."

"Well, that's not vague at all."

"I'm still figuring it out," she said. "Just trust me, ok?"

Riley drew her into a hug. "I always do." He turned around, dazzling their guest with his smile. "Hi, I'm Riley."

The girl's expression brightened immediately. Riley had the nicest, most approachable face Sera knew. When he smiled at you, you knew everything was going to be ok. He was using that gift to its full effect right now.

"How about you hand me those leaves over there, and we can grind up a new potion together," he said.

Sera left them to their potion-making fun. She walked off, smiling to herself. Her prisoner was in good hands with Riley.

"Hey, Sera," Riley called out.

She stopped and looked over her shoulder.

"You still haven't showered," he reminded her, waving his hand in front of his nose.

She held up the vial with the pink body wash. "Headed there now."

◆ ◇ ◆ ◇ ◆

It was freshly washed and dressed to kill in a full suit of battle leather that Sera stepped onto the platform of Sunset Tower. The top part of the tower hadn't survived the first battle of San Francisco. During the fight between the Dragon Born and the Crusaders, a dragon had knocked the top off.

After the initial few months of the war, there hadn't been any real battles. More like border skirmishes. Nowadays, both factions were staying mostly on their own side of the wall, neither one sure how they could take out the other without annihilating themselves in the process. It was more of a cold war at the moment—or at least a lukewarm one.

The ruined husk of Sunset Tower was open to the elements, and tonight the wind was making itself felt. Its icy fingers burned against Sera's cheeks, but the rest of her body was safe behind a thick layer of black leather.

Nearby, the magic of Monster Lake rose from the dark park like a thick and swampy cloud. The creatures trapped in there were unusually restless tonight. Every time one of those zombie beasts slammed against the wall, the fence sizzled.

They're trying to get out, Sera realized.

Maybe they also felt the weird magic hanging over the city tonight. That fog. That eerie fog. Kai seemed to think it was linked to the missing patrols somehow.

She'd have to ask him what he knew when he arrived—and hope that he was in a sharing mood.

Sera's people were hiding in the nearby buildings. Kai had said to come alone, but she knew he wouldn't. She could feel his people nearby too. He didn't trust her.

The feeling was one hundred percent mutual. Sera was extending her magic, trying to sense just how many Crusaders he'd invited along to join their private party, when she felt Alex closing in. Finally.

"She's sure cutting it close," Sera muttered to herself.

"Talking to yourself? So, it's true what they say about the Dragon Born. You really are all crazy," Kai Drachenburg's voice carried across the platform, piercing the wind like a spear. A long and very pointy spear.

"So it's true what they say about the Drachenburgs. You really are all ass—"

Sera's words died on her lips the moment she saw him step out of the shadows. With his eyes like blue glass and hair that shone like black dragon scales, Kai looked good—so good that if she'd seen him in a bar and didn't know who he was, she'd go flirt with him. Tonight, like every other time she'd met him, he was wearing jeans and a fitted black t-shirt, every dip and curve of his muscular chest stenciled into the fabric. Kai Drachenburg was, for lack of a better word, a beast. A dangerous beast with a body built to deal damage and take no prisoners.

But his body was the lesser threat. His magic was the real problem. It hammered against her magic, pounding out a hard, steady rhythm. Like a war drum. It felt like a raging bonfire on a cold and dark night, like a streak of lightning cutting across a stormy sky. It tasted of spiced apple cider and hot chocolate. His magic was, in short, divine. Like catnip for dragons.

Sera resisted the urge to purr. It would ruin her reputation as a badass. And then the guys would tease her later, especially Alex. So she just folded her arms across her chest and glared at him.

Kai grinned at her. "What's the matter, sweetheart? Cat got your tongue?"

She couldn't shake the foreboding feeling that he could read her mind. No, not her mind, she realized. Her magic. It had spiked as soon as it had tasted his. And it was now caught in a loop of wild frenzy. She pulled those wild horses back in.

Kai gave her a knowing smile, his eyes laughing like she was the biggest joke on the planet.

She kept her cool, saying quickly, "You didn't come alone."

"Neither did you."

Kai was a Sniffer just like she was. This whole thing was such a farce.

"Shall we get down to business?" she asked.

He smiled. It was a hard smile, strained to the breaking point. Ok, so he didn't want to be here any more than she did.

"You mentioned something about the fog?" she prompted.

"Ladies first." He extended his hand. How chivalrous of him.

She sighed. "Our patrol disappeared while

investigating the fog."

"That's it?" His dark brows drew together. "That's all you have?"

"When the fog came close to me earlier, I got a funny feeling. Like it didn't belong here."

"So, just to be clear, all you have is your 'funny feeling' about the fog and the fact that your people were foolish enough to run off after it?" he asked.

"Well, can you do any better?" she challenged. Yeah, this whole cooperation thing was really starting off on a great foot.

"One of our patrols was swallowed by the fog. Only one man escaped. He witnessed the fog roll over his teammates, and then they were gone. Like magic."

"Yeah," she said, her voice cracking with sarcasm. "Your intelligence is much better. Not vague at all."

"It sounds like spirit magic."

She knew what he was implying, and he was way off base. "Our Spirit Warrior didn't do this. It sounds more like a cheap Crusader trick."

"Cheap?" he repeated with disgust, as though the word were poison on his tongue. "I'm never cheap, sweetheart."

Of course not. Because that would just be uncouth.

"And why would we cast a spell that eats our own people?" he demanded.

"Oh, I don't know. Maybe you haven't worked out all the kinks yet. It wouldn't be the first time the Magic Council just jumped in and worried about the consequences later—or didn't even bother to worry about them later."

She waved her hand to indicate the broken city all around them. Her city. It had once been beautiful, peaceful, whole. Now it was in ruins. And all because of the Magic Council and their stupid Crusade against the Dragon Born.

The city was lit up with magic tonight. From up here, she could see the magic shifting and swirling, green and blue and yellow. It wasn't just the effects of the war. Something else was brewing. Something dark. Someone had cast a spell on San Francisco, and the city was singing out in anguish, a forlorn song of lost days and forgotten dreams. Everything was distorted, broken. Like someone had taken a baseball bat to a house of mirrors.

"Throwing blame around won't help us solve the problem," Kai said calmly.

He was right. They had to work together. Even if neither of them liked the other very much.

"Well, if we didn't cast this spell, and you didn't do it. Then who did?" she asked.

"Where did your patrols disappear?"

"You first," she shot back, smirking at him.

But before he could answer, streams of magic erupted all around them, like a bomb had gone off. The floor beneath them split and they fell into darkness.

6. War of Magic

AS THEY FELL, a cloud of swirling fog stirred and changed directions—like it had a life of its own. Kai tried to blast apart the bonds holding it together, but it wasn't made of mundane water vapor. It was born from dark magic. His spells passed right through it.

This was a trap, a Dragon Born deception. He was sure it was. But when he turned to look at Sera, he saw that she was blasting the fog with everything she had —also to no effect. Then the fog opened its dew-dripped jaws and swallowed them whole.

The air slowly cleared. Kai could see the ground below them coming up fast. He cast a wind spell to cushion his landing. Sera touched down a moment later, floating in on airy wings. Her magic-cast wings flashed green once, then melted away from her body like dandelion seeds on the wind. She shot him a smirk, challenging him to top that.

Not wanting to disappoint the lady, Kai set the

whole cave they'd landed in ablaze. His magic flames lapped across the crystalline walls and floor, basking the area in sunshine and fire. The lights bounced and danced off the mirrored ceiling. The hole they'd dropped through had sealed.

Sera looked around at the fiery lights, her eyes wide with wonder. She quickly shook herself and declared, "I could have done that."

Before she could make good on her promise, though, a shrill cry split through the cave, and a winged creature flapped through one of the four doorways. It had the body of a tiger and the wings of a giant eagle, but its eyes betrayed its true nature. They shone with demonic fire.

"A lesser demon," Sera said, drawing her sword.

Lesser demons lived in the spirit realm—or hell—just like demons. But unlike the demons, who could only survive in the inner three circles of hell, lesser demons were found throughout the spirit realm. Where they weren't found, however, was on earth. Their magic couldn't survive the journey across realms. Which could only mean that they were no longer on earth.

The tiger eagle shrieked again, shaking the walls, then it dove for Kai. He rolled together a fireball between his hands, pouring more and more magic into it until it was as large as a bowling ball. Then he unleashed it on the beast. It skirted aside with inhuman speed, but it did not escape the spell entirely. The fireball kissed the tiger's fleeing tail. The flying cat gave Kai an agitated hiss, then it spat a silver blob at its burning tail. Whatever was in that blob put out the fire immediately. As an added bonus, it had the delightful aroma of burning metal.

A second shriek announced the arrival of another tiger eagle. Sera's hands moved quickly, weaving together an icy net. She threw the net over the second beast. As net and creature hit the wall, Kai turned her ice to stone.

"Stop messing with my spells," Sera complained, turning to slash her sword clear through a third flying tiger. Both halves of the beast dissolved into dark smoke as they hit the ground.

"Earth is stronger than ice," he told her, punching his stone-spelled fist through the first tiger. It shattered like a broken mirror, the shards of lesser demon dissolving into smoke.

"You just wanted to show off," Sera shot back, sparing him an irked glower before she turned her attention to the swarm of tiger eagles pouring into the room from all four doors.

Kai moved back-to-back with her. "Says the woman who molded her magic into the shape of wings." He slammed a tornado of magic into the beasts in front of him. The tornado tore their phantom bodies apart, then began to swirl across the room, sucking in every beast that it touched.

She smiled at him. "My wings were pretty. And fully functional."

"They're ostentatious," he told her.

"That's rich coming from you, Mr. Tornado."

A layer of blue ice slid down her blade like liquid glitter. She slashed her sword through the air, shooting a shock wave of magic at the remaining tigers. The moment the spell hit them, the beasts froze—then shattered into shards of ice that dissolved even before they hit the ground.

"Well, this sure beats cleaning up after myself," she commented.

Kai watched her flick the remaining ice from her sword. The guys had been right about her. Her skill, the way that she fought with a seamless blend of steel and magic, was beautiful. So powerful. So fierce and unyielding. And yet she'd let his men go. Sera Dering was a contradiction. A puzzle.

"What?" she asked, noticing him staring at her.

"Behind you," he said as a new swarm of tiger eagles flew into the room.

They were faster this time, more coordinated. They rushed Sera as one, the ring of orange and black bodies overwhelming her. Beneath the onslaught, her steady magic hiccuped with the first hints of panic.

Adrenaline collided with magic, and Kai shifted into a dragon. He opened his mouth, pouring down a storm of elemental magic onto the beasts. Electrocuted, burned, frozen, and drowned, they shot in every direction, revealing Sera. He looked down at her.

"I was handling it," she snapped at him.

You're welcome.

The tigers were regrouping, the red glow in their shadowed eye sockets burning hotter than ever.

"Just try not to get in my way, dragon," Sera told Kai before she charged into their midst.

She was insufferable. Kai lifted his foot, stomping on a cluster of the beasts unfortunate enough to be in his way. He continued across the room, stomping and breathing magic onto the phantom creatures. Sera darted in and out between his legs, picking off the ones who evaded his attacks.

The beasts soon realized that the ground was not the smartest place to be. They flew higher, out of Sera's reach. She didn't let that stop her. She caught the end of Kai's swaying tail, using it to swing up onto him. She darted across his back, sliding and slashing, jumping and spinning to attack the beasts.

As the last demon turned to smoke beneath Kai's foot, he shifted back. Still standing on him, Sera dropped. He'd planned to test her, to see if she would recover or stumble, but something compelled him to catch her, some bizarre instinct to keep her from harm.

He held her in his arms for a moment, feeling her heartbeat quicken, her magic rippling against his. The rush of battle still pulsing through him, he couldn't stop thinking about how she'd fought. The fluid movement of her body. The feel of her magic, that aura of vanilla and cinnamon. He wondered if she tasted as good as her magic. Overpowered by the need to find out, he drew her in closer. Her hand grabbed the back of his neck, as though she wanted to find out too.

But at the last moment, she shook free of his hold, pushing him away.

"Easy there," he said. "I don't bite."

"I've heard otherwise. Bite, slash, stomp." She swallowed hard. "You're a monster."

"And what are you? An angel?"

"A dragon," she said proudly.

"I like dragons."

"You sure have a funny way of showing it, Commander," she snapped.

"I don't make the rules."

Her eyes narrowed. "You just follow them."

"No, not always. Only if they make sense."

"And sentencing an entire race to death makes sense to you?"

"The Dragon Born have killed thousands of people. Don't play the victim card here."

"Yeah, well if everyone were trying to kill you, you'd protect yourself too."

She might have a point. But then so did he. To be honest, this war had been going on for far too long, and no one seemed to be fighting for anything but the dubious honor of being the winner. To kill the other side, to wipe them out. To stand over their dead bodies, waving the glorious victory flag in the wind as their enemies' blood stained the battlefield of their defeat.

This war had already done enough damage. Humans, those without magic, had already been all but wiped out. Who would be next? This wouldn't end well. The only winners in the end would be the monsters, eating up the scraps left by this centuries-long war. They were already spreading faster than anyone could control.

Kai was sick of it. But he had to fight. Because if he didn't, the Dragon Born would kill everyone he'd ever known. He had already lost enough people he cared about to the war. He couldn't let a pretty face distract him from reality, no matter how magnetic the magic that came attached to that face might be.

"Look, I know you hate me," Sera began.

He didn't hate her.

"But we can try to kill each other later," she continued. "Right now, we have to get out of here. Wherever *here* is."

Kai looked around, trying to make some sense of this strange place. Like a house of mirrors, everything was warped, distorted by magic. When he stared at the wall, a twisted version of his own reflection stared back at him.

"Agreed," he said.

She winced.

"Sera?" he asked. "What's wrong?"

She pressed her hand to her side, and it came back drenched in her own blood. Kai pulled back her jacket to find that she'd bled through her shirt.

7. Between Realms

"WHEN WERE YOU going to tell me about this?" Kai demanded.

"I'm fine," Sera told the moody dragon. Damn, she'd been careless—and she hadn't even noticed. That's what she got for getting too caught up in the magic and adrenaline of battle.

"No, you're absolutely not fine. You're bleeding out everywhere. Sit down."

She glared at him. "You cannot just boss me around. I am not one of your soldiers, Kai Drachenburg."

"No, you're most certainly not one of my soldiers. My soldiers have the good sense not to question my orders," he said icily.

"Oh, I'm shaking in my boots."

"That's the hypothermia setting in."

"Haha."

But Kai wasn't laughing. That would have required

a sense of humor, a quality not found in dragon shifters. "I'm glad you're amused," he said. "Now sit down before I make you sit down."

"What are you going to do?" she challenged. "Sit on me?"

"If that's what it takes to heal you."

She must have heard him wrong. "You want to heal me?"

"Yes. Despite what you might think, I am not a monster. And I'm not going to let you die down here."

Sera had an unfortunate habit of trusting everyone. It wasn't a mistake she'd be repeating today. "Toss me the healing potion, and I'll do it myself."

He chuckled.

"What's so funny?"

He lifted his hands. The distinctive golden glow of healing magic shone on them.

Oh. "You're a healer."

She hadn't known that. It wasn't in his file, and she'd had no reason to think he could wield that kind of magic. He was a combat mage. His magic was made to deal damage, not to heal damage.

"Yes, I'm a healer," he said, his mouth hardening into a thin line. "Think you know everything about me? Think you've got me all figured out?"

Apparently not. Kai Drachenburg, it turned out, was full of surprises.

"Come here," he said, motioning her forward.

She held back. True, they'd fought together against those tiger beasts, but temporary alliances quickly crumbled as soon as the immediate danger of battle faded.

"I promise not to kill you," he said impatiently.

"Ever?"

"Until we get out of here."

Well, at least he was being honest with her. Sera sat down. As Kai peeled the shirt from her torn abdomen, she held back a gasp of pain. A tiny spark sizzled on his fingertip, which he used to cut the bloody fabric away, leaving her midriff exposed. He set his hand across her wound, and she felt a soothing warmth permeate her as his magic slowly stitched her damaged flesh together.

Sera ventured a look at him. He was staring at her, his expression almost perplexed. Blue fire burned in his eyes, the heat of his stare as unsettling as the feel of his magic pulsing through her.

"I didn't know you could heal," she said, looking away uncomfortably.

"I can't do as much as Dal, but I can handle the few cuts and scratches you have, princess."

She glanced up again, but the intensity of his stare hadn't faded out.

"I'm not a princess," she stated.

His brows lifted. "Oh, no? That's not what I heard. I heard that it's only a matter of time."

"What is *that* supposed to mean?"

"Rumor has it your Prince is quite taken with you." His tone was delighted, teasing.

Sera gaped at him. "Makani? You think Makani…" She shook her head. "Makani and I are not romantically involved."

"Oh?"

"He's very interested in my best friend. So, no, I'm

not with him."

He chuckled. He'd finished healing her wound, but his hand remained, warming her skin. "Good."

"Good?" she asked, her voice cracking.

"Yes. Makani isn't right for you. He's too crazy."

"I'm hardly the epitome of sanity myself."

He laughed. "You're a different type of crazy. Your Prince is all fire and brimstone."

"Whereas I'm more pizza and chocolate?"

He grinned. "Precisely. Pizza and chocolate. And roses." He leaned in, drawing in a slow breath.

Sera silently thanked Riley for the body wash. Kai's hand lifted to her face, brushing a strand of hair off of her cheek. For one insane moment, she wondered what it would be like to kiss him. But before she could find out, he pulled back, standing.

"All healed," he said, looking down at her.

She rose, steadying her shaky legs. It must have been the blood loss. It sure wasn't because of Kai. "Thank you."

"You're welcome."

She turned her gaze from his amused eyes. When she looked at him, her body betrayed her thoughts. The dragon was a handsome bastard, and he knew it. And his magic… She blocked it out. It was distracting.

"What is this place?" she asked, looking around the cave.

"I don't know. I've never seen anything like it. It appears to have been made with magic."

"Dark magic."

He nodded. "Yes, a dark spell spawned that fog and swallowed us up. This whole meeting was a trap."

"I didn't do it, if that's what you're implying."

He gave her a quick, assessing look, up and down, then said, "No, I know you didn't."

"It must be my trusting face."

"No, you're just a horrible liar. Your magic gives everything away."

"I take issue with that."

"Take issue all you want, but it is what it is," he said. "Be happy you're such a bad liar. It means I don't have to kill you."

"I'd like to see you try, Drachenburg."

"Just say the word, sweetheart."

"Stop calling me that," she snapped. "I'm not your sweetheart. Nor will I ever be."

Her assertion seemed to amuse him. "You're awfully adamant. Especially for someone who was begging me to go out with her."

The look in his eyes made her magic stutter—and she didn't even know why. He was the commander of the Crusaders. Her *enemy*.

"Begging?" she choked out.

"If you wish," he said.

"You are unbelievable. Insufferable. An insufferable, arrogant, demented, savage, insufferable—"

"You said that one already." His lip twitched. "Twice."

"Twice isn't nearly enough to cover it. Not even close!"

"By all means, continue. Don't hold back, sweetheart."

"I told you not to call me that," she growled

between her teeth.

"You certainly are excitable. Are you like this with all men, or am I just special?"

"A special pain in the ass."

"You're attracted to me," he said, as though that was that, no room for argument.

Well, she was going to argue all right. With fervor. "You're delusional."

He laughed. "Sweetheart, I can read magic well enough."

She glowered at him.

His smile persisted. "And your magic is screaming for me."

He extended his magic. As it brushed against hers, she felt a surge of heat rush through her body, head to toe, inside and out.

"I have this strange feeling whenever I look at you," he said, his hands stroking down her arms.

"Repulsion?"

He leaned in closer. "No, this feeling that we've met before."

"We have. Six times." Sera held up six fingers. "First at Witching Point, then at Magic Breakers, then…" She stopped when she saw his eyes light up.

"You remember every time," he said, as though that pleased him. She couldn't imagine why it would.

"I have a good memory," she said, stepping back.

"I remember every time I've met you too," he said, catching her hand. "Intimately."

She blushed, which didn't make any sense. She had nothing to blush about. Until now, they'd never even been alone together. She'd always gone with Makani to meet him.

Except in that memory, a voice in her head reminded her. Her dragon. She'd been uncharacteristically quiet today.

No, it wasn't a memory, no matter how real it felt, Sera told her. *It was an illusion. A trick.*

"I remember every time we've met," Kai repeated. "But that's not what I meant. I feel like there's something beyond that."

"Like we've met in another life," she whispered, her breath quickening.

"Yes."

She snapped herself out of the trance he'd put her in. "Do women really fall for those lines? Do they throw themselves at you when you whisper sweet nothings into their ears?"

Kai gave her a hard look, but she couldn't stop.

"I know your type, Kai Drachenburg. Whatever you're selling, I'm not buying."

"I'm not trying to seduce you, Sera," he said impatiently. "Though if you wish to throw yourself at me, then by all means get it out of your system now so that we can get back to business."

She flushed with embarrassment.

"What's the matter?" His hand closed around her wrist. "No clever retort? No snarky comeback?" He was so close that his lips nearly brushed against hers.

She felt herself arching toward him—then stopped herself. She was *not* going to kiss Kai Drachenburg, commander of the North American Crusader forces and sworn enemy of the Dragon Born. Even though she felt the same as he did. There *was* something between them, however that was possible. Maybe he was manipulating her mind with his magic. She could definitely feel him touching her body with his magic.

She broke free of his hold—and his magic. "Let's just get out of here."

"As you wish," he said, waving toward the doorway.

She walked through it, wishing they could just pass the rest of their hopefully short adventure together in silence. Unfortunately, Kai had other ideas.

"We need to talk about the fog," he told her. "And who is controlling it. Someone set us up. The spell that swallowed us was a trap, dropping us right into a nest of demonic monsters. We were meant to die in here."

"Which would escalate the war," she said.

"Exactly."

They'd just passed into another cave, similar to the first but much larger. Magic bounced off the mirrored walls, setting the spark for one phenomenal headache. Ghosts fluttered overhead in jagged, choppy movements, phasing in and out of sight, muttering and ranting in streams of incomprehensible sentences. They'd all lost their minds. Something about this freaky place must have driven them mad.

"Which of your people do you think is behind the fog?" Sera asked Kai.

"It wasn't one of my people. It was one of yours."

"The Magic Council has no honor. They would do anything to see the Dragon Born dead," she insisted.

"And yet these guerrilla warfare tactics are more in line with the Dragon Born's previous strategies."

She spun around. "Unlike you, we don't want to

fight. We're doing it to survive. We want a peaceful solution. That's why the Dragon Born came to North America centuries ago, to escape the Magic Council. But you followed us here. You eventually found us. And then the war started again. People fueled by hate that endured the passing centuries are the sort of people who would do anything—cross any line—to win."

Hate. That's what she felt in here, filling this room. It wasn't coming from her or even from Kai. It was rolling in through the doorway, trailing a stream of magic that reeked of burning rivers and apocalyptic nightmares.

"Demon," she gasped.

It wasn't a lesser demon like those tiger eagles. It was a full-fledged denizen of hell's inner sanctum. And it was headed their way.

Kai turned to face the doorway as a massive gold-skinned demon thundered into the room, its head of matted black braids swishing and swirling as it moved. Its bright eyes lit up when it saw them. A cruel sneer kissed the demon's lips. It pounded its fists against its tattooed chest, throwing back its head to unleash a war cry that pierced through Sera's magic like a spear. Kai just stared coldly up at the demon, his fists clenched, his magic primed.

"Let's go," she said, pulling on his arm.

He didn't budge an inch.

"You can't fight a demon" she told him.

"Watch me."

He was insane. Demons were immortal, unkillable. The only way she knew how to stop a demon was to break its hold over its host and send it back to hell. But this demon didn't have a host; it was in its raw form. Her trick wouldn't work. She didn't know anything that would.

"Get moving, you crazy dragon," she snapped at Kai.

"Run ahead if you're scared." A slow smile twisted his lips. "I'll catch up."

"Don't make me electrocute you, Drachenburg."

He glanced over his shoulder at her. "I don't run from battle."

"Do you like being carried unconscious from battle?" she demanded. "Because that's what will happen if you don't move your ass."

"Fine," he said, tackling her aside as the demon's fist hammered down. "Where to?"

"Through that passage," she said, pointing at a slender opening in the rocks. "The demon won't be able to fit in there."

"I'm not sure *I* will fit in there," he commented as he ran after her.

"If we hold our breath, I'm sure we can make room for your sizable ego," she said, pulling him through the gap.

They shifted and squeezed, slowly making their way down the narrow passage—until it abruptly ended. She pounded at the mirrored rocks, but they refused to give way. And when she tried again, she tripped over her own feet, falling into Kai.

"Ok, what now, genius?" he asked her. He looked amused, which was insane considering the situation they were in.

She kicked her feet, trying to dislodge her boots from the wall. "Well, there's one more thing I can try, but I'm not sure what will happen."

"If you're concerned, I can shift into a dragon. I know precisely what will happen."

"Oh?"

"The walls will split apart."

She gave him a hard look. "You want to create a rockslide on top of us. *That* is your plan?"

"It would bury the demon too."

Right, awesome plan. "But you want to create a rockslide *on top of us*."

He grinned, wrapping his arm around her. "Don't worry, sweetheart. If you snuggle up to me, I'll protect you."

That would be the day. "Did anyone ever tell you that you're really arrogant?" she growled, throwing his arm off of her shoulder.

"You did, just a few minutes ago. Everyone else has enough sense to be afraid of me."

"Well, I possess neither fear nor sense," she said to his great amusement. "So I think we'll go with my plan."

"Which is?"

"You'll see."

"Ok. But if it doesn't work, I'm bringing these walls down."

Sera wouldn't let it come to that. She pressed her hands against the walls, concentrating on the flow of magic around them. Here, everything was all mushed together, earth magic and spirit magic. This place—wherever it was—seemed to exist between realms.

They were on neither earth nor in hell. They must have been in some bizarre in-between region, which would explain the presence of the demons and why her and Kai's magic still worked normally.

In her former life as a mercenary, Sera had deported a few demons back to hell. She'd done it by breaking through the boundaries between realms. And that's what she was going to try to do now. Keeping her hands pressed to the wall, she concentrated on earth's magic. As she synched her magic to the earth's ebb and flow, the mirrored wall began to crack beneath her fingertips. The fractures split across the wall in every direction, drawing a web of fissures. The wall groaned once—then was silent.

"Well, that was anticlimactic," Kai commented after a few seconds of nothing happening.

Glass exploded all around them, melting into smoke—no, fog. The cave of mirrors disappeared, leaving them floating in a murky abyss. They hung in the air for a moment as the fog faded out, then they dropped. This time they only fell a few feet before hitting the ground.

"What the hell was that?" Kai asked, looking around. "And where are we now?"

Salt and selkie magic tickled Sera's senses. "Near the piers, I think. At least what's left of them."

"We've traveled across the city. To the Forsaken District."

"Inter-realm travel is not an exact science." She smirked at him. "If you snuggle up to me, I'll protect you from all the monsters."

His brows lifted. "Don't make promises you don't

intend to keep, sweetheart."

Yeah, this wasn't playing out at all like it had inside of her head.

"The fog seems to be related to the boundaries between realms," Sera said quickly. "The place it brought us to was kind of an in-between area, a mixing of both."

"I felt that too," Kai agreed. "The question is who is behind this. And what they're trying to do."

"This is dark magic."

"Hellish magic. Perhaps the demons are behind this. Your Prince was trapped in the spirit realm for a long time." He shot her a hard look. "Did Makani make a deal with a demon?"

"No, he was fighting *against* the demons. He wouldn't do that."

"Even to win the war?" he posed.

"Not even to win the war. The price of dealing with demons is too high. Makani knows that better than anyone. He wouldn't deal with them." Her brows lifted. "But the Magic Council might. They would do whatever it takes to defeat their enemy, even summon demons."

"Not everything. There are some lines that cannot be crossed."

"We'll see."

Sera didn't think that Kai was in on the scheme. But she *knew* the Council was. If she could prove it to him…

What, Sera? she asked herself. *It's not like he'd abandon his dynasty and all his friends just because you proved that they'd done something reprehensible. They've been doing reprehensible things forever, and he's still with them.*

She had to try, though. She had to figure out what was going on. And she had to stop it.

"I need to go speak to someone," she said. "Someone who might be able to help me get to the bottom of this."

"You mean, help *us* get to the bottom of this. We're working together, remember? And so I'm coming with you."

"I don't trust you," she told him.

"Whoever is behind this tried to kill me too, Sera," he replied, a hard edge to his voice.

"I don't trust you," she repeated. "Now that we're out of that cave, now that you're free of your promise not to kill me, what's to stop you from stabbing me in the back?"

"I promise not to kill you until we find out who is behind this." He held out his hand. "Can you promise to do the same?"

"Oh, please. I'm not so bloodthirsty," she said, shaking his hand.

"I am going to find out who set me up. And then I'm going to kill them." The look in his eyes told her that he was dead serious.

Maybe she *could* trust him to help her get to the bottom of this. And if she could get him to kill someone on the Magic Council—or even multiple someones—then he could solve some of the problem for her. But that didn't mean he wouldn't go after her next. She had to be careful. Really careful.

8. The Pier of Tears

SERA WAS STILL giving Kai a suspicious look. He wanted to remind her that she could trust him, but he didn't see the point. She wouldn't have believed him anyway.

Eventually, she stopped giving him the evil eye, her attention diverted instead to her phone screen. Humanity hadn't survived the war, but technology had. Miraculously.

"Pick up, pick up," Sera muttered into her phone. She tapped her fingers against her arm. "Alex, where are you? When you get this message, call me."

Kai pulled out his own phone and tapped out a message to the commandos, telling them he was alive.

Just a second later, Tony's response came back. *Of course you are.*

Callum added, *you're a tough bastard.*

Damn near impossible to kill, Dal contributed.

Kai chuckled, which drew a curious glance from

Sera.

"Just telling the guys I'm ok," he told her. "You've met them. Tony, Callum, and Dal."

"Ah, the commandos."

"Commandos, huh?" He nodded. "I like the sound of that."

"So did they."

"I bet they did."

A smirk twisted her lips. This was one of those rare moments where she forgot she was supposed to hate him.

"Riley. Thank goodness," she spoke into the phone.

Kai remembered from Sera's profile that Riley was her brother. He'd never met the guy. He wasn't Dragon Born like his sisters. In fact, he wasn't even a combat mage. His specialty lay in the magical sciences: mixing potions.

"Yeah, I'm fine. Don't worry about me," Sera replied to whatever he'd said. "But you need to tell me what's going on. I can't reach Alex." She paused. "What was she doing with Logan... Oh, I see."

She turned her eyes on Kai. Anger pulsed in them, sure and strong. So much for that moment of not hating him.

"Ok, if you manage to get hold of Alex again, tell her to call me," Sera said to her brother. "And have Eire check the wall's defenses. See you soon."

She tucked her phone back into her pocket, maintaining her glare the whole time. Whatever Riley had shared with her, Sera was blaming Kai for it.

"After we disappeared from Sunset Tower, the

Crusaders attacked my sister."

That had to be Blackbrooke's doing. The Director didn't know how to keep his nose out of other people's business—or his hands clean. He must have a man on the inside, someone spying on Kai.

"They had a lot of heavy duty weapons. And a team of combat mages. And vampires," Sera spat. "It was a kill squad, Kai. I went there in good faith, and you'd always meant to double cross me."

He didn't bother denying it. He tried to remind himself about the greater good, but that tired old argument was starting to wear thin.

"Luckily, my people got away," Sera continued, oblivious to his self-reflection. She probably thought he was just being obtuse. "Alex chased away your kill squad."

"All of them?" Kai said in surprise.

"Every single one." Sera smirked at him. But there was no amusement in that smirk. It was hard. Dark. Seething. "My sister is quite formidable, especially when she's pissed off. And she had help."

"The assassin," he realized.

"Yes. Your people were running away like their tails were on fire."

Blackbrooke, that idiot. He wanted Sera. He didn't give two hoots about the rest of them. So why had he attacked Sera's sister? He must have realized the squad didn't stand a chance against the Black Plague and Slayer. For a master of strategy, the man sure had a deficiency of sense.

Unless Blackbrooke had been deceiving him, unless he was using this meeting as a way to take out some Dragon Born, to lure them from their base. You couldn't trust a master strategist. They were always scheming, always lying, even to their own people. It was all about the mission—about victory. People were inconsequential to Blackbrooke.

Well, they weren't inconsequential to Kai. He tapped out another message to Tony, instructing him to pull in the troops. He hoped there were still troops to call back to base.

Sera glanced over at his screen. "You really didn't know about this, did you?"

"I didn't order them to attack your sister," he said. "Though I did know that Blackbrooke wanted to capture you."

"Duncan Blackbrooke?"

"Yes. Do you know him?"

"My fist knows him. I once punched him in the face," she explained.

"I see." It was a phenomenal effort not to laugh. "I will find out which of my people acted without my command." The thought of a traitor in his ranks hit him hard and cold. That knocked the humor right out of him.

"Don't punish them on my account," she replied, her smirk returning.

There was something incredibly infectious about her smile. But he couldn't afford to be infected. Not now. Probably not ever.

"I'm not," he told her.

She laughed softly. It was such an innocent laugh, one inexplicably untouched by the horrors of war.

They were coming up on the old wharf, where the

ferries had run back before the monsters destroyed the pier. Nowadays, you'd never have guessed this was once a bustling tourist area. Buildings were split open, their inner guts exposed. A few frail skeletons of boats were still tied to the docks. The rest had long since been destroyed—or washed away by the tide. There was a reason some people called this place the Pier of Tears.

"At one time, Alex and I and all the mercenaries here stood against the monsters," Sera said. "We were the wall that would not break, the line that monsters could not cross. But then the war came here." A dark look crossed her face, wiping away any hint of humor. "We had to turn from fighting monsters to fighting the Crusaders. Completely unchecked, the monsters moved in, feeding off of the hatred of magical discord. The first to fall were the humans. This was one of the last cities where humans had survived the war and the monsters. And then they were gone." She snapped her fingers. "Just like that. I don't even know how many of them are left. I swore to protect these people, and now they're gone. I failed them."

Her voice cracked with anguish; her magic twisted with helplessness. She really cared about those people. She wanted peace. There were so few people like that, driven by love rather than by hate. That was the problem with the world. Too much hate. Too much death. She put on a tough face and tried to be badass, but inside she was all sweetness and warmth. She didn't deserve to be hunted.

Sera cleared her throat. "Here we are."

They'd reached an old shop, one that looked more intact than its neighbors. The windows were completely boarded up, and a beast's claw had left its mark across the faded sign dangling over the door, but all of the walls were still standing. The fancy script text on the sign read 'Cloud Nine'.

"A magic shop?" Kai asked.

"It used to be," replied Sera, punching the magic barrier over the door. The silvery curtain of swirling magic froze…then shattered. Sera threw Kai a look over her shoulder. "Coming?"

As they moved inside, a man with spiked blond hair and eyes like a tropical ocean rushed forward, green Fairy Dust sizzling across his hands. Except it wasn't just Fairy Dust; it was Fairy Dust mixed with elemental magic. This man was a fairy-mage hybrid.

"Oh, I should have known it was you, Sera," he said as his eyes fell upon her. "There are few people who could have broken our shield. And Alex always first blasts it a few times for fun."

Sera shrugged. "Well, you know my sister."

"Yes, I—" He jumped when Kai stepped out of the shadows. His magic blazed back to life in an instant, and he didn't waste any time hurling it.

Kai caught the ball of glowing magic between his hands. "Pretty." He slapped his hands together, popping the spell.

The fairy-mage's jaw dropped.

"Should I show you mine too?" Kai asked him.

Sera glared at him. "Behave yourself." She turned to the fairy-mage. He was wearing a black athletic suit of stretchy synthetic fibers.

Kai rolled his eyes. Fairies.

"Cloud, he's with me," Sera told the man.

"You brought Kai Drachenburg, commander of the enemy's army, here. To *my* shop," Cloud spluttered.

"What did you want me to do? Blindfold him?" she demanded.

"For starters. Blindfold him and put him in iron chains. Or better yet, how about not bringing him here at all."

"He's a Sniffer. He could sense everything anyway, even through a blindfold."

"And iron chains tend to snap when I shift into a big, scary dragon," Kai added, flashing Cloud a wide grin.

"You are *not* helping," Sera snapped, moving in front of him. "Cloud, none of this matters. You're about to move shop anyway."

From the nervous look Cloud was giving Kai, he must have been one of the Dragon Born army's allies. A supplier of magical herbs from the look of the shop. Though it spanned two levels, the top floor was in a state of slow collapse. Here on the ground level, boxes towered in high stacks. Lanterns lit by magic fire hung from the walls, humming softly.

A second person, a fairy woman, stood behind a wooden counter close to Cloud, stuffing things into boxes. Her golden hair was braided back into two pigtails and accented with a black cloth headband. She wore a black dress and black leggings, the inevitable consequence of hippies meeting the apocalypse. Nowadays, everyone wore black. Bright colors were a death sentence inside the monster-infested war zone of San Francisco.

"Hey, Sera." The fairy woman gave her a little

wave.

"How's it going, Chakra?"

"Busy, of course. Having to move shop on account of the monsters and all." She stole a quick glance at Kai before her eyes flickered back to Sera. "I was wondering when Riley will be coming to see us again."

"I'm not sure."

"Tell him I have a new batch of Fairy Root," Chakra said with a sly smile.

"Will do," Sera said as Cloud moved in beside Chakra. "Hey, guys, do you happen to know where Naomi is at the moment? I need her help with something, and her phone is off."

"She's on Angel Island," Cloud told her.

"But Angel Island is overrun by monsters."

"That's why she's there. She's hunting," said Cloud. "The island's monster population is growing out of control. Their presence is starting to threaten Fairy Island."

"She went to Angel Island alone?" Sera asked.

"Yes."

"Thanks," Sera said, then turned and ran out of the shop.

Kai followed, matching her pace. As she ran, magic slid off of her back, crackling and glowing in the darkness.

"Wait," he said.

"I can't wait. My friend is alone on an island of monsters. I have to help her."

A dragon split from her, tall and magnificent. The moonlight shimmered off its iridescent blue-purple scales. Side-by-side, aglow in the same golden halo,

Sera and her dragon were two sides of a beautiful soul. The air sparkled and hummed with the song of their enticing magic.

"I'm going with you," he told her.

"Fine. See if you can keep up," she challenged him with a smirk as she jumped up onto her dragon's back.

Kai didn't wait. He shifted and launched into the air, staying right on her tail.

Hey, you're pretty fast, a voice said in his head, adding with a snicker, *for a shifter.*

Sera?

Yes and no. I'm Amara. Her dragon side. And you're Kai Drachenburg. The dragon turned her head to look him up and down. *You're not all that scary.*

You haven't seen me in battle.

Actually, I have. I saw you fighting alongside Sera. She enjoyed that.

So had he. Their movements had been so smooth, so coordinated. Almost as though they'd done it countless times before. Except they hadn't. Before tonight, they'd only ever been on opposite sides of the battlefield.

Sera likes you, Amara told him. *In spite of herself.*

Are you supposed to be telling me this?

Probably not. She chuckled. *I won't tell her if you don't.*

Kai liked this dragon. She had attitude. But they didn't have time to talk further because they were coming up on Fairy Island. They landed, and Kai shifted back as Sera's dragon folded back into her body. The golden halo still glowed around her, lighting up the dark night in that dark forest.

"Has anyone told you how beautiful your magic is?" Kai asked her.

She smirked at him. "Trying to get into my pants, Drachenburg?"

"Yes."

She snorted, giving him a solid punch to the shoulder. "Come on. I can feel Naomi nearby."

They moved down an overgrown path. A chorus of beastly howls cut through the night, and Sera accelerated to a full-out sprint. Kai ran beside her, blasting away any trees standing in their way. They came to a clearing scorched by spirit magic. And there a woman stood, trapped inside a ring of monsters.

9. The Spirit Warrior

SERA'S SWORD WAS out in an instant, and Kai had two fireballs flaming and ready to go. But Naomi was faster. She lifted her hands up in the air, splitting a hole in the curtain between realms. A stream of ghosts shot out of the tear, swarming the monsters. The beasts slashed and stomped, but their attacks passed through thin air.

Naomi skipped and hopped and waved her hands around in a kind of dance, directing the ghosts with her whole body—and her spirit magic. The otherworldly beings dove through the beasts, turning solid at just the right moment to tear them apart from the inside. Fifteen monsters rose into the air—then dropped dead to the ground.

The ghosts returned through the opening, and Naomi sealed it shut behind them.

"Naomi," Sera said.

The fairy spun around, her short green skirt flaring up. The air was still thick with spirit magic, a perfect balance of sweetness and tang wrapped up into one.

"Sera," she said, grinning. She strutted forward in her knee-high leather boots, moving like she was walking down a fashion runway, not through a monster-infested forest. "I simply *love* your new look."

Sera looked down wistfully at her cut-off top. "It was more of an impromptu modification."

"Those are the best kind. Chaos is so much more fun than order." To punctuate her point, she yanked the black bandana off her head, freeing her pale platinum locks.

"That's where you and Makani differ."

Naomi sighed, a dreamy look on her face. "We differ in more ways than one, honey, but that's the fun of it. Fire and ice. Water and lightning. Sometimes, you just need a little spark." She looked at Kai. "It appears you're starting to realize that. Hanging out with Kai Drachenburg, commander of the North American armies, are you? When you take the plunge, you don't fool around."

"I'm not plunging."

Naomi winked at her. "Though I could think of a few better places to bring him on a date than Monster Island." She wrapped her arm around Sera. "Then again, this place certainly is your style."

Kai snorted, and Sera shot him an irked look.

"Well, it's true," he told her. "Monsters are your style."

"*Killing* monsters is my style."

"Killing monsters in style is the way to go. Especially while on a date," Naomi added with an impish smile.

"Kai and I are not on a date."

"Oh?" Naomi asked. "So you just led him here to kill him then?"

"No," said Sera. "We were meeting to discuss the recent strange disappearances of our patrols when some of that creepy fog swallowed us up and dumped us into a warped mashup between earth and hell. We fought a demon, Naomi. A real demon. Not one inside of a human body. An actual demon in raw form."

The happiness and sunshine wilted from Naomi's lips. "The spirit realm has gone weird lately."

"The whole world has gone weird."

"Something bad is coming," Naomi said.

"What?" Sera asked.

"I don't know. This fog..." Naomi pointed at the creepy fog. "It's a mess, a tangled knot of mangled magic, a chaotic jumble where the earth and spirit realm have melted together. It's unnatural. Some spell caused it. A powerful one."

"What kind of spell?" Kai asked her.

"I don't know. I've never seen anything like it before. I haven't even heard of anything like it before."

"Neither have I." Kai looked at Sera.

She shook her head. She'd seen some pretty messed up magic, but nothing like this.

"Whatever this is, it's dark magic," Naomi said.

"It makes me feel sick just to be near it," Sera agreed.

"Could this magic have come from the spirit realm? From a demon?" Kai asked Naomi.

"Perhaps. The demons have a lot of magic

unknown to us. I could see one of them doing this." Naomi set her hands on her hips, tapping her legs as her gaze lifted in thought. "How about we go find out if one of them is behind this."

"How do you plan to do that?" Sera asked her. "Stroll into hell and ask one of them?"

Naomi's eyes twinkled with delight. "Exactly."

◆ ◇ ◆ ◇ ◆

Naomi waved her hands around, opening a portal into hell. "This might sting a little," she said, then pulled them through with her.

It didn't sting a little. It hurt like hell. Sera felt the drain immediately, the parasitic drip of the spirit realm's magic sucking out her own. It was like an anvil pressing down on her, pinning her to the ground.

Beside her, Kai put on a tough face and tried to pretend that it wasn't affecting him. Sera didn't buy it for a second. Hell was not an equal opportunity drainer. The more magic you had, the more it drained you. Unless you were a Spirit Warrior like Naomi. Her magic was spirit-based. Here, she was stronger than on earth, not weaker.

Naomi led them toward a grove of peculiar trees. With glossy purple trunks and even glossier pink leaves, they looked like a watercolor painting, soft and fluffy and all kinds of pretty. A wall of mountains hugged the grove, a silver backdrop to the purple-pink streaks and splotches.

Metal pots and pans grew from the branches of the tree they were standing under. Naomi snapped a small one from its branch, then set it over a hole in the ground. A fire roared to life beneath it. Naomi darted around the grove, breaking bits and pieces off the various trees, each of which grew a different kind of treasure. She poured everything into the pot, tugged free a spoon that had been poking out of the ground, and began to stir her bizarre creation.

"How long will this take?" Sera asked.

"Not long," her friend replied.

"Good."

"How much is this place hurting you?"

"I wouldn't call it hurting."

"What would you call it?"

"Well, it's more like my eyes are being pierced with a hot needle," Sera told her. "From the inside of my skull. How deep are we in hell?"

"The second circle of hell."

There were nine circles of hell. Demons only lived in the seventh, eighth, and ninth: the core of hell. They couldn't survive up here in the upper circles.

"How are you going to summon a demon here in the second circle?" Sera asked her.

"He's not exactly a demon. More like a half-demon."

"I didn't even know such a thing existed."

"Oh they exist all right," Kai said. "They're rare but not rare enough. They can live both on earth and in the spirit realm, moving between them as easily as crossing a room. I fought one before. Slippery beasts. Damn hard to kill."

"How did you manage to kill it?" Sera asked him.

"Stomped on it. Even a half-demon can't survive

the impact of a twenty-ton dragon."

Yikes. "Sorry I asked."

"But I burned it for good measure," he added.

Naomi was cracking up. "I like him," she told Sera. "He's not half as egotistical as you told me he is."

"Well," Sera said, glancing over at Kai. His face was unreadable, as hard as granite. "What can I say? You improve with time."

"Like a good whiskey."

"I thought Germans only drank beer," Sera teased him.

He grinned. "And I thought mercenaries only talked shit."

"Touché." She smirked. "That's *former* mercenary, by the way. And the phrase you're looking for is 'battle banter'."

"So you're only allowed to be snarky during battle?"

"Umm…." Yeah, she'd backed herself right up into that corner.

Naomi came to her rescue. "Sera's snark is dual purpose. It's not just useful when mouthing off during battle. The rest of the time it's called bedroom banter. Or pre-bedroom banter. Like right now."

Mortified, Sera's jaw dropped. Ok, maybe she didn't want to be rescued. Or at least she didn't want Naomi's idea of rescuing.

Naomi grinned at them. "Oh, sorry. I thought someone should say what we're all thinking."

Kai chuckled. "I like her."

Sera turned toward him. "You're not helping."

Kai lifted his hands. "Then by all means, continue

with your bedroom banter."

Naomi's shoulders shook as she tried to hold back another outburst of mirth at Sera's expense. Sera looked around to see if hell had a big enough hole for her to hide in.

"Don't worry, honey. Your banter is endearing." Naomi looked at Kai. "Isn't it?"

"I've always been fond of women who speak their mind." His eyes darted to her sword. "And carry a big sword."

"Should I leave you two alone?" Naomi asked.

"That won't be necessary," Sera told her. "I'm sure Kai can contain his enthusiasm for sword-wielding, shit-talking former mercenaries."

"Battle banter," he reminded her, his lip twitching.

"Whatever." Sera looked at Naomi—and her interesting concoction of hell's ingredients. "Is this how you're going to lure the half-demon to us?"

"Yes, he's quite partial to blood-bane stew. I can only make it in the spirit realm."

Sera leaned over to get a closer look at the stew popping and bubbling inside of the pot. The rancid smell of burnt meat and rotting cabbage wafted up. "Do I want to know what's in there?"

"Probably not."

Naomi broke a twig of flowering black blossoms from a nearby bush, crushing it to a powder between her fingers. She sprinkled the residue into the stew, along with a few drops of her magic. Green flames shot out of the top of the pot, creating a pillar of fire several hundred feet tall.

"He should be able to see it from anywhere in the

spirit realm," Naomi said.

"How do you know he's here?" Sera asked.

Magic cracked loudly, and a creature popped up right in the middle of them. He had the figure of a human, but the bright colors of a demon. His short spiky hair was midnight blue, his skin bright red. He was wearing only a pair of frayed capris—and nothing else. Not even shoes. Like his body, his magic was a mashup of earth and hell, sunshine and darkness with sugar and vinegar.

The half-demon's mouth spread into an eager smile when he saw the stew. He rushed forward, but Naomi cast a wall of spirit magic in his path. He shot her a sour look.

"You're not a very nice fairy," he told her. His voice echoed oddly, like it was reflecting off all the realms of hell and earth.

"I'm always nice, Onyx. But first a few questions." Naomi gave him a dazzling smile, the kind that short-circuited men's brains.

Her charms didn't appear to be working on him, though. He glared at her, but she just kept beaming at him.

"Fine," he said with obvious reluctance. "Ask away."

"Where did that fog come from?"

"There's a lot of fog in San Francisco. Even in San Francisco in hell."

Haha.

Onyx went for the food, but Naomi's magic pushed him back.

"Stupid fairies," he grumbled under his breath.

"You know what I mean, Onyx," she told him. "This unnatural fog we've had today. It was born from magic. Dark magic."

His eyes trained on the bubbling stew, he smacked his lips a few times. "Someone cast a dark spell. On earth and in the spirit realm."

"Who cast it?" Sera asked him.

"I don't know."

"A demon?" asked Kai.

"I don't know."

"It is powerful magic," Naomi said. "Powerful enough to make the boundaries between earth and the spirit realm bleed together into a big mess. You have magic in both realms, Onyx. Maybe it was *you* who cast the spell."

He stiffened, looking indignant. "Absolutely not. I'm quite fond of both realms. I have no desire to melt them."

"Perhaps a demon made you do it," Sera suggested.

"The demons don't make me do anything. I can go where they cannot. I have power they do not. I'm not scared of them."

"Then prove it," Kai challenged him. "Tell us who did this."

Onyx paused for a moment, then said quietly, "I don't know for sure if she was the one who cast the spell."

"Who?" Naomi asked.

"Rane."

"Who's that?" Sera asked.

To her surprise, it was Kai who answered. "A demon. One with power over perception. Over reality."

"The lines between the earth and spirit realm have been melted. We saw that in the fog," Sera said, thinking out loud.

"Yes," Naomi agreed.

"A demon could use this to get out."

"Maybe."

"One already did get out," Kai reminded her. "The one we saw in the fog."

"Right," Sera said. "And those lesser demons too. The tiger eagles."

"The fog is still not in this world. It's stuck between worlds," Naomi told them. "The demons cannot leave it to get to earth any more than you can use it to get to the spirit realm."

"But if this fog is breaking down the boundaries between realms, it's only a matter of time," said Sera. "And then the demons will get out."

"You don't understand."

They all looked at Onyx.

"The fog is not the spell. It's only a byproduct of the spell, of the breaking down of reality," he explained.

"Meaning?" Sera asked.

"This world is no longer what it should be," he said. "Someone has altered reality."

10. The World That Was

"WE'RE ALL LIVING a lie," Onyx declared. "This world, the world we think we've known, is a lie. This is all wrong."

Kai had certainly had the feeling that something was wrong, but he couldn't imagine anyone—even a demon—possessed the kind of power necessary to alter reality.

"How do you know?" Naomi asks Onyx.

"I can feel it," the half-demon replied. "The rhythm of the realms is wrong. It's hiccuping. Changing. The flow between realms has been affected. It's harder for me to break through."

"And you think the fog is a byproduct of the spell that changed reality?" Kai asked.

"There are weird echoes in the fog, kind of like mirror images, like ghosts of reality. Memories that aren't memories. It's like each person there is two selves."

"What does it mean?" Sera asked.

"I think the fog is a residue of the spell," Onyx said. "It's the bits of reality, mixtures of earth and the spirit realm, that clumped together when the spell was cast. They got all mushed together and formed this fog, this area where both realities co-exist, where earth and the spirit realm occupy the same space. Some people from both realities got trapped in there when the spell tore across the world."

"The whole world?" Sera asked.

"Yes," he said. "The entire world has changed."

"What about the people the spell trapped inside the fog?"

He shook his head. "You can't save them. The spell split them apart. They're no longer whole. Or sane. They're ghosts of their former selves: mad, aimless ghosts."

"What about people who get swallowed by the fog later, after the spell was cast?" Kai asked him. "How do they get out?"

"Well, how did you escape the fog?"

"I broke through," Sera told him.

"How very nice for you. Unfortunately, most people don't have magic-breaking power."

"Just the Dragon Born," said Sera.

"You're lucky you were with her," Onyx said to Kai. "How ironic that your sworn enemy is the reason you're still here." He laughed.

Kai glared at the half-demon, but he didn't get the hint. He just kept going.

"Without her, you'd still be floating around in there," said Onyx. "Well, unless the demon got you first. Which one did you meet, by the way?"

Kai smiled at him. "Can't say. You demons all look the same."

"As opposed to dragon-shifting mages?"

"The demon was male, I think," Sera said quickly. She shot Kai a hard look, as though she were afraid he was going to step on Onyx. Wherever had she gotten that idea from? "He had golden skin, black hair, and clubbed feet. And a wicked tattoo of a harp on his chest."

Onyx snorted. "Ah, you met Sin."

"Sin?" Sera gasped. "There's a demon named *Sin*? How delightfully original."

"Sin fancies himself the musical sort."

"His fists sure did try to thump out a melody on our skulls," Sera commented.

Onyx's shrieking laugh echoed through the grove. He sounded like a cat whose tail had been stepped on. "You're funny," he told Sera.

"How do we get rid of the fog?" Naomi asked him.

"It's fading on its own. Within a few days, the clumps of reality will smooth out. The fog will be gone. But that's not a good thing," he added quickly.

"Because that means the spell has set," Kai realized. "It's permanent."

"Exactly. You're pretty smart for a dumb brute." Onyx's lips twisted up into a saucy smile. "Until the point that it sets, it can still be reversed."

"How?" Naomi asked.

"I don't know. You'll need to talk to someone more familiar with this kind of magic."

"Is there even anyone familiar with this kind of magic?" Sera asked him.

Onyx shrugged. "Rane."

"The demon who cast the spell to begin with?" Sera shook her head slowly. "Somehow I don't think she'll be very eager to help us."

"I don't actually know that she cast it. I just said that she *might* know how to do it," replied Onyx. "This is powerful magic. These kinds of reality-altering spells need to be cast from both earth and the spirit realm at the same time. Otherwise the new paradigm doesn't set."

"There would be too many contradictions," Naomi explained. "People in each realm remembering a different reality. The spell would sizzle out as soon as it encountered a paradox."

"Exactly," said Onyx. "When you change reality, you need to do it all at once, on a large scale."

"How long ago was this spell cast?" Kai asked.

Onyx's eyes lifted in thought as he chewed his lower lip between pointy gold teeth. "In the last day, I think, going by the clumps in the fog."

"And yet it feels like things were always this way," said Sera.

"You wouldn't remember anything different," Onyx told her.

"How long do we have to change it back?" Naomi asked.

"I can't be sure. A few weeks maybe."

"Wait a moment." Kai lifted his hands. "Do we even want to change it back?"

Sera narrowed her eyes at him. "Are you serious? Of course we do. The world's supernaturals are at war, the humans are nearly extinct, and monsters roam the world, gaining ground every day. Why would you not want to change it back?"

"What if the World That Was was even worse?" he posed. "What if it was changed for a reason? Maybe some of us here were the ones to help change it."

Sera seemed to chew that over for a moment, then she shook her head. "No. I don't believe that. I believe that the world can be a better place."

"Just because it *can* be a better place, that doesn't mean it *was* a better place," replied Kai. "What if in the World That Was, demons roamed the earth? That would be worse than monsters."

"I just feel it," Sera said stubbornly.

"Wishful thinking?"

"A belief in a better world," she amended.

Her optimism was charming, if not naive. She had such a beautiful soul. So untainted. So pure. But the world wasn't populated by people like Serafina Dering. It was driven by hate. By conflict. Kai wasn't sure it could ever be any other way.

"There might be a way to figure out what the world was like before the spell," Naomi said.

"How?" Kai asked her.

"Echoes in the ether."

The confusion on Sera's face matched his own. "What do you mean?"

"If the spell hasn't settled yet, there should still be hints, fragments of the World That Was," Naomi explained. "We just need to find them."

"In the fog," Kai realized. "We ran into ghosts in there. Ghosts phasing continuously between realms, like something was broken in their magic. They must have been sucked into the fog when the spell was cast."

"They were all talking gibberish," Sera reminded him. "The fog jumbled up their minds. I'm not sure we can get anything useful out of them."

"I can try to talk to them," Naomi offered. "But I need to go chat with Gran first. She is the world's largest encyclopedia on weird magic, and she might have some tips for me on talking to crazy ghosts. She's on Fairy Island right now. I'll bring you back to earth, then head right over there."

Fairy Island was a sanctuary for peaceful fairies and mages. It had also been a popular tourist spot in the city. But when the war had come to San Francisco, the group's leader had closed off the island to outsiders. The people of Fairy Island wanted to live their lives outside of the fighting. Kai didn't blame them. He did wonder, though, how long their sanctuary would last before the bubble popped, before the war came to them. The monsters in the area were already threatening the island.

"How can I help you?" Sera asked her friend.

"Stay alive," Naomi told her. "You're one of the only people who can break through that fog. Plus, I'm rather fond of you."

Sera smiled. "Aw, I'm rather fond of you too."

The two of them squeezed each other into a big hug, and Naomi dropped the spirit magic barrier around the boiling pot. Onyx didn't waste any time. He used the chance to dash straight for the stew. Loud, slurping noises echoed off the pot as he messily gobbled down its burning contents.

"Ok," Naomi said, giving Sera a final squeeze

before stepping back. "Ready to go? I can bring you through a shortcut to save you the flight back to the city."

"That would be great," Sera replied. "Thanks."

The three of them left Onyx to enjoy his hellish snack. They passed weeping trees and burning grass. Finally, they made it to the shore. A stream of glowing green magic flowed across the large sheet of murky water, lighting the way to the city like a highway. Kai had heard there were many magic streams like this one throughout the spirit realms. Spirit Warriors, the otherworldly, and demons used them to quickly traverse the lands. Other citizens and visitors of hell were restricted to slower means. The streams could only be used by those with spirit or demon magic.

Naomi linked one arm in Kai's and one in Sera's, then jumped into the stream. Water and sky streaked by as the magic pushed them along like a high-speed moving sidewalk.

"How close can you get us?" Sera asked.

"There's an exit in the Presidio."

"That's Crusader territory," Sera told her.

"Yeah, right on the edge of it, sorry," replied Naomi. "There are only so many exits in the area."

"So you can just pop up in my territory," Kai said to Naomi.

Naomi smirked at him. "How else would I know that you run from Wizard's Beach to the Palace every morning at seven?" She gave Sera a conspiring wink, adding, "Topless."

Sera arched her brows at Kai, such a simple gesture with so many possible meanings. He wished he knew what she was thinking.

"And have you shared my routine with Makani?" Kai asked Naomi coolly.

"Leave her alone," Sera snapped. "Makani couldn't care less about your running attire—or lack thereof."

Naomi snorted.

"You two sure aren't taking this seriously. Need I remind you that we're at war? With each other," he added.

A pool of magic was swirling ahead of them, just off the side of the stream. That must have been their exit.

Naomi grinned at them. "Make love, not war, my dears."

Then she shoved them out of the stream, right into that swirling hurricane.

◆ ◇ ◆ ◇ ◆

They fell back to earth, landing on a dark, abandoned street. Kai knew the neighborhood. It was at the edge of the Presidio, close to the wall.

"Come on. I have a car nearby," he told Sera.

"You have a car parked near *here*?" she said in shock.

The place didn't look great for sure. The Crusaders called this area of a few square blocks Ghost Town because no one lived here. It was too close to the fringe, too close to the monsters. Even though they were on the other side of a twenty-meter magic-reinforced wall, you could still hear the monsters scratching at its defenses, testing them. Especially at night. A soft, constant hum—that of claws against magic—buzzed in the background.

People didn't come to Ghost Town unless they absolutely had to. Which meant the Crusader patrols came. But not the street cleaners. And most certainly not anyone with anywhere better to be. No one lived here except vagrants and spies.

"Yes, I have a car here. I have them all over the city. Sometimes it's useful to have one on hand. You never know when you might find yourself in need of a quick getaway."

"You shift into a dragon," she pointed out.

"Hard as it may be to believe, even my magic runs low on occasion."

She smirked at him. "I never would have guessed."

"And sometimes I don't feel like burning the required five thousand calories to make the shift."

She turned, looking in all directions. "I'm sure there's a steak house somewhere around here."

He could tell she was teasing him by the spike in her magic—and by the twitch of her lip. That smirk, that curve of her mouth, was so perfect. So full of attitude. So tempting. He resisted the urge to move in for a taste. He *had* promised her that he didn't bite.

Kai's phone buzzed in his pocket. He pulled it out and glanced at the screen to find a message from Tony demanding—in very polite words—an update.

Coming back to base soon, he wrote back, then sent off the message.

Tony's response was nearly instantaneous. *Where are you? What's going on, Kai?*

Later, Kai tapped out, then tucked his phone back

into his jeans.

"Your lover calling?" Sera asked him. She was *still* smirking.

"No."

The moonlight was shining down on her, illuminating her skin, lighting her up in a halo. Just like the halo he'd seen on her and her dragon.

Kai's phone buzzed again. It was Callum this time. He had the magic report from the scenes of the disappearing patrol team, but Kai had to return to the office to hear it.

"Another love letter?"

Kai snorted. "Yeah, from my team. Summoning me back to the office."

"Don't let me keep you."

She didn't even try to stop him, and she wasn't getting primed for a fight. She hadn't once tonight tried to stab him in the back. She'd worked and fought beside him like they were partners, like they were on the same side rather than sworn enemies.

"You're not at all what I expected," he told her.

"Neither are you." She nibbled on her lower lip. "You don't hate us, do you?"

"No. And you don't hate us."

"Hate is the whole problem here. Hate is what caused this war in the first place. It's what made the world into the living hell that it is. The problem isn't going to be solved by piling on more hate. It's only going to be solved by people putting their hatred aside. By understanding one another."

Her words were beautiful. Naive, but beautiful—just as he'd come to know her. Kai didn't think centuries of hatred in millions of people could be put aside so easily. Or could it? He wondered what such a world would be like, a world where he and Sera weren't on opposing sides of a meaningless war. One in which they really were partners.

"I want to understand you, Sera. I want you to trust me."

She stared at him for a moment, as though she were really seeing him for what he was. Not as the commander of the Crusaders, not as her enemy. Just as a man.

"I want to trust you, Kai." A slight smile touched her lips. "Really I do." She backed up, that smile fading, the mistrust gleaming in her eyes once more. "But you know I can't afford to."

11. Ghost Town

SERA FOLLOWED KAI to a reinforced gate, dually protected by magic and technology. As he pressed his glowing hand to the door to deactivate the gate's defenses, she considered his words. He claimed he didn't hate her, but that hadn't stopped him from commanding the army that was trying to annihilate her kind. He insisted she could trust him, but that wouldn't stop him from stabbing her in the back when the time came. The old magic dynasties, the leaders of the Magic Council, were proud, ruthless, and conniving. They would do whatever they had to win, for what they'd arrogantly declared the greater good. For them, that meant a world without Dragon Born mages in it.

Past the gate, an empty garage waited—empty except for a large black vehicle in the corner. Its markings claimed it was an SUV, but its outer dimensions and materials screamed *tank*. As far as vehicles went, in this time and place, a tank wasn't a bad choice. When darkness fell on the city, the monsters came out to hunt.

"It would be best if you let me drive you back to your territory," Kai told her as the car blinked in greeting.

"I know," she replied, sliding into the passenger seat.

He watched her for a moment, as though surprised by her quick agreement. Maybe she should have refused. Getting into a car with the commander of the Crusader army was kind of insane. Then again, so was trekking through the monster-infested Forsaken District that filled the broken expanse between his territory and hers. And she was too tired to fly or fight her way through all the beasts standing between her and her bed.

They drove through Ghost Town in silence, an invisible wall between them. She'd let herself get too swept up into Kai's charm. In his magic. He fought like no other. She bet he kissed like no other too.

Sera shook herself out of this daydream. She couldn't go down that road. They were enemies. All the wishful thinking in the world wouldn't change that. And even if they threw caution to the wind and ignored reality, reality would eventually catch up to them. It had a way of doing that.

Every so often, members of the opposing sides would fall in love and run off together. That story always had the same ending: their leaders would hunt them down and kill them both. There was no escaping hate. No escaping fate.

And besides, she and Kai weren't even talking about love. This was infatuation, plain and simple. Her magic was playing tricks on her. No matter what her magic said—no matter how it was telling her that there was something bigger between her and Kai—she knew it wasn't true. She hardly knew the man. And she didn't even know if she knew the *real* him. It wasn't like they had some great destiny to be together.

And maybe he was right. Maybe this altered new world was better than the old one. Maybe they didn't even exist in the other world. Maybe they hated each other. She didn't want to be consumed by the hate like others had, the hate she'd been resisting her whole life.

A loud crash jolted her out of her own mind. The car swerved to avoid a sudden stream of debris, knocking her hard to the side. Steadying herself, Sera looked through her window to see that a pack of monsters had broken down a part of the wall. The broken metal web hung at an awkward angle, clumps of stone dangling from it. The wall shook again, raining down broken debris, and then a pack of Blight wolves ran through the hole.

They streamed into Kai's territory, howling like this was their lucky night. These Blight wolves were bigger than the single wolf Sera had fought earlier tonight—and there were a hell of a lot more of them. Kai hit the gas pedal, and his car shot down the street.

They weren't fast enough.

The wolves were running with the speed of lightning, moving to surround the car. There must have been dozens of them—and they just kept pouring in from the Forsaken District. Sera slid open the sunroof. Unbuckling her seatbelt, she stood up to blast those beasts back where they'd come from. She scored a few hits, but it hardly made a dent in their numbers. Some of the wolves split off from the main pack, dashing up the ruined buildings that lined either side of the street. They tore across the rooftops, shingles flying everywhere.

A wolf landed in front of the car, and Kai spun the steering wheel to avoid a collision that even his tank might not survive. The force of the whirling car knocked Sera back into the car. Her head hit the dashboard, but there wasn't time to see stars. More monsters were surrounding them. Sera shook the magic from her frazzled fingers.

Kai turned down another street, driving off in another direction in an attempt to lose the pack. There were so many of them, a wall of fur and fangs and ill intentions. And they weren't giving up. One after the other, the beasts launched off the buildings toward their car. One of them slammed down right at the front bumper. Kai couldn't turn in time. The car slammed into the beast and hit a concrete wall.

The collision scored a second concussion to Sera's battered skull. She blinked back the light show of dizzying blobs dancing across her eyes. The car had stopped. They were sitting ducks. And a quick glance over at Kai told her he wouldn't be driving anytime soon. He was unconscious, and blood oozed down his face.

The wolves were still coming. They were nearly upon them. Sera jumped out and cast a ring of fire around the car, pushing the monsters back. As they began to prowl along the outside of her magic barrier, she ran to the driver's side and pulled the door open to deal with Kai. He was too heavy for her to lift, so she used her magic to move him across to the passenger seat.

Amara, keep the beasts busy, Sera said.

It would be my pleasure to show these riffraff the door.

Her dragon split from her, flying toward the pack of wolves howling on the other side of Sera's fire wall. She snatched two of the beasts up in her talons and hurled them back over the wall into the Forsaken District.

Sera hopped into the driver's seat and slammed the door shut behind her. She sped off down the road to the song of her dragon's laughter.

Are you sure you know how to drive this thing? Amara asked.

Sera hated driving under normal conditions—let alone with monsters hot on her tail, determined to paint the city red with her blood.

I know how to drive, Sera replied. *I just don't like to. There are too many crazies on the road.* She hit the gas to power through an old chain-link fence.

Crazies like you?

Sera stuck her hand out of the open window and blasted a pair of wolves who'd slipped by Amara's defenses.

Less chitchat. More killing monsters, Sera said.

She blasted a building with a lightning-earth-ice cocktail, blowing it up on top of the monsters. Her dragon swooped in, tossing another pair of wolves away. Sera made a sharp turn down a side street to avoid the avalanche of broken buildings.

The damn monsters followed. Didn't they have anything better to do than chase after her? One of them landed on the hood, howling and making a scene of how big and scary it was. Sera shot at it, but the beast evaded, sliding across the side of the car. Its enormous clawed paws caught on the driver-side back door, ripping it clear off. It hurled the black plate of metal over the car, and Sera had to swerve to avoid driving over it.

"You're really starting to piss me off," she growled.

As the beast slid past her window, she firebombed it off the car. The wolf rolled down the street, bowling over a cluster of his pack mates close on Sera's back bumper.

She was fast running out of magic, road, and time. Kai's base loomed nearby, casting a shadow over every other building in the area. Kai looked bad. She had to get him to his people so they could heal him. If she brought him to her own people, they would kill him—or at least torture him while they tried to use him as a bargaining chip, no matter what she said to stop them. He didn't deserve that fate.

So she turned toward Kai's base. She reached over and tugged to free Kai's phone from the front pocket of his jeans. Then she tapped out a message to Tony, *Coming in hot, monsters on my tail. Open the gates.* He seemed to be Kai's number two, so he'd be able to order the guards to open the gates—and, when the time came, order the guards not to shoot her. But she wasn't banking on that one.

The Crusaders would never open the gates if they

saw Amara. So Sera called her dragon back, feeling a warm rush of power as her other half absorbed into her body.

The gates of Kai's fortress, an enormous reinforced office building, came into view. They were still closed.

There was trouble from behind too. The monsters were running up on her side now, the side with a missing door. That was the tank's weak point, and they'd figured it out. Sera swore the beasts were smarter than people thought. She sent a spark of lightning magic across the car's outer shell, bombarding them with electrical energy until they let go.

Ahead on the road, the base's gates were starting to open. Finally, something was going right. She raced the car through the gates, watching in the rear view mirror as the guards swung their magic-charged sticks at the monsters to electrocute them. The gates swung shut.

While the guards were busy with their new friends, Sera drove into the garage. As soon as she parked, she jumped out of the car. She couldn't let herself be trapped in there when Kai's people came. There would be no room to maneuver if they attacked her. No, who was she kidding? *When* they attacked her. She was an enemy combatant, an abomination in their eyes. They'd shoot her in the head and not lose any sleep over it. And after everything that had happened already tonight, she didn't have enough magic left in her to make a reasonable magic barrier. She put up a crappy one instead, even knowing it wouldn't be able to stand up to anything. Sometimes crappy was all you had.

She opened the passenger door, trying to wake Kai. An unconscious Kai made her look suspicious. A conscious one could at least tell the guards not to shoot her. She slapped his face a few times, but the stubborn dragon continued to sleep.

"This is no time for a nap, Sleeping Beauty," she told him.

Her words had no more effect than her hands. He was still sleeping when she felt her barrier take simultaneous hits from twenty different magic sources. It tore apart like tissue paper, and the commandos surrounded her, their swords drawn.

12. The Enemy's Fortress

"PUT YOUR HANDS up," Tony told Sera.

All three commandos had their swords pointed at her, and over a dozen other Crusaders armed with guns were staring down from the walkways above, every single one of them with a clear shot of her head. So Sera held up her hands.

With those numbers, it was no wonder they'd been able to tear apart her wimpy barrier. They had the means and the desire. The Crusaders up on the walkways were glaring at her like they wanted to kill her. The commandos didn't appear to share that sentiment. Sera could use that.

"Kai is in the car," she said. "He was wounded when we tried to outrun the Blight wolves."

"Take a look," Tony told Dal, and the healer moved toward the open car door.

Tony and Callum kept their weapons and magic trained on her the whole time. Nice.

"Come on, guys," she said. "If I'd wanted to break

into this building, I could have used less ostentatious means."

"Why *did* you come here?" Tony asked her.

"Kai was hurt. I couldn't just abandon him to the monsters."

"You know, I think she's telling the truth," Callum said.

"Yes," Tony agreed. But he didn't put away his sword.

So they wouldn't let her go, even though she was telling the truth—and had just saved their leader. Ah, the cruel rewards of war. Sera supposed that meant she'd have to fight her way out of here. But how would she get rid of those soldiers up on the walkways?

Dal reappeared with Kai, who was still unconscious. Tony went to help Dal support Kai.

"Bring her," Tony told Callum.

That was her cue. Sera dashed away, hoping to get out of range before they could react. Like everything else tonight, things didn't go to plan. It turned out Callum had a fast draw—like Wild West, high noon shoot-out fast. Before she'd made it two steps, he zapped her with a gun that projected a wide beam of magic, disorienting her. Her balance thrown for a wild loop, Sera hit the floor.

She struggled against vertigo to get on her feet. Again, Callum was faster. He snapped a pair of fancy silver bracelets on her wrists that shot a wave of nausea through her. She grasped for her magic, but it was fading, blocked by the bracelets. Yellow and purple dots danced in front of her eyes, and she swayed to the side. The last thing she remembered before blacking out was Callum swinging her over his shoulder and carrying her out of the garage.

◆ ◇ ◆ ◇ ◆

No good deed goes unpunished. That was Sera's first thought as she faded back into consciousness. She should never have helped Kai Drachenburg. She should have left him there for the monsters to eat. If she had, then she wouldn't be in this mess. She would be soundly asleep in her bed.

The commandos carried Sera and Kai into a room five times as large as the room she and Alex shared. With its glass table and leather furnishings, it looked more like a business office than a war room. There were fresh oranges in a bowl on the desk. It had been *years* since Sera had eaten an orange that hadn't come out of a can. There was a bowl of chocolates next to the orange bowl. Now that was just unfair.

Callum and Tony cuffed Sera to an office chair while Dal set Kai down on one of the sofas and began to heal his injuries. The commandos were under the misconception that Sera was still unconscious, and she wasn't about to rob them of that idea. As long as they thought she was sleeping, they'd talk more freely in front of her.

"Have the patrols made it back?" Tony asked Callum.

"Two men made it back."

"Out of two dozen?"

Callum looked glum. "Courtesy of the Black Plague and Slayer."

Alex had certainly been busy tonight. Sera resisted the urge to smile. She was supposed to be unconscious. She almost wished she were unconscious. Whatever magic had been enchanted into those silver handcuffs, it was giving her the mother of all migraines. And she still couldn't access her magic. It was zapping the energy out of her, piece by piece. She had to get free before she didn't have any fight left in her.

Luckily, she knew how to use more than magic. Her hands were bound behind her back, but she stretched out her fingers until she freed the slender metal pin hidden inside her ring for times like these.

"The Black Plague and Slayer took out our guys?" Dal asked. "I thought Slayer worked for us."

"The assassin works for whoever pays him," said Tony. "His loyalty lasts only as long as his next paycheck."

"Then we should keep him on the payroll. We can't afford to have him work for the Dragon Born," Callum said.

"We've tried to. He doesn't want to work for us anymore."

"Why not?" Dal wanted to know.

"He's working with the Dragon Born," said Tony.

"What do the Dragon Born pay him that we can't?"

"How about we ask her?"

Sera heard footstep softly approaching—then magic surged through her body, flooding her with a dose of electrical agony. Sera pushed against her restraints, growling. The cuffs clanged against the metal chair legs, resisting her efforts to jump up and strangle the bastard who'd just electrocuted her.

"Rise and shine," Callum told her.

She glared up at him through a curtain of messy hair.

"We have a few questions for you," Tony said.

"I am *never* saving your lives again," she snarled. The aftershock of the lightning magic was still coursing through her body, making her twitch.

Her threat didn't seem to bother them. Neither did the murderous glare she was sending their way.

"How much are the Dragon Born paying Slayer in return for his services?" Tony asked her.

"Nothing."

"Nothing?"

"Not a damn cent."

"Maybe they're giving him something else. Something he wants more than money," Callum said to Tony. "Something we could give him too."

"Perhaps." Tony's fingers tapped across his folded arms. "Are you trading favors with Slayer?" he asked Sera. "Giving him access to the spirit realm? Giving him magic?"

"No, no, and no. Wow, you're really bad at this game," she told him.

"What are you offering him?"

She laughed.

Tony's face hardened. "This isn't funny."

"Actually, it is."

"You are being stubborn and defiant," Callum said.

"And you're being ridiculous," she countered. "You can't offer Slayer what we can, so this whole interrogation is pointless."

Tony wasn't giving up. "Our resources—"

"Are irrelevant."

"Whatever you offer, we can beat it," Callum declared with perfect confidence.

"No." She smirked at them. "You really can't. Slayer is working with us because he likes my sister, who is a Dragon Born mage. He's feeling very reluctant to help you kill her and everyone she cares about."

Tony frowned at Sera.

She smiled back. "This conversation isn't playing out like you'd imagined, is it?"

"No."

"Then maybe you shouldn't have started it by shooting the woman who saved your lives. And saved your commander from being eaten by monsters."

The commandos stared at her. They were good soldiers. Their bodies betrayed no sign that they felt bad about what they were doing to her. But she could feel it in their magic, that thick, sour scent of guilt. Her restraints might have been blocking her elemental magic, but her Sniffer abilities were functioning just fine. She could still sense all the magic brewing around her.

On the sofa, Kai was moving, slowly regaining consciousness. He blinked his eyes down hard a few times, obviously trying to find focus where there was none. The commandos all turned toward him, ready to catch him if he fell.

This was Sera's chance to move while everyone was distracted. She popped the lock on the cuffs and ran for the door.

But the commandos saw her and rushed forward, cutting off her escape. Before they could shoot her again with that magic ray gun, she dashed toward the window. As she moved, she wound up her magic, casting a storm of elemental spells all packed into one concentrated burst that would punch through the glass.

That was the plan anyway. Unfortunately, there was something weird about the glass. As her spell bounced off the window and slammed into her, her last thought before she blacked out was that no one could be this unlucky.

13. The First Day of a New World

KAI PUSHED TO his feet, ignoring Dal's warnings about his injuries. For a badass combat mage, he sure had a talent for fussing like a mother hen. As Kai stalked over to where Sera lay unconscious on the floor, Dal trailed him, waving his hands around to heal the last of his lingering injuries.

Kai stood over Sera, looking down at her. He wasn't surprised that she'd tried to run. He would have too under the same circumstances, chained to a chair in his enemy's stronghold, being interrogated by a team of commandos.

But he was putting a stop of this here and now. Few people had ever risked their skin to save him, and he wasn't about to repay the favor by locking her up in his dungeon.

Kai turned to face the guys. "What the hell were you thinking?" he demanded, his voice strained with barely contained rage. Magic splintered from him, shaking the ground. A few of the overhead lights popped.

It was Tony who spoke, his voice perfectly calm. "She is an enemy combatant, so we thought it prudent—"

"Prudent?" Kai roared, and books poured down from the quaking bookcases. "She could have left me there for the monsters, but she didn't. She put herself at risk for me." He stepped toward them. The ground shook beneath his feet, pounding out the beat of his anger. "She brought me here, where she knew she would be seen as the enemy. She saved my life. She spared yours only a few hours ago. That wasn't very *prudent* of her, was it?" Fury pounded against his chest, threatening to explode. He held it in with great difficulty. "And this is how you repay her?" He grabbed the device from Callum's hand and threw it at the floor, smashing it. "With this?"

"Kai, please calm down," Dal said calmly. "You're still recovering from a head injury. If you overexert yourself—"

"Stop," Kai said in a low growl. "Just stop."

He took a deep breath, trying to put out the inferno of rage inside of him. If he didn't contain it, he'd end up punching through walls. Or, worse yet, people. He didn't understand this rage—or why Sera was bringing it out in him. Like before in the cave, he was filled with this uncontrollable need to keep her safe. No, not just safe. Happy. And happy with him. He didn't want her to hate him.

He went back to Sera and lifted her from the ground, carrying her over to the sofa. He set her down, carefully spreading a blanket over her body. The corner of her mouth was lifted in a half-smirk. Even in sleep, she had attitude. He found himself unsurprised that she'd risked herself to save his life. That's just what she did; she threw herself into danger to help others. He couldn't decide whether he was furious or elated. Probably a bit of both.

Kai brushed a hand down her face. Then he stood to stare down the men she'd named his commandos. Their eyes flickered to Sera, then to Kai, who was standing as a shield between them.

"Kai," Dal said.

"What?" he snapped. A hurricane of rage was still stirring inside of him.

"If you don't let me pass, I can't heal her."

"Do it."

As soon as Kai stepped aside, Dal hurried to the sofa. He set a glowing hand on Sera's forehead, starting the sequence of spells to heal her body. Callum and Tony exchanged concerned looks, as though Kai and Dal had lost their minds by healing an enemy combatant. Well, Dal was a healer. He couldn't help himself. He didn't like to see people broken. And Kai…no, he had no excuse. He was the one who usually broke people.

"What happened after you two fell into the fog?" Callum asked him.

"We were attacked," Kai said curtly. "We barely got out of that fog again."

"Did you run across the patrols in there?" Tony asked.

"No." Kai looked at Callum. "What did you find

at the scene where our patrols disappeared?"

"Very bizarre magic readings," Callum reported. "I don't understand the meaning of them. The magic was all over the charts, earth and spirit magic melted all together, folded in on itself in a jumbled mess of funky readings and weird echoes."

"Funky readings and weird echoes? That's not very scientific," Kai said.

"Everything we know about the magical sciences was turned on its head at that scene."

And yet it sounded strangely familiar by now. It was looking more and more like that half-demon Onyx was right. Reality had been altered by magic.

Callum looked at Sera. "What do we do with her?"

"We should question her," Tony said. "She might know something about the fog. Her people might have cast it."

"I think you three had quite enough fun interrogating her earlier. And frying her with her own magic," Kai added with a stern look at Callum.

"I did what I had to do."

"Let's be reasonable here, Kai," Tony said. "Just because she brought you here doesn't mean she isn't behind the fog. Maybe she wanted to get onto our base, and this was her only way in. It's like you yourself said just a few hours ago. The Dragon Born have fooled us before. And they always have an ulterior motive."

"Whatever it is, this fog was made with old, dark magic," Callum chimed in. "I've never seen anything like it. Neither has anyone else down in Magic Research."

"We need answers. Dal, could you wake her up?" Tony asked.

"I'm not sure that's such a good idea. There was quite a potent charge on that window." Dal frowned at Callum. "Did you really have to design it to hit so hard?"

"The spell bounces back only what you hit it with," Callum replied. "She's quite a little powerhouse."

"In any case, she was electrocuted, frozen, drowned, set on fire, caught in a hurricane, and shaken by an earthquake all at once," Dal tallied off. "I healed her injuries, but I'd like to give her some time to recover from that trauma."

Callum rolled his eyes. "Hey, genius, you're not supposed to heal the enemy."

Dal smiled at him. "I'll remember that the next time you want me to heal you after I kick your ass in training."

"I guess we can question her tomorrow," Tony said.

"I will take care of it myself," Kai told them.

Tony's mouth thinned into a hard line. "Look, Kai, I know you two had a fun adventure killing monsters together—"

"You seem to be under the misconception that this is open for discussion. Let me cure you of that right now. I am your commander, and I said I will take care of it."

But Tony wasn't backing down. He looked him in the eye. "I need to know if your judgment has been impaired."

Kai wasn't offended. That was Tony's job after all.

If Kai's judgment became impaired, Tony had to make sure he stepped down. And then the Magic Council would send someone else to take over leadership of the North American army, someone who didn't know and didn't care about the shifted reality. Or worse yet, someone who *did* know and did care—care that they didn't change it back before it became permanent. What if Sera was right? What if the betrayer was not amongst the Dragon Born but someone on the Council? What if one of them had cast the spell? Like Blackbrooke.

If this someone had managed to protect themselves from the effect, then they would remember the World That Was. And now they would be making every effort to be sure no one put it back together. Sera and Kai had each been looking into the fog and the disappearances. Maybe they'd gotten too close, so the betrayer set them up to fall into the fog. If the fog was part of the spell they'd cast, they might be able to control it too.

Kai had to get to the bottom of this. He had to do it before the new reality set completely and it was too late. And he wouldn't be able to do that if he was relieved of his position—or worse yet, trapped inside of a prison cell or inside that fog. What happened when the fog finally dissipated? Did anyone trapped inside of it die?

If someone inside of his organization was behind this, then Kai couldn't afford to trust anyone. He glanced at the commandos. He could trust them. He'd known them for over ten years. Or had he? Today was the first day of this new world. If someone could change reality, he didn't really know anyone at all, not if they came from the World That Was. Which meant he couldn't trust anyone. Not even the guys.

"My judgment is just fine," Kai told Tony. In fact, he was seeing things more clearly than ever before.

Tony opened his mouth, presumably to protest, but Kai was faster.

"I want to do this my way," he told the guys. "As you said, Sera and I had an adventure together. She's more likely to spill her secrets to someone she trusts."

"And that's you?" Tony asked him.

Not really. Sera had been very clear about the fact that she didn't trust him. But the guys didn't need to know that.

"Yes," Kai said. "She trusts me. She'll talk. I just need to get her alone, make her drop her guard."

The commandos exchanged wary looks, but all Tony said was, "Ok, you're the boss. How do you want to play this?"

"Make sure my path to the garage is clear," Kai instructed him. "I'm going to drive her out of here."

"And where are you taking her?" Callum asked.

"Home."

14. Here Be Dragons

THAT BOUNCE-BACK of her own magic against the glass had hurt like hell, but it took a lot more than an enchanted window to keep Sera down. She drifted awake just in time to hear Kai tell his commandos that he'd find a way to make her spill her secrets. She wished she could have just kept on sleeping. Her dream had been so much better than this hot mess.

In her dream, she and Kai had battled on the beach, then when the smoke of their elemental storm had cleared, they'd made out in the sand. More memories of the World That Was? Or just her own wild imagination getting the better of her?

Whatever the case, she needed to come up with an exit strategy. They were on the move, Kai cradling her in his arms as he carried her through the halls. Sera didn't hear any other people nearby. She heard nothing but the soft rustle of his clothing and the steady rhythm of his heart. His chest rose and fell against her cheek; his arms held her in a tight embrace. So protective. So strong.

And she was in so over her head. She was not going to set down that road, she promised herself. The problem was she was already halfway there. She couldn't stop thinking about Kai—and she didn't even want to. This was bad. Bad, bad, bad.

The soft beep of a car announced their arrival in the garage. The sound was different than that of the previous car—the car she'd trashed fighting the wolves. She really did have a bad track record with technology. And heavy machinery.

Kai set her down on the car seat, his breath tickling her skin as he leaned over to fasten her seat belt. "You can open your eyes now, Sera."

She cracked open an eyelid to look up at him. "How did you know?"

"Your magic." He walked around the car and climbed up into the driver's seat. "It has a different hum when you're awake and when you're asleep." He started the car, which appeared to be a close replica of the previous one. "It changed about ten minutes ago, right in the middle of my epic conversation with the guys, right as I was telling them I'd pry the information out of you with medieval magic."

"So I heard. That doesn't sound very pleasant."

"It depends on who you ask." He turned to look at her, his eyes twinkling with magic. "And how you do it."

Whoa. Sera diverted her eyes out of the window. Looking at Kai right now was dangerous for her self-resolve. Ok, so she was pretty sure he was trying to help her by taking her away from his base, but she would almost have preferred the commandos torturing her. At least then she'd know where she stood. Unlike with Kai.

"Where are you taking me?" she asked as he drove out of the gates.

"To my house."

Bad idea. That way lay dragons. Going home with him wasn't any better than being imprisoned back at Crusader headquarters. In fact, it was probably worse. Much, much worse.

"I have a better idea," she said. "How about you bring me home?"

"No."

Sera gave him an annoyed look. "I see." She folded her arms across her chest. "So I am your prisoner after all."

"Of course not."

How reassuring. "I could blast my way out of here, you know." Well, assuming these windows weren't enchanted in the same way as the ones in his office.

He saw her squinting at his windshield and said, "These windows are enchanted only from the outside. So, yes, you could break out. But you're smarter than that. You know we need to work together to solve this problem."

"No, I'm not—and no, we don't," she said.

"Don't be stubborn. Whoever cast the spell is inside one of our organizations. Someone set us up back at Sunset Tower, someone who could control the fog. The bottom line is we need each other because we don't know which of our own people we can trust. Maybe it was your people who set us up, maybe mine."

"And maybe I don't trust you," she told him.

Yet she did. And the fact that he was willing to admit it might have been his own people behind the shifted reality made her trust him more.

She sighed. "Ok, fine. We'll do this together. But no medieval magic."

"I'll just have to think of another way to pry the information out of you." His look was serious, and yet there was humor dancing in his eyes. Those eyes like blue lightning, burning with magic. They were hypnotic.

And Sera was crazy. She cleared her throat. "Precisely how were you planning on prying the information out of me?"

A slow, sexy smile twisted his lips. "I haven't decided yet. The usual ways, I guess. Torture, interrogation, seduction."

Sera's mind was screaming at her not to run down that dark, scary alley that led into the dragon's den. She ignored it. She did love dragons. "You might want to work on your order there," she told Kai.

He laughed. "It's a work in progress."

God, he had a nice laugh. Strong, assured, but still honest. Genuine. Sexy as hell. And when he laughed, his armor dropped. Everything dropped, leaving him exposed, raw, naked. She blushed at the thought.

He glanced over at her and chuckled, low and slow. "You're always doing that."

"Doing what?"

"Blushing."

"I know." A heavy sigh rocked her chest. "My sister is always teasing me about it. She says I'm too reflective, always over-thinking things."

"Is this the same sister who charged into Sunnyvale and single-handedly slaughtered the town's entire monster population?"

"One and the same," Sera confirmed. "Alex doesn't think anything through. She just acts."

"That must make things simple."

"She claims it does. I'm not so sure. She makes even bigger messes than I do."

He laughed. There it was again, that perfect laugh. "You? Reckless? I can't imagine."

"Yes, I know it's hard to believe."

"Not really. Not after seeing the state of my SUV," he said, a hint of reproach in his voice.

"There was a pack of monsters after us. A horde even."

"One of the doors is missing."

She shrugged. "The monsters did it."

He shot her a dubious look.

"Fine, I'll just deduct it from your bill," she said.

"Bill?"

"The bill for saving your life. I figure with how valuable you are, I'm looking at a big paycheck," she told him.

"I thought you'd left your mercenary ways behind you." He looked more amused than outraged.

"I guess people don't really change."

He leaned across the divider, coming in close to whisper, "So, how would you like to be paid?"

His lips brushed past hers, soft and light. Heat flooded her, shooting tantalizing tingles all the way to her toes. Her breath stuttered, dizziness setting in, soon to be followed by madness. She dug her fingernails into her palms, trying to bring herself back to reality.

"You should keep your eyes on the road," she told him, trying to keep her voice hard and steady.

"I'm not taking driving advice from the person who wrecked my car."

"There were extenuating circumstances."

He chuckled.

"Kai, I'm serious. You could hit someone."

"No one's crazy enough to be driving at this hour in this city of monsters."

"Except for us," she pointed out.

"Sometimes you just have to be crazy."

As he kissed her again, she darted her tongue out to taste his. He swallowed her whole, devouring the inside of her mouth with unfettered hunger. The seat belt was restricting her movement, so she unraveled her magic, moving it where her hands could not reach.

The car swerved. Kai pulled back quickly, narrowly avoiding a building.

Sera smirked at him. "See? I told you that you need to keep your eyes on the road."

"There were extenuating circumstances. Your magic is wicked."

His magic brushed against hers, sending a jolt of liquid lightning cascading through her body. She'd never felt anything like that before. His magic was playing her body like a harp, making it sing with sensations she never knew existed.

"You're one to talk," she gasped.

The car came to a stop, and Kai said, "Sera, we're

here."

She peeled her eyes away from him to see that they were inside an underground garage.

"Astounding. We didn't die."

"I told you I could do it," he said with a satisfied smile. His hand lowered to her thigh.

Her heart rate spiking in a mixture of panic and anticipation, she jumped up and scrambled out of the car before she did something reckless. Like have sex with Kai Drachenburg inside of his car. She couldn't do that. She had to get her head back on straight. They were still enemies, no matter if they were working together on this one thing. And no matter how hot he was. Or how good his magic felt. Or how well he kissed, which was even better than she'd imagined. She touched her lips but dropped her hand hastily as he came around the car.

"I'm impressed we made it here in one piece," she told him, looking around the garage.

There was space enough for six vehicles. Two of the spaces were empty. The other four were occupied by big, egregiously expensive cars.

"As far as interrogation chambers go, this one isn't so bad," she said, smirking. "You have a thing for big cars?"

"It's easier to run over hindrances."

She laughed. "You really are a fan of the brute force method, aren't you?"

"I figured you'd appreciate that."

His hand slid past her ribcage, igniting the skin below into a state of eager panic. All her reasons for not sleeping with him were sounding really lame right about now.

"Well, I…"

He winked, then moved his hand further past her to open the door. "After you."

Turning to hide her scorching cheeks, Sera headed up the stairs. Well, at least Kai was a gentleman. Unless he just wanted to get a good look at her ass. She tried not to sway her hips too much as she ascended the steps.

The sign on the door at the top of the stairs read 'Here Be Dragons'. Sera snorted, then went inside. The first floor greeted them with a spectacular view of the bay through floor-to-ceiling windows. Sera paused to drink it all in. Kai stopped right behind her. His chest was rock-hard against her back, pushing against her as he breathed. Surging, retracting, surging, retracting. The teasing game of it was excruciating. He set his hands around her arms.

"Sera," he said, his breath hot against her neck.

She shivered. "Yes?"

"I want to show you something."

He took her hand and led her up the stairs to the next floor. From here, she could see all the way to Fairy Island. The magical wall that protected it was glowing bright and pink, a beacon of hope in the darkness of night.

"It's beautiful," she said, smiling. "You have a marvelous view."

"Yes."

Something in his voice made her turn around to face him. And then she saw he wasn't staring out of the windows at all. He was staring at her. She recognized that look in his eyes, a look of intent. Of promises she knew he had every intention to keep. His magic was pulsing, singing out to her, drawing her in with its seductive melody. She took an automatic step toward him—then stopped.

"Sera," he said.

"No."

"I haven't said anything yet."

"Let's just keep it that way, ok?" she pleaded. Every word that he spoke drove her closer to that edge, to the leap she couldn't return from.

"What are you afraid of? Me?" He set his hand on her shoulder.

She brushed it off. "Of you, of myself, of what's happening here. We are enemies, Kai."

"I am not your enemy." Stepping forward, he lifted his hands to her cheeks and met her eyes. "This has happened before. You and me. Can't you feel it?"

A rush of images flickered through her mind. She and Kai in a burning tower, monsters all around them. Vampires rushed Kai, burying him. Sera pushed them away. She pounded on Kai's chest, tears pouring down her cheek, mixing with her anguish. She shocked him awake with her magic. His hands massaged her back, hard and strong. His magic followed, pouring over her in a flash of white heat.

"Yes," she said, shaking herself free of the stream of forgotten memories. "But that was in a different world. We were different. How can we remember that?"

"No matter how much we study it, no matter how much we try to understand it, magic is a mystery." His arm hard across her back, he dipped her head back to give her a deep, deliberate kiss that made her knees buckle.

"The war," she protested.

"Does not exist between us," he said, pulling her in closer.

"Kai, if they find out about us…"

"They won't."

"I…"

She pulled away to catch her breath—and grasp for her fleeing sanity. Who would have known that madness could feel so good? Outside, the sun was rising over the horizon, bathing the bay in pink light.

"I'm interrupting your morning routine," she teased him with a small smirk. She couldn't hold it back.

He gave her a quizzical look.

"What Naomi said about your morning running routine." *With your shirt off.* Her gaze dipped to the hard muscular lines of his chest, clearly visible beneath his shirt.

He realized what she was thinking. "I'll take off mine if you take off yours." He grinned, fire creeping into his eyes.

She bit her lip, casting a long, sinful look down the length of his body. For one blissfully insane moment, she allowed herself to wonder what he would look like with fewer clothes on. She was about to throw caution to the wind and take him up on his offer when Kai's phone rang.

He ignored it. Instead, he nipped at her lip. A flash of heat shot through her as he teased it between his teeth.

"Someone wants you," she gasped.

"It can wait. I'm busy." He silenced his phone, then tossed it down onto a side table.

"I'm not sure—"

"Yes, you are. You're just still trying to talk yourself out of it. Let me help you make the right choice." His hands moved beneath her tank top, rolling it up with excruciating slowness as he lowered her back onto the bed.

The house phone rang. Kai growled under his breath.

"They're persistent," she commented.

His lips brushed against hers. "Give me just a moment, sweetheart." This time when he called her that, she didn't even mind.

"I'm not going anywhere," she promised.

"Good." He kissed her once more, then rose slowly from the bed, moving downstairs to answer the call of the ringing phone.

◆ ◇ ◆ ◇ ◆

Sera lay there alone, trying not to feel awkward. She was in Kai Drachenburg's bed! When she'd started out the day yesterday, everything had been so simple. She and Kai had been on opposite sides of a war that would only end in the other's complete annihilation. There was nothing more clear-cut than that. She'd never thought she'd ever work with him, let alone start to have feelings for him.

Because, like it or not, she had to admit to herself

that she was starting to care for him. And that was dangerous. She knew that. With Kai not right in front of her, it was easier to keep a clear head.

Maybe the world had been changed. Maybe they'd been together in the World That Was, but they weren't in that world anymore. What if they couldn't change the world back—or what if they decided they didn't want to change it back? In this world, the world they were living in, a relationship with Kai had very real consequences. It was about time she woke up and smelled the post-apocalyptic coffee. Reality was calling, and she needed to jump on board.

Sera's pants buzzed. She pulled out her phone to stare at Naomi's picture. "Hey, how's it going?"

"Hey yourself," her friend replied. "Man, you sound depressed. What happened?"

"Nothing." Just an appointment with reality. "What's up? Did you talk to your Gran?"

"Yeah, I did. She had some helpful tips for sweet-talking ghosts with a few of their marbles missing," said Naomi. "I was going to go diving in the fog to talk to some of the brain-muddled ghosts and their mirror selves, but I was sidetracked when I got a lead on Rane. So I thought I'd pay her a visit."

"You visited a demon? Alone?"

"Yep."

And Sera had thought Riley was reckless.

"And what did you learn?" she asked Naomi.

"Well, actually, not so much. Rane wasn't feeling very chatty. She threw me out of her house—uh, fire pit."

"Did you mouth off to her?"

"I'll have you know that I was the perfect charming fairy."

"So what went wrong?"

"She apparently doesn't like fairies," Naomi said. "And most especially not Spirit Warriors."

That wasn't uncommon among demons. Spirit Warriors were some of the only supernaturals who could hurt a demon, and that just didn't sit right with their big egos—or grand plans for world domination.

"Plus, it turns out she hates Makani," Naomi added. "And therefore me by association."

"What did our dear Prince of the Pacific do to her?"

"Oh, I don't know. According to him, they once had a disagreement of sorts. It was centuries ago, back in his demon-fighting days. He gave her hell's equivalent of a bloody nose or something like that, and now she hates him for eternity. Moody sort, those demons. Who holds a grudge for centuries?"

Demons, apparently. And the Magic Council. They really needed to get over that prank the Dragon Born played on them.

"If you can bring me to Rane's domain, I could try talking to her," Sera said.

"I don't know, Sera. If she hates me because I'm with Makani, then she might hate you too. You are his second in command."

Which was totally the same as sleeping with him.

"Rane doesn't have to know about that," Sera said.

"Well, she knew right away about me and Makani."

"Of course she did. I can smell his magic on you a

mile away. I bet she could too. Demons are sensitive to magic."

"She might smell his magic on you too, Sera."

"Unlikely. I haven't seen him in over a week. And I'm not that close to him. Which makes me wonder…" How to phrase this in a way that wasn't crude… "Naomi, did you pay Makani a visit before going to hell?"

"Yeah, I caught one of the spirit realm fast-track streams and went to chat with him about everything going on between realms and realities. I figured that since he'd spent so much time in hell, he might have some ideas. And he did. He was my lead on Rane. He told me where to find her." She chuckled. "We might have gotten a little physical."

Clearly, Naomi had no problem being crude. Then again, she never had. Naomi was the sort of person who told it like it was.

"Really? Now of all times?"

"There's no time like the present. And besides, I haven't seen him in like four days. A girl has needs, you know." Her smirk carried clearly over the phone line as she added, "You too, Sera. Have some fun. Why are you even talking to me instead of playing with Kai Drachenburg?"

Then without another word, Naomi hung up. She really was one to grab life by the horns and never let it go—and she encouraged everyone to live life the same way.

But Sera had a crisis to fix. If she had even a chance of fixing this world, she had to take it. She didn't have time to play with the dragon.

You were playing with Kai, her dragon reminded her.

Yeah, she had. And it had been fun while it lasted. Right now, though, she needed to focus, no matter how she felt about Kai. Step number one of fixing this mess was to talk to Rane. She needed to find out what the demon knew. After that… well, maybe then she and Kai could talk about this thing between them—and figure out what to do about it. Until then, she had the world to save. And who knew, maybe she'd end up saving herself along with it.

Sera hopped off the bed and took the stairs down to the next level. Kai stood across the living room, in front of a wall of glass windows, lit up by the sun's morning light. He was looking outside, his back to her, his magic bottled in. He must have been having second thoughts about their relationship too.

Sera was about to go to him, but before she could move, he spoke. "Sera." The ice in his tone froze her solid, like an arctic wind cutting through her body. He set his phone down on the table.

"Kai?"

He turned around to face her, his expression hard. His eyes burned with blue fire. "I should have known better."

"What's wrong?" she asked him. It must have had something to do with the call he'd received. "What's happened?"

He chuckled humorlessly.

"Kai? Tell me. You're scaring me."

"You should be afraid." Magic flames roared to life on his hands. "You have betrayed me."

15. The Winds of Fury

KAI GLARED AT Sera, anger burning inside of him. Anger at her. Anger at himself. She was the enemy, and he'd trusted her. But she'd been lying to him all along. He'd been such a fool. He'd never been one to trust so quickly, but something about her had scrambled his brain, overloading all sense. Tony had been right. His judgment was impaired, and Serafina Dering was the one who'd impaired it.

But no longer. He fed his anger to the fire burning on his hands. The flames surged higher and hotter, building up to a catastrophic release. A small voice inside of him reminded him that it probably wasn't a good idea to start a fire fight in his house. He silenced that voice, along with any self-doubt that would keep him from doing what had to be done.

Sera approached him slowly, lifting her hands. They were free of magic or weapons. She didn't even look like she wanted to fight. It was probably a trick.

Yet another lie.

"Wait," she said.

"No talking," he said in a low growl. "Ready your magic, draw your sword. Whatever. Stand and fight me."

He was not going to blast through an unarmed woman. Some things were just not done, no matter what she'd done. No matter what lies she'd told.

"I'm not going to fight you, Kai."

"I didn't take you for a coward."

She bristled at that. "No, I don't have enough sense to be afraid of anything. Even a big, bad dragon shifter like you."

There she was doing it again, disparaging herself.

"You are a lot smarter than you make yourself out to be," he told her.

And that was the problem. She was too smart. She was a better liar than he'd thought. She'd played out a sweet song of innocence and good intentions, and like a fool he'd drunk in every note, believing every word, every smile, every flicker of her seductive, duplicitous magic.

"Enough of these games," he declared.

"Indeed," she replied shortly. "Why do you want to fight me? What's wrong? I thought we were…" Her words choked off. "What happened to you?"

"*You* happened to me." He moved forward, hot fury pulsing through his veins with every step that he took toward her. "Your lies."

Her eyes drew together in a perfect imitation of confusion. "What lies?"

He was so close to her now, standing over her. The

sweet, spicy flavor of her magic teased his senses, exciting him as much as it infuriated him. This had to end now. The catalyst to his downfall had a name, and it was Serafina Dering.

His voice cracked with anger as he spoke. "The Dragon Born have gone too far. There are some lines you do not cross."

He pulled his cell phone out of his pocket and shoved the screen in her face, showing her the picture Tony had just sent him. The picture of the sister Kai thought he'd lost years ago. The little sister he'd thought was dead. Lara.

As Sera glanced at the picture, her magic stuttered. Its sweet song evaporated, leaving only the overripe stench of rotting fruit in its wake. Guilt flashed in her eyes.

"Kai, I—"

"How long have you had her?" he cut in, before she could smooth over her lies with sugar-coated promises. "How long has my sister been your prisoner?"

She blinked in surprise. "Your sister?"

"Yes, my sister. Who is in *chains* right now."

Things all over the living room exploded. Electronics fried. Books shot off the shelves. Windows shattered. The cold wind howled inside, swirling the chaos around, but Kai didn't care.

"I didn't know who she was," Sera insisted.

"Don't lie to me," Kai bit out. "Don't even try."

"It's not a lie. I found her yesterday, unconscious in the Forsaken District right before the commandos found me. I didn't know who she was. I wasn't going to just leave her out there with darkness falling and the monsters closing in, so I brought her to our base."

"You took her in, this stranger, all out of the goodness of your heart?" He barked a laugh.

"Yes," she said, defiance flashing in her eyes. "The people of this world need to start looking out for each other, not hating each other. That's the only way the killing will stop. The only way there will be peace."

He was too infuriated to be moved by her words. Not this time. They were probably just another lie anyway. Her whole story was probably a lie. His sister had died five years ago in a battle she'd been too young to fight. Another tragic casualty of this war. So either the Dragon Born hadn't really killed her—just taken her from the battlefield and kept her prisoner all this time—or the woman in that photo wasn't really his sister. This might be just another Dragon Born trick.

"Alex and I woke her," Sera continued. "But she doesn't remember who she is. We tried to use magic to help her remember—"

"You mean interrogate."

"Don't you dare pass judgment on me, Kai Drachenburg." She hurled the words in his face, anger burning in her eyes. "Your people sure weren't inviting me to a tea party when they tied me to that chair in your office. I saved their lives. I saved your life too. So you *will* hear me out." She hurried on, not giving him a chance to cut in. "Only after I'd brought her back to base did we notice the family tattoo. That's when we figured out she was a Drachenburg."

The Drachenburg family emblem was, unsurprisingly, a dragon. Every member of the family received a tattoo with that symbol. Enchanted with magic, the tattoo glowed when it was exposed to a special family spell. Every major magic dynasty had a similar mark. It was how they could distinguish their people from the imposters. The Dragon Born had quite a few fairies on their side, fairies who could change their appearance or even cast spells to make their allies look like other people.

But they couldn't hide what was inside. They couldn't change a person's magic. And magic didn't lie. Kai could always sense the Dragon Born from their magic, that potent cocktail so like his own magic. The problem was there weren't enough Sniffers to go around picking out imposters, and the tech for detecting magic wasn't that precise yet.

"So, yes, we figured out she was a Drachenburg," Sera continued. "But I didn't know she was your sister, Kai. If I had—"

"You'd have told me?" He laughed, and another window exploded.

Sera sighed. "Why must we distrust each other?"

"You can't erase centuries of distrust in one day."

"But you can create it in one day. Kai, we're not meant to be enemies. I can feel it. We're meant to be… I don't know. Allies."

And lovers. He felt it too in his gut. Until today, he'd always trusted his gut. He hated that he didn't know if he could trust it this time. Her magic had thrown off his equilibrium. What if this whole thing was one elaborate Dragon Born deception? What if there really wasn't a World That Was?

"We can fix this, Kai. We can make things right.

Lara..." She stopped, her eyes lighting up. "Lara is from the World That Was."

"What are you talking about?" he demanded impatiently.

"When Alex and I looked into Lara's mind, it was strange."

Kai had heard about Mind Breaker, a Dragon Born ability. He'd thought it was just a rumor. An old tale. The Dragon Born were viciously protective of their secrets. Why would she tell him now?

"I saw fragments that didn't make sense, like they'd come from another world," she said. "They must have been from the World That Was. Somehow she's from that world. She *knows* about that world. She must, somewhere deep down. We wanted to know if it's better than this one. Well, this is our chance. We have to see her. We have to help her remember."

Kai laughed at her.

Sera shot him an annoyed look. "Stop doing that. This isn't funny."

"No, it's not."

"You're psychotic."

"Sweet talk will get you nowhere."

"Start taking this seriously, Kai. We have to go see your sister."

"We can't see Lara," he said coldly. "Because your sister is about to kill her."

16. A Hell Like No Other

ANGER FLED SERA, leaving only dread in its wake. It twisted inside of her stomach, filling her with a sense of cold, hard inevitability.

"What are you talking about?" she said, fear straining her voice. Fear of what Alex had done. Of what she would do. And most of all, the fear that none of them would ever recover from the aftermath of that one cruel act.

"Your sister just sent us these." He shoved his phone into her hands.

Sera scrolled through the stream of photos. There were dozens of them, but they all featured the same dark scene. Lara was trapped against a concrete wall, chains bound across her arms, legs, chest, waist—over everything and anything that could move. The chains glowed, puncturing the murky darkness, lighting up Lara's contorted face. She was in pain.

The magic-charged chains chomped their

elemental jaws into her skin, a different element in each successive shot in the photographic series. Crackling flames of fire scorched her. Swirls of frost consumed her. Tendrils of sizzling gold lightning electrocuted her. Water drowned her. Earth crushed her. Wind choked the breath out of her.

A thick cloud of smoke permeated every photo, like the magic had been brewing for a while already. And in every shot, Alex stood behind her, a sword in her hand. Magic slithered down her blade, a demented smile cracking her lips as she swirled up the storm of elemental spells bombarding Lara. She was torturing Lara, and she wanted everyone to know how much she was enjoying it.

"Oh, god," Sera gasped.

"The Black Plague certainly lives up to her abominable reputation," Kai spat. Disgust dripped from every word. Anger pulsed behind every syllable. "Your sister is demanding that we release you at once. If we don't, she promises to cut Lara's throat."

Alex would do it too. She had no problem doing whatever it took to protect her family. And to win this war.

"She knows we have you," Kai continued. "She knows about what happened earlier tonight. How you drove onto my base pursued by a pack of Blight wolves. How the guys bound you and took you away. And how I drove you off the base again. You have a spy in my organization." Outrage bubbled in his magic. He obviously took that breach in his security personally.

"And you don't have one in ours?" Sera shot back.

She was sure he did. Makani had drawn out some of the Crusaders' spies, but they just kept popping back up. That was the problem with being desperate for allies. You couldn't torture everyone who came to you with an offer of help. Then people would simply stop coming. Not torturing their new recruits' intentions out of them meant they gained more allies, but it also meant some spies slipped through the cracks.

"Look, Alex is just looking out for me," she told Kai.

Sera didn't think Alex had actually enjoyed torturing Lara. She just wanted Kai to think that she had. She wanted him to think she was crazy enough to kill his sister slowly and painfully. Ok, so she probably really was just that crazy. Like Sera, family meant everything to Alex. In her eyes, the enemy had captured her sister, and she was going to do everything in her power to get her back. That's just what sisters did. The problem was Alex was always acting first and worrying about the consequences later. And she'd never met a consequence she couldn't hack her way through.

"I'll call her and set this right," Sera said, pulling her phone out of her pocket.

But Kai's hand flashed out, grabbing it before she could make the call.

"No calls," he said. "I won't have you compromising our position."

"Kai Drachenburg, you give me my phone back, or heaven help me, your position will soon be the least of your worries."

He tucked her phone into his pocket, then shot her a hard smile, daring her to try to reclaim it.

She stared him right in his insufferably beautiful eyes. "This is ridiculous. Stop being so hardheaded. I can fix this. I'll just go back to the Dragon Born base like Alex wants. I promise I won't let them hurt your sister."

His eyes hardened into ice. "Your promises are poison, your words lies."

"I never lied to you!"

"You had my sister, and you never told me. Maybe you didn't know she was my sister—or maybe that's just another lie—but by your own admission, you definitely knew you had a Drachenburg."

"I also have a bag of potpourri in my underwear drawer," she shot back. "Did you want to hear about that too? I don't tell you everything, you arrogant dragon."

"What were you planning on doing with Lara once you'd scraped all the secrets from her mind? You certainly weren't just going to let her walk away."

She opened her mouth to assert that, yes, she would have done exactly that. But she knew it wasn't true. Makani would have traded her off in exchange for some of their own people, or killed her to send the Crusaders a message. And Sera would have stood by and let him. She'd done it before, and before this war was over, she would have to do it again. Her hands were far from clean.

But that didn't mean she couldn't try to fix this situation. "I need to go talk to Alex."

"You're not going anywhere," he told her.

"I see," she replied, her smile strained to the breaking point. "Well, thank you for finally dropping the bullshit, Commander. I was your prisoner all this time after all. And to think I was actually starting to *like* you. My mistake. My first impression of you was spot on. You are an insufferable, arrogant, savage, demented psychopath."

"Are you done?"

"Oh, I'm just getting started," she said. "You sure have a fantastic way of showing your appreciation to the person who saved you from being eaten by monsters. Let's just set a few things straight right here and now. I could have escaped at any point."

"Then why didn't you?"

"Because I thought whoever cast the spell on this world was a bigger threat to us than we were to each other. Because I felt in my heart that we were meant to work together in harmony, not fight each other in hatred. And because, despite myself, I actually did feel something for you." Sera's eyes burned with unshed tears. She blinked them back. "But I guess you never really felt the same way."

"My feelings are irrelevant," Kai said, his words as free of emotion as his stone-cold face.

"That's just what people tell themselves when they're about to do something they know is wrong."

"Tell that to your sister. She doesn't just want you back. She wants me too."

"What?"

"We *both* have to come, you and I," said Kai. "You're not enough. If I don't surrender myself within one hour, she will kill Lara."

Sera wished she were shocked by this, but nothing shocked her anymore. She knew Alex would do anything to end this war. She must have found out who Lara really was and saw the perfect opportunity to snag the commander of the Crusaders' North American army. Had Makani been there, he'd have approved wholeheartedly. But Sera didn't. They couldn't act like this. They couldn't use innocents like this. That made them into the monsters the Council said they were.

"Let me talk to her." Sera's throat felt as dry as sawdust.

"I'm taking care of it."

Sera didn't like the sound of that. "What are you doing?"

Bombing the base? It was protected by magic, but what if the Crusaders had found a way around those defenses? What if they had a new weapon? What if there were enough spies in the inside to break the protection spell?

"Kai?"

"I'm going to return the favor," he said. "Your brother is fond of treasure hunting in the Forsaken District, isn't he?"

A cold chill cut through her.

"As we speak, my team is tailing him. He's just entered the site of an old magic factory. They once made healing sprays and drinks—up until the monsters chased them out. There must be a vast treasury of medicine buried in there. It's worth millions. Or, to a group with too few healers, priceless. He could set you up with healing supplies for months.

Even years." Kai's fingers danced rapidly across his phone screen. "*If* he survives the salvage."

"You cold bastard," she said. Every word cut like glass. "You stay the hell away from my brother."

He met her infuriated stare and was unimpressed. "Scary."

"If you hurt him," she snarled. "I will pluck your scales from you one by one and feed them to the Blight wolves."

Magic crackled between them, hard and angry. It was the sort of magic that didn't bend; it broke.

"You like to pretend you're a reasonable, peace-loving, hair-braiding, let's-all-hold-hands-and-sing-in-a-circle person, but when push comes to shove, you are no different from your sister, the Black Plague." His voice dropped to a rough whisper. "You are just a plague of a different color."

Anger abandoned her, allowing dread to take hold. Threatening him wouldn't save her brother. She had to try something else.

"Kai, please," Sera pleaded, grabbing his arms, pulling on him desperately. She wasn't above begging. "Don't bring that building down on him. Don't kill my brother."

Kai looked coldly at her hands, then peeled them off his arms with cool composure.

She tried again. "He's a non-combatant mage, Kai. He is no threat to you."

"Those bombs he makes are a threat to us," he shot back. "And just because he's not fighting on the front line, that doesn't mean he's not an enemy soldier."

"He is just a kid."

"So is my sister," he snapped. "The kid that your sister has threatened to kill."

Kai was too stubborn to listen to reason, and fighting him wouldn't solve anything. He was too powerful. She wasn't sure she even could take him down alone. But even if she managed to, would she use his life to save Riley's? Would she continue this circle of hate, this loop of escalating atrocities, further fueling the war already consuming the world?

She could escape him. Thanks to Kai's outburst, the windows were shattered. She could summon her dragon and fly away from here. But Kai would pursue her, cut her off, and she might not be able to get away in time to save Riley.

The only option left to her was to appeal to Kai's humanity. She knew he had it in him. She'd seen it. She'd felt it.

"Please," she said, meeting his eyes. "All I have left of my family are Riley and Alex. I can't lose them."

"Despite what you might think of me, I am not a monster. I will not murder an unarmed man. But my team will take him into custody. If Alex releases my sister, no harm will come to him."

Alex would give up Lara for Riley. Sera knew that she would. But that didn't mean it would end with that. Alex would find a way to get her revenge. They didn't call her the Black Plague for nothing.

"We have to put an end to this endless cycle of hate." She took his hands, squeezing them, trying to make him understand. "We need to work together, not against one another. Otherwise, there's nothing left of any of us that's worth saving. We're all just monsters.

To lose your humanity—that is a hell like no other."

Kai looked at her like he was finally starting to listen, maybe even understand. But then his phone beeped. He glanced down at it, and when he met her eyes again, that hard expression had returned.

"They got him. Let's go." He grabbed her arm, pulling her toward the door. "We have a date with your sister."

17. The Forsaken District

ALEX HAD AGREED to the prisoner exchange, just as Kai had expected. The Black Plague was a vicious killer, but she loved her brother and sister. She'd sworn at him, promising retribution of a thousand gruesome tortures, all while calling him a soulless bastard. He'd expected that too.

They agreed to meet at a neutral location in the Forsaken District, close to Fisherman's Wharf. It was near to where the commandos had found Riley scavenging in the old factory. It also wasn't far from the magic shop Kai and Sera had visited not so many hours ago.

A lot had changed in those few hours. The magic shop, the final holdout against the monsters, was abandoned now. With the barrier gone, the monsters hadn't wasted any time moving in. They'd already torn off the nailed planks over the windows. The splintered remains of the wooden barriers littered the ground in front of the shop.

A group of monsters was trapped inside a nearby parking garage, held in by a glowing blue magic barrier with the distinctive hickory smoke and rosemary flavor of Dal's magic. The beasts kicked and clawed, hissed and growled, banging against the barrier in the hopes of finding a way through.

Beside the garage, a second magic barrier shone brightly in the early morning light. It encompassed a high platform, one of many platforms the Dragon Born had built along the city's waterfront when the war came to San Francisco. They'd intended to shoot at Kai's army from way up there, to knock them out before they even got close, but Kai had sent spies in ahead of time to sabotage the towers. Most hadn't survived. This was one of the few that the Dragon Born had managed to save.

"Ladies first," Kai told Sera, waving his hand toward the tall ladder that led to the top of the platform.

She made a derisive noise, then started climbing. Kai followed closely behind, and as they reached the top, he saw his commandos waiting on the other side of a second barrier. They sure weren't taking any chances. They'd contained the monsters in the immediate area and set up a secure spot to make the exchange—and they hadn't even had much time to do it. There was a reason they were Kai's favorite team, and it wasn't only because of their wicked sense of humor.

Dal opened a hole in the barrier for Kai and Sera to enter, then closed it behind them. Riley stood between Tony and Callum. Relief flashed in Sera's eyes as soon as she saw him. But her relief soon hardened into cool rage when she realized his clothes were torn. Blood dripped from the ripped fabric.

"You hurt him." Her accusation pierced the early morning air still thick with fog. It was mundane fog for once.

"Actually, the building hurt him," Tony said. "A section of it collapsed on him when he tried to flee." He pointed down at an old wood building below whose roof was mostly caved in. "We pulled him out of there. Then Dal healed him."

Sera looked like she didn't know whether to thank them for saving her brother or tell them off for capturing him. She really was an enigma. Kai wondered if she even understood herself.

Maybe he'd been a bit hard on her. Yes, she'd had Lara in her custody and hadn't told him about her, but would he have done anything different in her place? It was hard for each of them to trust the other. Maybe they never would. The rage in Sera's eyes whenever she looked at Kai now seemed to indicate that she never would. No, it wasn't just rage. It was betrayal. And hurt. He couldn't stand to see her look at him in that way, so he kept his eyes forward.

He was angry too, beyond rage and reason. But Sera was not the one who'd tortured Lara, then sent him a slideshow as a souvenir. It was her sister Alex. The cursed Black Plague.

Kai stepped over a pile of mysterious glowing goo on the ground on his way to join his men. As he and Sera walked side-by-side, he kept his hand locked firmly around her arm. She didn't even try to fight him. She glared at him like she wanted to blow his head off, though. The six of them stood in silence, waiting.

They weren't kept waiting long. A change in the barrier's pitch preluded Alex's arrival. She was testing the barrier, poking it to find any sign of weakness. Kai was pretty sure she could have broken it if she'd wanted to. The sheer brutality of the Black Plague's magic-breaking ability was renown. She didn't believe there was any problem too small to knock down with a really big sword.

But she didn't break the barrier. Alex arrived on the platform, then waited at the top of the ladder for Dal to make an opening. She extended her hand down to pull a woman up.

Kai recognized his sister right away—not just her face but also her magic. His chest tightened with emotion. He pushed it right back down. He couldn't afford to betray any weakness. If he did, Alex would exploit it.

Kai was so overwhelmed at seeing the sister he'd thought was dead that it took him awhile to see something he should have noticed right away. "She is unharmed," he said as Alex led Lara through the opening in the barrier.

"I don't deliver damaged prisoners." Alex's eyes hardened as they fell on Riley's bloody clothes. "Obviously, the Crusaders don't hold themselves to the same standards."

"Those injuries were inflicted by a collapsing building, not us," Tony said calmly. "And we healed him."

"Oh?" Alex's brows lifted. "Well, how nice of you to heal him after you chased him into that building that collapsed on him."

Kai looked at Lara's dress. It was a yellow and pink sundress, the exact same one she'd been wearing in the pictures Alex had sent. In those pictures, the dress had looked burnt and ruined beyond repair, courtesy of the magic bombarding her. Right here and right now, however, it looked pristine.

"What's going on here?" Kai demanded.

Alex's mouth curled up into a mocking smirk. "We're doing a prisoner exchange, remember? Just like we discussed. Don't go senile on me now, Drachenburg. I still want to get my brother and sister back. And if you're too crazy to fight properly, this won't be nearly as fun." She flashed him a manic grin.

Wow.

"Did anyone ever tell you that you're crazy?" Dal asked her.

"And kind of scary," Callum added.

Alex turned that crazy smile on them. "Why, yes, as a matter of fact. Lots of people have told me that. Right before I run them through with my sword, by the way." She licked her lips. "Speaking of which," she added, looking at Kai. "If you don't want me to add Sunshine here to my very extensive death toll, then send my dear brother and sister on over. I don't think your delicate sister is enjoying my company too much."

Lara snorted.

Kai gave his sister a long, hard look. There wasn't a

scratch on her.

Lara blinked at him. She clearly had no idea who he was—or who she was either. After that initial outburst, she was trying really hard not to laugh. She...*liked* Alex. He could sense the adoration in her magic. She looked up to Alex. She obviously saw her like a big sister. Either Alex had cracked Lara's mind and she was now worshipping her captor, or...

"You never tortured her," Kai said, a cold anger taking hold of him as he realized he'd been duped.

"Impossible," said Tony. "We saw the pictures. We saw what *she* did to Lara." He shot Alex a wary look.

"Photos can be manipulated," Callum said. "Like that time we pasted Kai's face on the picture of a demon and stuck it on his office door."

The commandos' faces were completely, professionally blank. On the outside, they were the perfect soldiers. But their magic didn't lie. Inside they were laughing their heads off.

Beside Kai, Sera coughed down a chuckle. Alex grinned brightly, her gaze shifting from her sister to Kai.

"You were bluffing," Kai told her.

Alex smiled back.

Kai looked at Lara. "And you helped her."

Lara shrugged. "Alex said we were playing a game. I just had to act like I was in excruciating pain while she stood in front of me with her sword and one of her friends took photos."

Kai's jaw cracked.

"Aw, what's the matter?" Alex said to him in a mocking voice. "Is the big, bad, scary commander feeling embarrassed for overreacting?"

"He blew up his windows when he learned you'd tortured his sister," Sera told her.

Not only because of that. The belief that Sera had betrayed him had nudged him over the edge. Hence the windows. And the furniture.

"You have some anger management issues, Drachenburg," said Alex.

Kai narrowed his eyes at her. "I will get back at you."

Alex laughed. "For *not* torturing your sister."

"For making me think that you had."

"Well, would you have come here if I'd sent you a photo of your smiling sister eating a cookie?"

"I will tell everyone about what you did," he promised. "I will tell them that the Black Plague has gone soft."

The humor washed from her face in an instant. "You wouldn't dare."

"People's fear of your reputation is the reason you win your battles. With that reputation shattered, people will start to stand up and fight you."

Alex's magic crackled and spat. "My reputation is well-earned."

"As is mine."

Alex stared him in the eye for a moment, then threw back her head and laughed. She looked at Sera. "I can see why you're in love with him. He does have a certain ruthless charm to him beneath all that armor."

Sera's cheeks flushed. "I'm not in love with him."

Alex grinned. "Sure you are. I can see it in your eyes when you look at him. I can feel it in that sappy, gooey magic of yours. L-O-V-E."

"Can we talk about this later?" Sera said, nodding toward their audience. She was pointedly looking away from Kai.

While Kai couldn't tear his eyes away from her.

Alex's eyes darted from Sera to Kai. "Oh, dear. Did I make things awkward?" She looked more delighted than repentant. It must have been the gleeful way she wiggled her eyebrows up and down.

"It's fine," Sera sighed as Kai declared, "No."

Sera met his eyes for a moment, then hastily looked away. Her magic was all over the place, soaring and crashing in erratic patterns.

Alex noticed it too. "Whoa, what happened between you two? We saw the fog swallow you at Sunset Tower. And then you were gone."

"The fog brought us to a strange area between realms—and between realities," Sera told her.

"Realities?"

"We escaped the fog and went to see Naomi," Sera explained. "The short version of the story is we think someone cast a spell to change our world."

"Change it how?"

"They altered reality," Kai said.

"Kai and I keep getting flashes from this World That Was," Sera added. "It appears that before the spell changed our world, we were all allies. And more than that, we were friends."

"We were friends with them?" Tony narrowed his eyes at Alex in disbelief.

"So it seems," said Kai.

"And you think *I* am crazy." Alex shook her head

slowly as her eyes panned across the commandos. "I can't even begin to imagine a world where I would be friends with those clowns."

Callum winked at her, magic sparking on his hands.

Alex winked back, showing him her magic too.

"Don't provoke her," Tony told Callum.

Alex blew them an electrically-charged snowflake kiss.

"So what do you want to do about this?" Tony asked Kai.

Kai looked at Lara. Something about her presence now was stirring up memories inside his head, memories that wanted to be freed. Magic flashed before his eyes. He saw himself with Sera, Lara, Riley, and the guys. They were getting pizza together while chatting over the silly movie playing on the television. They were all so happy, so carefree. There was no fighting. No war. It was a better place, just as Sera had insisted. He thought she was right about Lara too.

"Lara is from the World That Was," Kai said. "If she got her memories back, we might be able to figure out what happened. And how to fix things."

Sera smiled at him, the warmth returning to her eyes, a silent *thank you* to him for trusting her intuition. And he really did trust her, he realized.

"Naomi can bring us to Rane," she said. "We can get to the bottom of this. We can help Lara regain her memories. We can help all of us."

Her hope was refreshing. So deliciously infectious.

He brushed his hand against hers, and a rush of memories from the World That Was flooded his mind, flashing past faster and faster until they settled into one distinct scene.

He and Sera were in a grand office with marble floors, expensive art, and his name on the door. She was sitting on the edge of his desk, speaking enthusiastically about the monsters she and the commandos had just taken out for him. He knew he should have been listening to her, but he couldn't concentrate on her report. He saw only those beautiful lips he wanted to kiss, that blush of her skin that he yearned to touch. A whisper of red lace from her bra was peeking out from her tank top, tempting him, making him want to pull down her strap and see more of what lay beneath. He reached out.

But she caught his hand and said, "I'm trying to be all responsible and give you my report, Kai."

"And I'm finding it hard to concentrate."

Her mouth quirked up. "Try harder."

"I'm trying as hard as I can, sweetheart, and it's just not helping." He touched her cheek with his hand. "You're just too beautiful."

Her tongue traced her lower lip, slow and deliberate.

"You are trying to tempt me." He looked at her clothes. At her skin-tight leather pants, fitting her every curve. At those high-heeled boots. At the touch of lace peeking out of her top. "This is a setup."

She grabbed him by the collar, tugging him roughly against her. Her lips brushed against his. "I've always wondered what it would be like to make out with the boss in his office."

Sera's magic split through the room, and the door

to his office slammed shut.

"You always wanted to make out in Simmons's office?" he teased her.

The skin between her eyes crinkled up. "Ok, yuck. Let me just amend that. Ever since I came to work for you, I've been wondering what it would be like to make out with the boss in his office."

"This is totally inappropriate," he said, kissing her.

She sucked on his lip, and a burst of hot pleasure burned through his blood, kissing every nerve, sparking thoughts too wild to contain.

"That's the whole fun of it," she said with a wink, pulling him onto the desk.

Kai snapped out of the memory. He glanced over at Sera. She was running her fingertip across her lip. When her gaze met his, that same desire he'd seen in her eyes in the memory shone there now. They must have shared the same flash.

Lara is bringing out these memories, he realized. *She is from the World That Was, our link to that reality.*

"Let's find Rane," Kai said to Sera.

"Thank you for trusting me," she whispered with a smile.

He looked at the guys. "Let Riley go."

"Are you sure?" Tony asked cautiously.

"Yes."

"Let Lara go too," Sera told Alex.

Alex didn't look happy about this latest development. "This is a trick, Sera. It must be." When Riley reached her, she looked him over, then met him in the eye. "Are you ok?"

"Fine," he said quietly. He looked embarrassed that

he'd been caught. He had no reason to be. Kai's team was highly trained and good at their job.

Alex was still pleading with Sera. "You can't trust these Crusaders."

Sera typed out a message on her phone, then gave her sister a half-smile. "Alex, this isn't a trick. Our world has been split apart, thrown into chaos and warfare, and we're going to fix it." She glanced down at her buzzing phone, then looked at Kai. "Naomi says she'll meet us here in a few minutes, then she'll bring us to Rane."

He nodded.

"Bring Riley home," Sera said to Alex. "Keep him safe."

"I don't like this."

"Please, Alex. You just have to trust me."

Alex sighed. "Ok. Fine." She shot Kai a look loaded with promises of cruel and unusual punishments. "But if anything happens to my sister, I'm going all Apocalyptic Alex on your ass, Drachenburg."

Dal dropped the barrier to let her out, and she and Riley climbed down the ladder.

"Go back to base," Kai told the commandos. "Make sure no one tries to stab me in the back while I'm gone."

They didn't look any happier about this plan than Alex had, but they didn't argue. They prepared to descend the ladder.

"Wait," Sera said, holding out her hand to stop Lara. She pointed down at the blue goo on the ground, which Lara had almost stepped in. "Go around it."

"What is it?" Lara asked.

"Bird poo."

"Is that all?"

Sera wasn't done. "Bird poo from a Northwestern Firebird. You don't want it on your shoes. It's highly flammable. Once you have that stuff on you, every tiny spark is a potential explosion."

The commandos stopped to stare down at the nearest glob of goo. The globs were all over the roof.

"Fascinating," Dal said, squatting down for a closer look.

"What part of 'highly flammable' did you not understand?" Sera asked him.

He grinned at her. "The part where I'm supposed to shriek like a girl and run away in terror."

Callum and Tony chuckled.

"This is no laughing matter," she told them. "That stuff sticks to everything. And you can't get it off. Trust me. I know." She grimaced, as though reliving an encounter with one of the birds. "When a bird explodes all over you, you need to shower in this disgusting spray that smells like acetone. That's one of only two ways I know of to get the goo off."

"What is the other?" Callum asked her.

"Freezing. But that comes with the risk of losing appendages." She looked at Lara. "Ready to meet a demon?"

The smile Lara gave her was strained. "Sounds lovely."

But before any of them could further contemplate the consequences of a trip to hell, a group of telekinetics and wind mages dressed in black uniforms landed on the platform. More soldiers were pouring up from the ladder opening.

"Did you tell anyone about this meeting?" Kai demanded of the commandos as the mages surrounded them.

"No, we didn't, just like you said," Tony replied, eyeing the new arrivals.

Kai had had his doubts about the three of them before, but no longer. The commandos of the World That Was were his friends. He'd felt it clearly enough in those memories. Then and now, their magic beat loyal and true. They weren't behind this spell; they weren't the ones who'd summoned the fog to swallow him at Sunset Tower.

"I am Kai Drachenburg, commander of the North American army of the Crusade," Kai declared to the soldiers surrounding them. "You will stand down."

"With all due respect, Commander, *you* will stand down," replied the telekinetic mage leading the group. "Director Blackbrooke has relieved you."

"Blackbrooke," Kai growled. The man was always interfering with his operation.

Kai took a closer look at the telekinetic's face. He wasn't one of his own men. None of the soldiers were. They were from the outside. Blackbrooke was obviously afraid that Kai's men were too loyal to betray him.

"Go," Kai said, giving the telekinetic a dismissive wave.

The man took an automatic step back—then stopped, grimacing when he realized he'd given ground. "You're not going to stand down quietly and peacefully, are you?"

Kai gave him a small smile. "If you even have to ask that question, you obviously know nothing about me."

The telekinetic sighed. "I have to bring you in, you know."

"You can try," replied Kai. "But you won't succeed." He gave the commandos a quick glance, which they understood immediately.

The look they gave him back said, *one distraction coming up*.

Callum lifted his hands, summoning a rain of falling fire. Simultaneous explosions went off all across the platform. He'd put the bird poo to good use. It was blowing up in every direction. The soldiers were scrambling to figure out what the hell was going on, where all those bombs could be coming from. They didn't seem to realize they were right under them.

In the confusion, a few of the soldiers tracked through the goo, and Callum set their boots on fire. A pair of elemental mages were busy trying to put out the fires on the platform—and save their comrades' footwear.

Chaos reigned on the platform. Soldiers ran around in every direction. Callum set off more explosions as Tony and Dal fought off any of the soldiers who got too close to Kai, Sera, and Lara. The fire was putting off a dark smoke, reducing visibility to near zero. The guys threw a few smoke bombs of their own at the soldiers.

"Oops," Tony said as Blackbrooke's men began to

pass out.

The guys' laughter sang out over the sounds of clashing magic and metal. True to their new name, the commandos were taking out the attacking soldiers with pure efficiency.

Too bad there were so many of them. The path to the ladder was still blocked off.

Kai took Sera's hand and squeezed it. She squeezed back, smiling. She had such a beautiful smile.

"I know you don't remember me, but I need you to trust me," he told Lara.

She stole a furtive look at Sera. It was strange to see his little sister, who'd always looked up to him, look now to another. Strange but somehow reassuring. His sister always had been an excellent judge of character. And she liked Sera.

"Let's do this," Sera told her.

Nodding, Lara took Kai's hand. Using the smoke as cover, he took off running for the edge of the platform. Lara's eyes widened in alarm, but she held tightly to his hand and matched his pace. Sera gave them both a final smirk, then dove off the edge.

Kai threw Lara into the air. He shifted into a dragon, and she landed on his scaled back. Beside them, Sera rode on her dragon through the sky. They were moving fast now, Kai and Sera's dragon flapping their wings in sweet synchronicity. They were clear of the smoke, but another dark cloud was approaching fast, rumbling with magic.

"It's following us," Lara said, glancing over her shoulder.

"It's the magic fog," Sera added, and her dragon

sped up.

Kai matched her speed. They tried to outpace it, but the vile magic snapped at their tails, slowing them. Then it opened its smoky jaws and swallowed them whole.

The air shook and rumbled all around Kai, like he was caught in a storm. A flash of magic split through the fog, knocking him over. For the first time he could remember, he lost control of the spell holding his dragon shape. His body shifted back, and he dropped out of the sky.

18. Of Beasts and Men

AS THE FOG overloaded Sera's magic, shooting her dragon back into her, she fell. She couldn't see a thing through the swirling mass of mist, but she could feel Kai and Lara. Following the scent of their magic, she reached out and grabbed their hands. In that moment, she broke through the fog. The barrier between realms hiccuped, and they fell into the spirit realm. A hellish San Francisco lay below, alight with slowly crumbling buildings and streams of glowing magic.

"Can you shift?" she asked Kai.

"No," he replied with perfect calmness, even in the face of their impending demise. "That fog threw my magic off. It needs a moment to resettle. Can you do any magic?"

"I'll try."

Sera tapped into her magic. Harassed by the energy of hell, it didn't come willingly, but she managed to cast a bubble of wind beneath them, slowly cushioning their fall.

The ground was coming fast. Sera wrapped another layer of magic around them, and they touched down on the grassy expanse inside the city. Their landing wasn't gentle, but at least they made it in one piece.

"Are you all right?" Sera asked them, shaking out her legs.

"Fine," Lara said.

"How did we get to hell?" Kai wondered, looking around.

Nearby, a hole in the ground belched up a geyser of fire, filling the air with the scent of sulfur and burning grass.

"There were globs of earth and the spirit realm whirling around inside of the fog," said Sera. "I broke through the fog while we were inside one of the spirit realm globs. So we ended up here."

"Globs?" Kai asked, his brows lifting.

"Yes, globs. They looked like globs."

His lip twitched.

"Don't make me set you on fire," she warned him.

"Is that a promise?"

"I can also just electrocute you."

"It might be worth it."

"Do you want me to give you two a few moments?" Lara asked them.

"No need," Sera said. "It shouldn't take me more than *one* moment to knock him flat on his back."

His gaze slid over her. "And what will we be doing once you have me flat on my back?"

"Uh…" Yeah, she'd walked right into that one. She had to stop doing that with him.

But before she could drive her foot in her mouth any further, an army of hellish men riding equally hellish beasts stampeded across the fiery plains and surrounded them, saving Sera from further embarrassment.

"How's your magic?" Sera asked Kai. Hers was hurting. Majorly. You had to love the magic-sucking, brain-piercing vibes of hell.

"I'm running a little low." He cast an earthquake that swallowed up half a dozen beasts and men.

Her jaw dropped. "A *little* low," she repeated, shock not even beginning to cover the flood of emotions swirling inside of her. Shock was joined by jealousy that he could still have so much power in hell and by amazement at the sheer force of that spell—and, finally, by an unwilling excitement at the ruthless sensuality of his unbending willpower.

Sera was about to scrape up some willpower of her own and blast the beast men over with a hurricane of hellish proportions, when Naomi popped up next to her.

"Miss me?" she asked with a cute wink of her glittery eyelashes. She cast a spirit barrier, trapping the beast men on the other side.

"How did you find us?" Sera asked her.

"You created a massive shock wave when you broke into the spirit realm. It rippled across the whole realm. I could have felt that from the moon." Naomi glanced at the beast men, who were charging at her barrier. The impact knocked them off their beasts. "Trust you to attract the only demonic army within fifty miles of here."

"They were waiting here when we dropped out of the sky," Sera told her.

Naomi smiled.

"Did you say *demonic* army?" Kai asked her.

"Yeah, they work for one of the demon lords. Which means we need to get out of here. That barrier won't hold them forever."

The beast men kept charging at the barrier. Hairline cracks were starting to form, shooting across the glowing pink wall of magic.

"Link hands," Naomi instructed, grabbing Sera's hand.

Sera connected to Kai, who connected to Lara. A chain of bodies, they jumped into the stream of light and magic as the spirit barrier broke. The highway carried them away, and Naomi waved goodbye to the beast men running in futile strides to catch them.

Or not so futile. Beasts and men flooded into the glowing stream after them. Naomi's smile wilted from her lips.

"They can use the stream?" Sera asked Naomi.

"That's new. Their demon must have given them the power."

Roaring out a vicious war cry, the beast men charged forward. Naomi shot spirit magic their way, which Sera ignited as it hit them.

"Cool," commented Naomi.

But the beasts were still getting closer. Picking them off one at a time wasn't going to cut it.

"Take Naomi's hand," Sera said to Kai.

If any of them let go of Naomi, they'd fall out of the stream. Only someone with spirit magic could surf the highways of hell.

Kai shot Sera a quizzical look, but he grabbed hold of Naomi's hand as Sera slipped out of the way. She grabbed onto his shirt to hold herself in place, their noses brushing together.

"If you wanted to get close to me, all you had to do was ask, sweetheart," Kai whispered against her face.

"Maybe later," Sera whispered back. She didn't even know if she was joking or serious. "Get ready to catch me," she told Lara.

Then she rolled across the front of Kai, slipping past Lara to kick away a beast man at the front of the pack. Lara reached out and grabbed hold of her wrist, and Sera bounced back, blasting the nearest beast man with her magic. He stumbled and rolled, taking three others with him as he fell out of the stream.

"You're insane!" Kai called out to her over the howl of the storming stream. It didn't seem to like all of the earth magic they were hurling around.

She shot him a wide smirk and called back, "That's already been established!"

"How did you know I'd catch you?" Lara asked her.

"I trust you." She smiled at Lara.

Lara smiled back.

"We're getting close to your stop," Naomi announced, her voice piercing the raging storm. "I'm going to open up a hole so you can get through. Rane will be on the other side."

"What about you?" Sera asked her. "You're going to fight a whole army by yourself?"

"I'll be fine. I have a few tricks up my sleeves."

She cast a ball of swirling silver streaks into the stream. Then, unlinking from Sera, Kai, and Lara, she pushed them inside. As Sera slipped through the hole between realms, she saw Naomi launch herself off the stream like it was a trampoline, making the magical highway wiggle and shake so much that she knocked the beast men off of it.

◆ ◇ ◆ ◇ ◆

They landed in front of a small cave with a purple door built into the mountains. Since there wasn't anything else in sight except black bushes growing out of the blanket of ash on the ground, Sera figured the cave must be Rane's place. She knocked on the door, but no one answered. She looked back at Kai, who shrugged and pushed his way inside.

The door was unlocked. Maybe demons didn't need locks. No sane person went knocking on a demon's door—or entered a demon's home without invitation.

Inside, the cave walls were as smooth as glass and as shiny as a mirror. Magic echoed off the mirrored surfaces, a million voices blended into a single chorus. The voices sang a song as old as time itself, a song of forgotten ages and fractured realms.

"This doesn't feel like the spirit realm," Sera commented.

"No," Kai agreed. "It's something else. Something outside the realms."

"How very perceptive of you," a woman's voice cut

through the echoes. "For mortals," she added with a low chuckle.

A youthful woman with long blue hair tied up with a golden band melted out of the shadows, her high ponytail swaying as she stepped gracefully toward them. She wore a crop top and short skirt, both a lighter shade of blue than her hair, and golden sandals. She was a head shorter than Sera and as willowy as a model. She looked like a nymph, but Sera wasn't fooled. Beyond the pretty facade, her magic was pure demon: thick, heavy, and snapping like the jaws of hell.

"Serafina Dering." She pointed at Sera, her gold bracelets jingling. Then she moved down the line to Kai. "Kai Drachenburg." As she finally stopped in front of Lara, her gold eyes lit up. "And his little sister Lara. You, my dear, are an anomaly."

"You know why we're here?" Sera asked the demon.

"Of course. The world has changed."

"Did you change it?" Sera asked.

Rane put her hand in front of her mouth and giggled like a young schoolgirl. "Onyx told you this is my doing, did he? Yes, I do have power over reality and perception." She ran her hand down her ponytail, turning the hair red. "I could perform such a spell, but I find myself completely unmotivated to cast it."

"So you didn't do it?"

"No."

"Then who did?" Kai asked her.

Rane smiled.

"You don't know," he said.

"Of course I know. No one can alter reality without me finding out about it. I can sense the ripples of change. I—and this place—exist outside of the realms, outside of reality." Rane touched one of the mirrored walls, and it turned to stone. A web of vines slid across the rocks, blossoming with red roses and purple morning glories. "Changes to the world do not affect us here."

"So you remember the World That Was?" Sera asked.

"Dear girl, I remember every world that ever was."

"So this isn't the first time someone has changed reality," Kai said.

Rane clapped her hands once, loud and clear. The sound echoed off the walls, blending into the melody of voices.

"Can it be changed back?" Sera asked.

"Yes."

"And are you going to tell us how?" Sera prompted her.

"I'm not quite sure."

"Not sure how to change it back or not sure whether you want to tell us how?"

"Exactly," Rane said. "Reality is complex. Every strand of time and space is interconnected. You cannot just start pulling randomly at strands. Merlin should have known that."

"Merlin?" Sera asked. "As in the wizard of legend?"

"No, not that Merlin." She giggled. "My former protege."

"So we're talking about another demon," said Kai.

Rane smiled at him.

"Fantastic," he said.

"So how did Merlin change reality?" Sera asked. "Like you changed that wall?" She pointed at the rocky wall, which by now was blossoming with twenty types of flowers.

"No," Rane gave the wall a dismissive wave, and the vine dissolved into smoke. The rocks turned back into the glossy mirrored surface from before. "That was not real. It was merely an illusion. Or, to borrow an old human expression, smoke and mirrors. Illusions are easy to create. Fairies do it every time they change their appearance. When you cast an illusion, the reality beneath still exists. But when you cast a reality spell, you change the very fabric of the world itself. It's very powerful magic. Very dangerous. Very hard to cast. If you don't do it properly, you might rip apart reality completely, creating a big melted mess."

"Like the fog," Sera realized.

Rane nodded. "Yes, the fog is one such place, but it is dissipating. Merlin seemed to have avoided a complete catastrophe, albeit only by the skin of his teeth. This kind of magic is unwieldy. It takes a true master, which Merlin, no matter what he thinks, is most certainly not, not even after all these centuries. When you cast such a spell, you must realize that you can never predict all variables, can never know if it will turn out the way you want it to. So many things can go wrong. Merlin doesn't ever think about consequences. He never did. He's obsessed with making deals with you mortals. You could call it his addiction."

"Who made a deal with him? Who wanted to

change our world? Was it the Crusaders?" Sera asked her.

"The Council has done many things in this war, but even they wouldn't go so far as to make a deal with a demon," said Kai.

Rane laughed. They looked at her.

"Let me show you something." She motioned for them to come closer.

As they moved toward her, she hurled a ball of glowing magic at the wall. The glob of yellow magic splattered against the mirrored surface, which began to ripple like water. Mist wafted up from it, filling the cave. Figures formed from the mist.

A group of mages, fairies, vampires, and ghosts stood in a circle, a potpourri of magical scents thick in the air around them: Crushed Velvet, Sunshine Leaf, and Cream of the Abyss. Dread twisted and turned inside Sera's stomach. They were summoning a demon.

She recognized some of their faces from the files she'd read on the Crusaders. These were high-up members of very old dynasties. This was the Magic Council.

A vision of Kai made of mist and magic walked past her to stare down the Magic Council. "You are summoning demons," he growled. "Real demons. The Dragon Born are not our enemies. The demons are. And you are inviting them into this realm."

The mist swirled, then Sera saw herself fighting the leaders of the Magic Council as the doorway to hell began to open. And Kai was fighting right alongside her.

"What was that?" Kai asked as the mist dissipated,

melting back into the mirrored wall.

"That was an echo from the World That Was," Rane told him.

"It's…shiny."

"I believe the battle took place inside a casino."

Kai turned to Sera. "We were still fighting."

"But not each other. I told you we were on the same side." She gave him a half-smile. "And of course we were fighting the Council if they were trying to summon demons into the world." Sera looked at Rane. "No offense."

The demon sighed. "I don't make deals with mortals. They always try to double-cross you after the fact. They promise to let you out, then they try to stuff you back into hell. Well, I'm fine right where I am, thank you. I don't feel the need to burn the earth to the ground while laughing over the dying, spasming bodies of my victims. That seems like an awful lot of effort to expend to prove I'm the biggest, baddest, most powerful demon in the land."

Sera was getting the feeling that Rane was not like other demons.

"So you're suggesting the Council made a deal with Merlin for a spell to change the world," Kai said to Rane.

"I didn't say that. I only showed you that they have no problem making deals with demons."

It wasn't a real answer, but Sera didn't think they'd be getting one. Rane might have been different than other demons, but she shared her kind's love of elusive, cryptic answers.

Sera had to try anyway. "So who made the deal

with Merlin?"

"Maybe the Council. Maybe someone else." Rane shrugged. "You would have to ask Merlin."

"And where can we find him?"

"No idea. We haven't spoken in centuries. But it doesn't matter. He wouldn't tell you who worked with him anyway."

Great. "How can we reverse the spell?"

One step at a time. They didn't have time to play twenty questions with a demon. They could worry about finding the person who'd made a deal with Merlin *after* they fixed this mess. If Naomi's half-demon friend was right, the clock was ticking. They didn't have long until the spell became permanent.

"Reverse the spell." Rane nibbled on her lip. "Good question."

"How about you give us a good answer then," said Kai.

"Careful, dragon. I already threw one person out of my house today."

"I think you'll find me harder to throw than a fairy."

She looked him up and down. "Oh, I don't know. I have a good arm."

Sera had to intervene before magic started flying. And demons and dragons.

But Lara was faster. "If you don't know how to reverse the spell, we'd of course understand," she said to Rane. "It is very complicated magic."

Rane wagged her finger at her. "I know what you're doing."

Lara smiled innocently at her.

Rane squinted at her. "You don't belong here. You are from the other world. Before the change."

So Sera had been right about Lara.

"But how did you get here?" Rane wondered. "People caught in the fog when the spell was cast were quickly driven mad by the contradictions and mirrored selves. But you...you're not mad. Are you?"

"I don't remember anything. Not even who I am," Lara told her.

"You have no counterpart here," said Rane.

"My sister died five years ago," Kai said.

Rane nodded. "Yes, that's it. You have no other memories to fill your head. But then why are you here? You *shouldn't* be here. When the spell swept the world, you should have ceased to exist."

Rane began pacing, muttering to herself. "And yet you are here, a fragment of the other world." She waved her hands around. Magic rose from them, coalescing into distorted shapes. "We can use this, I think."

The glowing magic latched onto Lara, and then *she* began to glow.

Kai tensed, but Rane just flicked her hand dismissively. "Don't mind the glow."

She might as well have told him to stop being Kai Drachenburg. He'd just gotten his sister back. He certainly wasn't going to let her be whisked off to oblivion.

But before any of them could do anything, the glow on Lara surged, shining as bright as the sun. A white flash exploded, blinding Sera. When she could see again, Lara hadn't been sent away after all. She was still standing there, albeit looking completely disoriented.

"What do you remember now?" Rane asked her.

Lara looked at Kai, then at Sera. "Everything. I remember everything."

19. Memories of a Lost World

LARA RAN FORWARD, slamming into Kai to give him a sisterly squeeze. Then she grabbed Sera's hand, pulling her into the hug.

"Thank you," Lara told Rane.

The demon looked flustered. Maybe no one had ever thanked her before.

"Thank you," Kai added, laughing inside when he saw her confusion compounded. It appeared he'd been right. She wasn't used to appreciation.

"How did you do it?" Lara asked her.

"Your memories were all there, locked away behind a haze caused by the shift in reality. I just put your body and mind back into sync."

"Lara, what happened?" Kai asked her. "Do you know how the world ended up this way?"

"The last thing I remember, Sera and I were in the Fairy Queen. A dress shop in the city," she said in response to their perplexed looks. "We were picking out a wedding dress."

"You're too young to get married," he told her, he hoped calmly.

"That's just like you, Kai, always thinking you know best. If I want to find a nice vampire to settle down with—"

"No," he growled.

Lara sighed. "Stop being such a hard ass."

Sera covered her laugh with an unconvincing cough. Kai glared at her. He could still feel her magic laughing.

"Chill out, Kai," Lara said. "I'm not marrying a vampire. I'm not marrying anyone, in fact."

"Then who's getting married?"

Lara smirked at him. "You are, genius. To Sera."

Kai looked at Sera. She wasn't laughing now. She looked like she wanted to flee actually. They stared at each other in silence, the air heavy with things unspoken. Rane watched them all, munching down on something that looked an awful lot like popcorn—well, except for the sulfur-like smell wafting up from it.

Lara looked from Kai to Sera. "Wow, I think that's the first time I've ever seen you two stunned to silence. You're always talking, flirting, bantering."

Sera's lip twitched. "Battle banter?" she asked Kai.

"Bedroom banter?" he shot back, a smile tugging on his lips.

Sera snickered.

Lara let out a heavy sigh. "Get a room. Seriously. Go at it like rabbits. I don't know what this world has done to you two, but the sexual tension between you is so thick that it's giving me a migraine. And your magic!" She looked at Kai. "Have you no shame? You've been feeling her up right in front of your sister."

"I have been doing no such thing," he said calmly.

"Believe me, I wish that were true. I wish I could forget what I've seen."

Kai had missed her, really he had. Teasing and all. But he had to sigh at her comments anyway. It was his brotherly duty.

"Anyway, so Sera and I were trying on dresses," Lara continued.

"Oh, you too?" Sera asked her, her eyes flicking briefly to Kai.

The two of them were insufferable together.

"I couldn't resist," Lara said. "The dresses were so pretty. I reserved one. I billed it to you, Kai. I knew you wouldn't mind."

Kai dropped his face to his hand.

"Do you have any potential grooms picked out?" Sera asked Lara.

"I'm still considering my options."

"I hear vampires make excellent lovers." Sera was pointedly ignoring the searing gaze Kai was shooting at her.

"Nah, too cliché," Lara decided.

Sera chuckled, low and wicked. "Of course." Her eyes twinkled at Kai.

She was just as bad as Lara. And he loved her for it. Wait, where had that come from? He loved Sera?

"Please continue with your story before Kai fries us with his fiery stare," Sera told Lara.

Ah, so she *had* noticed him looking at her. Why

did that make him happy? He was fighting a grin from breaking out on his lips. This was so messed up.

"Ok, so we were trying on the dresses," Lara said. "Suddenly, everything got really dark, like an eclipse. And then buildings started shattering. It was like a scene out of some post-apocalyptic science fiction movie. We saw a magic shock wave tearing down the street. The whole building was shaking. Sera pushed me down, shielding me as the windows exploded." She shivered, holding herself. "And that was everything. When I came to, I didn't know who I was."

"She shielded you with her body?" Rane asked Lara

"Yes, all heroic like." She grinned at Kai. "You would have approved."

"I'm pretty sure I wouldn't have approved of my fiancée throwing herself into danger."

He glanced at Sera. She was giving him an odd look. Almost contemplative. She was looking at him like she was allowing herself to really see him for the first time, without overthinking it, without analyzing the consequences. Just feeling it.

He could feel her magic venture forward to his, but it wasn't sexual or seductive. It was curious, warm, affectionate. Like she was embracing that connection between them.

Lara laughed. "Oh, yes, you knew what you were getting into," she told Kai. "Sera does crazy stuff like that all the time. Like that time she sacrificed herself to save us all."

Kai was enjoying his magical connection to Sera, but annoyance sparked in him at Lara's words. "Why would you do such a thing?" he demanded.

"I don't remember," Sera replied. "But I guess there was no other way to save the people I loved."

"There is always another way." He wrapped his arms around her protectively. It felt so natural, so right—like part of a pattern. He drank in her magic, the rhythm of her breaths. Magic was swirling around them, but he hardly noticed it. He saw only Sera.

"Don't ever do that again," he told her, kissing her forehead.

Sera's eyes lit up in challenge. She rose to her tiptoes and looked him in the eye. "Kai Drachenburg, I know you're not trying to tell me what to do."

"And what if I am?"

"There will be strong words," she told him.

"Oh, *strong words*, you say? Well, in that case, I'd better find something to hide behind."

"Don't make me kick your ass."

"That's more like it. Sweetheart," he tacked on with a grin.

"You call me that again, and you'll be eating your words, fiancé or not."

He grinned at her. "Sweetheart."

"Ok, you asked for it."

She moved to take a swing at him, but he locked his arms around hers, pinning them to her sides. She struggled against them with no success. He had no intention of letting her go. She zapped him with her magic, but still he held on. It was exhilarating. His body lapped up her magic, craving more. She hit him again with her magic. He continued to hold on, even though that last one had made him dizzy. He blinked down a few times, then looked down at her to find her smirking up at him. Her magic slid against his, tasting it, even as she zapped him again.

He leaned in, whispering to her, "Are you enjoying this as much as I am?"

"God, yes," she whispered back. Her lips brushed against his jaw, electrifying his aura.

Lara cleared her throat. Kai released his hold, and Sera took a step back.

"How disappointing," Rane sighed. "I was hoping they'd fight. Or screw." She set down her popcorn on a table as glossy as the mirrored walls.

"You're really crude you know," Lara told her.

"I'm a demon, dearie. Of course I'm crude."

"So, uh, let's get moving." Sera turned away from Kai. "Rane, can you help us find Merlin?"

"I don't know where he is."

"But you can find him," Kai told her.

A demon with her power level could find him. She could sense distortions in reality, and right now, Merlin was at the center of them all.

"Perhaps," said Rane. "But I have no desire to."

"Don't you care at all about what he's done?" Sera demanded. "He's wrecked the whole world."

"It doesn't affect me. Not here in this place between realms, between realities. This limbo land."

"You trained him. You made him powerful. This is your responsibility to fix the mess he's made," Kai told her.

Rane shook her head. "I can't help you."

"But you helped Lara remember who she was," Sera said. "You have power. You could help us fix this."

"I've already done too much."

"You're afraid of Merlin," Kai realized.

She let out a hard, derisive laugh. "Don't be ridiculous."

But Kai knew it was true.

"If you won't help us, then we'll just have to do it alone," Sera said, not giving up. Her eyes shone with hope, her mouth was set with purpose. She wasn't giving up—not now, not ever. Her stubbornness was positively endearing. "How long do we have before the spell is permanent?" she asked Rane.

"A few days. A week at most. Then the World That Was will be lost forever."

"I hate to be selfish here, but what happens to me when the other world is gone?" Lara asked.

"You are dead in this world. When the other world fades, you will cease to exist," Rane told her.

Lara's spark faded, her magic growing glum.

Sera grabbed Lara's hand. "We won't let that happen." She took Kai's hand next. "We'll fix this. For all our sakes."

20. Breaking Minds

"IN OUR WORLD, the Dragon Born and the Magic Council are not at war," Lara explained as they left Rane's cave. "The Council long ago killed all the Dragon Born. Or so they thought. A few survived, and occasionally a pair of Dragon Born twins is born, a miracle of magic that no one understands. To avoid discovery, you and Alex spent most of your lives pretending to be human."

"Are you saying that we shouldn't try to change the world back?" Sera asked.

"Not at all. The World That Was isn't perfect, but it's better than this place. For one, it hasn't been destroyed by centuries of magical warfare," said Lara. "And I think that the Council's views of the Dragon Born are changing, mostly because of you. You did save the world a few times. Plus, Kai roared and stomped and shot magic out of his nose in the Council chamber until the other members behaved themselves."

"I would never do such a thing," Kai stated. The expression on his face was perfectly convincing, but Sera wasn't fooled for a second. She knew his style, and roaring, stomping, and shooting magic was definitely it.

"You would and you did. And stop interrupting." Lara's lips curled with amusement. "So, recently the Council found out that Sera is Dragon Born. Many on the Council tried to have her killed. Right now, we're stuck at a bit of a standstill. Officially, the Council is pretending that Sera isn't Dragon Born, but that hasn't stopped a few members from speaking out against her. One of them is Blackbrooke." She arched her brows at Kai.

"You think Blackbrooke is the one who made the deal with Merlin," Kai said.

"Perhaps," Lara replied.

"His men *were* present both times the fog attacked us," Sera pointed out. "If he realized we're onto him, he'd try to stop us from putting the world back to the way it was."

"Which is so stupid," Lara said. "Who would want this world, a world where so much is destroyed? Where monsters are slowly taking over?"

"People aren't always rational," Kai told her.

"Especially when driven by hate," Sera added, breaking through the in-between realm to return to earth.

They popped up inside a section of neutral territory south of Golden Gate Park. Neither the Dragon Born nor the Crusaders held the area, and the monsters hadn't moved in yet either. It might have had something to do with the ghosts. Rumor had it the area was haunted.

As soon as Sera's phone got reception again, she tried to call Alex. Her sister's phone went straight to voicemail.

"Problem?" Kai asked.

"I can't reach Alex. I wanted to ask her to help with our new operation."

"Which is?"

"To ask Blackbrooke if he made a deal with a demon."

Kai's mouth tightened into a hard line. "That's not what we're doing."

"Oh? Did you have a better suspect?" she asked him brightly.

He said nothing, his face hard, his eyes unyielding.

"I didn't think so," she said with a smile. "He set us up at Sunset Tower. He intended to send a kill squad after me. He took over your base. Sent soldiers after us. Need I go on?"

"No."

"He looks guilty as hell, Kai. Probably because he's been there."

Lara snorted.

"Very well. We will talk to him. But *just* talk," Kai said.

A few feet in front of them, hiding in the shadows, a car beeped. Kai kept walking toward it like he owned it.

"You do not have a car parked here," Sera said in disbelief, staring at the black SUV that, sure enough, looked like a tank.

"As you can see, I do." He opened the door for her. "I told you I had cars parked all over the city."

"Well, yeah, but I didn't actually *believe* it," she replied, getting in.

He leaned in closer and whispered, "You'll find I'm full of surprises." His words fell upon her lips, melting softly into them.

Then he pulled back and went around to the driver's side. Lara hopped into the back seat, laughing.

"I can't believe you have these tanks parked all over post-apocalyptic San Francisco just like you do back home," she told her brother as he started the engine.

"Tanks?" Kai asked, one eyebrow arching upward.

"Sera's name, not mine."

His eyes slid over to Sera.

"Well, they do look like tanks," Sera said with a smile.

"This vehicle does not have sufficient armor to classify it as a tank."

He said it so matter-of-factly that Sera couldn't help but laugh. "A mini tank then."

He bristled. "That is *not* a dignified name."

"I like it," said Lara.

"So do I," agreed Sera.

"Why am I not surprised?" Kai shook his head, then sped off wildly down the street.

Sera wondered if he drove like this in the World That Was, where there actually were other cars on the road.

"I messaged the commandos," Kai said. "They'll be meeting up with us soon."

"Where?" Sera asked.

"Back at Sunset Tower, where this adventure began," he told her. "Blackbrooke's forces have taken over my base, so we can't meet there."

"Good."

Kai gave her an odd look.

"Not good that Blackbrooke has taken over," Sera explained. "Good that we're not going to your base. I do not have fond memories of that place. Or of your team at that place. Are you sure we can trust them?"

"In the World That Was, the commandos are like brothers to you," Lara said. "And when it came down to it, when they found out what you are, they sided with you."

"But this world is different."

"I trust them," Kai declared. He sounded certain, but still…

"How reassuring."

"Well, there is one way to find out for sure," Lara said. "Mind Breaker."

"Mind Breaker," Kai repeated, as though he didn't like the taste of the word.

Sera looked at Kai, wondering if he was going to be a problem in this operation. The commandos were part of his army, and more than that, they seemed to be his friends.

But rather than protest, he just said, "Do it."

"Really?"

"Really," he confirmed. "I trust them, but if this is what it takes for you to trust them too, then do it."

Sera nodded. Kai was surprisingly reasonable—once you got past the dragon scales and hellfire.

"By the way, thank you for saving my sister back in

the World That Was," he said.

Sera smirked at him. "Now that wasn't too hard, was it?"

He sighed. "You're reckless."

"For saving your sister?"

"For provoking me. I've stomped on people for less."

Her smile widened. "No, you haven't. You just like to tell people that so they're scared of you."

He grinned at her.

"You wouldn't step on me," she told him, at least eighty percent sure of it. "I'd run my sword through your foot."

He reached over and flicked a strand of hair out of her face. "And when I knock your sword away?"

She caught his hand in hers. "Then I'll run my magic through you."

"Please do." He lifted her hand to his lips, kissing her fingertips. "And focus on my back. There's an itchy spot I can't reach."

She pulled her hand away, glowering at him. "You are insufferable. I can't believe I made out with you."

"And you enjoyed it too," he stated with perfect satisfaction.

"On second thought, I'm not sure I want to put the world back. Obviously, the Sera of that world has seriously impaired judgment. No way in hell would I ever have agreed to marry you."

He chuckled, low and confident. "You just keep telling yourself that, sweetheart."

Sera glanced back at Lara. "Is he this insane in the other world?"

"Of course. And so are you."

Sera didn't know what to say to that, and it turned out she didn't have any time to respond anyway. Kai brought the car to a stop at the base of Sunset Tower, parking in the shadows.

They stepped out of the car, moving toward the entrance in hurried silence. Unlike their previous meeting on the roof, they went inside this time. The lower floor had once been a lobby, as was immediately evident by the high ceilings, as well as the reception desk in the corner. Flipped onto its back and split down the middle, the desk had seen better days. Then again, so had the rest of the lobby. Furniture and parts of the building that had broken off the crumbling walls were littered across the floor like the candy that had exploded out of a birthday piñata.

And in the middle of the urban wasteland, standing right in front of one of those debris piles, were the commandos. Sera didn't waste time or words. She strode forward in hard, determined steps, blasting a wave of magic in front of her. Her magic shot through their bodies, breaking through their minds. She'd never broken three minds at once, and she didn't think she'd ever try it again. Visions flashed through her head, a jumbled mass of their memories from the last day. The scenes were zipping past too fast to catch everything, but she didn't need to. She could feel the loyalty beating beneath their magic. They would never betray Kai. In fact, they'd been doing nothing but trying to help him.

"They're clean," Sera told Kai, releasing the commandos' minds.

Tony looked up, rubbing his head as he met Kai in the eye. "You don't trust us?"

"I do. She didn't."

"Damn woman, that hurt," Callum complained to her.

"So did having my magic bounce off the window and slam into me."

"I guess we're even then."

A maniacal noise Sera hardly recognized as her voice burst from her lips. "Not even close."

"What do we have to do to make it up to you?" Dal asked her.

"Get me a pizza."

"We can order pizzas later," Kai said, then he turned to the commandos. "What's happening back at base?"

"Blackbrooke has taken charge," Tony reported. "He's called all Crusaders back to base."

"He isn't looking for us?" Kai asked.

"He's gathered all the Crusaders, getting them ready for a big operation," Dal said.

"What kind of operation?"

Callum's eyes flickered to Sera. "Against the Dragon Born."

"Blackbrooke has a new weapon," Tony said. "One he intends to use on the Dragon Born."

"Believe me now?" Sera said to Kai, pulling out her phone.

"If they are dealing with a demon…" Lara began.

"They might have new magic. Demon magic, which might be strong enough to break our defenses." As the phone rang, Sera tapped her fingers impatiently against the wall.

"Sera," Makani answered. "Naomi told me what happened."

"We're working on it. But listen, the Crusaders have a new weapon. It might be powered by demon magic."

Nothing seemed to shock Makani. He just kept going. "Naomi and I are headed back to base now," he told her. "If the Crusaders think they can beat us with demon magic, they've got another thing coming. Try not to get killed going after whoever cast the spell on our world."

Then he hung up.

Makani had fought demons for centuries. He was powerful and experienced. He never showed weakness. Still, if the Crusaders were backed by the magic and might of a demon, even he might not be strong enough to stop them.

Sera couldn't worry about this now. She had to trust that Makani could protect the base. After all, it wasn't like she could do anything he couldn't. She had to go after Blackbrooke. And for that she could really use Alex. Sera pulled out her phone to try calling her again, but her sister still wasn't answering. So she tried Riley. He picked up after the first ring.

"Riley, listen. The Crusaders are planning to attack the base. Makani and Naomi are on their way, but I'm not sure if they'll arrive in time. I need you to get everyone ready for battle. The Crusaders could strike at any moment with their new demon weapon."

"I'll spread the word," he promised. "And get a few surprises ready for them."

"Thanks," she replied. "Hey, have you heard from Alex?"

"No. After we returned to base, she went out again. She hasn't returned. She's not answering her phone."

"I know. That's why I'm starting to get worried."

"Alex can take care of herself."

Sera sighed. "How are you?"

"Fine."

"You don't sound very convinced."

"Just recovering. It doesn't feel nice to be crushed by a building."

"I did warn you about going treasure hunting in those buildings," she said.

"I guess I should listen to you."

"Oh, definitely." A smile tugged at her mouth. "Forever and always."

"I'll take it under consideration."

"Good."

Riley was quiet for a moment, then his voice pierced the static, "Sera?"

"Yes?"

"Watch out for yourself." His voice was strained with emotion. "The Crusaders don't pull any punches."

"Neither will I," she told him, hanging up the phone. Then she turned to the commandos. "Have you seen or heard from Alex?"

"Not recently," said Tony.

"Your sister doesn't exactly send us love letters," Dal added, chuckling.

"We saw her briefly in the Forsaken District after the smoke cleared from our battle with Blackbrooke's men. She said she was looking for her weapons dealer." Callum gave her a bemused look.

"Slayer," Sera said.

"The assassin?" Kai asked.

"Yes. I believe you know him."

"I have his number," he said cautiously.

So Sera decided to tease him. "Why do you have Slayer's number?"

"I've hired him a few times." He said it with a completely neutral face.

The commandos had been talking about Slayer last night—and asking her about him.

"You hired him to spy on us," she told Kai.

"Yes." He didn't look embarrassed. In fact, he wasn't betraying any hint of emotion. "And to steal things. The assassin is quite competent at that."

"Because he's also a professional thief."

"I haven't forgotten." Annoyance flashed in his eyes.

Sera laughed. "He stole something from you, didn't he?"

"Yes," he admitted.

"Why did you hire someone who stole from you?"

"It wasn't my idea. It was a mandate that came down from Blackbrooke."

"That man causes all kinds of trouble for you, doesn't he?" she observed.

"You have no idea." He pulled out his phone, scrolling through his contacts list. "I don't trust Slayer."

"Because he stole from you?"

"Because he would steal from his own mother for

the right price."

"Alex seems to like him."

"Your sister is even more reckless than you are."

Sera couldn't argue with that. Prudence wasn't one of Alex's virtues. But who cared? Alex had more than enough other virtues to make up for it.

"Don't mind Kai," Lara said to Sera. "He gets grumpy when people take his playthings. You should have seen him with his toys when we were kids."

Sera couldn't imagine Kai as a child. Or playing with toys.

"What kinds of toys did he have?" she asked Lara.

"Tanks and dragons. And lots of armies. He made them fight one another."

"Of course."

"The battles were quite violent," said Lara.

"They were meticulously laid out," Kai insisted. "Full of strategy."

Lara rolled her eyes. "You meticulously lined them up to create the most violent battles."

"I wouldn't expect you to understand the finer points of my strategy."

"The battles always ended the same way. With the dragons charging the tanks, throwing them around and stomping them to bits."

"Sounds vaguely familiar," commented Sera.

The commandos chuckled.

Kai narrowed his eyes at them. "Traitors."

They flashed him matching grins.

Kai put his phone away. "Slayer isn't picking up," he told Sera.

"And neither is Alex. I wonder where they are."

"Knowing the two of them, up to no good—and lots of it."

"Well, then we'll just have to go chat with Blackbrooke without them," Sera said.

Kai expelled a resigned sigh. "Ok. Just talking. But no shooting. Most of the people on that base are mine."

"I'm sure we can think of something."

It was probably just as well that Alex wasn't coming. She'd have insisted on charging in a fury of steel and magic. This operation would require a bit more subtlety.

But as they set off toward Kai's base, Sera couldn't help but wonder where Alex was. And whether she was all right.

◆ ◇ ◆ ◇ ◆

Kai's base was lit up in a blinding array of spotlights and magical lanterns. Add a freaking enormous glowing wall into the mix, and you had yourself one impenetrable fortress.

Luckily, Kai had the entry codes. It turned out Blackbrooke was more arrogant than paranoid.

Soldiers were everywhere, but none of them were Kai's. Blackbrooke had brought along his own army. They were clearly getting ready for their big Dragon Born operation. They didn't seem to expect the battle to play out here. Sera and the others snuck past them with surprising ease. They even made it all the way to the inside of the main building.

And that's where their problems began.

A small army of soldiers was waiting for them in the lobby. Blackbrooke's army. The supernatural soldiers quickly surrounded them. Sera should have known it wouldn't be that easy.

"We don't want to fight. Just talk," Kai told them, lifting his hands slowly.

The soldiers misinterpreted his gesture. Fearing he was about to unleash the fires of hell upon them, they opened fire. Magic and bullets shot toward Sera's group, but they never met their marks. Dal cast a defensive barrier around them that absorbed the Crusaders' attacks. That didn't stop the soldiers from continuing to fire.

"It wasn't supposed to go this way," Kai said, watching the hail of bullets and spells light up Dal's golden barrier.

"I don't think Blackbrooke wants to talk," Sera observed. "He just wants to kill us."

Kai sighed. "Let's get him."

"Blackbrooke is upstairs."

"Yes. I can sense him up there," Kai replied with thinly concealed wrath. His voice dropped to dangerously low levels. "In my office." He turned to the commandos. "We need a distraction."

"Allow me," Lara said brightly.

She thrust her hands up in the air. A thick, shining beam of magic shot out of them. The stream split into two, and from each emerged a glowing dragon. One was green, the other blue, but both were woven from strands of magical light held together by the sheer willpower of a mage summoner. The two dragons shot over the Crusaders, trailing flaming tails of lethal beauty. They opened their mouths, breathing magic. The sheer power of the shock wave shattered every window in the room. A second breath of magic sucked up the soldiers and blew them outside.

Lara ran at the open windows, quickly picking up speed. Between one step and the next, a spell of shifting magic exploded around her, and then she was a dragon. An elegant blend of shimmering scales the color of rubies and wings that shone like gold, Lara made one beautiful dragon. She followed the two smaller dragons outside, and together they harassed the Crusaders, diving and roaring and breathing magic. Now *that* was a distraction.

"Your sister is really kind of sexy," Callum told Kai.

Tony and Dal nodded in agreement. All three commandos were watching the dragons with pure awe.

"Don't even think about it," Kai said to them. "Just keep these guys off our backs."

Tony gave him a crisp, professional nod, and the commandos turned to face the fresh wave of soldiers who'd just stormed the lobby. As Sera and Kai ran toward the elevators, a few Crusaders dropped down from the upper levels. Kai cast a swarm of whirlwinds, blowing the men out of their path. But more were coming. Sera spun around and hammered her fist against the floor. An earthquake shook violently beneath the Crusaders' feet, knocking them over. The elevator doors swooshed open. Sera and Kai dove inside, and he mashed the button for the twelfth floor.

They arrived at the roost that housed Kai's office without anyone else trying to kill them. Blackbrooke's head snapped up at the sound of the opening elevator.

His eyes narrowing, his magic hiccuping, he scrambled out of his chair and hit the alarm button on the wall. The act was superfluous. All the alarms on the base were already going off at full volume.

"Get away!" he shouted.

Sera moved forward, calmly avoiding the marble paperweight he threw at her. "Tell me about the new weapon you have against my people."

He backed up, his frightened eyes darting to Kai. "Why are you just standing there?" he demanded, his voice strained with panic. "Attack the abomination!"

Kai's glare was hard and cold. "You've ordered my own people to kill me."

Any semblance of hope died in Blackbrooke's eyes.

"Answer her question," Kai told him.

Sera kept moving forward. Blackbrooke ran around the desk, knocking chairs over without any rhyme or reason. The man had clearly never been in an actual fight. He didn't have any offensive magic. Just an offensive personality. Sera grabbed his arm as he fled, slamming her magic into him to break his mind.

A stream of memories flooded her, finally coalescing into a single moment in time. She saw Blackbrooke at the center of a large chamber, addressing his audience of mages, fairies, vampires, and otherworldly. The Magic Council.

"Everything is going to plan," he declared with satisfaction. "We've located the hidden community of Spirit Warriors."

"And you think they will help us?" asked an elderly female mage in the audience.

"Of course. They understand that their families

will be our guests until they've fulfilled their part of the bargain." Blackbrooke smiled. He really was evil.

"And how will you proceed?" a vampire asked him.

"The Spirit Warriors will cast a spell around the entire Dragon Born base," Blackbrooke explained with relish. He really liked being the center of attention. "This spell will send everyone inside the base to the deepest corner of hell. Then we let the demons deal with them."

"What about the Spirit Warrior allied with the Dragon Born? She can get them out again," a fairy pointed out.

"We're sending a team to Fairy Island. We will destroy the barrier and take the island," Blackbrooke replied with a cruel smile. "Her cooperation with us will ensure her family's survival."

The urge to electrocute Blackbrooke faded away to confusion. So the Magic Council was sending the Dragon Born to the demons, not taking the demons out of hell. And Blackbrooke was at the helm of it all.

But as despicable as he was, he wasn't the one who'd made a deal with Merlin to change the world.

The blinding lights of the Magic Council's chamber melted away to a darker room. Blackbrooke stood across from a man dressed in a high-tech synthetic black bodysuit. Weapon belts filled with knives criss-crossed his chest and were strapped around his arms and legs.

"I've been tracking the Black Plague and Slayer as you asked," the assassin said. Sera recognized him. His name was Nightshade, and he was a first tier telekinetic. He had enough magic to single-handedly level a city block. The knives were just for show.

"And?" Blackbrooke asked.

"They are dabbling in dark magic," Nightshade reported. "I saw them converse with a demon. The demon offered them the power to take out the armies of the Crusade."

"And they agreed?"

"Yes. They did," the assassin said.

Sera's heart sang out in agony. This couldn't be happening. Not Alex.

"Then we'll need to act fast," Blackbrooke decided.

The memory faded out, hurling Sera back into the jaws of cold reality. She stumbled away from Blackbrooke, sagging against the wall.

The Director met her eyes. "Abomination," he spat through bloody lips. Then he turned his glare on Kai. "You've brought the Dragon Born here. You've betrayed us."

"This whole world was changed," Kai told him. "Because of you."

Except it wasn't Blackbrooke. Sera tried to process what she'd seen in his mind, but she just couldn't. Her heart couldn't take the strain. It would break.

Blackbrooke was more than happy to speak for her. "It was the Black Plague," he said with cruel satisfaction. "She made a deal with a demon."

21. Fallen Alliances

SERA COULDN'T FORM the words. She couldn't even think about it. It hurt too much to even consider the possibility that her sister had betrayed her.

The Crusaders rushed into the office, saving her from further reflection. As they tried to paint the room red with her blood, she blasted them aside, her survival instincts kicking in. Fighting them was so simple, so easy. So black and white. Not like Alex's betrayal.

Kai fought beside her, his eyes hard. Fury raged beneath the cool composure at the surface of his magic. Whether he was angry at his own men for trying to kill him or at Sera for convincing him that Blackbrooke was the one behind the spell of shifted reality, she did not know. She almost didn't want to know. She'd convinced him to attack his own people. And she'd been wrong about Blackbrooke all along. The thought that Kai might not ever forgive her ate at her almost as much as the hard fact that she didn't really know her sister at all.

"You caused this!" Blackbrooke called out as two of the Crusaders whisked him to safety. "The Dragon Born brought this hell on the world!"

And the horrible, insane truth of the matter was he was right. The Magic Council had spearheaded many atrocities throughout the millennia, but this one sat firmly in the Dragon Born court.

The Crusaders continued to stream into the room, overwhelming Sera and Kai, backing them up across the room. With every backward step, they were losing ground. They'd soon be right up against the window—the very same window that had bounced back Sera's magic, knocking her unconscious the last time she'd tried to break through it. If she hit it with her magic enough times, it would break. *Everything* broke eventually. She probably had the raw power to do it, but her body didn't have the endurance to take that many hits. It hadn't been able to withstand even one blast of her own magic, let alone five or ten or however many it took before that window's magic defenses overloaded and shut down. No one could withstand that.

So what if she didn't have to?

"Hey, guys!" Sera called out to the Crusaders with a contemptuous smirk. "Is your magic so weak that you have to hide behind those guns?"

They took the bait, lifting their hands to blast a wave of elemental and telekinetic magic at her. Their magic shot forward, a glowing ribbon of energy. Sera threw herself against Kai, then turned the tackle into a roll to move them out of the way. The Crusaders' magic hit the window and bounced back hard at them. The magical overload knocked them unconscious.

Sera rose to her feet and walked over to the window, brushing her fingers across the glass. The magic protecting it hummed in low, weak notes, barely holding a tune. It was weak now. Sera could see the holes in the magic lattice. She thrust her magic through one of those holes. All at once, the magic and glass crumbled from the window frame. Still not meeting her eyes, Kai cast a funnel of wind magic out of the open window, and they used it like a slide to reach the ground.

Down here, the battle was raging in full force. Lara was back in her own body, grappling with the soldiers by hand while her two dragons swooped and swiped freely at the army surrounding her. Dal and Tony were engaging the Crusaders with their swords, while Callum blasted them with a dizzying stream of elemental spells.

Without a word to her, Kai turned and walked toward his team. He'd trusted her, believed her, even taken up arms against his own people for her—and her sister had been behind everything from the beginning. Sera didn't know if she could fix this, but she couldn't help but try.

"I didn't know," she called out to him. "Alex has always been willing to do whatever it takes, but I didn't think…"

He just kept walking, not stopping for a moment. She wished he would turn around and shout at her, fight her, or even curse her name. That's what Kai did. He didn't just walk away. Except here he was, doing just that. She could feel his magic simmering with cold rage beneath the mental wall he'd put up—and yet he wasn't attacking her. He was holding himself back. She wasn't sure what to make of that, but she didn't dare hope.

Sera was alone now, without allies, deep within enemy territory. She had to get out of here. She turned and hurried toward the wall. Sometime during the fight, the magic protecting it had overloaded. Riley stood on the wrong side of it, a magic bomb in each hand. He looked ready for a fight.

"I came to help," he declared, looking around for an unlikely Crusader to throw his bomb at.

If the situation had been different, she might have laughed. Instead, she frowned at him. "You shouldn't have come. It's too dangerous here."

Like always, he shrugged off her concern. "The base has been warned. Makani can handle things. I couldn't just stand by while my sister stormed the Crusaders' headquarters." He hurled his bomb over her head. Light exploded in a flash, and the four Crusaders who'd been running toward her passed out. "I am going to help."

"The fight is over." She watched Kai and the commandos turn their backs on her and walk away. "This is all over."

Lara dropped down in front of Sera, carried in by her blue dragon. "I'll talk to Kai. Wait here." Then she ran off after her brother.

Sera couldn't wait. She and Riley were alone amongst enemies. "We have to get out of here," she told him.

It had hurt to watch Kai walk away from her. Lara was arguing with him, but he didn't bend. He looked at Sera across the field, his eyes burning with fury. He'd come with her. He'd taken her side against the Council, and they'd been wrong.

Pain bombarded Sera from two fronts: Kai and Alex. She bottled that pain up. There was no time for it right now. She brushed the sweat and tears from her eyes, then took Riley by the arm. She had to get them out of here before the Crusaders caught up to them.

Magic shot past her, and she threw herself over Riley, shielding him as they fell to the ground. She jumped up quickly and spun around. Alex stood across the lawn, magic burning on her hands.

"I know, Alex." Flames erupted from Sera's hands. "I know what you did. You crossed a line we swore we'd never cross. You made a deal with a demon!"

"I wasn't going to hold up my end," Alex said, moving forward. "I was just using him to get the power we needed."

"And that's supposed to make me feel better? You changed our world, Alex. It doesn't matter if you let the demon out of hell because your actions have put us all into hell."

"What?" Confusion rippled across her magic. "What are you talking about?"

"You and the demon altered reality. You made this hellish world. You sent the fog after us, to trap us. Why?"

"Sera, I don't have anything to do with that fog. The damn stuff swallowed me and Logan, and we barely got away. I haven't used the demon's spell yet.

And it doesn't control the fog. It's a spell to drain the magic of supernaturals. Hell in a bottle. I was going to use it to weaken the Crusaders during battle."

Her magic ran true. But that didn't make any sense.

"But if you didn't cast this spell, then who did?"

Sera was so busy staring down the false threat ahead of her that she didn't see the real one from behind. Magic surged through her, overloading her senses. She fell to the ground.

She looked up into Riley's face. It was a cold face, a hard face, one she hardly recognized. Magic as dark as midnight pulsed up and down his arms. Alex lifted her hands to shoot him, but he was faster. The dark magic swirled like fog and enveloped her, pinning her to the ground. Where had he gotten that magic?

"Sera," Riley sighed as the dark magic wrapped around her wrists, constricting tightly. "I love you, but I can't let you interfere."

22. Shifting Magic

KAI WATCHED SERA struggle against the magic wrapping itself around her body. Shining like the midnight sky and oozing with evil intentions, it didn't feel like anything from this world. Kai had never felt any magic like it before—except for the fog consuming San Francisco, the fog that was a byproduct of the spell that had changed reality. The fog that the demon Merlin could control.

Riley stood over Sera. He was supposed to be a noncombatant mage, and yet he was making this midnight magic bend to his will. His magic came from the same source as that fog. His master was one and the same. Merlin.

Kai prodded the boundaries of Riley's magic, looking for any hints of demon possession. A demon on the loose was dangerous. But Kai didn't sense a demon living inside of him. All he felt was that dark magic. It permeated Riley, thick as the fog. He was in league with a demon. He was clearly a threat.

Sera kicked at the magic crawling up her legs, shattering it. The spell hadn't hit her hard enough. It hadn't had a chance to sink its teeth into her yet. She freed her hands, and a surge of joy flooded Kai. But he contained the feeling. He contained all of his feelings. They were what had gotten him into this situation to begin with. What had he been thinking, attacking his own base, his own people? He'd allowed himself to get swept up in the whole adventure with Sera. He should have checked before accusing Blackbrooke. But he'd been so sure that the Director was up to something. And he was. Sending the Dragon Born and their allies to hell? That wasn't right.

Not that the Dragon Born were innocent. Alex had made a deal with a demon to weaken the Crusaders. And Riley had made his own kind of deal with another demon, and together they'd ruined the world.

Sera was on the move. Riley tried to shoot her, but she rolled away. Alex was still on the ground, trying to push at her magical restraints. Kai could feel the pulsing echo of her magic-breaking bursts pound against the restraints. But they weren't breaking. She'd received a stronger dose of Riley's magic. The spell holding her was out of phase with this world, between realms and reality, just like the fog.

Kai began to move forward, keeping a close eye on Riley—and on that black magic too. He couldn't let it hit him.

"Stop right there, Drachenburg." Riley pivoted around to stare him down. "Not another step."

Kai didn't step, but he did shoot. He unleashed a stream of elemental spells. Riley threw up a magic shield that ate them right up.

"My turn," he said with a wry smile.

Glowing balls of darkness whooshed at Kai, one after another. As Kai evaded them, he felt the magic singe the outer edge of his aura. Even though the magic barely touched his own, it stung like hell. That sure was potent stuff. No wonder Alex was still trapped beneath it. From what Kai had seen of her, she could break through anything. But not through this.

"I never thought you were one to run from a fight, Commander," Riley said coolly. Magic sizzled up and down his arms. Across his chest. His hair.

Sera gaped at her brother in horror. "What have you done to yourself?"

He spun to face her. "I'm doing this for you and Alex. I'm trying to protect you."

"By working with a demon?" she demanded. "You know better. Deals with demons never work out the way you expect. What did the demon promise you?"

"He gave me this new magic to fight the Crusaders, to protect my sisters. The war wasn't going well for us. I had to do something," he insisted.

"In the World That Was, there wasn't any war," Sera replied.

"There is no World That Was. The Crusaders have brainwashed you. They've woven this deception to confuse you from the truth."

"And what truth is that?"

"That they are the enemy," he stated. "I'm trying to protect you."

"How could you think betraying us would help us?" Alex demanded.

"I didn't betray you."

"All those times you went treasure hunting...you were meeting with *him*," Sera realized. "Did you spy on us for Merlin? Did you tell him I was meeting with Kai last night?"

"Yes," he said reluctantly. "He told me the Crusaders' commander was dangerous, and he was right."

"We were getting too close to the truth, and Merlin told you to keep us busy," Kai said.

But something about this didn't make sense. As Sera had pointed out, there was no war between the Magic Council and the Crusaders in the World That Was. Why would Riley have made a deal with a demon to make the world worse? Even if he'd been duped by the demon, why would he continue to work with him?

"Enough talk. I won't allow you to deceive me as you have my sister," Riley told him.

Magic swelled around him like a tidal wave, surging higher and higher toward an inevitable tipping point. A storm of black lightning rushed toward Kai and the commandos, who'd come to stand with him. It ate through Dal's barrier, washing Kai's allies away. Lara dashed toward Riley, but a second storm hit her. Her body froze, suspended for a few seconds as the cloud unleashed bolt after bolt of lightning on her, then she fell. As his sister hit the ground, rage ruptured the bindings of Kai's self-control and he charged, spells ripping out of him in rapid succession. Riley stumbled back under the onslaught, but he wasn't giving up. He countered with a hurricane of dark magic that hurled Kai against the wall. Kai was back on his feet in an instant, but Sera was faster. She ran between him and Riley's next barrage—and the spell hit her instead.

"Sera, what are you doing?" Riley demanded, his eyes shaking as he watched her wipe away the blood dripping from her nose.

"I'm not going to let you hurt him," she said, planting herself firmly between them.

"Get out of the way."

"No. I won't."

Riley tried to nudge her aside with his magic, but she wouldn't bend. She just kept standing there, refusing to move even as he hit her again with magic.

"Move," Kai growled at her.

"You're hurt," she told him.

"*You* are hurt." Kai could feel the pain pounding through her with every beat of her pulse. He couldn't stand it. He reached out to heal her.

She caught his hand. "Save your strength. I'll be fine."

"You are barely standing."

"I am standing just fine."

"You are insane," he said, a low growl buzzing on his lips. "I won't let you stand there and take damage for me."

She threw a smirk over her shoulder at him. "Well, that's the great thing about free will, you see. I can stand here if I want. And we've already talked about you not ordering me around."

"You are insane."

"On that we can agree," said Riley. "Sera, this is between Drachenburg and me. Stop being a martyr."

"Then stop shooting," she countered.

"He is the commander of the North American Crusader army. The enemy. They want to kill all Dragon Born. They want to kill *you*."

She looked at Kai, smiling, then back at Riley. "He's different."

Riley glared at her. "No, he's not."

"Back in the World That Was, we were all friends," Lara said, walking toward him. "I remember it all. We're not lying to you. Merlin is."

Riley paused. Something about Lara brought out the first spark of doubt in him. But just as quickly as it came, that spark was gone. His face hardened; his magic surged.

"Stop," a voice said with such force that the magic on his hands winked out.

Rane had appeared out of nowhere in their midst. The demon strode toward, her now-white ponytail whirling up in the wind. She wore knee-high black leather boots and a floral chiffon dress.

"Listen to them," she told Riley.

"You came," Sera said, surprised.

Rane sighed and looked at Kai. "It's about time I took responsibility for the mess Merlin has made."

"Who is this?" Riley demanded.

"Someone else who was betrayed by Merlin," Rane said. "I taught him everything I knew. I made him strong. Then he took that power and stabbed me in the back. He used me. Just like he's using you." She moved closer to him.

"Stop," Riley warned her, lifting his hands.

But she didn't stop. She just kept coming. Riley shot his magic at her. With effortless ease, she caught the magic around her arm, dissolving it.

"Your magic doesn't work against me," she told him.

"And yours doesn't work against me." He pulled out two magic bombs and threw them at her.

Rane darted aside with inhuman speed, avoiding the explosions. As Riley reached for two more bombs, she moved in, grabbing him by the face. With a hand against each cheek, she held him there, her spell weaving itself around him. Magic flashed, and then Riley was on the ground. He looked up, his gaze shifting from Rane to Sera to Kai.

"Oh god," he said, guilt cascading through him.

"You remember the World That Was?" Sera asked him.

"Yes," he said, standing to face Kai. "Man, I'm sorry. I thought I was helping, but I just screwed everything up."

"What happened in the World That Was?" Alex asked as the magic holding her dissolved. "Why did you help Merlin?"

"I'm not sure. I remember Merlin coming to me in our world yesterday. He said he had a way to help us with the members of the Council who wanted to kill my sisters. His hand flashed out…" Riley rubbed his head. "And then I don't remember anything else from that world."

"Merlin gave you some of his power," Rane told him. "He infused it into you. He gave you a magic that exists outside of time and space."

"Why?" he asked.

"To control you," she said. "The magic is very potent, very hard to resist—and for someone who was unprepared to receive it, impossible to fight. He fed off your love for your sisters, in both the World That Was and this one. He twisted that love, manipulating it so he could control you. Your mind was clouded. Merlin made you cast the reality-changing spell for him. And because this magic exists outside the realms and realities, you can cast it on earth and the spirit realm at the same time."

"Why would Merlin make Riley cast it?" Sera asked.

"He wanted to avoid the consequence of that particular spell."

"Which is?" Kai asked.

"There's a chance the person who casts the spell dies as the magic explodes across the world. And when you *did* survive, he decided to use you again. He manipulated you, drawing on your fears for your sisters' lives. He fed off your love for them, using it to drive you to do insane things. To trick you into spying on them for him. Into keeping them from finding out the truth."

"But how does Merlin know the truth? How can he remember the World That Was when the rest of us don't?" Sera asked Rane.

"I live outside the tides of reality, and so does Merlin." Rane set her small hand on Riley's shoulder, meeting his tormented eyes. "Don't blame yourself. You couldn't have done anything to fight his control."

"And he will do it again. He will control me again."

"I've broken the bonds of his control, giving you the magic to fight his influence," she said. "It won't be easy, but it *is* possible."

"You knew all of this when we met with you," Kai said to her. "And yet you told us nothing."

"It took some digging in the stream of memories to learn the full story." Guilt bubbled to the surface of her magic before she hastily pushed it back down. A demon who felt guilt? That was new.

"There is more to the story. What is your history with this demon?"

Rane looked at Kai like she wanted to argue, but she just sighed instead. "Merlin is not a demon, but it's as good as a classification as any other. Or as bad as." She glanced at Riley. "Once, long ago, he was a lot like you. A noncombatant mage. A student of the magical sciences. That's probably why he picked you to give his powers to, to cast the spell for him."

Riley didn't look like he liked the comparison.

"Merlin came to me, begging for knowledge. He was very talented, very inquisitive, especially regarding the magic of perception and reality. I decided to take him on as my student. I gave him powers that no mortal should have. He grew very quickly in power and knowledge. Too quickly. I didn't realize until too late that he'd gone too far. He did…terrible things. He'd used me to gain power. I cast him out, but he didn't stop. He had already grown too powerful, and he found ways to steal more magic."

"What does he want?" Sera asked her.

"He wants to change reality to suit him. And only him."

"We will stop him," Kai declared.

"I hope you can," Rane said. "And I'm going to give you a fighting chance."

Magic burst out from her like a shock wave. As it hit Kai, a deluge of memories hit him, pulling him under. The spell snapped, slamming Sera into him. He reached out, his arms closing around her in a protective embrace as they fell to the ground. Sera lifted her face from his chest and looked down at him. And in that moment, it all came into focus, this world and the one that was. He remembered every moment.

23. A Storm of Spells

SERA PROPPED HER arm up on Kai's chest, unable to contain the smile spreading across her face as she looked down on the man she loved.

"You remember?" he asked her.

Her smile grew wider. "Yes." She leaned down and kissed him. Then she punched him in the shoulder. "You did it again. Trying to boss me around, you insufferable dragon."

"What can I say? Old habits die hard." He set his hand on her back, pulling her in. "I missed you." His mouth brushed her neck, every word pulsing out a ruthless, sensual beat.

"I missed you too," she said, her senses igniting, overwhelmed by the closeness of his magic. "We have to fix this world."

"Indeed." He chuckled. "You still have to make good on your promise."

"What promise?"

"Your promise to let me help you try on dresses. And take them off."

"You are a wicked man, Kai Drachenburg."

"So you've told me. And that I'm insufferable, arrogant, and a bunch of things that are undoubtably true."

"Did I hurt your feelings?"

"Irrevocably." His mouth curled in sinful promise. "Care to make it up to me?"

"After we save the world, sweetheart." She grinned at him. "I'm sorry for calling you names. Even though you totally deserved it."

A soft chuckle permeated their private reunion, reminding Sera that it wasn't so private after all. She climbed off of Kai. Their arms still linked, they rose to their feet.

"I'm not forgetting about how you guys tied me up," she told the snickering commandos. From the looks on everyone's faces, they all had their memories back.

"You know we love you, Sera," Tony said.

"But it was war. And some of us were a bit overly diligent." Dal looked at Callum.

Callum grinned at Sera. "It takes more than a few zaps to stop a tough Dragon Born mage like you."

She folded her arms across her chest and continued to glare in an appropriately menacing manner.

"Though maybe you and Kai aren't so tough after all," he added. "After all, you were the only ones to fall over from that memory-joggling spell."

Alex laughed. "They were just looking for an excuse to make out."

The commandos were cracking up. Riley didn't join in, even though he was practically one of them by now.

Sera touched her brother's shoulder. "Are you all right?"

"No, I'm not all right. I messed up. I betrayed you."

"Hey, that wasn't your fault." Alex swooped in to gave him a rough hug. "Merlin messed with your mind."

"He's quite adept at this magic. Even against demons," said Rane.

Sera was getting the feeling more and more that Merlin had worked his magic over Rane too. And if he could fool a demon, he could fool any of them.

"So now that we know who we are again, let's fix this messed up world," Alex declared.

It was so weird having these memories in her head, this world and the other, all mixed up, conflicting.

"The old world is still there," Rane said. "Buried, but still there. But as this new world settles, the old fades away. Soon there will be nothing left of it. And when it fades, so will your memories. You will remember only this world."

"This world where we're enemies. Where we hate each other," Kai said to Sera.

She squeezed his hand tightly, fighting the sinking fear that if she let go, she would lose him again.

"We had a connection," she said, holding onto hope. "We didn't hate each other. Not really."

"Your bond is strong. Strong enough to cut through to this world from the one that was," said

Rane. "But once the other world disappears..."

"So will that bond," Sera finished. She looked at her friends and family, all united once more. "So we'd better get to work."

Thunder trailed her words. She looked up at a sky swirling with magic. Black lightning flashed across dark storm clouds. A spell was rolling in. It felt like the reality-distorted fog but bigger. Much, much bigger.

"Why do I get the feeling that Merlin sent his creepy magic storm to come swallow us whole because we know too much?" Alex said.

"Probably because that's exactly what he's doing," Sera told her.

"Yeah," Alex agreed, blasting the storm with fire.

The clouds shifted, swallowing her spell. Alex tried again. They all tried, hitting the storm with everything they had.

What they had wasn't enough.

Nothing they shot at it got through. The storm chomped down on elemental magic and bounced back Sera and Alex's magic-breaking spells. Riley lifted his hands, trying to control the storm with the magic Merlin had given him.

"It's not working," he said between clenched teeth, sweat beading up along his hairline. His body was shaking, convulsing.

"Let go," Sera told him.

"No." His face set with stubbornness, he kept hitting the storm with every ounce of magic and willpower he had. Blood dripped from his nose.

"Enough," Alex barked, putting magic behind the word.

Riley staggered sideways, the magic on his hands fading out. "Not...strong...enough," he heaved out in staggered breaths.

"But I am," Rane declared, pushing forward.

She marched right up to the storm that had just touched down on the ground, and she stared down the raging cloud. Whips of sparkling green magic slid out of her hands. She cracked the whips at the cloud. Her magic *did* have an effect. The cloud roared in agony. Rane kept up her onslaught. Step, slash, step, slash—she drove it back.

A bolt of black lightning split out of the cloud, wrapping itself around one of her whips. A second followed quickly and did the same to the other whip. Blinding white magic shot across her whips, moving toward her. Rane released them, and they fell to the ground. The magic sizzled out on them, then the spell that bound their magic together dissolved, turning to smoke. Rane stared at her broken spells, the shock evident on her face.

A blood-curdling laugh pierced the storm cloud, a voice born from the bowels of hell. "You have grown weak in your old age, Rane," it said. "I am more powerful than you."

"Merlin," she growled, her eyes pulsing with crimson light.

She wove strands of rainbow magic between her hands, twisting and twirling them into an enormous glowing sword. She swung it two-handed at the cloud, slashing across its smokey belly. Merlin's voice shrieked. Whatever Rane was doing, it was working.

She brought her sword around for another swing,

but a pillar of magic thrust out from the cloud to meet her strike. The magic sword shattered upon impact. The storm sprouted tendrils of shimmering magic, black as the abyss. They moved toward Rane, coiling and curling, striking and snapping in a series of fiery kisses and frosty bites. Again and again, they attacked from all sides, their numbers doubling with every passing second, leaving her no room to fight—and no hope of escape. Finally, when the smoke and snowflakes had finally cleared, Rane lay unconscious on the ground.

Sera unloaded everything she had at the storm cloud. Around her, the others were doing the same, but for every wisp of cloud they blasted away, two new ones took its place. It was the hydra of storm clouds.

"There is something seriously wrong with that magic," Alex commented as she tried to drown the storm in a tidal wave.

Merlin's spell ate her magic and spat it back out at her. It crashed against her and Lara. They fell. The commandos fell too, followed by Riley. Merlin was knocking them down like they were nothing.

"Any brilliant ideas?" Kai asked, blasting the cloud with a firestorm of cascading magical explosions.

That *did* have some effect. The storm stopped swirling for a moment, but quickly recovered. And it struck back. Forks of lightning opened the sky, unleashing a torrential downpour of magic. The glowing drops latched onto Kai like leeches. A crackling net of energy formed between them, bombarding him with enough electricity to take down even a dragon. And Kai did fall.

Sera ran to him, ignoring the lingering electricity zapping at her fingers as she touched his face. He was ok. Unconscious but still ok. She jumped up, blasting the storm with her breaking magic. It stalled for a moment, then kept on going.

"You're far too much trouble," Merlin said to her from beyond the storm. "I tried to do this the nice way."

"Nice way?" Her laugh could have cracked granite. "You turned the world into a living hell."

She blasted the storm again, drawing on every magical reserve she had. The clouds froze solid, but once again the effect only lasted a moment before they began to swirl again. She needed to get closer. But how to do that without getting sucked in?

"Don't be so picky," Merlin told her. "Your world wasn't all sunshine and rainbows either."

"It was better than this. Why did you change it?"

"You need not worry about that. I'm going to put you in timeout, little Dragon Born. You and your friends. Don't worry. I'll let you out again. Eventually." He chuckled.

"When this reality is permanent and we don't remember anything."

"Exactly," he said. "Then you and the shifter can go back to hating and killing each other. It's simpler this way, you know."

The storm was coming closer. It was nearly upon them. Sera hit it again, agony burning through her blood as the spells tore out of her.

"It's admirable how you don't give up, even in the face of certain defeat," Merlin commented.

Sera had to go into the storming fog. Destroy its bonds from the inside. It was the only way. She took a step forward.

A hand caught her around the ankle. She looked back at Kai, who was barely conscious but still holding onto her with an iron grip.

"Don't you even dare," he snarled.

She leaned down and kissed him softly. "I know you're not trying to boss me around again," she said against his lips.

His other hand gripped her around the back. "No."

"I'll be back before you know it."

"We don't know what that cloud will do to you."

Sera kissed him again. "I love you."

"I love you." His eyes were shaking, his magic howling out in anguish.

"Have faith in me," she said, her eyes burning.

"I always have," he said, letting her go.

Wiping away her tears, she jumped up and ran at the storm, which expelled a gasp of surprise as she punched through the spell's outer boundaries. The storm raged all around her. She could barely see outside of it anymore. She blasted Merlin's magic left and right, breaking the bonds that held it together.

But it fought back. As the final strand of this storm of spells broke, something slammed into her head. The ground opened up beneath her feet, and she dropped into the abyss.

Epilogue

KAI WATCHED AS Sera fought the spell inside the storm. Strand by strand, cloud by cloud, she was breaking it. But it was breaking her too. He struggled to his feet, blinking back dizziness as he ran toward the storm.

The spell cracked once more loudly—and then it was just gone. *Sera* was gone.

Kai roared as agony tore through him. He'd just gotten her back. And now he'd already lost her again.

"She isn't dead," Riley said.

Kai spun around, grabbing his shirt, shaking him, latching onto any sliver of hope.

"She got sucked down a tunnel of magic, through folds in reality," Riley told him.

"He's right," Rane said, standing shakily. "I can feel her falling into Merlin's domain." She looked at Riley. "You have his power now. The power I gave him, he also gave to you."

Alex got to her feet. "If you gave Merlin his power, can't you just take it away?"

"It's not so simple."

"That psychopath has my sister. I'd say it's pretty damn simple," Alex declared.

"He's grown too powerful. I can't beat him with raw strength."

"But I can. Bring me to him. Demon mage or not, I'll kick his ass."

"He is out of my reach," Rane said.

"How is that?" Alex asked. "You came here to earth, something I thought no demon could do. And yet here you are, proving that the impossible is possible. If you can do that, you can bring us to Merlin."

"Once, that was true. But no longer. His fortress is untraceable," Rane said.

"We'll see about that." Alex pulled out her phone and immediately began typing. "I happen to know someone who can track anyone."

"Slayer," Kai said.

"You got it."

"Even if you could find Merlin, I can't enter his fortress," Rane said.

"Can't or won't?" Kai asked her.

"Can't. He sealed his barriers with my blood. I can't enter."

"Does that even work?" Kai asked Riley.

"Only against demons," he replied. "It's an old ritual people used to use to ward against people possessed by demons. From what I understand, it involved a lot of chanting and mixing the blood of the demon you wanted to keep out into a solution that you sprinkled around your house. Since demon blood is hard to come by, not many people could actually properly perform the ritual."

"But we're not demons," said Alex. "We can enter Merlin's fortress."

"In theory, if you can find it," replied Rane. She turned to Riley. "You will need to gain better control of your magic if you're going to help them fight Merlin."

"Are you offering to train me?"

"My last apprentice didn't work out so well." She looked him up and down. "Something tells me you'll turn out better."

"I will," Riley said, his jaw set with determination. "We will find Merlin. And Sera."

"Yes," Kai agreed. "We're going to save Sera. And then we're going to put the world back the way it was."

BOOK TWO
Midnight Magic

1. Wicked Wasteland

KAI TREKKED ACROSS the plain of burning trees. Overhead, thick storm clouds stirred in silver swirls around the midnight sky, drowning out the stars. The storm hadn't come yet. It was as if it were waiting for something, some special signal to rip open and let loose.

It had been a day since Sera had disappeared inside Merlin's storm of spells, and Kai hadn't slept since. How could he? She was out there somewhere. He couldn't feel her magic, not here in this wicked wasteland beyond the borders of reality, but he knew she was here. She hadn't given up on him when the Grim Reaper had taken him, and he wasn't going to give up on her now. Not now. Not ever. No matter where she was in this world or any other, he was going to find her. Merlin could be torturing her this very moment. He could be killing her.

Kai stopped—that hard, knotted ache in his chest

clenching up. He refused to think like that. He was going to get Sera back, and everything would be fine. Well, except for Merlin. When Kai was through with that shadow mage, nothing would ever be fine for him again.

"We're going to get her back, Kai. And then we'll teach Merlin what happens when you mess with dragons," his sister Lara said, echoing his thoughts. "In fact, I wouldn't be surprised if Sera is already teaching him that lesson. Have I told you how thrilled I am that you're marrying her? I'm going to have the Mistress of Mayhem for a sister!"

Kai shot Lara a darkly appreciative look. "You and Sera will be back to spreading mayhem before you know it."

She punched him in the shoulder. "You bet we will."

"Why do dragon shifters show affection by hitting each other?" Riley asked them.

Lara turned to him, her eyes twinkling with magic. "Aw, what's wrong? Feeling left out?"

"Yes. Please hit me," he said drily.

Lara obliged. To his credit, Riley didn't even cringe. He'd always been tough, but lately he'd gotten even tougher. The Shadow World had hardened him and so had his new magic. It was losing his sister, though, that had changed him most of all. Kai had never seen Riley look so determined.

"Can you sense Sera?" Kai asked him.

That's why they were here in this realm, one of many thousands of twisted realities that littered Merlin's kingdom like tiny worlds trapped inside of glass snow globes. These worlds, castoffs of Merlin's magic experiments to change the real world, littered the area surrounding his fortress, forming a labyrinth of paths. In order to make it to the center, they'd have to find their way through these shards of discarded realities. Merlin called these lands his kingdom, but others had dubbed the area the Dump.

Merlin's storm had brought Sera to his lands. Riley and Rane had used their shadow magic to determine that much. They couldn't, however, pinpoint her exact location. Merlin had warded his domain against his former mentor, which meant Rane could neither enter it nor track magic through it. She'd sent Riley in her stead. Unfortunately, he still didn't have a very strong handle on his magic. At this point, Kai and the others were operating with at least as much guesswork as actual magic. In the hours since Sera's disappearance, they'd already been to eight other worlds looking for her. They'd come up empty every time.

"Riley?" Kai prompted him again. "Can you sense Sera?"

"She is close," Riley said, his voice a harsh rasp. His forehead crinkled in concentration. "I can feel her. That way."

Riley pointed across the plains, his green eyes burning bright in this dark, desaturated wasteland that smelled of burning leaves. A mad laugh echoed on the wind, its eerie call whistling through the spindly trees. Past those trees, on the other side of this patch of twisted earth, a city lay in wait. Tall and crooked, it was a jumbled mess—like larger pieces from several different cities had been pulled out of the ground, transported here, and then stuck together with a hot glue gun. Bridges, skyscrapers, cathedrals, and houses were thrown about with no sense of rhyme or reason.

"Alex and Logan are checking out the city," Lara said.

"Then let's join them," replied Riley. "There's nothing out here."

The three of them moved toward the city, the thick grains of rough, red sand shifting beneath their boots, pouring into the web of fissures that crisscrossed the ground. Kai sidestepped a pothole that could almost be called a crater. The air was hot; it suffocated him like a wool blanket in the heat of summer. Sweat beaded up all over his skin, saturating his shirt. It stuck to his body with the tenacity of superglue.

"This place is creepy," Lara commented as a beam of moonlight broke through the clouds. It shone down on the city like a searchlight, bathing the skyline in crimson light. The taste of broken dreams and insanity saturated the air.

"Do you hear that music?" Riley asked.

Kai was trying hard *not* to hear it. The moment they'd arrived in this world, that constant low hum of out-of-sync magic had begun playing in a loop inside of his head, and it was building steadily louder. The beat seemed to shift with the wind, growing faster, thumping harder. It was giving him a hell of a headache.

"The soundtrack of this world," Lara commented. "I feel like I'm at a Halloween party."

"Or stuck in a horror movie," added Riley.

"Yes. Exactly that." A sly smile curled her lips. "If I

faint out of terror, do you promise to catch me?"

Riley snorted. "You don't faint."

"True," she agreed, brushing her hair off her shoulder.

Riley watched her long, bouncy locks cascade like a red waterfall down her back.

"No," Kai said.

"No what?" Riley asked with such innocence that Kai nearly believed it.

"You may not sleep with my sister."

Riley blinked. "That was…direct."

"I'm a direct kind of guy."

"No kidding. I guess I should be happy you didn't fire a warning shot across my chest."

"Friends don't set friends on fire."

"Good to know," Riley said, chuckling.

"This isn't funny," Lara snapped, her lower lip quivering with annoyance. She shot Kai a sidelong look. "What makes you think you can tell us what to do, you big hypocrite? You're dating his sister."

"I never said I was fair."

Lara glowered at him. "If you think—"

"What would you say if I asked your sister out?" Riley asked Kai. He looked almost amused.

"You're free to go out with her. With a chaperone."

Lara rolled her eyes. "What is this, the eighteenth century?"

"You are my sister," Kai said. "And until a few months ago, we all thought you were dead. You can't blame me for being protective."

"There are all these crazies in the world, and you're worried about Riley? He's never hurt anyone."

"To be fair, I did cast a spell to change the world, throwing everyone into war."

"You're not helping," Lara snapped.

Riley folded his hands together and smiled. He even batted his eyelashes at Lara. Her expression softened. Apparently, magic wasn't the only power he had at his disposal. No man should have eyelashes that long. Why had Kai never noticed them before? Oh, that's right. Because he hadn't been hitting on his little sister before.

"I know he has it under control. Merlin won't be able to control him again," Kai said to Lara. "I'm more worried that he won't be able to protect you from danger."

Riley's expression darkened. He was obviously embarrassed about his inability to control his new magic. He had no reason to be. Shadow magic was Rane's magic, demon-based magic—potent, deadly, unwieldy. It wasn't something you could master in one day, which must have been frustrating for a magical sciences genius like Riley. He'd probably never before faced a problem he couldn't study his way out of.

"You've gained some very powerful magic," Kai said.

"And I'm not giving up until I've mastered it."

"Even if it takes years?"

"Even if it takes years," Riley confirmed, his eyes shining with conviction.

"And some day he might finally be a worthy protector of your precious, delicate little sister," Lara said sarcastically, rolling her eyes. "That's where this was headed, wasn't it, Kai?"

"Of course." Kai tried to keep his face neutral, but a smile tugged at his mouth.

Lara threw him an irked look.

"I was kidding, Lara."

Her eyes narrowed.

"Ok, mostly kidding," he said. "You do need someone to look out for you. I wasn't joking about that."

"I can protect myself, thank you," she snapped. "I shift into a dragon, in case you forgot."

"A small dragon."

"And I can summon dragons too," Lara growled at him.

"You have a lot of power, Lara, but you have no control. It's all chaos, all wild magic. I'm not surprised really, not after that decade the Grim Reaper's people had you. They didn't know how to teach you to deal with your power."

"I can deal just fine."

"Your dragons nearly set the office on fire last week," Kai reminded her.

"Stop crowding my space, Kai. Unlike Sera, I don't want your overbearing help."

"But you *do* need it."

"I'm not ten anymore. I'm an adult. I can handle my magic."

Kai wasn't so sure that she could, but pushing her into a corner would just make her fight harder. She was a Drachenburg, after all. So he let it go. For now.

"Ask me out," Lara said to Riley.

He blinked, looking from her to Kai. "I refuse to get in the middle of this."

"Do you want to go out with me or not?" Lara twirled a lock of her hair around her finger. "Or should I take Cutler up on his offer?"

"What was Cutler's offer?" Riley asked Lara.

She shot him a coy look. "Use your imagination."

Cutler was an incorrigible skirt chaser. It didn't take much imagination to get inside of his head. Kai added Cutler to his black list—then remembered that the telekinetic was already there.

"Will you be my date at Sera and Kai's wedding?" Riley blurted out.

Lara smiled demurely. "What a marvelous idea. I'd love to be your date. Now, what do you say we go rescue the bride before Nelly sells the wedding dress Sera and I picked out?"

"Is this the red one Sera mentioned?" Kai asked as they reached the edge of the city.

Lara frowned at him. "It's a surprise. You are not seeing it before the wedding."

He flashed her a grin. "Sera will let me see the dress."

"Over my dead body."

"That won't be necessary. Over your unconscious body should more than suffice."

"Funny, Kai. Almost as funny as the time you told me your sweaty socks smelled like strawberries."

"I seem to remember you falling unconscious then too," he said.

Lara's nose wrinkled up.

"It was your fault for smelling them," Kai pointed out.

"I was five years old!"

"The hard lessons need to be learned early in life."

Lara threw up her hands. "Big brothers are the most annoying people on earth." She looked to Riley for support.

"I only have big sisters. And when I was a kid, they let me eat cereal for dinner."

"Cool."

"I always thought so."

Kai didn't ruin their illusion by pointing out that neither Sera nor Alex could cook. Making peanut butter and jelly sandwiches was *not* cooking, no matter how much Sera insisted it was—or how much she insisted that those bizarre sandwiches were real food.

"Where to now?" Kai asked Riley. "Where's Sera?" It was annoying not being able to sense her here, like his magic-sniffing power was being bounced right back at him.

Riley pivoted in place. "I think she—"

A pillar of fire shot into the air. It had erupted from deeper inside the city.

"That's Alex's signal," Riley said.

"Yes," Kai replied.

He didn't waste time. He reached for his magic—the magic that linked him to the power of the beast—and shifted into a dragon. Before Lara could protest, he swooped her and Riley up, tossing them onto his back as he flew toward the pillar of red fire. The sky was just as red. The hot dry air singed his tongue. It tasted like sawdust with a bonus serving of acid.

Kai spotted Alex and Logan down below, trapped between the Empire State Building and the Sydney Opera House. They were surrounded on all sides by a horde of monsters. Their bodies dripping decaying old flesh, the monsters looked like they'd been raised from the grave. Alex and Logan cut and slashed with brutal efficiency, their movements devoid of mercy or regret. They fought well together, every step coordinated like an elaborate dance, like they were one person. That must have been a consequence of their blood magic bond.

Could Sera and I have such a bond? Kai wondered. *Could we be inside of each other's heads? Could we be magically linked, so that we are one when we fight. Perhaps through dragon magic?*

The magic that allowed him to shift into a dragon wasn't that different from Sera's magic. They were just two kinds of dragon magic—and similar magics could bond.

But there was no time to think about that right now. Kai began to descend toward the battle. Lara, reckless as always, jumped off his back. A burst of magic exploded all around her. When the smoke cleared, she was riding on the back of a blue dragon. Formed from manipulated strands of magical light, her summoned dragon shone brightly in the stormy sky. Grinning wildly, Lara gripped her dragon as it dove for the ground. Its mouth opened, and blue fire poured down upon the monsters. Several of the creatures caught on fire, but they just kept coming at Alex and Logan as though they didn't feel the flames melting their flesh.

Kai flew lower, and Riley jumped off to land beside Alex, throwing vials of magic at the monsters. The glass exploded, drenching them in a pale white fluid that quickly froze, encasing them in ice. Kai shifted back and landed amongst the frozen bodies.

"They are undead monsters," Kai said as ice shattered all around him.

"Yes," Alex growled, gritting her teeth as she continued hacking through them.

But even torn apart, the monsters kept coming. Logan was launching so many knives into their midst that Kai couldn't help but wonder where all those weapons had come from. The assassin had a magic all his own.

"I hate these undead things," Alex commented, slashing a monster in half. "They don't know when to quit."

"They're dead. They have no will of their own," Riley said. "They're being controlled by a necromancer."

"Anyone see this necromancer?" she asked.

"Over there!" Lara called out from above.

Kai looked where she was pointing. A man in a cloak stood a few floors up inside of the Empire State Building.

"That's the guy we were tracking earlier," Alex said. "The one we chased here from the world with the purple sky."

"Where's Sera?" Kai asked Riley. "You said you felt her here."

"I did," he replied. "And now she's gone. Like she's vanished into thin air."

"Can you fake someone's magic?" Alex asked.

"I didn't think so, but this place is strange," said Kai. "It reflects magic. Perhaps someone projected

Sera's magic to lure us here."

"The necromancer. He led us into this undead trap," Logan said calmly, as though he were discussing the dinner menu.

"But why?" Riley asked.

"Let's ask him," Kai said, preparing his wind magic to pluck the necromancer off his perch.

"I'll get him!" Lara called out as she and her dragon surged forward.

Her flight was short-lived. Like a swarm, the undead monsters leapt up, covering Lara and her dragon, pulling them to the ground.

"Damn it, Lara," Kai growled, heading toward her.

Alex's hand shot out, catching his. "Logan and I will help her. You get that necromancer."

As she and Logan jumped into the bed of monsters crawling all over Lara, Kai cast a lasso of wind magic. He snapped it out, ringing it around the man in the building—and then he gave the lasso a hard tug. The necromancer had turned to flee, but it was too late. He shot through the air toward Kai, landing at his feet.

The necromancer scrambled up. Before Kai could restrain him, Riley swung a punch at the man's head. The magic holding the dead monsters popped the moment their puppet master fell unconscious. The false life left them, and they went limp. Bodies and parts spilled to the ground.

"About time," Alex commented, kicking away the monster impaled on her sword. "That was getting gross."

"At least they didn't explode all over you like last time," said Logan.

Alex shivered. "I'm trying hard to forget those exploding zombies, thank you."

The commandos had told Kai about how they and Alex had once fought zombies. Like Sera, Alex seemed to attract trouble, even more so than most supernaturals.

Kai grabbed the necromancer and swung him over his shoulder. "Let's get out of here. We need to have a chat with our prisoner and see what he knows about Sera's whereabouts."

2. The Demon's Domain

RILEY'S SPELL BROUGHT Kai and the others back to Rane's domain. Like Merlin, the demon who'd given him his power lived in a realm beyond reality, a place where the events of the earth and the spirit realm did not touch her. And neither did reality-altering spells.

Reality functioned differently here in her haven. Her world was always changing. Rane could shape it into whatever she wanted it to be. Most of the time, the environment was a reflection of her mood. And right now, she wasn't happy. Thick, dark storm clouds hung like a ceiling of doom overhead, like they could split open at any moment. The soft, distant rumble of thunder echoed off the stones that formed the rocky landscape. It was a steep climb over rocks and wobbly ledges to reach Rane's house.

"A cynical person might say she doesn't want any visitors," Lara said as they ascended the narrow mountain path.

Alex smirked at her. "You think she wants to be alone with the commandos?"

"Good point. I wouldn't mind being alone with them." Lara wiggled her eyebrows.

"Maybe you should ask them to the wedding too," Riley said drily.

"All *four* commandos? What a great idea!"

"There are only three commandos," Riley told her.

"Three plus you."

"I'm not a commando."

Lara cast a long, delighted gaze down the length of him. "You're a commando where it counts."

"Are you hitting on my brother?" Alex asked, her eyebrows drawing together.

"Of course."

"Good."

Riley coughed. "Good?"

Alex beamed at him. "You need to have some fun."

Lara grinned back. "Riley, have I told you how much I absolutely *love* your sisters?"

"Of course you do. Everyone loves them."

"Except Blackbrooke and his Dragon Born hate club," commented Alex.

"I will deal with Blackbrooke," said Logan.

"No, *we* will deal with him," Kai told him. "Killing him won't solve anything."

"What makes you think I was going to kill him?"

"You're an assassin."

"And you're a mage who shifts into a multi-ton dragon. That doesn't mean you spend your days burning villages and raining down terror on major cities."

"Fair point," Kai allowed. "But let's put Blackbrooke on the back burner for now. We have more important problems at the moment."

"For once we agree, Drachenburg."

They'd reached the entrance to Rane's house, which right now looked more like a cave than a house. Kai turned the knob in the rocks and the door swung open easily, as though it were made of wood, not stone like it appeared.

Beyond the door, the cave wasn't a cave at all. It was a castle. Like the landscape outside, her house changed with her mood. Every time they came here, it looked different.

Right now, Rane's mood equalled a heavily fortified medieval fortress with tall ceilings and dusty banners hanging on the walls. They passed rooms bursting with disorder—potion bottles scattered about in every direction, spell books stacked in messy piles, spell scrolls lying about. They came to a grand dining hall where all of the furniture hung upside down from the ceiling.

"Cool," Alex said, looking around in wonder.

"Hanging from the ceiling isn't as exciting as it sounds," commented Logan.

A black streak rained down on Kai. He reached out, catching the falling cat. Purring loudly, she nudged his hand with her head, then jumped to the ground. The cat belonged to Rane, which meant she changed color too. When they'd left the house earlier today, she'd been bright purple with long hair. Now she was black with short hair. And her eyes were green instead of gold.

"I think she likes you," Alex said to Kai as the cat rubbed against his leg.

"I prefer dragons."

Her lips curled with wicked delight. "I'll bet you do."

The cat meowed once at Kai, then took off running across the room. She was leading them to Rane.

They found the demon sitting in a lounge with dark cherrywood floors and antique furniture. Sunlight streamed in through the windows, which were partially curtained. The light had to be magic-made because there were no holes in this rocky mountain from the outside, no way to let in any light. Such trivial things didn't matter to Rane. She could bend reality, making the impossible possible. That was the nature of her magic.

Rane and the commandos were enjoying a late night snack. A red-and-gold woven carpet lay under the coffee table that held a serving tray packed with tea cups and tiny bowls of sweets. Rane sat in a soft armchair that resembled a throne. Behind her, the wall of paintings that featured peaceful countryside scenes stood in stark opposition to her demonic origin. But Rane was no ordinary demon. She wasn't like the others of her kind. Because of her unique magic, she could go outside of hell without possessing a human host. And she simply wasn't interested in things like taking over the world or ending everything in a flourish of death and chaos. She was more academic actually. Like a little professor. Ok, she had a warrior side—and that had definitely come out when she'd fought Merlin—but most of the time she was reflective and calm. She did have the pride of demons and a nasty temper. But she also had a sense of humor, which the commandos were enjoying right now.

"You and your commandos have certainly had a lot of adventures," Rane commented as Kai entered the lounge. She lifted her tea cup to take a dainty sip.

"Yes," Kai agreed, looking her over.

Rane was wearing a long flowing white dress trimmed with lace. She wore a pair of black leather boots under the dress. That was Rane, black and white all in one. Her hair was midnight blue today and pulled up into a high ponytail. The commandos were wearing all black, their usual uniforms.

Logan passed in front of Kai and dropped the still-sleeping necromancer at Rane's feet.

"I've always appreciated gifts," she commented, setting down her teacup. She glanced down at the man. "Who's this? A ritual sacrifice?" She sounded completely serious.

"He is a necromancer we found running around in one of the worlds inside Merlin's domain," Kai told her.

"That explains why I haven't spied him before."

Merlin had sealed the borders of his domain in Rane's blood, so she couldn't get into his kingdom. It was an old spell against demons, but Merlin was old himself. Because of the spell, Rane was blocked from entering Merlin's territory, whether by teleporting in or through more mundane means. Rane had the ability to use mirrors to see into parts of the world, but Merlin's spell kept his domain shrouded from her sight.

"He lured us to him by faking Sera's magic," Riley told her. "How was he able to do that?"

"If I could guess, I'd say he used a magic mirror to bounce her magic into that world," Rane replied, snapping her fingers.

Tendrils of dark magic slithered across the necromancer's body, moving toward his face. They merged into twin streams of shadows, which then shot up his nose. The necromancer jolted awake, jumping to his feet.

"What is your name, necromancer?" Rane asked, her voice deep with magic.

"Kieran." His gaze darted wildly around the room, unable to focus on anyone or anything for more than a moment.

"Do you serve Merlin?"

"Who is Merlin?" he laughed, his voice trilling with madness.

"The master of the domain you were wandering around."

"The Wizard?"

"Yes, the Wizard," Riley said. "Tell us about your master the Wizard."

"I know no master, only a mistress. A sweet and beautiful mistress."

"Who is this mistress?" Alex asked her.

"She would be angry with me if I told you."

Alex glared at him. "I will be angry with you if you don't."

He laughed again, his voice echoing off the smooth walls.

"He's insane," Lara commented.

"Twinkle, twinkle, little star. All those worlds so near and far." The necromancer's eyes danced with madness.

"He's been stuck in Merlin's domain for too long. His mind is gone," Kai said, turning toward the necromancer. "How long have you been traveling those worlds near and far?"

"Since the beginning. Since that spark of magic created the first world. And every day, there are more and more. New worlds burying the old."

"Seven hundred years ago, Merlin's domain was formed from the magical waste of his first spell. It's like a magic garbage dump of recycled scraps of remodeled reality," said Rane.

"What spell?" Kai asked.

"The spell that changed the world," Rane told them. "Seven centuries ago, Merlin cast a spell that altered reality."

"How was the spell broken?" Lara asked.

"It wasn't. The world he created is the world you know."

"The world we're trying to get back," Lara said.

"Exactly."

"Wait, so if Merlin already changed the world, why did he change it again?" Alex asked her.

"Because, despite what he believes, he doesn't really know what he's doing. All those worlds in the Dump are his failed experiments, microcosms of altered reality that he created but never cast on the real world."

"What is he after?" Kai asked. "What does he want

to change?"

Rane shook her head. "That I do not know. But if you can figure it out, we'll be one step closer to stopping him."

A hard, shrill laugh cut through the room. It was coming from the necromancer. Insanity flashed in his eyes, igniting them with magic. Kai felt a chill crawl up his neck, like the grave was reaching out its icy hand to claim him.

"I'll have none of that in my house," Rane said with a sharp snap of her fingers.

A warm, salty breeze washed across the room, melting the cold hand of death away. Kieran clenched his fists and pushed against her magic, trying to open a doorway to the souls of the underworld.

"I am a demon, dear boy," Rane told the necromancer in an almost bored tone. "I am the only one who will invite hell into this house."

Kieran slouched, his magic sapped. "You don't play nice."

"I should hope not," Rane said, straightening with indignation.

He threw back his head and laughed.

"Where is Sera?" Kai asked him.

"Who?"

"Sera. The mage whose magic you were using to lure us in."

The necromancer shrugged. "Doesn't ring a bell."

"I think someone has rung his bell far too often," Callum commented.

"I was just thinking the same thing," Dal said. "Kai, his mind is obviously not all there. Perhaps if

Alex were to use her magic to break his mind, she might be able to catch a glimpse of some memory that might help us."

"That is a *marvelous* idea." Grinning, Alex stepped toward the necromancer.

"Don't break him too hard, love," Logan said. "He's already crazy."

Alex shot him an impish grin, her magic crackling with delight. "I can be subtle, thank you."

"As subtle as a surgeon with a jackhammer," commented Tony.

"In our crazy world, that's sometimes exactly what the job requires."

Kai found himself agreeing with her. Lately, their problems had been requiring more force than subtlety.

Alex strode forward, and without a hint of ceremony or subtlety, she grabbed the necromancer by the collar. With his magic blocked, he wasn't in any position to put up a fight. Alex met his flickering eyes and slammed her hand against his chest.

"Where's my sister?" she demanded, her voice cold and calm. It was almost unearthly.

"Who?"

"Sera. The Dragon Born mage whose magic you shot up like a beacon for us to find."

"I don't recall—"

Kai pulled a picture of Sera from his pocket and shoved it into the necromancer's face. "Remember her now?"

He chuckled. "She's pretty."

"Where is she?" Kai demanded, pushing down his rage. This necromancer was toying with them. He'd been toying with them all day, leading them on a wild goose chase through the worlds in Merlin's domain.

"Answer the question," Alex said. Her magic washed across Kieran's chest, climbing his neck. "Where did you see Sera?"

"Once upon a time," he croaked out, wheezing for breath.

Kai looked at Alex. "Your magic isn't working."

She shook her head. "Some spell is protecting him."

"Can you break that spell?"

"I won't stop until I do." Her eyes narrowed with determination. Magic spat and hissed across Kieran's body, covering him in a web of magic-charged light. "Tell me about the worlds in the Dump."

"There are thousands of worlds in the Wizard's Dump. It's a maze." A dreamy look fell over the necromancer's face. "You won't ever find your friend without help."

"You will help us," Alex told him.

"Ok." A short laugh burst out of his mouth

"Where is she?"

"Not at the Wizard's castle," he called out in a sing-song voice. "She's out there in the Ether, lost, cut off from her loved ones. Alone. Forlorn."

"Are you capable of saying anything useful?" Kai demanded.

The necromancer turned his blood-shot eyes on him. "Of course not. I am mad. Nothing I say has any meaning."

Laughing, he rushed forward, tackling Alex to the ground. He scrambled to his feet and made a run for it. Logan launched a knife at him, cutting him off from the door. The commandos circled around, closing the gap. The necromancer charged head-first at them, trying to bowl them over, but Kai's team was too well-trained. They grabbed hold of him. Kieran thrashed about, slapping and kicking the commandos. Logan moved in, but as his hand closed on the necromancer's, he jumped back.

"I thought you'd neutralized his magic," he snapped at Rane.

"I neutralized his necromancer powers, but that's not the fairy's only magic," she said, yawning.

"Watch out for his Fairy Dust!" Alex called out as she ducked to evade a cloud of sparkling black magic.

Lara and Riley jumped on top of the necromancer, trying to pin him down. Six mages and a magic-enhanced super assassin, and they couldn't handle one necromancer? This was getting ridiculous.

"You're not going to help, are you?" Kai asked Rane.

"Why should I? He will wear himself out eventually."

Demons could be really aggravating, even the not-completely-evil ones. Kai wasn't foolish enough to think Rane would be on their side forever. She was too unpredictable, too easily swayed by her own whims.

The necromancer was making a run for it. Kai moved into his path and grabbed him, pinning his arms to his sides.

"This is over," he said.

"Oh, no." The fairy's eyes lit up purple. "The game is only just beginning."

Then he vanished into thin air. A wave of dizziness crashed against Kai. His vision blurred. He blinked, but his eyes didn't clear. The world was spinning, shifting. He stumbled off balance.

He caught himself before he fell. As the dizziness melted away, he realized it wasn't Kieran who had disappeared. Kai was standing in the middle of San Francisco. But it wasn't the San Francisco he knew. Something was different about it. Something was wrong. But before he could figure out what it was, magic glowed green beneath his feet. A glyph opened up and swallowed him whole.

3. The Beast

THE GLYPH SPAT Kai out into a dark cavern that made Rane's demonic dwelling feel cozy by comparison. Being dumped into a creepy cavern never ended well.

Kai could barely see past the curtain of darkness that shrouded the cave, but there wasn't anything wrong with his other senses. Unfortunately. The air was dank. A penetrating chill clung to Kai's body like a wet blanket, saturating his skin. Even worse, the whole place smelled of old mushrooms and mold.

Kai summoned a fireball. As it flared to life in front of him, the light of the magical flames bounced off the smooth walls, lighting up the whole cavern in orange fire. The walls themselves appeared to be on fire. Kai reached out to touch the glossy surface, and his magic rippled and pulsed, dancing over the rocks like fingers over piano keys.

"Kai?"

"Sera?" he called back.

"I'm here." Her voice echoed off the walls. So sweet, so seductive, so beautiful.

"Where?" He began moving, hurrying toward the voice.

"I'm trapped."

He waited for her to speak again. When she didn't, he said, "Keep talking so I can follow your voice."

Silence crashed against his words.

"Sera?"

A beastly snarl roared through the cavern, shaking the walls. Kai kicked off into a run, following the tunnel to the end. The path spilled into a large chamber. The walls were made of hard granite—all except for one, and it was made of glass. Sera stood trapped inside of that glass prison, her hands pressed against the clear surface. When she saw him, her eyes lit up. A single tear rolled down her cheek, her pain cutting him deep. Kai surged forward, casting a quake at the glass wall. The ground thumped and rattled, but the glass wall held.

"This isn't ordinary glass," Sera told him, her voice as clear as if she were right beside him. As if there were no wall between them.

"You can't break it?" he asked her, knocking against the glass.

"It is impervious to magic." She moved her hands so they were in front of his. Only that damn wall stood between them.

"Nothing is impervious to magic. You're just not hitting it hard enough."

Sera smirked at him. "Be my guest, hot shot."

Kai withdrew his hands, clenching them into fists. Magic slid across his skin—a sizzling, burning, biting combination of lightning, fire, and ice. The magic layer closed over his arms like armor. He thrust his fists forward, slamming them against the glass wall. Magic ignited against magic. The force of the explosion hurled him across the room.

"I told you it's impervious."

Kai jumped to his feet and looked at the glass wall. It didn't have a scratch on it. He, on the other hand, had a bloody lip and a dislocated shoulder. Gritting his teeth, he popped it back into place.

"We'll just have to find another way," he told Sera.

She opened her mouth to speak, but a savage growl drowned out whatever she was going to say. Kai snapped his head around to see a great beast enter the chamber.

It looked a lot like a dragon, but its proportions were all wrong. Dragons were beautifully balanced creatures, but this beast was neither balanced nor beautiful. It was a hideous mismatch of dragon and other beastly parts. It had the head and the body of a dragon but the claws of a tiger. Its tail was that of a scorpion, and its wings looked like they'd been ripped off of a very large butterfly and glued onto the beast's back. A warped dragon. What a travesty. Dragons were beautiful, elegant, perfectly-proportioned creatures. They weren't...this.

The Beast opened its mouth and roared. Carried along the notes of that primal sound, magic poured out. Like a cloud of glowing, glistening pestilence, the stew of distorted magic rolled toward Kai. There was something odd about it, like it existed between states. It was neither gas nor liquid, neither earth magic nor spirit magic. Kai put up a barrier of ice, but the Beast's breath melted right through it. His ice barrier crumbled to the ground like the broken shards of a shattered mirror—and the dark cloud just kept coming. It bit through his clothes, scorching his skin in fiery agony.

The Beast snarled, snapping its jaws at Kai. It stomped down one of its feet. Kai darted out of the way—but only just barely. He took a deep breath, settling himself for the shift... Nothing happened. Something was blocking his spell. He could cast elemental magic, but his shifting and magic-sniffing were out of commission. What the hell was going on?

"The Beast is too strong."

Kai pivoted around to find Sera standing beside him. "How did you get out of the mirror?"

"What mirror?"

Kai glanced back at the mirror, but it wasn't there. Something had turned the wall into stone.

"Sera, what's going on?"

Surprise flashed across her face. "Your head is bleeding!" She rushed forward, lifting her hand to his head.

Pain flared up across his forehead. "Stop," he caught her hand. Her fingers were dripping blood. His blood. "We have to fight the Beast. Together."

She shook her head. "I told you. The Beast is too strong."

"It's not like you to give up."

"Escape while you can, Kai. I'm not going

anywhere." She glanced down at the chain around her ankle that held her to the ground.

Where had the chain come from? It hadn't been there before.

"Something is wrong," he said. "The Beast. It's the Beast."

"Forget the Beast. It's gone."

Kai looked past her, but the Beast had vanished. A smile touched Sera's lips, a smile so sweet that Kai would have kissed her to taste it. But something was very, very wrong.

"You're not really here," he said, the realization twisting inside of his gut. "You're an illusion. The Beast is messing with my head."

"Don't be silly. You've been looking for me, and I'm right here." The blood faded from her hands. Sera lifted her finger to his mouth, her touch soft against his lips. It sure felt real. In fact, it was the most real thing he'd felt since Sera had disappeared. "We're together again. Everything is going to be all right." When she smiled, his mind was hers. It believed every word, every caress, every breath.

But his heart wasn't fooled. That wasn't Sera. She felt...wrong. It took every shred of willpower that he had to pull away. And when he did, he saw the Beast right behind her, lying in wait.

"You should have listened to me," Sera said sadly. "It would have saved you a great deal of pain. Now there will be no escape, no blissful death."

She pulled out her sword, and in a single, swift motion, she stabbed herself through the stomach. "There will be only suffering." Blood poured down her body. She staggered to the side, then collapsed dead to the ground.

Kai's throat choked up. Yes, she was only an illusion created by the Beast, but she was an illusion with Sera's face. And seeing her die in front of him hurt, whether or not it was real.

"I will see you burn," Kai promised the Beast in a savage hiss.

Then he turned and did something he just didn't do: he fled. There was a patch of sunlight on the other side of the chamber, and Kai ran right for it. That was his way out of this cursed cavern.

"Kai, stop! Help me!" Sera's voice called out in pain inside of his head. "Don't let the Beast get me!"

He kept running. This wasn't a battle against the Beast. It was a fight against the strongest instinct he had: the instinct to protect the woman he loved. His partner. His mate.

The Beast's laughter howled cruelly in the chamber, growing louder with every echo. And then a far crueler sound followed: screams of agony. Sera's agony. The sound cut at Kai, slashing his skin, burning his flesh.

"It's not real," he muttered to himself, pausing beneath a hole in the ceiling.

A beam of bright light shone down on him. It wasn't the sun. It was the moon, and an incredibly bright moon at that. There was magic in that light. Hope. Kai cast a funnel of wind to shoot him out of the cavern.

The fake Sera was right about one thing, Kai thought as he landed on the street. *The Beast is too strong.*

He needed a plan if he was going to defeat it—a plan plus some way to get his dragon-shifting magic back. A defense against the Beast's mental manipulations wouldn't hurt either.

"I will be back," Kai promised the Beast raging down in the cavern.

A melody of magic hummed like chimes in the wind. Kai knew that sound. A magic ward. Someone had trapped the Beast down there. And Kai had a sinking suspicion it was the same someone who had teleported him down there to meet his end.

4. Alone

THE MAGIC STORM dissolved around Sera. Merlin's spell was broken. She hung suspended for a moment, caught in the wake of shattering magic, consumed by it. Falling in slow motion, she was frozen in that single moment in time.

Then the magic snapped, and she fell into darkness. The abyss swallowed her whole, not even bothering to chew first. Emptiness consumed her, filling her with a profound loneliness she'd never before experienced. Out here, wherever here was, she was alone, cut off from everyone she cared about. She could feel the bonds of love snapping with wretched finality. A biting wind brushed across her skin, chilling her soul. She reached out, knowing it was desperate, that there was nothing to catch her.

But then her dragon *did* catch her. Sera fell against Amara's back, her tears of anguish and joy sliding across her dragon's purple-blue scales. The world had shrunk to just the two of them, caught inside of a dark cloud. She couldn't see what lay beyond—*if* anything even lay beyond its black borders. Merlin had boasted that he was sending her to 'time out'. Maybe that's all this abyss was, a place for you to drown in your own eternal loneliness.

No. Sera shook her head. She wasn't giving up. Not now, not ever. Maybe she couldn't see anything right now, but she knew the world was still there. She felt it deep inside of her heart, which was beating in time to the thump of Amara's wings. Sera clutched tightly to her dragon, feeling the smooth scales beneath her fingers. They were flying faster than they'd ever flown before.

Where are we? Sera asked as the blackness lightened to wisps of fog.

I don't know, replied Amara.

You're flying blind at this speed? That's very impulsive of you, Sera teased her.

I am flying toward the bright spot up ahead. The fog is thinner there.

Sera didn't see the bright spot. All the fog looked the same to her.

It's there, Amara assured her.

Sera didn't dispute her words. If Amara said it was brighter up ahead, then it was brighter up ahead. Dragon eyes saw far better than her human eyes.

And after a minute, Sera could perceive the fog thinning. It swirled across her skin, its icy fingers trying to cling to her as Amara burst out of the cloud. A bridge loomed in front of them, tall and imposing.

"The Golden Gate Bridge," Sera muttered.

Except it wasn't the Golden Gate Bridge. Its shape was unmistakable, but it was so…gold. Not red. Gold. It shimmered in the early morning light, millions of tiny golden glittering particles rising up from it like a halo of stars.

This isn't the San Francisco that we know, Sera said.

Perhaps Merlin changed the world again, her dragon suggested.

They were passing over the city now. The skyline looked different than her world, different than the Shadow World too. Some of the buildings were not there, some had been replaced by different ones. Architectural remodeling? What was Merlin up to?

Well, there's only one way to find out, Sera said. *Let's get down there and see for ourselves.*

As they descended, Sera realized that the city was intact. Unlike the San Francisco of the Shadow World, the buildings here stood tall and unbroken. There was no sign of decay or destruction. She didn't see any monsters. She couldn't feel any monsters either. But it wasn't just the monsters. She didn't feel any magic whatsoever. Blind, crippled without her magic-sniffing ability, she felt cut off from some part of herself.

Something is blocking our ability to sense magic, Amara said.

Sera didn't need to be able to sniff out magic to know something rotten was amiss. The streets were too clean, too quiet. Even at this early hour, people should have been out and about, hurrying to their jobs, picking up their morning coffee. There was no one. These eerie empty streets… It felt like a ghost town. If it weren't so damn clean, she'd have expected some tumbleweed to blow across the street to the tune of a slow, forlorn violin.

They set down on a cold, abandoned street like a hundred other in this bizarre city. Amara faded into a cloud of sparkling magic that melted back into Sera. Feeling her dragon back inside of her blasted back the coldness, warming Sera to her core. She wasn't alone or forgotten.

Not like this forlorn city, Sera thought, walking down the empty street. Something tugged at her senses. It was trying to tell her something.

We're being watched, declared Amara. Her dragon's senses were heightened even when she didn't take corporeal form.

Gravel slid and crunched behind Sera. She turned around, expecting a monster. She found a tabby cat instead. It opened its mouth and let out a soft little meow.

"Well, you certainly are the cutest monster I've ever faced," Sera told the tiny cat.

Purring, it bounded down the street in pursuit of a leaf caught on the wind.

Spreading happiness to small creatures. I think our work is done here, Amara.

Don't celebrate just yet.

I hear them.

Sera turned to find a dozen soldiers in dark red uniforms blocking her path. They were dressed a lot like the commandos, but the dark looks on their faces were nothing like the humor the commandos exuded. These soldiers' eyes were hard and cold. They were full of hatred—and that hatred was pointed right at Sera.

"We saw that little flying stunt," one of them said, swinging a dark baton in his hand. From his stance, he was the one in charge of this band. "Impressive."

His crooked smile broadcast loud and clear that he wasn't the least bit impressed. Rather, he looked like he would take great pleasure in hurting her—and he had no intention of denying himself that pleasure. His companions appeared no more amicable.

Sera gave the Hate Squad a wary look. "What do you want?"

"We're going to take you into custody. There's no point in struggling," the leader said, his eyes gleaming with demented delight. "But, honestly, I'm really hoping that you will struggle. And I have a feeling you're going to grant me that wish, aren't you?"

"I haven't done anything to you."

"You were born," he replied in a low snarl as the soldiers closed in around her.

Sera's lips buzzed with annoyance. Why couldn't she—just for *once*—land in a world that didn't hate the Dragon Born?

The soldiers attacked all at once, swinging their batons in quick, brutal arcs. A surge of agonizing energy slammed into Sera everywhere their weapons hit. Her body blossoming with pain, she fell shaking to the ground. Like a rabid dog, the aftershocks of that cruel, unknown power ripped apart her magic layer by layer, piece by piece. Sera held onto her magic, even as it began to fade away. She pushed it all into a single concentrated burst of wind that blasted the soldiers away from her. The flames of her fire barrier surged as she rose from the ground.

"There it is." The leader licked his lips. "Magic."

He pulled the shield off his back. Thrusting it in front of him, he pushed through Sera's barrier. The fire wall collapsed, its magic drained. The shield pulsed in quiet victory.

She gaped. "How did you do that?"

The leader laughed. "You're not from around here, are you?"

"No."

He was getting too close. Sera cast ice. Frosty jaws split out of the asphalt, freezing his feet to the ground. Completely unconcerned, he lifted his foot. The ice cracked, then shattered to pieces. He repeated the motion with his second foot.

Sera shook her head. "This is impossible."

He chuckled, low and cruel. "You supernatural scum think you're so special, so powerful, but you're not. Your pathetic magic is nothing but tricks. And once it's gone, you have nothing left."

Sera drew her sword, countering the strike of his baton. A shock of energy jumped across from his weapon to hers, tearing across her body like a tornado. Her muscles spasmed, and her sword fell to the ground. The leader kicked it away. She lifted her hand to blast him, but only a gentle breeze answered her call. He knocked her upside the head with his baton. She couldn't stop the soft whimper that broke her lips as her magic was roughly ripped away.

Amara? You have any magic left? Sera asked as the soldiers closed in again.

No. Those weapons neutralized it.

Sparks sizzled and spat as twelve batons hammered

down on Sera. Blood streamed down her face. They rose their hands to hit her again, but she ran forward, breaking through their circle. All that time—those many long years—she'd spent tackling big, bad monsters was coming in real handy right now. She rolled out of the tackle and sprang to her feet.

The leader laughed, walking up to her. "You are pretty resilient for a mage. In this game, the mages usually hide in the back, cowering in fear. Once the warriors fall, they are easy pickings."

"Game? What game?" she demanded.

"You really don't know anything, do you?" he replied, smirking.

He lifted his hand to smack her with that cursed baton once again, but Sera caught the stick on the downward swing.

"It is *you* who know nothing. You attacked a mage who knows how to fight without magic," she told him.

Sera stomped down on his foot with the heel of her boot. He growled in pain, his grip loosening on the baton. She grabbed it out of his hand and, with sweet satisfaction, knocked the supernatural-hater over the head with his own weapon. He fell to the ground.

"How?" He looked at her, his face twisted with shock.

"In my world, I spent most of my life fighting without my magic. I absolutely don't need it to kick your ass." She flipped the baton over once in her hand, then slammed it against the side of his head, knocking him unconscious. "Who's next?" she asked the eleven other haters.

They gaped at her, frozen in shock, as though the

people they bullied had never before fought back. They looked at Sera like she defied the laws of nature. Well, she'd never been very good at following the rules. The battle was quick. Before they'd recovered from their surprise, she had them all sleeping on the ground.

She looked down on the twelve people who had cornered and attacked her. "You should have left me alone."

Loud, crisp claps echoed down the empty street. Sera turned to find a man in a black hoodie standing there, giving her a standing ovation.

"Very impressive," he said, smiling widely. "Very impressive indeed."

He looked completely unlike the soldiers she'd just fought. Sera's magic-sniffing ability still had not returned, but she knew he was a mage. There was something about the way he carried himself that gave him away.

"You're a mage." She grabbed her sword off the ground and sheathed it.

He nodded, looking her up and down. "You don't even need your magic to know that, Dragon Born?"

Sera sighed. "Do we have a problem?"

"Dragon Born mages, always so suspicious," he chuckled.

"That's what happens when everyone wants to kill you."

"Not everyone. And not here."

Sera gave the twelve napping soldiers a pointed look.

"They want to kill us all. All supernaturals. It's a big game to them," the mage said.

"They said that too. A *game*. What did they mean by it?"

"In this world, the humans are the hunters and we supernaturals are the prey. It's a game they play, a hunt. A hunt with prizes awarded for killing supernaturals. Kills are scored based on the power level of the prey, and the hunters move up the ranks when they accumulate enough points."

"That is sick," Sera said with disgust. "Why don't you fight back?"

"Our greatest asset is our magic, and as you saw, their weapons neutralize it."

"There must be a way."

His eyes shone with hope. "I'm hoping you can help us with that."

"How many hunters are there?"

"Five thousand."

"Five thousand. What can I possibly do against five thousand hunters?"

"A lot," he said. "But first, we need to get out of here. More patrols will be coming."

Sera followed him. She should have been working out how to get herself the hell away from this world, but all she could think about was the poor supernaturals being hunted. Back in her San Francisco, she'd been the hunter, the slayer of monsters and nightmares. But in this San Francisco, she was the hunted. She was the monster.

"Where are all the monsters?" she asked the mage. "Or do you not have any here?"

"Oh, we have them all right. They are always there but rarely in sight. They live in the shadows. In darkness. You never see them until it's too late. There's only one warning that they're near. If you feel an icy chill creeping down your back, you have to run. Don't even try to fight. The shadows cannot be defeated."

"Everything can be defeated," replied Sera. "There's always a way."

He grinned at her. "That's what I love about you Dragon Born. For you, it can always be done. There's never any challenge that cannot be overcome."

"If only everyone were so fond of the Dragon Born."

"You'll find that the supernaturals here are different."

Being hunted must have given them some much-needed perspective, commented Amara. *How about we grant Blackbrooke and his supporters that same perspective by throwing them into this game?*

I'll add it to our to-do list. Maybe we can fit it in somewhere between getting the hell out of here and saving the world.

"How did this game start?" Sera asked the mage.

"I don't know. It's just always been the way of this world. But it wasn't until a few months ago that the hunters developed weapons which turned the tables against us."

"The ones that zap you of your magic."

"Yes, they are quite effective. I'm surprised you were able to take so many hits before your magic gave out. But that is the power of the Dragon Born, isn't it? Your capacity for magic is unmatched. That's also why the hunters target you above all. You are the prime prey, the biggest prize. Every hunter here wants to make a name for themselves, and killing a Dragon Born mage is a sure path to glory."

"I knew it was too good to be true, a world where supernaturals do not hate us. Humans who want to hang our heads on their walls is no better than the world I know. We have done nothing to anyone, and yet there is no world where the Dragon Born are not hated and hunted."

"It is a *bit* different here than in your world."

"How do you know so much about my world?" Sera asked.

"I don't, but as you said, the Dragon Born are hunted wherever they go. We don't have any more Dragon Born left here, but we have had them visit us from the other worlds. The story is always the same, century after century. That same sad tale from every Dragon Born who has ever come here. But you need not fear us. Here, you aren't the problem."

"No? Then what are we?"

"You're the solution. You are our salvation."

5. Witch Burning

AFTER DROPPING THAT little bomb that Sera was supposedly some kind of savior who would lead the supernaturals of this world to a better life, the mage didn't say anything more on the matter.

"What's your name?" Sera asked him as they navigated the dark streets. After that brief burst of sunrise, the sun had decided to take a nap. It was hiding behind a thick layer of fog.

"I'm Talen."

"Sera."

"Sera," he said slowly, as though savoring the sound of her name on his tongue. "We must hurry, Sera. When the streets are dark, danger lurks behind every corner. The vampires are still out, which means more hunters will be on patrol. They like to set traps for the vampires, knowing their hunger makes them desperate."

"Have you ever thought of setting your own traps for the hunters?" she asked.

"Not as long as they have those weapons. Without our magic, we cannot win."

"You could learn to use a sword."

"Some of us can. But not enough of us." He motioned her forward. "This way. Through the alley. The hunters patrol the main street."

Their turn down the alley pushed them into darkness, lit only by a few flickering street lamps. As they walked, a cool chill tickled Sera's senses. With every step, she felt as though sandpaper were scraping against her soul. A slow, steady tap popped, punctuating the silence. Sera pivoted around, but she saw nothing except shadows. Those shadows grew, billowing up to swallow Talen. She could almost see the forms of beastly shapes shifting inside of the shadows, but what were those shapes supposed to be? Lions? Dragons? Birds? They were like a mangled union of many different beasts, all melted together, all hissing and whispering their toxic song.

Sera grabbed Talen, pulling him away from the shadows. They ran until they reached the end of the alley, and then they ran some more. The shadows rushed forth like a black tsunami, snapping at their heels. Sera's breath froze on her lips, ice pouring down her throat, swallowing her heart.

"I was right about you," he said, his eyes wide with terror as he watched the shadows retreating. His terror turned to hope as he looked at Sera. "You are our savior. Come on. It's not far to our hideout."

He led her across the street to an old house with chipped blue paint. Once, the color must have been cheerful, but it had faded long ago. Next to the bright orange house and the sunshine-yellow one on either side of it, the blue house looked downright despondent. Talen stepped up to the house and, never slowing, walked right through the wall.

Sera took a deep breath and followed. She passed through the magic curtain, watching the battered blue wall melt away before her. Her skin still tingling, she landed on the other side. She was standing in a rust-stained warehouse bay far too large to fit inside of that skinny blue row house.

"Now, that was an impressive illusion," she commented, running her fingers across the seams of the invisible magic curtain.

"It's not just an illusion. It's a ward. Only mages can enter here," he told her.

Sera glanced at the pair of mages practicing their magic nearby. They'd paused to gawk at Sera, which made her realize just how awful she looked at the moment. Her face was caked with dry blood and her pants split with a web of tears at the knees. Not that the mages looked much better. A large group of them —twenty at least—were walking straight for her and Talen. Most of them wore clothes that were just as torn as Sera's. All of them, in fact, except for the woman at the forefront. She was sporting a suit of pristine dark brown battle leather.

"Calliope," Talen called out to her. "You'll never guess what I've found."

The woman's gaze shifted to Sera. "A mage."

"Not just any mage," he replied, practically bouncing with excitement. "A Dragon Born mage. Our salvation."

"That is good news," Calliope agreed.

There was something about her smile that made the hackles rise up on the back of Sera's neck. She took a preemptive step back. Before she could take a second, magic blasted out from every mage in the room. Again and again, the mages' magic hit Sera, a constant barrage of spells that brought her to her knees. She tried to stand, tried to draw her sword, but the bombardment was too much. Maybe if the hunters hadn't weakened her defenses already, she might have stood a chance. But not like this. The spells didn't let up. They pounded hard and fast, as relentless as a rainstorm. The mages' magic washed over her, pulling her under.

◆ ◇ ◆ ◇ ◆

Sera woke up tied to a post with firewood piled all around her. This sure wasn't how she'd expected her visit to the mages' hideout to go. Damn her trusting nature. The mages tossed more firewood onto the pile. Talen stepped up to Sera, flames dancing on his fingertips.

She glared at him. "What the hell do you think you're doing?"

"I'm convinced you're our salvation," he replied, sprinkling tiny magic flames over the firewood. "But the others still need some convincing."

"You need to prove you're the real thing. That you're really Dragon Born," Calliope said. Logs shot over her shoulder, landing in the smoking pile. Telekinetics. They always had to show off. That appeared to be a constant in any reality. "We've been burned before."

"And so you *burn* me?" Sera demanded.

"Show us your dragon, and we'll let you go."

"The hunters zapped us pretty hard. We don't have enough magic for her to take corporeal form."

"That is unfortunate," said Calliope. "But the Dragon Born are both powerful and resourceful. If you really are what you claim to be, you'll be able to free yourself."

So this was a good old witch burning. Fantastic.

Sera's gaze darted to Talen. "You could tell them what you saw."

"He did," Calliope said. "He saw you grab a baton and use it against the hunters. Clever, but it proves nothing."

"And trying to burn me alive proves what exactly?"

"Everything."

"This is madness," Sera growled.

"You aren't the first person to come looking for us. The hunters have sent in many before, trying to find us, to exploit us, to trick us. We sent them the imposters' burnt remains in a basket."

Sera struggled against the restraints, even as the fire crackled over the wood all around her. "I never asked for anything. You dragged me here. You begged me to save you."

Calliope said nothing. No one said anything. They just watched calmly as the fire closed in on Sera. She didn't have time to convince them of the madness of what they were doing. She had to concentrate on getting herself out of here, not on verbal sparring matches with crazy mages. Living in this horrible world had clearly cracked their minds.

Sera could feel her magic returning—slowly, painfully, as though someone had ripped her skin away, and now it was starting to regrow. She drew on her elemental magic, pouring water over the flames, but the fire was too hot. Her water hissed, dissolving into smoke. She cast a cloud of ice. The fire died out.

As soon as the flames went down, they burst back up. Sera cast ice again and again, but the fire just kept popping up. It was like a trick candle on a birthday cake, except there was nothing funny about this joke. There had to be a way to put out the spell for good. If she could just string together enough elemental spells, maybe the constant barrage of changing magic would overload the original spell. The question was whether she had enough magic left in her to pull it off.

Sera took a deep breath, then unleashed her magic. The spells tore out of her with unfettered ferocity. Ice followed earth, lightning followed water. Around and around, they went. A dozen spells. Two dozen spells. Three dozen spells. Sera cast one after the other without pause. The spells were sapping her dry. She drew on her reserves—and her dragon's magic. The bonds that bound the never-ending fire spell burst apart, exploding into a flood of fireworks. Tendrils of lightning slid around Sera's wrists, snapping the restraints holding her to the pole.

"Dragon Born," the mages gasped, staring at her in wonder as she stepped over the charred, still-smoking firewood.

They were looking at her as though she gave them

hope. No, it was more than that. They looked at her as though she would save them from this hellish world. Sera's heart ached for them—how could it not? But she had no idea how she was supposed to save them.

"Savior," they murmured above the soft hiss of smoke.

"I'm just a mage," she said. "Like all of you."

"No, not like us," said Talen. "You are Dragon Born, the supernatural savior, the one who will save us from the humans' hunt."

"How?"

"Legend tells us that only the Dragon Born have the power to unite the supernatural community against the hunters," Calliope said. "But there hasn't been a Dragon Born savior in years. We don't get many visitors here."

"Why is that?"

"It's true of all the worlds in the Dump," Talen told her.

"The Dump?"

"The worlds created by Merlin's magic experiments."

Merlin. Now they were getting somewhere. "How do I find Merlin?"

Talen paled. "Why would you want to do that? Merlin is a monster."

"He changed my world, and I'm going to make him put it back."

"You come from out there, from beyond the mist. Earth," Talen gasped. "How did you find your way here? The only way in or out of Merlin's domain is with shadow magic."

"It's a long story," Sera said. She wasn't ready to tell them everything. She didn't quite trust these people. They had just tried to burn her at the stake after all.

"I'd love to hear it," replied Talen.

"Maybe some other time. I need to find Merlin. Can you help me find the way?"

"We need you to stay and help us."

Sera clasped her hand together behind her back, priming her magic just in case they tried to make her stay against her will. "Merlin made this world. It's his fault that you're in this situation. I'm going to end his reign of terror one way or another. So don't you see? Helping me find Merlin *is* helping yourselves."

"She's right." Calliope met Sera's eyes. "We will help you. But first, where is your other half? Your twin?"

"Well…" Would they refuse to help her if she told them Alex wasn't here? You never knew. They might consider Dragon Born twins an all-or-nothing sort of deal.

"We must find her before the others do."

"The hunters?"

"No, the vampires or the fairies."

"I thought they are your allies."

Disgust washed across Calliope's face. "Most certainly not."

"The Dragon Born are the ones who will unite us," Talen reminded Sera.

"Says some prophecy?"

"It's not just a prophecy," he said. "It's a legend. It's happened before."

"How many times?"

"Once, long ago, at the dawn of this world." He beamed at her. "And soon history will repeat itself."

"So you're saying that centuries ago, two Dragon Born mages united the supernaturals in this world and led them to freedom?" she asked him.

"Precisely."

"Ok, if the Dragon Born led all of the supernaturals from this world, why are you still here?"

"We aren't the same supernaturals. After the exodus, Merlin looked for new prey. He gathered us from a thousand different worlds in his domain and dumped us here, into this game."

"But *why*? What is the purpose of the game?" she asked.

Talen's forehead crinkled up in confusion. "We're not really sure. All we know is that the Dragon Born are going to save us."

No, they hoped that because two Dragon Born centuries ago had saved the others, a different two Dragon Born could save them now. Hope was a powerful force. But was it really hope or just plain, simple desperation?

"You said the Dragon Born saved the supernaturals long ago by uniting them?" Sera asked.

Talen nodded. "That's right."

"Ever consider forming an alliance with the other supernaturals instead of waiting for someone to come and save you?"

"We've tried. Believe me, we've tried. But the others are so unreasonable," Calliope told her.

I bet the vampires, fairies, and ghosts would say the same thing about them, Amara commented.

No doubt.

"We really must find your twin before the vampires or fairies do," Calliope continued. "They always screw things up when they find the Dragon Born first. The vampires, driven mad by hunger, sometimes eat them. And the fairies are even worse."

"Worse than being eaten?"

"You don't want to know."

"What about the otherworldly?" Sera asked.

"Talking to them is pointless. They're in a perpetually foul mood on account of Merlin trapping them in his domain, cutting them off from both the earth and the spirit realm. They'll hiding in this domain's freakish version of the spirit realm."

"More freakish than the actual spirit realm?"

"Yes."

The false wall in the building rippled, and a mage in a faded cloak sprinted through the illusion, coming to a stop in front of Calliope. "At sunset, the Huntsman and his hunters will engage in a huge, coordinated attack on every major supernatural hideout in San Francisco."

The mages in the room began muttering. Fear rose up from them, sucking all the hope out of the room.

"Who is this Huntsman?" Sera whispered to Talen.

"One of the warlords who hunts the supernaturals of this city."

"Then I'd say it's time to turn the hunt around. Today."

"Look around," one of the mages said. "We don't have the numbers to take on the Huntsman's army."

"You give up too easily. The Huntsman is attacking

all the supernaturals in the city tonight. You have a common goal, a common threat. What better reason than that to unite together against the hunters?"

"It wouldn't make a difference. You saw their weapons. They neutralize magic!" another mage called out.

"Then you just have to neutralize their weapons before they neutralize yours. If the supernaturals of this city could just put your differences aside for one day, you'd have the numbers and the power to defeat the hunters. You could end this game yourselves."

The mages all looked to Calliope. She nodded, smiling.

"The Dragon Born mage is wise. We have chosen well to follow her."

Sera gritted her teeth. They didn't need her. They needed one another. Why couldn't they see it? Why couldn't they move past their hate?

The illusionary wall rippled once more, spitting out another mage. "The Witch Slayer has struck again," he said immediately.

"The Witch Slayer? Another warlord?" Sera whispered to Talen.

"Yes."

"How many warlords does this city have?"

"Just the two. And they don't get along very well. They are fighting for control of this city."

"The Witch Slayer has captured two mages," the messenger continued.

"Who?" Calliope asked.

"They are not our own. One is a magical scientist. The other is a red-haired dragon summoner and shifter."

"Riley and Lara," said Sera.

Calliope's eyes flashed in surprise. "You know these mages?"

"Yes." Sera looked at the messenger mage. "Where are they being held?"

"At the Witch Slayer's castle. She is going to execute them at midnight while the whole city looks on. She wants everyone to see what happens to supernaturals, that we cannot hide, that our magic cannot save us."

Sera's throat constricted. "Not if I have anything to say about it," she said, her voice thick with emotion.

"You can't go to the Witch Slayer's castle. You have to help us fight the Huntsman! The hunters are going to kill us all!" one of the mages shouted, his lips quivering with the onset of panic.

"We're safe here from the Huntsman," another mage said calmly. "The spells around this place will keep the hunters back."

"No," said the first messenger, the one who'd brought word of the Huntsman's impending attack. "The hunters have a new weapon, one that can break through magic barriers. I saw them use it on our northern base. Everyone died."

"We have to run!"

"Go somewhere they'll never find us!"

"There's no use! If they can break through our protective wards, there's nowhere we can go!"

Their panic rumbled at the surface, like a big pot of popcorn ready to explode. If they kept working themselves into a frenzy, they'd stampede into the street, running right into the hunters' hands. Sera looked at Calliope. She was their leader. It was her job to calm them. But the telekinetic was just standing there, wringing out her hands, her eyes flickering back and forth from the exit. She was psyching herself up to run. And where the leader went, the others would follow. Someone had to stop her—stop all of them.

"Enough!" Sera shouted, casting a ring of fire that cut them off from the exit wall.

The mages froze, shocked to silence.

"In my world, I have faced many evils," Sera told them, her voice cutting through the silence. "I've fought many battles. There are times to flee and times to fight. This is a fighting time. You cannot run. You must fight."

"Staying here is suicide!" someone shouted.

"I didn't say anything about staying here. I said you have to fight. You must join with the other supernaturals of this city and make a stand against the hunters. And I will help you. Together, we will stand against the Huntsman's attack. Together, we will stop the Witch Slayer. I cannot do this alone." She held out her hand. "And neither can you."

Calliope met her eyes, her fear fading. Nodding, she set her hand over Sera's. "It's about time we stood up to the hunters and broke out of this sick game. If you will lead us, Dragon Born, we will follow. We will be your army to command."

As the mages' voices lifted in agreement, dread took hold of Sera's heart. These people were looking at her like she had all the answers, and she didn't have a clue of what she was doing. She didn't know this world, and she was no leader.

"We will fight for you," the mages chanted. "We will be your army. Where you lead us, we will follow."

Kai was a leader, someone who could command loyalty and armies. But Kai wasn't here. The mages were stuck with her instead, a former mercenary who'd never wanted to command anyone. They stared at her, as though they expected her to say something.

"Are you ready to take back your world?" she shouted out, covering her anxiety with pure volume. She knew it wasn't the best pep talk, but the mages didn't seem to care.

"Yes!" they shouted in unison.

"Good, then let's get to it," she said.

"Where do we begin?" Calliope asked her as the others grabbed their weapons.

"The hunters have greater numbers and devastating weapons in their favor, but they are divided. The Witch Slayer and the Huntsman are competing, not working together. We're going to use that against them," Sera decided.

"How?"

"By getting one of the warlords to help us fight the other."

The question was how to get either one of them to listen to her without trying to kill her.

6. City of Shadows

HAVING ESCAPED THE dragon-like beast in the cavern, Kai walked down the streets of San Francisco. Except it wasn't San Francisco, at least not the one he knew. Drachenburg Industries had no presence in this world, nor did any other magic company. The buildings were simply missing, replaced by unfamiliar ones, buildings without soul or purpose, like they were just empty shells. The streets were empty too. Kai hadn't passed a single person yet. In a city the size of San Francisco, that was odd.

Kai's magic-tracking ability was still offline, and his other senses picked up only hints of magic. An ancient symbol painted onto a building, the scent of magical plants on the wind, the soft hum of a ward somewhere nearby—there was very little here, in a place that was a supernatural hotspot in his world.

The supernaturals were hiding, keeping their distance. Kai could see them shifting in the shadows, keeping just out of sight. Scouts. They weren't just being stealth because that was their job. They were afraid, Kai realized. He could smell the fear everywhere, swirling in the air like a cloud of impending doom. What were they afraid of? The Beast?

Kai looked around. What was this place, this city of shadows where supernaturals hid and magic failed. He'd almost have thought it was hell, except his magic wasn't being drained. It was just being blocked—or at least some of it was. He could feel his elemental magic ready and waiting to be unleashed, and now that he was out of the tunnels, his shifting magic was back too. It was just his magic-sniffing power that was out.

No, it wasn't hell, at least not in the literal sense. It was another one of Merlin's broken castoff worlds, the refuse of his demented experiments to change reality. But how had Kai gotten here? The last thing he remembered before coming here was fighting that necromancer…

The sounds of steel and magic shattered the eerie silence. Kai ran toward the battle. He had to get an idea of what was going on here, of what war had torn this world apart, forcing the supernaturals into hiding.

He turned the corner to find a band of a dozen soldiers dressed in crimson. Five vampires lay bleeding and unmoving on the ground behind them, but the soldiers were still advancing, surrounding two warriors. A knife cut through the air, shimmering in the dim light, and one of the soldiers fell. Lightning cracked, snapping out like a whip, forcing the soldiers back. And then Kai saw who the two warriors were: Alex and Logan.

One of the soldiers pulled the shield off his back, thrusting it in front of him. The moment it made contact with Alex's magic, the lightning sizzled out. She shook out her hand, casting a fireball. Before she could launch it at the soldiers, they all lifted their batons in unison and swung. Alex avoided most of them, but one strike got through. As the baton slammed into her stomach, she expelled a low gasp, and her fireball went out.

Kai rushed forward to help her, but Logan was faster. He launched a fleet of knives so fast that his hands were a blur of movement. A moment later, the soldiers all hit the ground.

"You weren't supposed to kill all of them," Alex complained. "We wanted to question one of them."

"Sorry, darling. I couldn't risk it. There's something very wrong about their weapons. I saw how they affected you. I couldn't let them get in another hit."

"I'm fine."

Logan caught her as her shaking legs gave out. "You always think you're fine."

"And I always am," she replied, grinning at him. "Those batons dealt a nasty shock to my magic, but I can stand by myself."

"As you wish." Logan let go of her. His head snapped around to Kai. "You're late, Drachenburg."

And here Kai had thought assassins had no sense of humor. "Who were those soldiers?"

"The city's crazy anti-supernatural squad," said Alex.

"They set a trap with blood for these vampires and then attacked them," Logan added, glancing down at the vampires. "Here the supernaturals are hunted like trophies, their deaths granting great glory to the hunters."

Alex frowned down at the soldiers. "Disgusting. I spent years hunting monsters, but humanity has the capacity to be the greatest monster of all. We should drop the anti Dragon Born crowd in here for a few days to see how much they like being hunted like animals. Then maybe they'd understand how completely moronic it is to kill people for the way they were born."

Alex had a point. A very good point, in fact. Kai wondered how Blackbrooke would hold up in here. Maybe it was vicious and vengeful to think about throwing Blackbrooke into this world, but after all he'd put Sera through both back in the World That Was and in the Shadow World, Kai wasn't feeling especially magnanimous. Blackbrooke had taken his base, usurped his people—and forgiveness wasn't a quality dragons possessed. Sera's ability to see the best in people was nothing sort of astounding. She was a better person than he'd ever be.

When Kai thought about all she'd suffered, he wanted to tear into anyone who had ever hurt her. It was an anger that he could scarcely control. It burned through his veins, igniting an old and primal rage that threatened to consume him. He'd spent so many years in perfect control, but then he'd met her. He'd fallen for her. And now he couldn't imagine life without her. She broke down every layer of control in him, leaving him completely bare. Without her, he was unraveling. Something was boiling inside of him. Fear, anger, pain.

Only the need to find her was keeping him on the path of sanity. Only that gave him focus.

The necromancer had said he'd seen Sera. Kai had to believe it, even though the man was crazy. He had to have hope. Riley and Rane had insisted that Sera was in Merlin's domain, that she was alive. And Kai was going to find her.

Logan gave him an odd look. "You ok, Drachenburg? This is no time to fall apart."

"I am *not* falling apart."

A soft moan escaped one of the humans. He was still alive. Surprise flashed in Logan's eyes. For once, Kai didn't blame him. No one should have been able to survive that swarm of knives. Kai went over to him and looked down. The man wasn't dead, but Kai could scarcely call him alive. His wounds were beyond grotesque, and the pain that contorted his blood-stained face showed he felt every cut.

"Have you seen her?" Kai demanded, shoving Sera's picture in the dying man's face.

"You will all die when the Witch Slayer comes," he snarled, his glee cutting through the pain. "The heads of all abominations will decorate her castle's walls."

Abominations. That's just what the supernaturals of Kai's world called the Dragon Born.

"Who is this Witch Slayer?" he asked the man.

A look of pure devotion washed over his face. "The Witch Slayer is the all and powerful true ruler of this city."

"True ruler? So that means she isn't ruling it now," Logan observed.

"No." The man's expression soured. "The

Huntsman is fighting her for control of the city. But that pretender is no match for her magnificence. And neither are you supernatural scum," he added with vicious delight. "She will wipe you all out. The end is near, and it begins tonight at midnight."

"What happens at midnight?" Alex asked.

"The Witch Slayer will execute two of your kind. Their heads will decorate her throne room, dripping blood down the walls."

Alex's nose twitched in disgust. "Charming."

"The redhead's blood will flow freely, pouring onto the head of the dark-haired one who tried to save her."

Kai's gaze darted to him. "What kind of supernaturals are these?"

"Mages." The man spat the word like it was poison. "A female dragon summoner and a potion-throwing male."

"Lara and Riley."

Alex's shoulders tensed up.

"What about her?" Kai tapped Sera's photo. "Have you seen her?"

"Yes." The man laughed hysterically.

"Where is she?" Kai demanded.

"Another Dragon Born mage." His eyes flickered to Alex. "Oh, goody. We'll kill them both and reap the rewards twofold."

Silver flashed, and the man's head hit the ground. Kai turned to look back at Logan. His sword was dripping blood. He wiped it off his blade casually, then put the sword away. Anger burned coldly in his eyes. He was standing at the precipice of rage. Maybe Logan should have been worrying about himself, not about

Kai.

"You ok, Slayer? This is no time to fall apart."

"I am not falling apart."

"You killed our only source of information," Kai pointed out.

"Another one is alive." Logan indicated another hunter, who was, sure enough, stirring.

Alex walked past all of the dead hunters and stopped in front of the stirring man. "Talk."

He laughed, blood splattering his lips. "The Witch Slayer will see your carcasses hung from her walls."

Alex rolled her eyes. "So we've heard. Let's just skip to the point where you tell me something useful."

"Your blood will water her garden, your screams will sing her to sleep—"

Alex set her boot on his bleeding shoulder and crunched down. The man spasmed in pain, curses spilling out of his mouth.

"Oh, I'm sorry did that hurt? Maybe that's because this isn't a game!" Alex snarled. "You bleed as surely as we do, and if you don't want to bleed any more than you already are, talk. Where is my sister?"

"I don't know."

"Where is the Witch Slayer holding Riley and Lara?"

"At her great fortress, of course. It is impenetrable, so don't even try going there." A smile cut across his mouth. "No, actually, go there. I want to see you burn."

"You're not going anywhere," Alex told him. "At least not until you tell us about all the defenses around the fortress."

The man laughed. "I will do no such thing."

Logan drew two knives. "You will." His eyes hardened into cold granite.

The hunter's gaze darted around desperately. He looked truly afraid for the first time. "Why are you helping them? You're not a supernatural," he said to Logan.

"No, I'm not a supernatural. I'm something much worse, neither human nor supernatural. Some people call me a monster. I'll let you decide for yourself." Logan took a slow, deliberate step forward.

"Wait," the hunter said, his voice cracking with fear.

But before he could speak, the shadows stirred, billowing out from the darkest corner of the street. The temperature dropped twenty degrees, as though winter had just landed in San Francisco. But Kai saw no frost and no snow; all he saw was darkness, and that darkness opened its icy jaws and swallowed the hunter whole.

Alex gaped at the shadows. "What the hell…"

One of the vampires rose from the ground. "The shadows are cursed."

Wretched noises snarled and crunched from the shadows. Kai could hear the hunter dying an excruciating death. And then there was silence.

"The shadows do not remain satiated for long," said the vampire. "We must hurry. See, they are stirring once more."

As smooth as oil, the blanket of darkness slipped across dead hunters and vampires. Alex cast a wall of fire, but the shadows passed right through it.

"What is your name?" Alex asked the vampire.

"Dax."

"Ok, Dax. What else do you know about these shadows?"

"No one knows anything about them. Except that they are always hungry. They prefer to consume magic, but they will also feed on the life force of humans."

Kai shot a bundle of lightning-wrapped ice at the shadows. They paused for a moment, then smashed right through his spell.

"That won't work," Dax said. "We have to run."

But the shadows were swarming in from every direction. They'd even formed a ceiling of darkness overhead. There was no way out of this trap but to fight. But fight them with what?

Light, Kai realized. The enemy of darkness was light. He extended his hands high in the air. The shadows had consumed Alex's fire because she'd been focusing on heat, on burning them out with pure power. He'd done the same thing with his spells.

"I need you to cast the brightest light you can," Kai told her. "Forget about power. Forget about touching the shadows. They have no substance. What we need is pure light."

He cast a ball of sunshine, hurling it overhead. Alex added her own magic to his, forcing it brighter. Blinding white light flooded the street, crashing against the darkness. The shadows retreated, and then slowly, screeching and protesting, they fizzled out. Kai clapped his hands together, putting out his light.

"How did you know that would work?" Alex asked, cutting off her magic too.

"I figured shadows couldn't penetrate the light."

Logan gave him an inscrutable look. "You're smarter than I thought, Drachenburg."

"Of course I'm smart. I run a multi-billion dollar company."

"Not in this world, you don't."

Kai shrugged. "The world might have changed, but I'm still the same person."

"The person who steps on people who annoy him."

"You're one to talk." Kai glanced at his knives.

"Ok, boys. You can fight later." Alex stepped between them. "But first we have to save Riley and Lara. And find Sera."

"What do you have in mind?" Kai asked her.

"I don't know." Alex chewed on her lower lip. "Sera's the brains of our operation. I'm the muscle. But I think if we're going to infiltrate the Witch Slayer's castle, we'll need some help."

Logan's brows lifted. "Thinking things through before charging in impulsively?"

Alex grinned at him. "Well, I'm not completely incorrigible. Maybe only ninety percent incorrigible."

A hint of a smile twisted the assassin's lips. "Ninety-five percent at least."

"Let's debate math later." Kai looked at the vampire. "Do you know where the Witch Slayer's castle is?"

"Yes." Dax's eyes danced wildly, burning with pure terror.

"Bring us to your people," Kai pressed on. "We have some things to discuss."

"Ok." Dax exhaled in relief, obviously happy to get

off the streets—or at least happy that Kai wasn't demanding that he bring them to the Witch Slayer's castle right then and there. "Follow me."

◆ ◇ ◆ ◇ ◆

The vampires' hideout was located inside an office building that stood at the edge of where Golden Gate Park should have been. There was no large recreational park in this world's San Francisco, however. The city was just rows and rows of buildings street after street, all mushed together without borders or districts.

Their vampire guide led them into the building, past a pristine lobby that looked like it hadn't been worked in since it had been built. Past the lobby, the hall opened up into a large room that was dark, dank, and completely empty. Not a single person was in sight, vampire or otherwise. The air was stale, at least a decade overdue for a good airing out. The ceiling loomed ten meters overhead. A row of windows near the top had been painted black and taped shut.

"This place feels like a tomb," Logan commented.

"Let's hope it's not actually a tomb," Alex said as they crossed the room.

They found no bodies. There wasn't even a drop of blood in the room, which was surprising considering who lived here.

"They've all fled," Dax realized.

"Why?" Kai asked.

"In times of great danger, when our base is compromised, we retreat to our safe house."

"So the hunters found you," said Alex.

"It would appear so."

"We're going to need you to lead us to that safe house," Kai told Dax.

"Yes, we'd best get there quickly, before the hunters find us here," he agreed.

They were turning around to go back the way they'd come when a trap sprang up, swooping them up into a netted cocoon.

7. When Evil Clashed

SERA SNUCK QUIETLY through the dark room, the magic stone in her hands pulsing ever faster, leading her onward. The mages had given her the stone before retreating to their second hideout. They would come out of hiding when—and *only* when—she had convinced the vampires and fairies to join her cause. And they weren't going to help her gain the other supernaturals' loyalty either. The mages were flaky allies at best, but Sera didn't have many options here, in this unknown world. She needed their help to save Riley and Lara before the Witch Slayer executed them for the crime of being supernatural. Sera couldn't decide what was worse: the hunters' unwavering prejudice or their single-minded drive to earn their hero diploma by murdering innocent people in this twisted game.

She stepped softly, inching forward. The Huntsman, the Witch Slayer's arch nemesis, and his army of hunters were systematically butchering their way through the city's supernatural population this evening. Somehow they'd learned the locations of the supernaturals' bases and how to break through their defenses. That's why the mages had run. The vampires had fled too. Anyone with a lick of magic and even a drop of sanity was running, but not Sera. She needed to have a little chat with the Huntsman.

His hunters' easy victories had made them sloppy. They'd set off her alarms the moment they'd entered the building. She'd been a few blocks over laying down more traps when the stone had begun to pulse, calling her back. The Huntsman had to be with them. According to the mages, he was personally leading the 'cleanup' of the supernaturals' hideouts tonight. This was the best—maybe the only—chance Sera would get to talk him into an alliance. If she could just get him all tied up, maybe she could convince him to make a deal. She needed him to tell her how to turn off those anti-magic weapons so they could infiltrate the Witch Slayer's castle.

The Huntsman hated her kind, but she had a feeling he wanted to beat the Witch Slayer at this game more than he wanted to kill her right here and now. He wouldn't pass up an opportunity to score a victory against his arch nemesis, especially since she was already winning this Game. If Sera's experience with evil masterminds held true, when evil clashed, the underdog was always looking for a way to beat the other. And it didn't matter what he had to do to get it, even if it meant making a deal with someone he despised. The trick was getting the supernaturals united before the inevitable double cross went down.

Overhead, the net swayed and creaked in time to the crackle of magic slithering across the ropes. The stone in her hands was flickering rapidly, its song a furious hum of supercharged notes. She was closing in on the trapped hunters. Lowered, hissed voices rained down on her, and it was then that she realized her mistake. She hadn't captured the hunters at all.

"They're almost here. Can anyone reach my sword?" Alex whispered.

"It won't cut through those ropes," Logan said with a serenity that bordered on boredom. "They were woven together with magic."

"What are magic-hating hunters doing using magic?" Alex asked.

"You could say the same about my family," Logan replied.

"True… What are you doing?"

"Fighting magic with magic," Kai's voice said, and a bright light flashed to life, filling the dark room.

Sera blinked back the blinding ribbons of light streaking across her eyes. Her vision clearing, she looked up into Kai's face. The moment she saw him, hope stirred inside of her. That cold, lonely rock that had been crushing her heart since she'd dropped into this world melted away, replaced by happiness. Her gaze shifted to Logan, then an unknown vampire, and finally to Alex.

"You're here," Sera said. She couldn't stop grinning.

"I'm glad you find this amusing, sweetheart," replied Kai.

She winked at him. "Give me a moment, and I'll

have you all out of there."

Sera lifted the small rock above her head, cutting a few patterns into the air. Stone shifted to steel, and the sphere elongated into a dagger. She slashed the blade across the net. The ropes split, dissolving into smoke, and her friends dropped.

"Ow," Alex moaned, rubbing her back as she rose from the ground. "It's a good thing my sword wasn't out, or I'd have skewered myself on it."

Sera blinked, sheathing the dagger. "I didn't know the net would *literally* vanish in an instant. I thought I was just cutting a hole into it."

"What did you think would happen? That the spell would just let us down gently?" Alex's smirk stretched her mouth to the limits.

Sera couldn't help but grin back. She'd missed her sister so much.

"I'm glad you're not dead," Alex told her.

"I'm glad I'm not dead too." Sera grabbed hold of her sister, pulling her into a hug. She squeezed hard, not wanting to ever let go.

"Must…breathe…"

Sera pushed back, releasing her. "Sorry."

Alex chuckled, then glanced back over her shoulder. "Hey, are the rest of you all right? Logan, what's wrong? You alive?"

Logan was suddenly beside Alex. "I was giving you and Sera a moment."

She grinned at him. "I'm relieved you didn't slay yourself on all those knives."

His hand curled around her waist. "I assure you that I keep my knives properly sheathed."

Alex's lips quivered, like she was having a hard time holding back a lewd joke. Her shoulders shook with suppressed laughter.

"Would you like a sedative?" Logan asked coolly.

"No, I can control myself."

Logan looked utterly unconvinced. He turned his gaze on Sera. "I'm glad you're safe."

"Wow, that was almost sentimental." She smirked at him.

"Your sister is a bad influence."

Kai stepped up beside Alex and Logan, his eyes locked on Sera. She couldn't feel his magic right now, but she could read his emotions clearly enough in the blue storm raging inside of his eyes.

"Uh, hi. So, how are you?" she asked him, feeling suddenly shy beneath the intensity of that stare.

"How do you think I am?" he said, a soft growl simmering beneath the surface of his words. "You threw yourself on your sword. Again."

"Not literally."

Fire flashed across his eyes. "Not this time anyway."

They kept staring at each other, the abyss of awkwardness growing between them.

"Well," Sera said finally, when she could take the silence no longer. "It all worked out."

Kai's hand flashed out. He caught her arm, pulling her in. Her face hit the hard wall of his chest. "I'm keeping you close, Serafina Dering," he said, low and quiet, as his arms wrapped around her back. "You're mine and I'm yours. You agreed to marry me, so it's too late to run."

"I'm not running."

"And if you do run," he continued, his heart pounding against her ear. "I will chase you to the ends of the earth. I will not give up on you. Not ever, you hear me?"

"Of course you won't. You're too stubborn for that." Sera relaxed against him.

One hand cupped her chin, tilting her head up as his other hand curled around the back of her neck. "I missed you."

He closed his mouth over hers in a slow, deep kiss that jolted awake every nerve in her body. Sera dug her fingernails into his back, pulling him closer. She could scarcely breathe, but she didn't care. Her head spun with a thousand delightfully wicked thoughts. Suddenly, he pulled back, leaving her flushed. She tried to hold on, but he slipped right through her fingers.

"It feels like you've been gone for an eternity," Kai whispered against her ear as his hand stroked slow, deep circles into her back.

"After Merlin's storm swallowed me, I fell through the abyss. Time seemed to slow. I was stuck there," said Sera. "How long have I been gone?"

"About a day."

She exhaled in relief. "So it's not too late to break the Shadow World spell, to put things back to the way they were."

"Sera," Alex said. "The Witch Slayer, one of the players of this game, has taken Riley and Lara. And she's going to kill them at midnight."

Pain pinched Sera's heart. "I know. That's why I

came here to the vampires' hideout. The other player, the Huntsman, is going through the city, attacking the supernaturals' bases tonight."

The vampire stepped forward, a web of worry lines marring his face. "What happened to my people?"

"They fled before I got here," Sera told him. "This place was empty. I set my trap, hoping to catch the Huntsman unawares when he came here. I caught you instead."

"So the Huntsman is still headed this way," said Alex.

"Yes." Sera drew the dagger and waved it in the air, going through the pattern of movements the mages had taught her to turn the blade into a pair of knitting needles.

"Taking up knitting?" Alex asked, her eyebrows arching in amusement as Sera began weaving another magical net.

"Just preparing a little surprise for the Huntsman," she replied. "As you saw, these nets are resilient against magic, muscle, and steel."

"That enchanted rock is very powerful," the vampire said. "I have only ever seen one like it—in the possession of the mages."

"They loaned it to me."

"How generous of them, considering it does not belong to them."

"Let me guess," Sera said. "You're going to tell me the stone's rightful owners are the vampires."

"The fairies made the stone for us, infusing it with great magic. That was centuries ago, but we immortals do not forget."

"I'm sure," she replied drily, continuing to weave the net. "But for right now, the stone is mine to use. If we're going to stop the hunters, all vampires, mages, and fairies will have to stop fighting over trinkets and presumed offenses. You have to work together. There will be time to be petty later, *after* we've defeated the hunters and saved my friends."

The vampire dipped his chin. "Agreed."

"Peachy." Sera glanced at Kai. "How did you find me? Magic-sniffing doesn't work in this world."

"We didn't find you," he replied. "At least not on our own."

"We were looking for you, but we couldn't track you down," Alex added. "We caught a necromancer who had lured us to him using a whiff of your magic."

"Where did he get my magic?"

"We believe he was projecting it."

"What is with all the dramatics?" Sera commented. "So much intrigue, so many games. Whatever happened to just walking up to someone and declaring your evil intentions. Say what you want about Blackbrooke, but at least he's always direct."

"The necromancer was less about the dramatics and more about the madness," Alex told her. "He obviously knew where you were, but nothing he said made any sense. He tried to run off, and we stopped him. Then, just like that, Logan and I popped up in this world, right into the middle of a fight between the hunters and some vampires. I don't know how we got here."

"The necromancer. He sent us here," Logan said.

"But how?" Alex asked.

"Some fairies have the power to teleport people," Kai said. "The necromancer must be one of them."

"He teleported us between worlds," Alex pointed out. "They don't teach that kind of magic at fairy school."

"We have bigger issues than an over-juiced necromancer right now," Sera said. "The Witch Slayer is going to publicly execute Riley and Lara in just a few hours. The mages will help us attack her castle, but they won't come out and play until we convince the vampires and fairies to join us."

"Even together, we don't stand a chance as long as the hunters have their anti-magic weapons," the vampire said. "Not so long ago, we were getting stronger. We had enough power to fight back. But then the hunters developed these weapons to short-circuit our magic. Overnight, they turned the tables against us." Woeful icicles dripped from his joyless laugh. "The tables are *always* turned against us in this game. No matter what we do, we lose. But this will change." He shot Alex an adoring look. "The Dragon Born will save us."

"Apparently, we're considered some kind of savior in this world," Alex told Sera.

"Yes, I know." Sera sighed. "So, what did the vampires do to you?"

"Do to me? Nothing. Why?"

"The mages' test consisted of burning me at the stake to prove I was the real deal, a genuine Dragon Born mage."

"Wow." Alex's jaw dropped. "That sucks."

"Yes, it really did."

"We would never try to do such a thing," the vampire told Alex.

Her eyes narrowed into suspicious slits. "You weren't in any position to test me."

I bet that's what he was bringing them here to do—to overpower them so the vampires could test them, Amara said.

Sera relayed the comment.

Alex's eyes sizzled with magic as she snapped her head around to glare at him. The sheepish look he gave her in response was answer enough.

"I saved your life, you crazy vampire. And you don't trust me?" Alex snapped with unmasked annoyance.

"If you'd spent all these years here, you wouldn't trust easily either. The hunters are devious, and they've tricked us before. Those tricks cost us greatly. We're more careful nowadays."

"Tell me about this *test*," Alex ordered him.

The vampire said nothing.

"It involves blood, doesn't it?"

His eyes pulsed once.

"Damn vampires," Alex grumbled. "It's always about blood with you." She turned to Sera. "So what's the plan? Do you have a way to neutralize the hunters' weapons?"

"Of course I do." Sera tied together the final bindings of the magic net and lifted it up. "We're going to trap the Huntsman and convince him to help us."

"You'd better leave the convincing to Logan."

"No, not that kind of convincing. We're going to

talk to him. He'll tell us how to neutralize those anti-magic weapons so our growing supernatural army of mages and vampires can attack." Sera glanced at the vampire, who was nodding in approval. "And we will help the Huntsman defeat the Witch Slayer at this game. With the game over, the supernaturals will be free."

"It sounds like you've got this all figured out," commented Alex.

"Well, we are the saviors, after all."

"You bet we are, sister." Alex took the other end of the net. "Ok, crazy game world, bring it on."

Laughter echoed through the room, a blend of madness and…well, more madness.

"I know that laugh," Kai said quietly.

"Things aren't so simple here, you see." Magic flashed, and a man in tattered robes appeared in front of them.

"The necromancer," Logan said, drawing his knives.

The man's face rippled with delirium. "My mistress is coming. And she's going to get you."

"We don't have time for this madness," Alex said.

"But there is truth beneath his madness," commented Logan. "I hear someone coming."

The doors to the room flung open so hard that they nearly flew off their hinges. A woman in a long crimson cloak strode in, her black battle leather creaking with every step. Her hair was as dark as a starless night, her eyes shining as brightly as unfiltered sunshine. Two guards dressed in red walked beside her.

"The Witch Slayer," the vampire muttered, his

voice cracking with fear.

Sera moved quickly, casting a strong breeze beneath the net. The braided rope shimmered silver, then shot at the Witch Slayer. The woman sidestepped with fluid grace. As the net swept around for another pass, the Witch Slayer drew her sword and swung it fast and hard. The blade split the magic bindings apart. The net dissolved, blowing away like smoke on the wind.

"That's impossible," Sera gasped. "The mages assured me that net was immune to your weapons."

The Witch Slayer's laugh sang out like diamond tiaras and shattered dreams. Teeming with a woefully broken intelligence, it was as beautiful as it was cruel.

"Yes, it is immune to my hunters' weapons. But not immune to me." Her mouth drew up into a crescent smile. "Aww, what's the matter? Did the poor Dragon Born mages come to the party with all the wrong toys?"

"This isn't a party. And it isn't a game," Alex snapped.

"See, that's where you're wrong. It *is* a game, the greatest game in all of the worlds." The Witch Slayer shrugged. "Or at least it used to be. It's grown rather tiresome of late. What this game needs is a proper adversary."

The doors burst open once more, and six hunters filed inside. They wore the same leather superhero suits as the Witch Slayer's hunters, except in forest-green rather than blood-red. Superheroes, bah! It never ceased to astound Sera how many villains painted themselves as the hero. She shot the two groups of hunters a hard glare. No way, no how. She was not going to be some delusional psychopath's hero quest.

"Speak of the devil," the Witch Slayer whispered as the green hunters' line split, opening the path for a man in thick leather armor.

The Huntsman walked down the aisle as though he already owned the room and everything in it, which currently consisted of a dozen empty crates and an impressive collection of cobwebs. There was an unwavering confidence about the man, which was impressive considering how badly he was losing his war game with the Witch Slayer. That confidence might have had something to do with his size. He towered a full head over everyone in the room, and he was built like a bulldozer. If Sera ever found herself with a castle wall to break through, the Huntsman would be way at the top of her list of likely battering rams.

He looked at the Witch Slayer, his eyes gleaming like obsidian daggers. "What are *you* doing here?"

"I could ask the same about you. I didn't expect to find you out and about after the bloody nose I dealt you at our last battle." Her crimson lips shimmered brightly, accentuating the saccharine-shelled words spilling from her mouth.

"A minor setback that shall soon be corrected," he replied. "I do not allow my previous misfortunes to consume me. I am not a child who stomps her feet and throws a tantrum when things do not go my way. How long did you lock yourself into your room after your last defeat?"

Her nostrils flared as her eyes narrowed to angry

slits. "I cannot recall. It's been far too long since my last defeat."

"You will taste that bitter medicine soon enough."

"You'll never win this game," the Witch Slayer snarled. "You have already lost. You're just too blind to see it."

The way the two of them spoke was so unreal, as though they didn't care about the world or any of the people in it. All that was important to them was winning their precious game. The necromancer bobbed up and down beside his mistress, his eyes darting erratically from her to the Huntsman.

The Witch Slayer yawned. "I'm growing bored of this. How about you do something sensible for a change and just surrender, Huntsman?"

"No," replied her stony-faced opponent.

She winked at him. "Let me know if you change your mind."

"I won't change my mind."

"Spoilsport."

"You don't have to lose," Sera said quietly to the Huntsman.

He turned his head to give her a wary look.

"Sometimes victory lies down the most unexpected path."

"Oh, no. No, you don't, you devious girl." The Witch Slayer pointed at Sera. "Let's just break up this happy little team."

Glowing blue glyphs pulsed to life on the ground. The harsh snarl of ripping fabric cut across the room, and then Kai, Logan, and the vampire guide were just gone. Only Sera and Alex remained. They were alone, trapped between two warlords who wanted nothing more than to make a hunting trophy out of their still-breathing bodies.

8. The Game

KAI FELT THAT familiar tingle, like ants crawling across his skin, and then the rough tug of teleportation. The journey was slower than he was used to—slower and smothered in a cloud of magic-charged fog. As icy as a post-blizzard stroll, the air cut through him like a shot of adrenaline.

When the swathes of magic cleared, Kai saw that Sera was not here. Neither was Alex. Only Logan and Dax had come along for the ride. The glyphs had already gone out, but the light they'd brought along lingered on, hovering overhead like a swirling galaxy. As the light expanded, the room came into focus...or rather the cave. Kai was right back where he'd started, stuck in the Beast's cavern.

The walls were shining eerily—oily, black, glossy. They were like canvases of pure darkness, tapestries that absorbed all light. Dark magic patterns rippled across them, shifting slowly like reflections on a lake's surface. Kai heard the slurping swoosh of water across smooth rocks, but there was no water in sight. The ground and ceiling were as glossy as the walls. It was like standing inside a room of blackened mirrors.

"Where are we?" Logan asked.

"Somewhere we don't want to be," said Kai.

"You're scared?" Logan's brows crept up. "*You*, the great Kai Drachenburg, the dragon, the Mages Illustrated cover model?"

Kai shot him a hard look, but the assassin just remained unperturbed. In fact, he looked amused.

"He's right," Dax said. "We don't want to be here. She's teleported us to the Beast's cavern."

"So the Witch Slayer is a witch of sorts herself," said Logan.

Dax swallowed hard. "She has many powerful spells. One of those is the ability to teleport people."

"How ironic that a supernatural is on a quest to rid this world of supernaturals," commented Kai.

"She doesn't care about that. She doesn't care about anything but *winning*. She has to beat the Huntsman no matter what. That is her goal above all else. This is nothing but a game to her. It's not even real. We are not real. We're here solely for her amusement," Dax said.

"It's time that changed. It's time you fought back," Kai told the vampire.

"Legend tells us the Dragon Born will save us from this hellish game." A smile spread his lips as he looked up, his eyes twinkling with hope. "They will lead their followers to freedom."

"That's why you're tagging along with us," Logan

observed.

"Yes. When the Dragon Born train departs this world, I have every intention of being on it."

"Before we can depart this world, we have to get out of this cave. There's an exit that leads to the surface." Kai brushed his hand across the wall. The dark patterns swirled up, then settled back down. "But the paths and walls have shifted since I was last here."

"They say this cave is like the labyrinth of worlds that surrounds Merlin's fortress," said Dax. "The path out of here shifts constantly. Once you fall into the Beast's lair, you are forever doomed."

"That's ridiculous. I made it out," Kai pointed out.

Dax nodded. "Yes, but you are blessed by being the consort of the great Dragon Born savior."

Kai coughed. "*Consort?*" He'd never had a title other than his own.

Logan laughed. "You should see your face, Drachenburg."

"I wouldn't be so amused if I were you, Slayer. You're the *consort* of the other great Dragon Born savior."

The assassin's expression hardened. "Perhaps we need a more active title."

"Concubine?" Kai suggested. He just couldn't help it. Man, Sera's snark was really starting to rub off on him.

Logan cleared his throat. "Let's just concentrate on finding the way out of here."

"You can't track magic in this world," Dax told them. "It works differently here. It's at a different frequency, a frequency that impairs magic-sniffing. It's like trying to detect magic in a house of mirrors. It bounces off of everything, mangling it up into a big, unfocused mess."

"I don't need magic to track." Logan inhaled deeply. "This way. The air is cleaner down here."

"I have a bad feeling about this," Dax muttered as they followed Logan down a tunnel that seemed to grow darker with every step. "This place is a web of traps. We could be walking right into one of them."

"I know what I'm…" Logan stopped moving, freezing at the threshold of a large open chamber. "Weird."

"Slayer?"

"The path has changed. Look at the walls."

The dark magic on the walls was bubbling up like a boiling pot. The ripples shifted, the colors changed. A soft hum buzzed, growing steadily louder. The Beast stepped out from behind a forest of monster-sized stalagmites. It turned its red glare on Kai and expelled a huff of smoke that rumbled like an old car engine.

"That is one ugly dragon," Logan commented.

"I don't believe it is a dragon," Kai replied as the Beast extended its butterfly wings and scraped its catlike claws against the rocky ground. "At least not a true dragon. It's like a chimera of monster parts."

"According to legend, the great Beast once had fur," Dax told them. "It was supposed to look like a very large lion. But the Beast was cursed with an appetite for magic. As it fed on the magic of its victims, its appearance changed. Its body warped."

"Is the Beast the Witch Slayer's pet?" Kai asked him.

"No, the Beast belongs to no one. It is a vile creature, a product of this world made with the darkest of magic, twice cursed. Its appetite can never be satiated. When it can't find magic to feed upon, it consumes the life force of humans instead." Dax's eyes flickered from the beast to Kai. "The Beast hungers for you. You escaped it before. I can see it in its eyes. I've seen that look before in my kind. It's the look we vampires get when we've chosen our prey. The Beast will not stop until it has caught you and drained the magic and life out of you."

"Sounds like you're as good as dead, Drachenburg," Logan said with a crooked grin.

"Indeed. I might as well lie down and wait for the end to come."

The Beast didn't have the patience for that. Its eyes pulsed with crimson delight, and then it charged forward, the erratic tufts of wolf hair shifting and sliding between its hard scales as it moved. Logan dashed off in a flash, launching a barrage of knives as he moved. But the blades bounced off the scales with a resounding clunk and fell to the ground. Logan came around for another pass, drawing his sword this time. He swung it in a wide arc, slashing at the Beast's legs. The blade didn't go through; it bounced off the scales as uselessly as the knives had.

Logan stopped beside Kai. "We need something that will pierce that armor. Something like your talons. Shift into a dragon and make a few gashes in the Beast's side."

"I can't," Kai said, much as he hated to admit it. "Something in this cave is blocking my shifting magic."

"What are you good for then?" Logan said, rushing off for another pass at the Beast. He didn't sound annoyed. In fact, he said it like he was merely stating a fact. You knew things were serious when Logan locked into his professional assassin mode.

Kai couldn't shift into a dragon, but that didn't mean he was just giving up. He blasted the Beast with fire, and when it didn't react, he cast an earthquake, sinking the ground beneath its feet. He strung spell after spell together, but the Beast just took it like it didn't feel a thing.

It charged, breaking down the bindings of Kai's spell, tearing through Logan's traps like they were nothing. The spells turned brittle and snapped, raining to the ground like broken cracker crumbs. Dax dashed forward, but he didn't make it far. The Beast's eyes met his, pulsing, and then Dax turned and ran away, screaming in sheer terror.

"Don't kill her! Stop! Wait!" the vampire bellowed, sobbing. He waved his hands wildly in the air, batting at enemies that weren't there.

The Beast had captured his mind and was driving him to the brink of madness. Kai caught him as he was about to run right into the monster's open jaws. Logan jumped off the Beast's head, throwing something into its eyes as he dropped. Its roar of agony shot through the cavern, splitting fissures across the rocky walls. Dry powder drizzled down from the ceiling.

"That will only hold it off for a minute or so before the poison wears off," Logan said as the Beast stomped blindly around the room.

Dax was holding himself, rocking back and forth. "We're going to die, we're going to die," he repeated over and over again.

"Shut up," Kai told him.

But the vampire didn't stop. He kept rocking and muttering, his mind caught in a waking nightmare, a prison it could not escape.

"This isn't working," Logan said to Kai. "The Beast is immune to every weapon we have. That poison should have eaten through its eyes. Instead it gave the monster the equivalent of a shot of pepper spray to the eyes."

"Suggestions?"

Surprise flashed in Logan's eyes. "You're asking *me* for suggestions?"

"Do you have any?"

"There are some battles that cannot be won."

"Is that written in the assassins' handbook?"

"Yes."

Kai rolled his eyes. "Why am I not surprised?"

"Haven't you ever been in a battle you could not win?"

"Quitters never win."

"You quit last time you faced the Beast," Logan pointed out.

"That wasn't quitting. It was regrouping."

"Fine, then let's 'regroup'," said Logan. "We need more firepower to take that thing out. And we don't have time for this. Alex and Sera are surrounded by the Witch Slayer's forces *and* the Huntsman's forces. That is a battle worth fighting, not this one."

"You know, I actually agree with you."

"Try not to sound so irked by that."

"I'm getting the feeling you two don't like each other very much," Dax commented. The Beast must have been too distracted fighting the poison to maintain its mental lock on him.

"What ever would give you that idea?" Kai asked him.

Dax shivered. Since vampires didn't get cold, it must have been a lingering aftershock of the Beast's control. Or the vampire was just scared shitless.

"What happened between you two?"

"I stole something from him once," Logan said.

Kai held up two fingers. "Twice."

"I distinctly remember it was once."

"Once in each reality. Twice altogether."

Logan's brows drew together in annoyance. "That doesn't count. That's like saying you were born twice."

"I think the Beast can see again," Dax gasped, taking a step back.

"Good," Logan said. "You wanted a plan, Drachenburg, and here it is. The beast is blocking the exit." He pointed at the stream of light pouring through the rocky mound behind the Beast. "It wants you. So you have to get it to chase you to the other side of the room, away from the exit. Then we'll incapacitate it and escape."

"The only way we have to incapacitate it is that poison. You'll need to throw more of it in the Beast's eyes," Kai told him.

"That thing is heavily armored. Do you know how close I had to get to throw the poison in its face? I'm not even sure I can do it again."

"You can because you want to stay alive long enough to save Alex," Kai said. "It's the same reason I won't let the Beast maul me to little bits. I need to save Sera."

Logan extended his hand to Kai. "I think we have an understanding, Drachenburg."

They shook hands quickly, then sprang into action. The Beast was still blinking, clearing the green liquid from its eyes, but it could see well enough to glare at Kai.

"Over here, you blind pussy cat!" Kai shouted up at it.

The Beast didn't waste time. It shot straight for him, moving fast for something that size. Kai threw up a wall of ice, but the monster smashed right through it, chasing him with single-minded determination. Dax ran for the high pile of rocks blocking the way to the exit. He threw them off, every toss fueled by vampire strength supercharged with fear.

Logan swung around behind the Beast, jumping onto its thrashing tail. Even as he ran up its back, it ignored him, focusing its attention solely on Kai. Its tongue slid across its fanged teeth in eager anticipation.

"Sorry, you won't be eating me today," Kai told the Beast as Logan kicked off its head and somersaulted in the air, throwing the poison in its face.

Kai ignited that poison with fire. The Beast let loose a howl of rage, and it blindly ran forward, slamming hard against the wall it didn't see. Kai and Logan darted around it, joining Dax at the rocky mound. The vampire had nearly cleared the way, and they quickly helped him throw the last blocking boulders aside, then ran for the exit. They scrambled up the ladder, emerging on a dark street. It wasn't the same spot Kai had come out last time. It seemed that not only were the tunnels shifting, but so was the exit.

And they had another problem. The shadows were swirling all around them, closing in. Kai cast a bright light, but it went out immediately.

"That won't work," Dax told him. "Not this time. We're too close to the Beast."

"The Beast controls the shadows?" Logan asked.

"The shadows *are* the Beast," replied Dax. "The monster is cursed to be stuck down there in those tunnels, but it can send smaller parts of itself out here to hunt people and bring them down for dinner. We might have escaped the tunnels, but the Beast isn't letting us go."

9. The Witch Slayer

"WELL, ISN'T THIS fun?" the Witch Slayer said, looking from Sera to Alex.

She didn't spare a glance for the Huntsman. She'd turned her back on him like he didn't even matter. That meant she didn't see the hard glare he was shooting like a machine gun at the back of her head.

The Witch Slayer was small, even slight. She almost looked like a doll next to her opponent, a doll with perfectly braided black hair pinned up onto her head princess-style. Her eyes, as bright as her hair was dark, danced with a strange light, a combination of intelligence, amusement, calculation, and madness all wrapped up into one cute package. Her black leather bodysuit looked entirely out of place on her, but the red cloak was right on the money. If Little Red Riding Hood were a villain, this was exactly what she'd look like. Her sword was the only weapon she wore. Not that someone with that kind of magic needed a mundane weapon. Whoa, was she powerful! Even with Sera's magic-sniffing ability down, there was no missing the hum of magical energy surrounding the Witch Slayer like a halo. What was a mage doing hunting down other supernaturals?

Her opponent, the Huntsman, was as large as she was small. His blond hair was cropped nearly to his scalp, hugging his body as tightly as the suit of green leather he wore. Large, muscular, and decidedly badass, he was the quintessential warlord. Weapon belts covered his body, packed with a combination of blades and guns. His hazel eyes gleamed with an intelligence that rivaled his opponent's. Yet there was a roughness there not present in her eyes, like he'd survived the kind of horrors that had broken lesser men but only hardened him.

"What are you doing here?" the Huntsman demanded. "This is my place. My night."

The Witch Slayer laughed softly. "Until you win our little game, my dear Huntsman, this city belongs to no one." Her words were crisper than his, more refined. "I may come and go as I choose."

"You may come and go at your own risk." He spoke with a rough and rugged intelligence that clashed harshly with her perfect intonation.

The differences between the two players were striking, and yet here they were, caught up in the same game, spearheading the same atrocities in the name of sport. The Witch Slayer was more genteel, more regal. Like a princess. There was nothing royal about the Huntsman. He was just a regular guy. A regular guy who had been forced to adapt to an irregular situation.

Whatever they had been before the Game began—good or evil, regular or royal—the two players were tearing this world apart. To them, it was nothing but a playground, the arena where their darkest desires played out in full color.

A smile curled the Witch Slayer's lips. "Are you threatening me?"

"I can assure you," he replied. "When I make a threat, you will know it. There will be no need to ask."

She laughed. "You really are great fun, you know. I'll be so sad when our game is over."

"Giving up already?"

"Oh, no." Madness flashed in her eyes. "The end is near, Huntsman. And you won't like where it leads you."

The Witch Slayer was two people, two sides: a sane, competitive warrior and a little princess driven to madness. The Huntsman, on the other hand, was simply a cold-blooded killer. Such lovely choices for allies, but Sera had already picked her poison. A calculating killer was the better choice. A crazy person would turn on you just because it sounded funny. The insane weren't driven by reason. They were impossible to predict. And it was that unpredictability that made them dangerous. If the Witch Slayer didn't know when she was going to stab Sera in the back, then how could anyone else see it coming?

So that left Sera with the cold and cunning Huntsman. "Your game isn't going so well, is it?" she said.

He shot her a hard, sour look. What was it Dad had always said about not poking a nest of hornets?

"Classic. Positively perfect." The Witch Slayer laughed. "I'm glad I didn't send you off with the others. I wouldn't have had a chance to see the look on his face just now."

"Why did you send our friends away?" Alex asked her.

"Friends?" Light danced across her eyes. "Let's not be coy, dears. I know they mean more to you than friendship. A whole lot more, in fact. But they matter not." She gave her hand a dismissive wave. "I want to speak to you. The Dragon Born."

The Huntsman shifted his weight, his expression darkening.

"What's the matter?" she asked, chuckling behind her hand. "Don't tell me you didn't know what they are." She glanced at her two hunters. "Stop and drink in the sight. We are in the presence of a miracle, an event that happens only once in a lifetime. The Dragon Born walk among us again."

Her tone was equal parts mockery and sincere wonder. Two sides, two selves, the Witch Slayer was like a chocolate and vanilla ice cream swirl—after the chocolate and vanilla had melted into a big pile of mush.

"It's been so long since any of your kind have wandered into our little war game," she continued. "And it was great fun the last time, wasn't it, Huntsman?"

He folded his arms across his chest. "As I recall, last time you tried to feed me to the Beast along with the Dragon Born."

"Surely you aren't still upset about *that*. It was

decades ago." She gave Sera a conspiring wink. "The last time Dragon Born mages walked among us, it was a delightful pair from the Netherworld."

"I wish you wouldn't use those ridiculous names," the Huntsman said.

"Why ever not? My names are much better than names like World 126."

He sighed like they'd had this discussion a thousand times before—to a thousand unsatisfying conclusions.

"What can I say?" She grinned at Alex. "I'm an incurable romantic."

"I have a cure for you all right," the Huntsman grumbled.

"What's that, dear? I didn't quite hear you. If you want people to take you seriously as a warlord, then you really must stop muttering."

His hand caressed the hilt of his sword.

"I find your silence uninspiring. Once more, with feeling this time!" she said, lifting her arms in the air.

Sera felt like she was in high school again

A really twisted version of high school, said Amara.

"What happened to the Dragon Born last time?" Alex asked the Witch Slayer.

"Ah, you're referring to that 'prophecy'. Or was it an urban legend? I really can't recall… Well, I have to tell you that I don't believe there's any truth in it. Don't get me wrong. The last Dragon Born to grace this world with their presence were good fighters, but they weren't chosen. And they certainly were no saviors. They came, played, and then departed this world."

"What do you mean by 'departed this world'?" said Sera.

"Oh, they didn't die, dear. I meant they *literally* left this world. They realized it was a battle they couldn't win and left. Smart mages, those two." She smiled widely. "So, you see, there is no prophecy. Not a real one anyway. It's just a story the supernaturals of this world tell one another to give them hope. Don't let them rope you into it too."

"So, that's why you wanted to talk to us," Alex said. "You think you're going to convince us to leave."

"Oh, no. I don't care if you stay or flee."

"We couldn't flee even if we wanted to," Sera said.

The Witch Slayer ignored her. Apparently what she had to say was more important than reality. "Though if you stay, I could use your help with something."

"You're trying to recruit them?" the Huntsman said, indignant. "Really?"

She arched her brows at him with perfect calmness. "No need to be moody that you didn't think of it first." She glanced at Sera.

"No deal."

The Witch Slayer turned to Alex next.

"Like my sister said, no deal."

She sighed. "This is because I'm insane, isn't it?"

"No, this has to do with you being a villain. We don't make deals with the bad guys," Alex told her. "Especially ones who are making a game out of hunting down innocent people."

"You were trying to make a deal with him." She pointed at the Huntsman. "He was just too dense to notice it."

Surprise flashed across his face.

"You're oddly astute for a crazy person," Sera told her.

"Thank you. And you are surprisingly sweet for a menace." She didn't even sound like she was insulting them. She actually seemed to mean it as a compliment. "You look rather smug," she said to the Huntsman.

"While you ladies were chatting, my forces were surrounding this building," he said, a smile twisting his lips. "If you turn and leave now, I'll even tell my soldiers to let you go, *dear*."

The Witch Slayer giggled. "You are hilarious. This is so much fun. We really must get together more often. And since you were such a gentleman, let me extend the same offer to you. If you turn and leave now, I'll let you go."

His eyes narrowed. "My hunters have this place surrounded."

"Indeed they do," she said, smiling brightly. "Do you wish to surrender?"

He shook his head. "You're getting madder each day."

"I'm waiting for an answer, Huntsman. Do you wish to leave here unharmed or in chains?"

He glanced at her two guards. "You couldn't."

"I can."

"You seem to be short an army, and mine has this building surrounded."

The doors opened, and more green hunters rushed inside. The Huntsman's victorious smile faded as soon as he realized his hunters were wounded.

"What happened?" he demanded of them as they

barred the door.

"Did you really think I would leave my castle without my army in attendance?" The Witch Slayer smirked at him. "While your soldiers were so diligently surrounding the building, my soldiers were surrounding *them*."

The doors thundered and shook, like it was being hit with a battering ram. Wood cracked and splintered from the door, falling away in shaved slivers.

"Tick-tock, Huntsman."

What was left of the door hit the floor with a heavy splat. Red hunters stormed inside, pushing the green hunters back.

"I have more where that comes from, waiting right outside," the Witch Slayer said. "You are outnumbered. Maybe you shouldn't have tried to launch six simultaneous strikes in one night." She met his glare with a pleasant smile.

The Witch Slayer might have been mad, but the Huntsman was stubborn. He waved his hunters forward. As the two armies clashed, Sera grabbed Alex's hand.

"Let's go," she whispered. "Now, while they're distracted."

"What about the Huntsman?"

"Forget it. This was clearly a big mistake. We'll have to find another way to neutralize those weapons."

Sera and Alex ran, zigzagging past the hunters in red and green. They were too busy fighting one another to take notice, even as the sisters slipped outside. The Huntsman was waiting on the dark street. They reached for their swords.

"Wait," he said, holding up his hands. "You wanted to make a deal."

Alex's eyes narrowed with suspicion. "And you want to make one too?"

"Yes. As you've realized, I've been losing ground recently. I need a victory against the Witch Slayer, or this war is all but lost. So I will help you, even if it means annoying Merlin."

He said the name like it was holy. That set off alarm bells in Sera's head.

"What is your connection to Merlin?" she asked him.

"I serve him."

"You're *his* warlord, his dirty hand of justice in this Dump, aren't you?" Alex said.

"Yes. I keep order between the worlds."

"And here you destroy order," Sera commented.

"There isn't much to do in Merlin's domain when I'm not crushing the occasional bloody rebellion. This is just a game."

"A diversion?" Alex suggested.

"For her, yes. She grows bored with all the time Merlin spends lost in his lab, engrossed in his work. For me, it is training, something to keep my mind and body alive."

"These people are dying so you can feel alive," Sera growled in disgust.

Alex squeezed her hand. "You know who we are," she said to the Huntsman.

"Yes, I do. And I know you want to put the world back to the one you know." He sounded like he didn't care one way or the other.

"And you are ok with that?" Sera said in surprise.

"It doesn't affect us here. And, besides, Merlin is just going to change the world again anyway. He's not happy with the way it's turned out."

"What is he actually trying to do?" Sera asked him.

"The same thing he's been trying to do for centuries: save his sister."

"What happened to his sister?"

"Centuries ago, Merlin changed the world with magic, but something happened that he did not expect: he erased his sister from existence."

"That's horrible," Sera said. She wasn't fond of Merlin, but his sister certainly hadn't deserved to pay the price of his magic.

"It truly is a great tragedy," the Huntsman agreed. "And he's been trying to bring her back ever since."

"But how can he bring her back?" Alex asked. "Even if he could reverse those changes, this happened centuries ago. His sister would have died already."

"Oh, she's not dead," said the Huntsman.

"You said Merlin erased her."

"She's here. But not all there. As you saw for yourself."

"Wait, you're saying the Witch Slayer is Merlin's sister?" Sera gasped.

"Yes."

"How is that possible?" Alex asked. "If he erased her, how is she here?"

"That is a very long story."

10. The Huntsman

"HER NAME IS Arianna," the Huntsman began. "Seven hundred years ago, Merlin's experiments with reality-changing magic wiped her from existence. As his spell's magical shock wave tore through the world, as he saw his beloved little sister fade before his eyes, he opened up a portal to this domain. It is a sanctuary outside of time and reality, a place he created for her. And it's where he experiments before casting a spell."

"So the worlds that litter the Dump—" Sera began.

"Some are castoff worlds from before Merlin changed the real world, others are his failed experiments of the centuries that followed the first spell," the Huntsman told her. "Here, we all exist, whether or not we exist out there in the real world."

"So if Arianna left Merlin's domain, she would cease to exist?" Alex asked.

"Yes. By pulling Arianna into this in-between

realm as she was disappearing Merlin saved his sister. Her mind, on the other hand, is split. It's broken."

"In other words, she's crazy," said Alex.

"She hears voices in her head. One moment she is completely sane, and the next you wonder where her mind has gone. That makes her unpredictable."

"Unpredictable in your game. That's why you can't beat her," Sera realized. "She's powerful and smart and unpredictable. You don't stand a chance."

"With this alliance, I will."

"Wait, you know she's insane, and still you can think of nothing but winning this game? What the hell is the matter with you?" Sera demanded.

"You know she's insane, and you care only about stopping her brother so you can put your world back. That is your game. How is it any different?"

"Because we want to help people, not kill them," Alex told him.

"If you shatter the Shadow World, some people will die and others will live. Who are you to decide which world is better?"

"The Shadow World is one torn apart by war," Sera said. "It shows us what happens when hate wins. It is not better, not by any measure."

"Merlin," Alex growled. "Everyone is suffering because of him. The people here, the people in the Shadow World. His own sister. She is in this situation because he just couldn't leave the world alone. What gave him the right to change it?"

"The world you know, the world you consider real, is the one Merlin made so long ago," the Huntsman pointed out. "Think about that for a moment."

"I'm trying not to," said Alex. "It's messing with my inner sense of serenity."

"You shouldn't feel bad for Arianna, you know," the Huntsman told her. "She will use that against you. She might be crazy, but she is far from stupid."

"Instead we should trust you?" Sera asked, lifting her brows.

"Making a deal with me was your idea."

"One of our worse ideas, I'm beginning to think," Alex commented.

"If it doesn't sit well with you, you could just give up now."

"You obviously don't know us very well."

"Can you deactivate the anti-magic batons?" Sera asked him.

He laughed. "Make one of my best weapons useless? I think not."

"What's more important to you: beating the Witch Slayer or killing supernaturals?"

"I don't take pleasure in killing these people," he said.

"And yet you do it anyway."

"War is not pretty, little girls. Only a man with neither soul nor sense fails to see that."

"This isn't war. It's a twisted game you play for sport," Alex told him, frowning.

"There are no real wars to fight in this domain. None that matter," he said icily. "Merlin told me to keep his sister amused, and this is how I do it. A mad mind is easily bored. Do you really think things would get better here if Arianna won the game? She would execute people for the sheer amusement of it."

Alex rolled her eyes. "And we're supposed to believe that you're a saint?"

"What I am is a soldier."

"That's no excuse," Sera said.

"I'm not asking you to excuse me. I neither need nor want your approval. But you *do* want something very much: two people you care about that Arianna is holding prisoner. The question you have to ask yourself is how far you're willing to go to save their lives."

"What do you want?"

"My offer is simple. I and a small team of my hunters will help you infiltrate Arianna's castle. The bulk of my forces will engage her army, drawing her attention away from us."

"You want us to bring you with us? How do we know you won't try to stab us in the back?" Sera demanded.

"You don't. But what choice do you have?"

Alex laughed. "You have to love his honesty."

"It's positively refreshing," Sera said drily.

"So," Alex said, looking at the Huntsman. "Why are you insisting on coming with us? What is it you're looking for in her castle?"

"Weapons," he replied immediately.

The man really was chronically honest. That didn't make him one of the good guys, though. No one truly good would ever serve Merlin, the man who'd decided to try and 'fix' his monumental screwup by ripping reality apart.

"What kind of weapons?" Sera asked. She wanted to see just how far she could push the Huntsman's honesty.

"All you have to know is there's a magic barrier protecting the armory—and that I'm going to need you to break it."

"These weapons must be pretty spectacular—" The realization hit her hard and suddenly. "You don't know how to make those anti-magic weapons. She made them, and you've been stealing them from her hunters. That's why you can't help us deactivate them. You don't even know how they work."

The Huntsman's face remained impassive.

"What's in her armory?" Sera asked him. "The schematics to create the weapons yourselves?"

"Yes."

"So, you expect us to help you arm your hunters to kill supernaturals?"

"I don't expect anything. As I told you, you're going to have to decide how far you're willing to go to save your friends. I know how to get you into her castle. Without me, you will never save them in time."

Sera didn't like this. Not one little bit. Making a deal with the devil never turned out well, even if that devil was a clean-cut warlord with an penchant for honesty.

"Think about it," the Huntsman said. "If you decide to take my deal, light up the Golden Gate Bridge tonight, and my army will come to you. Or just let your people be executed by Arianna at midnight. Your choice. But make it quick before it's too late."

He shot them a cool smile before he turned to walk away, as though he knew what they were going to choose. Sera sure didn't know. Of course she wanted to save Riley and Lara, but she couldn't put any more of those weapons into the Huntsman's hands. It was bad enough that the Witch Slayer could make them. She'd probably not yet outfitted her whole army with them only because half the time she was too crazy to think straight.

"We have to do it, Sera," Alex said. "Whatever it takes to save Riley and Lara."

Sera sighed, fearing her sister was right. Well, what had she expected when she'd come up with the idea to make a deal with the Huntsman? She'd known anything he wanted wouldn't sit right with her, but the Witch Slayer wasn't going to just let Riley and Lara go. Why would she? She was winning her game with the Huntsman. Plus, she was, well, insane.

"Let's go find the mages," Sera replied. Maybe there was a way to turn this all around. If she could get the weapons' schematics to the mages, they might be able to come up with a defense against them. Then it wouldn't matter that the Huntsman could make more.

They hurried down the streets, avoiding the shadowy corners where unseen dangers lurked, ready to devour anyone who wandered too close. The hunters were nowhere to be seen. They must have still been fighting one another back at the vampire's base.

"Where exactly is the mages' hideout?" Alex asked.

"Apparently, it looks like a stationary shop from the outside."

"I've been wondering about all these buildings," Alex said. "There are so many shops all neatly set up, but no one is inside. No employees, no customers. In fact, I haven't seen anyone besides the hunters and the hunted in this city since we arrived."

"The mages told me the original inhabitants of this world left here in a fiery blaze of glory, led by the Dragon Born. And then Merlin gathered supernaturals from his many worlds to populate this one. Perhaps he had the city remodeled before bringing them here to play in this game." Sera's stomach clenched up. "It's all so sick." She stopped in front of a store window that featured tidily-packaged notebooks and pens against a pink-and-white checkerboard backdrop. "This must be it."

They stepped inside, moving quickly down the aisles. Highlighters and coloring books gave way to glitter pens and greeting cards, which in turn blended into pots and sleeping bags. At last, they came to a black curtain fluttering in a gentle breeze that seemed to come from nowhere. Sera pushed past it to enter the mages' hideout.

No one was there. Large enough to comfortably fit twenty cars, it was home to nothing but a scattering of broken furniture. There was no blood, no bodies. That made Sera dare to hope the mages were all right. Maybe the mages had gotten away before the hunters could close in on them. But where were they now? Calliope had told her about this base—and this base only. If the mages had retreated to another building in the city, they would have a hard time finding them. Neither she nor Alex could track magic in this world. As for Kai…

"I hope the guys are all right," Sera said quietly. Her voice echoed horribly in the empty room.

"They're fine. They know how to take care of

themselves," Alex assured her.

"You're right, of course."

"Well, that is, if they don't kill each other."

Sera snorted. "I think they can control themselves at least for a little—"

She paused, pointing at the shifting curtain. Someone was coming through. Sera drew her sword and moved to one side of the doorway. Alex dashed to the other side, drawing her sword, preparing to strike.

The silken layer parted, and Talen came through, the lingering magic of the ward spilling in streams of tiny sparks down his body. "Sera, we need to—" His eyes flickered to Alex. Sera had lowered her sword, but Alex was still poised to attack. "Is she your twin?" he asked Sera, his eyes never leaving Alex.

"Yes, this is Alex."

"Another Dragon Born." Talen bowed his head. "What a pleasure to meet you," he told Alex, smiling widely. He didn't even look bothered by her sword anymore.

Alex chuckled, extending one hand to shake his as she sheathed her sword with the other. "Likewise."

"Talen, where are the other mages?" Sera asked him.

"The hunters were coming, and we knew we couldn't fight them. Not with their numbers and the weapons they have. The others had no choice but to take sanctuary with the fairies."

"And the fairies are bad?" Alex asked.

"Not bad exactly, but they are dangerous," he replied. "I stayed behind to free the other mages when it's safe again. Well, as safe as it gets here."

"What do you mean by 'free them'? Have the fairies imprisoned them?"

"Well…in a manner of speaking."

11. Secret Garden

FROM THE OUTSIDE, the fairies' San Francisco hideout looked like a rose tree no different from its thorny neighbors. The trees were planted at precise intervals, forming a neat line along the street. Their branches were freshly pruned, the faded yellow leaves plucked away. Sera hadn't seen a gardener in the whole city, but she'd seen more gardens than she could count. Who was taking care of all the plants? Either the beasts that lived in the shadows had a green thumb, or there was magic afoot.

Sera was going with the latter. After all, the pink-yellow blossoms that adorned the rose trees were so beautiful that they had to be magical. A sweet, floral perfume hung as thick as whipped cream in the air. The scent was potent, almost intoxicating.

"It's beautiful," Alex commented. "What a fitting hideout for the fairies."

"Great danger lies beneath that beauty." Talen

pointed at the thorns. "Be careful in there."

"You're not coming?" Sera asked him.

"I will remain here. Try not to get lost. It's only a few hours until midnight."

The hour at which the Witch Slayer would execute Riley and Lara. Sera took a deep breath—and grabbed Alex's hand—then the two sisters stepped through the magic tree.

A fairytale garden paradise awaited them on the other side. With its system of streams and koi ponds, accentuated with sweeping red bridges, it put to shame any garden the city had to offer. Sera and Alex followed a stone path lined with roses and daffodils and flowers of a thousand different varieties. Soft, lacy baby's breath bobbled in the wind, singing like bundles of tiny sleigh bells. Water lilies sat with picturesque beauty atop serene ponds of lazy fish. Overhead, butterflies danced on air. One of them set down on Sera's shoulder, its touch as soft as whispered kisses.

There was no furniture in this garden, or at least not what you'd typically think of as furniture. Sofas woven from enchanted bushes, daybeds grown from fairy rings, living trees carved into chairs—that was where the fairies here lounged. Their clothes were soft and airy, made of silk and chiffon. No one was wearing shoes. They danced barefoot and free, turning and twirling between party tables filled with treats. The air tasted of sweet desserts and candied desires, of flowers and trees, sugar and spice.

At the end of the garden path, soft curtains blew in the breeze, reminding Sera of that curtain in the mages' hideout. It appeared that the fairies' secret garden had another layer. She pushed the gauzy barrier aside to enter a circus tent. But rather than trapezes and trampolines, the massive canvas-walled interior was outfitted like a casino. Bright, flashing lights turned overhead, projecting a light show of changing colors onto the ceiling. Fairies and mages and vampires drank and laughed and played at the game tables.

"It appears every supernatural in the city fled to this place," Alex commented.

"The hunters broke through the magic that warded the mages' and vampires' hideouts. Why weren't they able to do the same here?" Sera wondered.

"Because we make better wards, that's why!" a nearby fairy declared, lifting his glass in the air. He nearly fell off his bar stool in the process.

A flash of movement caught Sera's eye. Past the game tables and the bar, people were fighting. Punches flew and kicks snapped, but this wasn't a typical bar fight. A crowd surrounded the fighters, cheering them on.

"Fighting rings," said Alex.

A mage slammed his fist into his opponent, who doubled over, spitting out blood. The crowd cheered, their song of revelry rising above the heavy and hard mood music. The garden had been sweet and innocent, but this place was rougher and harder, the city's supernatural underworld. People danced and drank, fought and fed. Primal roars thundered from the fighting rings. Moans of pleasure rose from the sofas, where supernaturals made out like no one was watching.

"They're all drunk," Sera commented.

"Drunk or drugged." Alex pointed at the snack platters and shot glasses sitting on every table. "You remember the tale of the lotus eaters? Well, I think we've found this world's equivalent."

"I've found something else. Or rather *someone* else. Commandos."

Sera pointed at the lounging area closest to the fighting area. Tony, Dal, and Callum sat on a gargantuan white leather sofa, drinking bright blue jello shots out of the bellybuttons of the three fairies lying across them. "Let's go. We have to help them."

Alex tilted her head to get a better look. "I don't think they want our help."

"But we need theirs to save Riley and Lara." Sera walked over to the sofa and waited for the commandos to notice her. When they didn't, she cleared her throat. And when that didn't work either, she said, "Hey, guys."

Callum glanced up, a drunk smirk twisting his lips. "Hey, Sera. How are you?"

"I need your help."

Laughing, Tony lifted up a small glass. "Care for a shot of…" He looked at the others. "What was it again?"

"Apple juice," Dal told him.

"Right. Apple juice."

Tony shoved the glass into Sera's hands. His coordination was away on vacation, so he spilled half of it on the floor. The fairies giggled, then strutted off, swaying their hips. The commandos watched them leave and sighed.

"Now look what you did, Sera." Callum's mouth

couldn't decide if it wanted to frown or smile. "We were having a very invigorating conversation."

"Yes, I'm sure the insides of their bellybuttons are really invigorating," she replied drily.

Dal snorted. "Did you see what she did there, guys? That's Sera snark."

"We love you, Sera," Callum said.

Dal and Tony nodded vigorously.

"Aren't you going to drink your apple juice?" Tony asked her, nodding at the half-empty drink in her hands. Or was it half-full? Right now, she just wasn't sure.

"That is not apple juice," she said, even though her nose was telling her it was. She set the glass down on the tea table. "It's drugged. You're drugged."

"Don't be silly, Sera. We would know if we were drugged," Dal said, downing another shot.

"Which we most certainly are not," declared Tony.

The commandos laughed. Dear God, she was never going to get them off that sofa. Their minds were too far gone.

"How long have you been here?" she asked them.

"Since..." Callum looked at the others. "How long has it been?"

"Since we were teleported out of Rane's house." Tony scratched the stubble on his chin. "So about five minutes maybe?"

"That happened hours ago," Alex whispered to Sera.

"This place is obviously affecting them."

Mischief flashed in Alex's eyes. "You think?"

"We don't have time to take incriminating photos

of them to tease them about later."

"I was not going to do that."

"Of course you were."

Alex sighed. "Ok, fine. I was. But can you really blame me? Kai's team of super soldiers drunk off their asses? Look at them. They're not even wearing pants!"

"I'm trying not to notice."

Alex snickered.

"And neither should you," Sera said.

"Fine." She folded her arms across her chest, pouting out her lips. "Spoilsport."

"How about you put that diabolical mind to work and help me figure out how to snap everyone here out of this trance?"

Alex's brows swept her hairline. "All of them?"

"Every single one. They are our army."

Alex watched two vampires run past, throwing blood-filled balloons at each other. "Some army."

"I'm sure they'll be more formidable once they sober up."

"Good luck with that."

They turned toward the voice—and found a pixie with spiked pink hair. She was half Sera's height, the size of a child, but she had the body of a grown woman. She was accentuating that body with a black skintight top and a pair of shiny silver leggings.

"The Fairy Queen's palace has woven its spell around them," the fairy told them. "They don't want to sober up, and they certainly don't want to leave. This place makes you want to stay forever."

"That's why Talen didn't want to come in," Sera said to Alex. "This is a prison. A prison you never want to leave."

The fairy shrugged. "I suppose that's one way of looking at it. This place eats magic and free will. But when you're here, you don't need either."

Alex rubbed her head. "That would explain the headache I feel coming on. This place is sapping my magic."

"You know the best remedy for a headache, right?" The fairy pointed at the half-empty glass on the tea table. Yep, Sera had decided that it was definitely half-empty. "Consume lots of fluids."

Alex frowned at the pixie. "You're not helping."

"When did I ever claim to be helping?" she posed, then turned and walked away.

"How are we going to get everyone out of here to fight for us if they don't even want to leave?" Alex asked Sera.

"The fairies have made them like this, so they can unmake them. They can reverse the spell. We just need to talk to the person in charge here."

"Over there. Let's ask that guard." Alex pointed at a fairy wearing a pair of beach shorts and no shirt.

Well, at least it's not the other way around, commented Amara.

I've already seen too much here.

Or too little.

"Are you sure he's a guard?" Sera asked as she followed her sister to the cabana boy.

"Of course. The uniform is a dead giveaway."

Sometimes Sera didn't follow her sister's logic, but when Alex was sure about something, she was rarely wrong.

"Hi," Alex said as they stopped in front of Cabana Boy. "Nice togs."

He flashed her a sparkling white smile that would have made any normal woman go weak in the knees. It was a good thing Sera and Alex were badass mercenaries.

"We want to see the fairy in charge," Alex told him.

"The Fairy Queen is very busy. But I would be happy to tend to your needs." There was enough suggestion lathered into those words to drown a donkey.

"You're cute, but we'd really prefer to see the queen," Alex said with a bright smile.

"I'm afraid she is not taking appointments today."

"Doesn't she know what's going on in the city right now?" Sera demanded.

"Our queen is well aware of the situation."

"And she doesn't want to change it?" Alex asked.

"Out there, we are vulnerable. In here, we're safe. Our wards will protect us from the hunters."

"Until they don't," said Alex. "The hunters have broken the mages' wards and the vampires' wards too. It's only a matter of time before they break yours. The hunters will come here. They will take you all out at once, all the supernaturals in San Francisco. And drugged as everyone is, you wouldn't put up much of a fight."

Cabana Boy's perfect forehead crinkled in agitation. "Are you questioning the Queen's wisdom?"

"What wisdom?" Alex muttered.

"Look, we just want to talk to her," Sera told the

fairy.

He said nothing.

"Doesn't she want to change the world? Don't you?" Sera asked him. "If all the supernaturals worked together, we could fight this game."

"You must be new here," he replied coolly.

"Yes, we are. In fact, we're just passing through from another world."

"Have a pleasant trip."

Sera wasn't going to let him shut her out. "We're Dragon Born."

His face transformed in an instant, hope shining through his skin.

"Don't you guys have a prophecy about us?"

"Yes," he said quietly. "We do." He turned, motioning them forward. "Come with me."

"Now we're getting somewhere," Sera whispered to Alex.

They didn't get far. The fairy stopped in front of the first fighting ring. Over the ring hung a banner with smudged, illegible letters finger-painted in blood.

"What's the meaning of this?" Alex demanded.

"You will fight."

"Like hell we will."

"Before you can see the Queen, you must prove you are really Dragon Born."

"Great, another test."

"You misunderstand. This is not one test but rather seven," he told them. "The prophecy tells us two Dragon Born mages will free us by conquering the sins of this wretched world." He pointed at the ring, where seven vampires stood in a line like perfect little soldiers, their heads held high in the air. "That is your first challenge, the first sin you must conquer: pride. They're called the Proud Seven, and they haven't lost a fight in over a century."

"You cannot be serious." Alex was shaking her head in disbelief. "You want us to fight 'pride'? Haven't you ever heard of allegory? I don't think the prophecy was meant to be taken so literally."

"That is for us to decide. If you wish to see the Queen, then you will prove your worth in the way that we see fit."

"This is really messed up," Sera commented.

"The world is messed up," replied the fairy guard. "What will it be? Fight or flee?"

Sera looked at her sister. "Fight."

"Fight," Alex agreed, stepping into the ring.

She charged right at the Proud Seven, catching them off guard. While their attention was fixed on Alex, Sera ran around behind them. She lifted her hand, blasting the vampires with wind magic. They didn't go down. Instead they pivoted to glare at her.

"I think they're wearing magic-proof armor," Alex commented from the other side of the ring.

"Yeah, I just figured that out."

The vampires moved in unison. Like they were performing a dance, four whirled around to Alex as the other three surged toward Sera, who tried not to feel offended by the fact that they considered Alex the bigger threat. Raised voices cheered from the sidelines. They'd only been in the ring for a few seconds, and they'd already attracted an audience. The hunters weren't the only ones who liked games.

Sera evaded the first vampire's fist, but the second took her in the stomach. And the third hit her so hard in the head that her vision blacked out. It returned a moment later—just in time to see a boot stomping down on her face. She rolled away.

"This isn't going well."

"No," Alex agreed. One of the vampires had both of his hands around her throat.

Sera jumped to her feet, blinking back the stars still flashing yellow and purple across her eyes. She slammed her fist against the back of the vampire's head. Roaring in fury, he released his hold on Alex and stumbled back. Sera grabbed her sister's hand and pulled her away from the vampires. They'd reformed their perfect attack line. Proud indeed.

"They're strong," Alex commented, agitated sparks shooting out of her fingertips.

"Strong, but proud," said Sera. "We need to use that against them."

Alex's eyes lit up. "I know what you're thinking, and I love it."

Sera hurled a fireball at one of the vampires. It hit him in the head, and his hair promptly caught on fire. Roaring in fury, he broke formation and ran straight at her.

"You're not wearing any armor on your head," Sera said with more delight than she should have felt. She turned and ran.

"None of them are."

Grinning, Alex ran at the line of six vampires, unloading a rapid sequence of spells on every unprotected part of their bodies. Lightning cut across their naked hands. Frost crusted their hair. Wind tore at their cheeks. Sera added her magic to the mix. The ground rumbled beneath their feet, knocking them around the ring. Enraged, the vampires abandoned their pride, and everything crumbled. Their line broke apart as they ran wildly at the sisters, their eyes pulsing red. The fight didn't last long after that.

"Not bad," the fairy commented after the last vampire had fallen.

Alex smirked at him. "We excel at baiting vampires."

"All that pride, all that perfect discipline, won't help a vampire trapped in blood lust," Sera added.

The fairy guard plunked two cocktails down on the table. "Congratulations. You have conquered Pride. Now drink."

"A drinking game?" Alex asked.

"I thought only the losers had to drink in these games."

"They'll have to drink too," he glanced over his shoulder at the sleeping vampires. "When they wake up. You get to drink now. Then you can face your next challenge."

"I can't decide if that's a punishment or a reward," Alex said, sipping her drink. "Yum. It tastes like chocolate."

Sera took a sip. The jolt of sugar-coated magic went straight to her head. The room was spinning like a carousel, and not in a bad way either. Sera tried to hold off the impending symptoms of magic intoxication.

"Your next challenge awaits."

The fairy guard pointed at the banner hanging over the ring. The text faded from 'Pride' to 'Gluttony'. A blob entered the ring. Sera blinked down hard, and the smudges and swirls hardened into the form of a ten-foot-tall mage. Or was he a giant? Fire crackled across the massive battle sword in his hands.

"Hello, Gluttony," Alex said, slurping down the last drops of her cocktail.

"Seven times," Sera told her. "We have to do this seven times."

Alex grinned. "This is by far the most twisted drinking game I've ever heard of."

12. Dark Impulses

THE BEAST'S SHADOWS were unrelenting, but at least Kai could shift into a dragon again once he left the cave. He flew Logan and Dax out of the shadows' reach, but as they landed, darkness rose up, rushing across the ground like a black river. Kai cast a ball of blinding light. The stream of shadows screeched, then retreated. It appeared they were far enough away from the Beast for that trick to work.

"The Beast is tracking us," Logan said with perfect calmness.

"You cannot track magic here," Dax reminded him.

"There is more than one way to track." Logan pointed at his nose.

"You're saying the Beast can smell me from across the city?" Kai said.

"I can."

"Funny, Slayer."

"You smell like dragon," Logan said. "Obviously, the Beast craves that."

Dax nodded. "He's right. The Beast's favorite dish is Dragon Born magic. Other kinds of dragon magic are a close second."

"The Beast isn't the only magic hunter around," Logan commented, his hand flashing up to catch a knife. He sniffed the blade. "Poison."

A storm of knives and arrows shot toward them. Logan zigzagged down the street, catching and discarding the weapons. They dropped to the ground in a continuous stream behind him. Red hunters charged out of the buildings on all sides, waving the batons in their hands.

"The Witch Slayer's hunters," Dax muttered softly.

Kai cast a wall of fire between them and the hunters. Logan came to a halt beside him.

"They're going right through your barrier," the assassin observed.

"Thank you, I'd noticed." Kai cast several more barriers, but the hunters' shields dissolved his magic upon contact.

"We're caught between the hunters and the shadows," Dax said, pointing at the stirring darkness behind them.

Kai and Logan exchanged looks. The assassin nodded, then ran right at the hunters. Surprise caught them off guard. Their line faltered but quickly recovered, and when it did, they were pissed off as all hell.

"You're not a mage or vampire or fairy," one of them said, swinging his baton.

Logan caught the weapon. "No, but I'm not human either."

He snatched the baton out of the hunter's hand and threw him into the shadows, which billowed up to swallow him. A single scream pierced the darkness before it was silenced. The hunters stopped and stared at the shadows in terror.

"Go," Kai told them.

The hunters' faces hardened, and they lifted their batons in the air. Logan and Dax circled around them, attacking from the sides while Kai charged forward. He grabbed the nearest one and tore the armor plate from his chest. Then he slammed the heel of his hand against the man's chest, shooting a jolt of electrical energy through him. As the hunter fell, another one flew over Kai's head, sinking into the shadows on the other side.

"They're getting close again," Dax said, giving the shadows a wary look.

Kai cast another light. The hunters froze, blinded, and Logan hurled them at the retracting shadows. Its black, wispy tentacles gobbled them up.

"That spell works equally well on hunters and shadows," Logan commented, watching mercilessly as both faded away.

"That is the key," said Kai. "The hunters' armor and weapons shield them from magic, but it doesn't protect their senses from being overloaded."

"Until the Witch Slayer adds sunglasses to their uniforms," Dax said. "And, believe me, as soon as she realizes the weakness in their armor, she will plug it. She's done it every time so far."

"Let's end this before it comes to that." Kai looked at Logan. "You said you could track me from across the city. Can you track Sera and Alex too?"

"I don't have to. I can feel Alex..." Logan frowned.

"What's wrong?"

"She's gone." He blinked. "No, she's back again. My bond with Alex has been tumultuous of late."

"That bond was made in the World That Was. When Merlin created the Shadow World, changing reality, he changed us," Kai told him.

"And in the Shadow World world, Alex and I never bonded," Logan realized. "So the magic linking us is diluted." He began walking. "Let's fix this mess."

They followed Logan for twenty blocks, to a street lined with rose trees on either side. He paused in front of a tree with yellow-pink blossoms as large as apples. The scent of cotton candy fluttered softly on the wind. It was so sweet that it made Kai's teeth hurt, but it sure beat the stench of rot and despair that the shadows exuded.

There was magic in that tree. Even with his Sniffer power crippled, Kai could feel it. As he took a step toward the tree, Logan darted off, disappearing into a pristine white house with shiny blue shutters. He returned with a man in a black hoodie in tow.

"He smells like Alex and Sera," Logan said, holding tightly to the back of the hoodie.

"I know him," Dax said. "He's one of the mages in this city. Talen."

"So you're one of the mages who tried to burn Sera at the stake," Kai said, his eyes burning.

"I'm helping the Dragon Born," the mage insisted,

his gaze flickering wildly between Kai and Logan.

"If you're helping them, then where are they?"

Talen pointed at the tree. "They've gone to see the fairies."

"And that's a bad thing?"

"They've been in there for hours," the mage told them. "People lose themselves in there. It brings out your darker self."

"Darkness is not always bad. Sometimes you need to embrace your inner darkness, not fight it," commented Dax.

Talen rolled his eyes. "That's the vampires' motto. You use it as an excuse to eat people."

"And you tried to burn the savior at the stake," Dax shot back.

"That was a test. We didn't do it for fun."

Dax laughed. "Mages don't even know how to have fun. I bet your people are in there, sitting at the sidelines, clutching their drinks while everyone else has a good time."

"Enough," Kai said. "Do you think you two can keep from killing each other for a few minutes while Logan and I go inside?"

"I promise not to set the vampire on fire," Talen said.

Dax rolled his eyes. "And I promise not to snap the mage's neck and feast on his blood."

"Let's go, Drachenburg," Logan said. "If they kill each other, it's not our problem."

Kai stepped into the tree. The cotton candy scent grew stronger, and the streets and buildings dissolved into streams and flowers. A warm, golden light shone over a fairytale garden where vampires and mages were getting along much better than the two outside. Along with the fairies, they ate and drank together. There was even a vampire and mage couple making out on a bed of flowers.

"A little fairy magic can cure anything, it seems," Kai commented. "Even long-lasting grudges."

"Yes, it would seem that the solution to all the world's problems is a fairy orgy."

Laughing, Kai pushed past the curtain at the end of the garden path. Here, in an enormous circus tent, the party was rougher. Beyond the gilded gambling machines and marble-topped bar, past the feasting tables, past the sofas of unfiltered debauchery—there lay the fighting rings. People crowded around them, blocking Kai's sight, but even over their cheers and laughter, he could hear the snaps and thumps of several brutal battles playing out all at once. As he moved toward the fights, magic swirled around him. His feet grew heavy, his head light. The fairies' spell was trying to work its magic on them. He clenched his jaw and plodded on, dark and dangerous impulses pushing against his self-control. Talen had been right. This place was dangerous.

The crowd was thickest around the first fighting ring. Kai turned toward it. Over the gleeful grins and starry-eyed stares, he saw something that made his heart stop. A huge mage towered over Sera and Alex, pummeling them with fists the size of bowling balls. The giant hit them again and again, unchecked, as though he couldn't even stop himself. His body roared with laughter, strands of blood-stained spittle dangling from his crooked, pointed teeth.

Kai pushed against the crowd blocking his way to Sera, but they hardly moved. They barely noticed him. Magic sizzled to life on his hands, as though it had a mind of its own. He blasted the spectators away, opening a path in the crowd. As the people fell to the sides of Kai, they laughed hysterically. None of this was real to them. Their minds were clouded by magic. They were living in a dream.

"You lost," the giant mage declared, grinning down at Sera.

She kicked out hard, hitting the giant's leg. Howling, he dropped to both knees, and Sera slammed her heel into his groin. The giant doubled over, and Alex jumped onto his back, locking her arms around his neck. He ran back and forth across the ring, batting wildly at Alex, trying to displace her from his back. Alex held on.

Sera grabbed one end of the string of twinkling lights tied around the rope barrier that surrounded the ring. She circled the hysterical giant, looping the band around his legs a few times. Then she retreated to the sidelines and gave the rope a hard tug. The giant tripped, and as he fell, Alex jumped off. He hit the ground so hard that it shook. He continued to howl and thrash. With every movement, he grew more and more entangled in the lights.

Sera grabbed a giant decorative urn from the sidelines. "You know what they say. The bigger they are…" She tossed the urn to Alex.

"The harder they fall," her sister finished, crashing the urn over the giant's head.

His eyes rolled back, and his head hit the ground. The audience roared in approval. A male fairy dressed in a pair of beach shorts lifted up two cocktail glasses swirling with thick black liquid. Sera and Alex each took a glass and drank. And then before Kai could get to them, they disappeared.

"Where did they go?" Logan asked.

"They were teleported away to their next challenge."

Kai pivoted around. The fairy in beach shorts was suddenly there, though he'd stood beside the ring just a moment ago.

"What challenge?" Kai demanded.

"You will not interfere with the testing."

Magic spun around him and Logan, weaving a net. Kai blasted the silver wires of the net, but his magic just bounced back at him, cutting strikes of agony across his body. Logan pushed against the net, but even his strength could not break it. He didn't even bend it.

"That's fairy-made steel, magic woven into it as it was forged," the fairy said. "You aren't going anywhere."

13. The Seven Deadly Sins

THE SEVEN DEADLY sins weren't much fun when they were kicking your ass. After their fourth battle, Sera and Alex asked the fairy guard for a break. His response?

"There's no rest for the vanquishers of the wicked."

In the end, they'd convinced the fairy to give them two minutes to catch their breath. They'd spent half of that time dousing their bruises and cuts in healing spray. The other half had been taken up by a round of victory cocktails. The fairies were not only making them fight the personifications of sin in a bizarre supernatural gladiator showdown; they'd also named their drinks after those sins. Greed tasted the best, but it made Sera paranoid that everyone was trying to steal her drink. Envy just made her want Alex's drink. Pride was shiny and all, but too sweet. Not enough substance. Gluttony had too much substance, like a milkshake infused with alcohol.

The bell rang, signaling the start of round five, and Cabana Boy pushed them into the fighting ring to fight the fairies' personification of Wrath. Sera stumbled, trying to regain her balance. There was more than alcohol in those cocktails. Each one contained enough mind-mangling fairy magic to make them forget their own names, and they'd had four cocktails each. Sera's self-control was dangling from a thin strand, and from the manic spark in Alex's eyes, she wasn't faring any better.

All thoughts of bathing naked in the gigantic chocolate fountain beside the buffet table died when Sera saw their next opponents. Four monsters stood opposite them. Each one had the body of a men—albeit covered in a thick carpet of fur—and the head of a different large cat: a white tiger, a cheetah, a panther, and a lion.

"They're like ancient Egyptian gods or something," Alex commented.

"Or shapeshifting magic gone wrong," added Sera.

"They might have been hot if not for all that hair," Alex said with a silly smile.

Sera squeezed her sister's hand. "Are you all right?"

"No, I'm drunk as hell, but I'm not going to let that stop me from putting those monsters in their place."

The lion opened its jaws and unleashed a bone-chilling roar.

Alex smirked at the monster. "Just try it, kitten."

The beast men surged forward, moving fast. The white tiger and the panther went for Sera, the cheetah and the lion for Alex. Two-to-one weren't fair odds, especially when each of those two outweighed you by over two hundred pounds. Claws flashed, slashing Sera's shoulder. Pain split across her skin like an earthquake with five epicenters. The wound hurt like hell, but it wasn't gushing blood. The damned battle cat had given her the beastly equivalent of a paper cut.

Her arm still pulsing with the aftershocks of the pain, Sera drew her sword. She pushed the panther away with a gust of wind magic. Sharp spikes shot out of the ground, encasing him inside a stony prison. One down, one to go. She swung her sword at the tiger, but he blasted her with a blizzard. Ice spread across her skin, freezing her sword to her hand. What kind of freaks had the fairies put them up against?

Pushing back with fire, Sera melted the ice. Steam rose from her body. She grabbed hold of that steam, using her magic to wrap it into a thick fog. She twirled the fog around the tiger's legs, infusing the smoky tendrils with earth magic to hold him in place. The beast man pushed, his muscles bulging against the restraints.

"I guess you're not so tough after all," Sera told him.

The tiger heaved against the ropes of stone. They crumbled, raining down his body like gravel. The beast's eyes burned with blue fire.

"Shit."

A savage snarl tore out of his mouth, hitting Sera on a deep and primal level. This was about magic. It was about fear. And it was about the food chain Sera was suddenly finding herself at the bottom of. The people gathered around the fighting pit scattered like mice. It took everything Sera had not to turn and flee with them. She was a badass monster hunter. She did not run away from beasts or men or any combination thereof.

"This isn't going well," Alex said, pressing her back to Sera's.

The lion was trapped inside a magic cage beside the panther, but that still left two beasts. The cheetah and tiger circled around the sisters, creeping forward with cruel, deliberate slowness. A low rumble filled the empty silence.

"What is that sound?" Sera asked.

Alex's mouth drew into a thin line. "They're purring."

"Getting a bit excited, are you?" Sera said to the beast men.

The tiger expelled a roar that rang inside her ears.

"Oh, I'm shaking in my boots," she quipped, forcing her voice to remain steady.

Yeah, she was scared. Only a lunatic could look into those savage beasts' eyes and not feel the bone-crushing weight of their power. Well, Sera would just have to stuff down her fears and play the part of the lunatic for a while.

"Come on, boys. Are you going to attack or just prowl around all day?" she demanded.

Alex yawned loudly. "We're getting bored."

The cheetah shot forward, tackling her across the fighting ring. Sera turned to intervene but the tiger was faster. He grabbed her arm, holding her in place. But Sera still had one hand free. She blasted fireworks into his beastly face. Anger burning in his eyes, the tiger roared. He pulled hard and threw her against the ground. Sera pushed up to her feet, her right arm screaming in agony. The tiger had broken it.

She had to think of something—and fast. The tiger wasn't playing with her now; he was fighting to kill. His body tensed, singing with a fury that was ready to explode. Wrath had blinded him. She had to use that against him.

The tiger leapt at her. She cast a wind spell beneath him, shooting him at the cheetah wrestling with Alex. The cheetah hissed, the tiger snarled, and the two of them rolled across the fighting ring, a ball of fur and claws. Sera grabbed Alex's hand, and together they blasted the beasts with enough spells to knock out Godzilla. And when the beasts finally stopped rolling, the sisters hit them again for good measure.

Applause erupted from the audience around the ring. Sometime during the fight, they'd wandered back over. Magic shifted, popping like a big balloon. The fur melted from the tiger and cheetah to reveal Kai and Logan.

"It was all an illusion." Sera snapped her head around to glare at the fairy guard.

He shrugged. "Who better to play Wrath than the dragon shifter and the assassin?"

Alex's hands clenched into fists. "We could have killed them. Or they could have killed us."

"Yes, that's typically how these kinds of matches go." The fairy guard held up two bright red cocktails.

Sera shot the glasses a look of pure loathing. "You're sick."

"No, I'm merely thorough. I can't just let anyone

see the Queen. You do want us to give you an army to save your friends, don't you?"

"Screw this. Let's save Riley and Lara ourselves, Sera," said Alex. "We've never needed an army before."

"We do this time. The Witch Slayer commands three thousand hunters. We cannot take them on alone."

Kai's hand closed around hers. "And you won't."

"Hey," Sera said, looking down at him. She squeezed his hand. "You look…better."

"I look like shit."

"Well, at least you're not all covered in fur anymore."

"I prefer scales anyway."

Sera snickered.

"What in heaven's name did you hit us with?" Logan asked, blinking.

"An elemental cocktail of spells." Alex grinned at Sera. "Kai taught it to us."

Logan shot Kai a cold stare as they both stood. "I knew I should have killed you long ago, Drachenburg."

"You only kill for money."

"I was once offered five million dollars to kill you."

"I suppose there's no point in asking who made you that offer."

"It was Blackbrooke." Logan watched him closely. "Surprised?"

"That he made you that offer? No. I *am* surprised that you didn't take it."

"Blackbrooke is trying to kill Alex. As soon as I find a way around his security, I will be coming for him."

"Tick-tock, boys and girls," the fairy guard sang out.

Sera grabbed one of the cocktails. Alex took the other. As if by magic, two more glasses appeared in the fairy's hands.

"I wouldn't want you to drink alone," he said with a crooked smile.

Alex rolled her eyes. "How generous of you."

"Drink up. All four of you are invited to the next match."

"What's going on here?" Kai asked.

"The city's entire supernatural population is in thrall to the fairies," replied Alex. "And the Fairy Queen will only release them to the true saviors."

"If we want to gain an army to take on the Witch Slayer and save Riley and Lara, we have to convince the Queen that we are those saviors," Sera added.

"I thought you'd already proven that to the mages."

"Yeah, well, the fairies have their own test."

"A test that involves defeating the seven deadly sins. You guys were Wrath, by the way," Alex told them.

Logan looked uncharacteristically perplexed. "This is bizarre."

"You said it. And to top it all off, every time we beat a sin, we have to drink a cocktail of the same name." Sera nodded toward the two drinks in the fairy's hands.

"What is the purpose of this?" Kai asked the fairy.

"It wouldn't really be a challenge if the contenders were sober."

That was fairy logic for you

"The next fight is about to begin," the guard said. "Drink."

"Fairies are nothing but trouble," Logan commented, taking a glass.

Kai took the other. The four of them clinked glasses, then drank. Wrath's flavor bore a disturbing resemblance to blood. Sera tried not to think about that and just kept drinking.

"Your arm is broken," Kai commented as she set down the glass with her left hand.

"You did that."

"I wasn't myself." He set his hand over her arm. Magic poured out of his fingertips, spreading across her arm like a warm, soothing blanket.

"Stop," she said. "You shouldn't use magic. Every time you do, it opens you up. It helps this place work its spell on your mind."

His hand flashed out, catching hers before she could disrupt his spell. "I am not letting you go into battle with a broken arm."

"Are you always going to order me around?"

"That depends." He held her still, speaking with infuriating calmness. "Are you always going to throw yourself on your sword?"

"If this is about me stopping Merlin's storm yesterday—"

"It's about more than just that, sweetheart. Do you even know what it does to me when you sacrifice yourself? It *kills* me a little every time. But you don't care. You just keep doing it!"

"I do it because I *do* care. Because I can't bear the

thought of you dead."

"But you don't think about what it would be like for me if you were dead. You are selfish."

"I…" Her throat choked up. Her eyes stung with unshed tears.

"If you cared about me, you wouldn't do this to me," he growled, anger swirling red inside his eyes, staining his blue irises.

"I love you." She set her hand over his. "I'm not perfect. Far from it actually. I might not always act with my head, but every choice I make comes from my heart." She set his hand on her chest. "And that heart is yours."

"Sera…" He shook his head. "I'm sorry. I don't know what came over me."

"Something is happening." She looked from the empty drink in his hand to the fairy. "What did you do to him?"

"It's just the lingering effects of Wrath. It should settle down in an hour or so."

Sera glowered at him.

"It appears you're suffering from the same problem."

"So," Alex said quickly. "What did you guys see when you fought us?"

You knew things were bad when the impulsive sister was trying to keep the peace.

"You don't want to know," Logan told her.

Alex winked at Sera. "Do you think we had scales or fur?"

"Or both."

"That would be—"

Thick fog spilled into the fighting ring in gurgling purple waves, cutting them off from everyone else in the room. There was something eerily familiar about that fog.

"Merlin's magic fog," Sera whispered.

Alex paled. "He's found us."

14. Stuck in Time

WHEN THE PURPLE smoke cleared, Merlin wasn't waiting. Neither was another hellish dimension or warped reality. The Pacific Ocean spread out before Sera. The blue water stirred, frothing into a white foam as waves rolled up the sandy shore. The warm wind kissed her bare arms. Soft sand poured through her naked toes. Kai lay beside her, his fingers braided with hers.

"I don't ever want to leave this place," Sera whispered to him.

They'd come to this Pacific island after their defeat of the Grim Reaper. Here they were free. Free from hate. From pain. From fighting whichever latest psychopath was trying to ruin the world.

"I don't want to leave either," Kai replied. "But we're not really here, Sera. It's not real. It's a fairy illusion."

It sure felt real—more real than the game world,

more real than the Shadow World.

"We have to get back," Kai told her.

"Just a little bit longer." She settled her head on his chest. "I don't think I'm ready to go back to the world after everything that's happened. It's so peaceful here, so far from the craziness of the real world."

"That's the problem. The world is changing all around us, and we are stuck. If we stay here, we'll be washed away by the tide."

The tide tickled her toes. "I'm tired of fighting, Kai. It never ends. All we do is fight, and what difference does it make? There's always another evil to fight."

"I know. And I'm sorry." He squeezed her hand. "But we have to stop Merlin. As long as he's out there, changing the world, there is no safe haven for us. There is no peace."

Sera sighed. "I know."

Hands linked, they rose from the ground, shaking the sand from their clothes. The blue sky darkened to a purple mist that swallowed the peaceful beach.

Sera's vision cleared just in time to evade a punch to the face. She pivoted around the attacking fairy, knocking him in the back of the head. The magic that encased the fighting ring trembled as he fell unconscious to the floor. Kai was grappling with another fairy. Six more stood in a perfect circle at the edge of the ring, chanting a heartbreakingly beautiful song. The banner swaying overhead read 'Sloth'.

Alex and Logan were frozen in place, not moving, hardly breathing. Wisps of purple mist swirled over their bodies. They were still caught in the fairies' spell.

Sera waved her hand in front of Alex's glassy eyes. When that didn't work, she grabbed her sister's hand. Magic ignited between them. The room spun, knocking Sera off balance. She reached out, catching herself on a fence. Faded paint chips crumbled from her hands, pouring to the grassy ground. Across the lawn lay a house Sera hadn't set eyes on in eight years, not since she and Alex had burnt it to the ground.

"The lights aren't on inside the house," Alex said.

She was standing beside Sera, wearing a miniskirt, knee-high boots, and a white-and-gold tank top with the logo of their old high school on the front. Alex had only worn that shirt once. She'd put it on in the morning, and by the evening it was stained with blood and ashes. This was that day, the day their lives had forever changed. Alex was stuck at the turning point, and she clearly had no intention of moving forward.

"Riley is staying with a friend tonight," Alex continued. "But Dad is inside. The lights should be on." Tears streamed down her cheeks. "Why aren't they on!"

"You know why," Sera said quietly, squeezing her hand.

Alex shook her head, lifting her chin in defiant protest. "It's not true. He's fine."

Sera's heart beat in agony, her throat constricting, choking her words. "No." Her eyes stung. "He's not fine. He's dead."

Wet sobs exploded from Alex's mouth.

"It happened a long time ago," Sera told her, wiping her eyes. Seeing that house again brought back more than the memories of that day; it bombarded her with every emotion she'd felt. "We have to move on."

"I can't move on. I can't go further." Alex swallowed hard. "Because as soon as I step inside that house, it becomes real."

"Alex…"

"This is all my fault. It's my fault Dad is dead."

"An assassin killed him, not you."

"He was alone because of me! If I hadn't gotten it into my head to rebel—if I hadn't run off—you wouldn't have had to go out after me. And then we would have been there to fight the assassin when he came. Instead, Dad had to face him alone. So, yes, it is very much my fault."

"You were sixteen, just a kid. Kids rebel all the time."

"It's no excuse."

"Alex, you need to stop torturing yourself," Sera told her. "There was no way you could have known what would happen. We'd lived years without anyone finding out about us."

"That doesn't matter."

"You have to move past this."

"Don't you get it? I can't move past this. The moment I walked into our house that day, I changed. Something inside of me broke. I killed the assassin, Sera. I *liked* killing him. A rage like none I'd ever felt consumed me. When I took his life, it wasn't about protecting us. It was about revenge."

"That day changed us all."

Alex gave her a sad smile. "Not you, Sera. You always stayed the same. You never welcomed darkness into your heart."

"We may not have the power to change the past, but we can decide our future. We are in control of what kind of people we want to be." Sera smiled at her. "Let's take the first step toward that future now. Together."

Her chest still quaking, Alex nodded. They walked through the open gate, across the soggy lawn, and entered the house of their childhood. As they pushed open the front door, the mist swallowed them and spat them back into the fighting ring, right into the midst of a firefight. Kai was hitting the fairies protective barrier with a barrage of firebombs. Five fairies hid behind the besieged barrier. A sixth was running away from Logan, throwing blasts of Fairy Dust over his shoulder. But he was too slow. In a flash, Logan was in front of the green-haired fairy. He punched him in the head, and Green went down.

And then Logan was beside Alex. "Are you all right?"

"I'm fine. Thanks to Sera." Alex cleared her throat. "What did you see when you were trapped in the fairies' spell?" she asked him.

"Nothing."

"That bad?"

"No, that good." A wistful look touched his face. "I didn't ever want to leave that moment." He turned his eyes on the fairies, his expression hardening. "They made me never want to leave."

"If you kill them, the Fairy Queen won't help us," Sera warned him as Kai's spells finally shattered the barrier.

Logan's eyes never left the fairies. "I won't kill

them, but that doesn't mean I'll be gentle."

He dashed forward, grabbing a fairy fleeing the collapsing barrier. He pulled hard on her arm. Her shoulder didn't pop; it snapped. The fairy fell to the floor, cradling her broken shoulder. Alex cast a cloud of ice around a silver-haired fairy, but he broke through the frosty mist before it could freeze around him.

"I've been so slow lately," she commented.

"Your mind remembers our world, but your body is from the Shadow World," Logan told her, throwing a knife at the silver-haired fairy. He stumbled when it sank into his thigh. "In the Shadow World, you were never bitten by a vampire-fairy hybrid. You don't have the vampire's speed and strength. Or the fairy's resistance to this fairy magic."

Sera ran toward Kai, who was shooting fairies down left and right.

"Don't use so much magic," Sera told him. "This place makes you crazy, and the more magic you use, the easier it is for the fairies' spell to work you over."

"Did you tell your sister that?" he said, glancing at Alex, who'd just knocked out the last fairy standing with a cloud of frost.

Sera laughed. She wasn't sure why she did it, so it must have been the fairy magic muddling her mind. "Don't eat or drink anything in fairy land either."

"You're not very good at following your own rules, are you?" he observed as she drank her victory cocktail.

"Nope." She burst into laughter.

Beside her, Alex was laughing so hard that she stumbled into Logan.

"They have been compromised," he said to Kai.

"I'd noticed."

Kai wrapped his arm around Sera, leading her from the ring. They sat down on a bright pink sofa with yellow star patterns all over it. It was so tacky that it made Sera laugh. She was doing a lot of that lately. Alex and Logan took the sofa on the other side of the coffee table. It was orange with blue stripes. Sera snorted.

"Sera, I need you to focus," Kai said.

She rested her head against his shoulder. "You smell yummy."

"I smell like sweat."

Logan coughed.

"Something in your throat, Slayer?" Kai asked, his dark brows drawing up.

"No." He raised his cocktail in the air.

Kai clinked his glass against Logan's, then gave the drink a perplexed look, as though he didn't remember how it had come to be in his hand.

"If you don't want it, I'll take it."

Sera reached for his cocktail, but he quickly drank it down. So she grabbed a bowl of chocolate instead. He caught her hand before she could sample its contents.

"Spoilsport," she pouted.

"Why are we here?" he asked, blinking.

"We…" Contentment swaddled her like a warm and sunny day. "I'm sure there was something we had to do here."

"Talk to the Fairy Queen," Logan said.

"Oh, right. We're going to tell her to give us a

supernatural army," Alex said.

"While we're at it, we should totally make the Fairy Queen release the commandos," Sera told her.

"The guys are here?" Kai asked.

"Yep, and I'm going to get them out of here, just you wait and see. Them and everyone else in here." Sera raised her glass in the air.

Alex raised her glass too. "The saviors will save you!"

"How many of those have you had?" Sera asked her.

"Not enough but more than I should have." Alex tossed her a bag of chips.

"Where did you get those?"

"I can't remember."

"I don't think the saviors are in any condition to get anyone out right now," Kai commented.

"Least of all themselves," agreed Logan.

Kai touched her cheek. "Sera, I need you to focus. Where are the guys?"

She set her hand over his. "Which guys?"

"Callum, Dal, and Tony."

"The commandos are here? Where?" Sera looked around.

"You said they're here," Kai told her.

"Did I?"

He clenched his jaw.

"You look so adorable when you try to be a badass," Sera told him with a smirk.

"I don't need to try. I *am* a badass."

"We all are," Alex declared, grinning.

"Badass, table of four, the Queen will see you

now," the fairy guard announced.

Sera glanced up at him. "How long have you been standing there?"

"Too long. Now, get moving. The Queen is a very busy fairy."

15. Between Two Worlds

THE FAIRY GUARD brought them to a waiting room, then left without another word. Kai figured he was going for 'strong and silent warrior', which would have worked better if he'd been wearing shoes. And a shirt.

There were no chairs in the waiting room; there were tree stumps instead. Four of them, in fact, as though they'd sprouted up just for them. Flowering trees jutted up out of holes in the oakwood floor, filling the air with the sweet citric scent of oranges. The walls were glass, revealing an aquarium where brightly-colored fish swam in a continuous loop, pushed along by a stream of rushing water. Warm mist saturated the air, smothering the room in steam. It felt like a rainforest in here, so hot and humid. A sweat broke out on Kai's skin.

"Did we fight all of the fairies' sins?" Sera asked, sitting down on one of the stumps.

The crazy thing was she wasn't even speaking in metaphor. Or at least not *only* in metaphor. The fairies had always put too much stock in legends and prophecies, but Kai had never imagined they would take things so far. The hunters weren't the only ones putting people through games. The fairies were doing it too.

"I don't know if we fought them all," Alex said. "For some reason, I'm having trouble counting to seven right now."

Sera snorted. "I know how you feel."

There weren't any cocktails or fairy finger food in the waiting room. Even the fruit on the trees wasn't ripe yet. The danger was in the air. There was magic in that mist. Ever since entering the fairy's hideout, Kai had felt their spell chipping away at his self-control. The spell that had blinded him to Wrath had done most of the damage. He'd fought with Sera. Not bantered, not battled. A darkness had come over him, and he'd lashed out in anger at her, spilling the worst part of himself. It wasn't anger. It was fear. Fear of what would happen to him if Sera actually died.

"I'm sorry," he said, pulling her close.

"Was that a 'preemptive' sorry for pulling me off my stool?" she asked, her eyes twinkling in delight.

He didn't deserve to have her look at him like that, not after what he'd said to her. "I shouldn't have said those things."

"No, what you shouldn't do is hold your pain in. It will only make you explode."

That's exactly what had happened. The fairies had worked over his mind, using those feelings, twisting them into anger. They had turned him into Wrath.

"When did you get to be so wise?" he asked her.

"I'm just repeating the same words you once said to me. You were talking about magic, not pain, but I think it applies just as well," she replied, smiling.

It had been a long time since they'd been alone. It felt like an eternity. In the Shadow World, they weren't friends or lovers. They weren't even allies. They were enemies. Those memories were still buzzing around in his head. Kai pulled her tightly to him.

"Hey...not so hard," she gasped.

He loosened his hold, but only a bit. "You told me I should talk about my feelings. Well, here they are. I'm never letting you go, Serafina Dering. Not after you tried to sacrifice yourself to save us. Again."

"I'm still here."

"And I'm going to keep it that way, even if it means handcuffing you to me."

"That will make using the toilet difficult."

"I'm serious."

Sera flashed him a grin. She was so beautiful it made his heart ache, so sweet that he could hardly resist a taste. He looked down to find that his hand was on her thigh. He withdrew it.

"Kai," she said, catching his hand. "I missed you. It feels like we've been apart for a lifetime." She put his hand back where it had been. Her smile was half-shy, half-inviting—and completely bewitching.

Kai took a deep breath. No, not here. Not like this. They weren't alone.

Except that they were. Kai blinked. He and Sera weren't in the waiting room anymore. They were in their apartment, alone, standing inside their walk-in closet. Sera's clothes had changed. In place of her leather pants and tank top, she wore a long red dress that hugged her curves all the way down to her hips before fluffing out in soft, beaded ruffles.

"We would have ended up together in any world, Kai." She set his hand over her heart. "I can feel it. Can you?"

"Yes," he said, his voice a deep croak.

It was taking every shred of willpower he had to keep his hand still. Unfortunately, willpower seemed to be in short supply around here. He could see himself tearing that dress off of her.

"I can't sense your magic," she said. "Without it, I don't know how you're feeling."

"I'm sure you don't need magic to know what I'm feeling right now, sweetheart."

"Our minds remember the World That Was, but our magic is still trapped between two worlds, two realities. And our bodies are of the Shadow World," she said coyly.

He lifted his gaze from the ruffled slit in her skirt. "Yes."

"And this body has never known yours. I feel so… empty."

A feverish heat broke out all across Kai's skin.

She leaned in closer, whispering against his lips, "I want you."

Madness was taking hold of him. It pounded against him, cracking his self-control like a shattered windshield. His hand dove beneath the slit of her ruffled skirt, stroking her thigh slowly. Sera's lips teased his with soft kisses, but her hips ground against him. It wasn't just an invitation; it was a demand.

Kai had never been able to ignore her demands. The last strands of his control snapped open, exploding. Slamming her hard against him, he kissed her with an urgency that pulsed through every part of him. Her lips parted, expelling a soft gasp, and he plunged his tongue into her mouth. He drank her in. The desire to devour her was overwhelming, unstoppable. He had to possess her—and to be possessed by her. His mind was slipping away. There was nothing left of the world except the two of them and the shrinking space between them.

A soft sound tapped at the door of his subconscious. It was so distant, so quiet, hardly more than a trickle. That's what it was, he realized. Water. He was hearing the rush of water flowing through the aquarium in the waiting room.

"What's wrong?" Sera asked.

He'd stopped kissing her. That was wrong. He should have been kissing her and then some. But he could not give in, even if every part of him wanted to.

"We aren't really here. The fairies are messing with our heads again. This is a test," Kai told her. "It's the final one. Lust."

"I know." She rose up to kiss him.

"Stop." He pressed his finger to her lips. "We have to stop. We can't stay here. We have to save Riley and Lara and put the world back before the spell becomes permanent."

"Just one more moment," she pleaded, her fingernails combing through his hair, massaging his scalp in slow, seductive circles.

In another moment, he wouldn't be able to hold back anymore. Desire was tugging at him, trying to drag him under. It didn't help that this body didn't know Sera's—and that it really, really wanted to. His body snarled in savage, jealous protest, wanting to experience the ecstasy his mind remembered only as a dream. He had to see if it was real.

"Sera, I'm breaking. Please." His voice hardly rose above a whisper.

Sera smirked at him. "Are you asking me to continue or to stop?"

"Both."

She laughed. "Later then."

"Is that a promise?"

"You bet it is." She kissed him once more before stepping back.

As she peeled away from him, he resisted the urge to groan in frustration—or to hold to her. She brushed down the wrinkles in her skirt. Why did that sweet, innocent gesture make him want to throw her down and make love to her?

"I really like that dress." He tried not to sound like a lech as he looked her up and down.

"I can tell." She winked at him. "Well, red is a sexy color."

"Is that what your wedding dress looks like?"

"You'll just have to wait and see," she said, mischief dancing in her eyes. She took a deep breath. "Ok, ready to do this?"

"Yes."

Hands linked, they walked toward the open door,

turning their backs on the soft bed beckoning them. Magic flashed, and then Kai was back in the waiting room, sitting in his chair. Sera was beside him. Past her, Alex and Logan were trying not to look at each other.

"That was intense," Alex said to her sister.

"I'm surprised you made it out of there," Sera teased her.

"So am I," she replied, perfectly serious. "I have my cold-blooded assassin to thank."

"It was clearly a trick," Logan said.

"Yes, *clearly*," Alex repeated with emphasis. "Which is why you took off your shirt before realizing it wasn't real."

"It was itchy," he replied, his face inscrutable.

The sisters laughed.

"You know, you're more palatable when you're drunk," Kai told Logan.

The assassin dipped his chin. "Likewise. In fact, you should never be sober."

"Behave, boys," Alex said, folding her hands together on her lap. "We've got company."

A fairy in a bright yellow sundress stopped in front of them, smiling warmly. Between her hands, she balanced a tray set with four cocktails. "Follow me, and I will lead you to the Queen's throne room."

16. Unbreakable

THE FAIRY QUEEN'S throne room was like a picture out of a fairy tale book—a children's fairy tale book. Kai had lived through enough real world fairy tales to know that the reality was far darker than the fantasies of the innocent.

The queen's sanctuary was more a forest than a room. Blossoming vines dripped from the canopy. Every inch of them was covered by butterflies. A warm breeze whispered through the leaves, and the butterflies fluttered into the air, their wings sparkling like crystals. Woodland creatures sipped from the gently flowing stream that coiled through the magic garden. Flowers grew along either side of the path that led to the queen's throne.

The throne itself looked like an enormous flower that had sprouted out of the largest tree in the forest. The Fairy Queen was perched on her seat of cream-colored petals, her hands folded serenely in her lap.

She wore a pink lace gown with chiffon streamers for the skirt. Delicate ballet slippers capped her tiny feet. Her hair was braided back from the sides of her face, falling in a cascade of golden curls over her shoulders. She was petite, beautiful, and undeniably regal.

And Kai recognized her face. The queen of the fairies was none other than Nelly Winterspice, the fairy who owned the Fairy Queen dress shop back in the San Francisco of the World That Was.

"Nelly," Sera said.

Surprise flashed in the Queen's eyes. "You know me."

"We all do," said Alex. "You make the best dresses in all of San Francisco. Maybe even in the whole world."

"Not in this world."

Nelly slid off her throne, the train of her skirt slithering behind her as she descended the three mushroom steps to the ground. She closed the distance to Sera and Alex, moving with balletic grace. She looked at the sisters with eyes as golden as her hair. Magic shone deep within them.

"You are Dragon Born."

"You don't sound so sure," Sera said.

"Oh, I'm sure." Nelly clapped her hands together once. "Now, let's move on to business, shall we? The prophecy tells us that the Dragon Born will conquer the world's sins and free us from this perpetual hell."

Alex frowned at her. "And you decided to take it *literally*."

"How else would you have me take it? You may think my tests silly, but they were necessary. I had to make sure you were really the ones, the true saviors. Many people can fight monsters, but it takes a true savior to conquer the demons within. That's what stands against us: what's within. The Dragon Born have a tenacity beyond all others, and together, joined, you two are unstoppable. Together, you cannot fail because you each hold the other up, you each keep the other on the right path. You defeat temptation. You know what really matters."

"That's a tough order to live up to," Alex said to Sera. "I think I preferred it when she didn't trust us. This world-on-our-shoulders thing isn't all it's cracked up to be."

"But you two have had the world on your shoulders before, haven't you?" said Nelly. "Many times in fact."

"How do you know?" Sera asked her.

"It is the way of the Dragon Born, to save others. It's in your nature, woven into the very fabric of your magic. You are protectors." Nelly stepped closer, her eyes narrowing.

"Yeah, dragons are all cuddly and protective," Alex commented.

Nelly continued without pause. "I can see in your eyes what you've been through. You've saved the world before."

"This isn't our first rodeo," Sera agreed.

Alex snorted.

"And I know you are the saviors because I've been in your mind." Nelly tapped a finger to her head.

"We're not fond of people rummaging around inside of our heads." Alex glanced at Sera. "Well, unless they're family."

Sera wrapped her arm around her sister's waist.

"You are very unusual saviors," Nelly told them.

Alex's lip twitched with amusement. "You don't say."

"But you are strong," Nelly continued. "Your bond to each other, to your lovers, to all those you love—those bonds are what make the Dragon Born unbreakable. You never give up, and you never turn away. That is why the warlords kill all Dragon Born who come here. It's the reason the Dragon Born are the biggest prizes in the hunt. You are the greatest threat to this twisted game."

Nelly stepped forward, her dress fading away, melting into battle leather as she walked. "I pledge my forces to your campaign against the Witch Slayer. We will help you rescue your loved ones from her evil clutches. The mage and vampire leaders have done the same. Together, under your command, we will defeat the tyrants who hunt us, who have turned this world into a living hell." The flowers all around her exploded into fireworks of potpourri, spreading their sweet scent to every corner of the throne room. "We will end this game once and for all." Her eyes glowed like liquid gold. "There is just one final test."

"Haven't there been enough tests?" Alex demanded. "We already fought your seven deadly sins. And drank them. Lust could use some work, by the way. It's a tad too sour. Too much lemon juice, I think."

Nelly chuckled. "I like you."

"Of course you do. I put your sins to shame."

Logan set his hand on Alex's shoulder, but he looked at Nelly. "What is your final test?"

"Oh, it's not my test. The prophecy says after the saviors defeat the seven sins of this world, the path to the Original Sin will open up and they must defeat it."

"The Original Sin? What is that?" Sera asked.

"I think there was an apple involved," Kai told her.

She shot him a smirk. "Smart ass."

"No one knows what the Original Sin is," Nelly said. "We only know that after you defeat it, the path to our salvation will open, freeing this world."

"That's not vague at all," Alex commented.

The fairies' prophecy was held together by wishful thinking, but it was better to have hope than to drown in despair.

"The Original Sin," Logan repeated. "That could be Merlin. His sin of messing with reality created this world and all the others out there. Perhaps defeating him is the key."

"If so, this will not be an easy battle," Kai said.

Logan's brows lifted. "Worried, Drachenburg?"

"Whatever it is, we will face it together," Sera said quickly, reaching out to take Kai's and Alex's hands. "United, there's nothing we can't face."

Nelly inhaled deeply, a slow smile curling her mouth. "I haven't tasted such pure optimism in years. It's refreshing."

"Perhaps you need a line of new cocktails?" Alex suggested. "Hope. Tenacity. Friendship. Love."

Nelly nodded at one of her fairies. "Make it so."

As the fairy began scribbling furiously on her notepad, Sera turned to Alex. "So, sis, we have our army."

"Yes, but it won't be enough to save Riley and Lara. We need to take the Huntsman up on his offer."

Kai looked at Sera. "What offer?"

"The Huntsman has offered to add his army to our forces and help us infiltrate the Witch Slayer's castle."

"How generous of him," Kai said drily.

"Of course he wants something in return."

"What does he want?"

"To come with us when we break into the Witch Slayer's castle. He needs us to shatter the magic around her armory so he can steal the schematics for those anti-magic batons she developed." Sera chewed on her lip. "You know she is a mage?"

"I had my suspicions after she teleported us across the city," replied Kai. "A mage hunting down supernaturals." He shook his head. "That would be like—"

"A Dragon Born mage helping the Magic Council kill their own kind."

"Yes," he said. "It doesn't make sense."

"The Witch Slayer isn't just any mage. She is Merlin's little sister. He erased her when he changed our world seven hundred years ago. She only exists because she is here, in this realm outside of the real world. Something happened to her mind all those years ago, Kai. She's not right in the head."

"She is indeed crazy," Nelly agreed. "But she is also brilliant. She developed the anti-magic batons. As horrible as their purpose is, I can't help but admire the genius of her design. The batons are magic themselves, and none of us have been able to find a way to neutralize them."

Alex looked at Sera. "If Riley were here, I bet he could figure it out."

"Then we just have to break him out of the Witch Slayer's dungeon," Sera declared.

"To do that, we first need to get into her castle. We need the Huntsman to keep her army busy. We should take his deal, Sera. It's the best chance we have."

"I don't trust him. He will turn on us the first chance he gets."

"Then we won't give him that chance," Alex told her.

"We'd be giving him the power to make more of those weapons, which his hunters would use against the people in this world."

"We will free the supernaturals before that happens." Alex looked at Logan.

"The Witch Slayer's army is enormous, and she has powerful magic. The Huntsman's forces will even the odds a bit," he said.

"I hate to say this, but I agree with the assassin," Kai said.

Sera looked at him in shock.

"Sorry, sweetheart. They're right. We're running out of time. The Witch Slayer has promised to kill Lara and Riley at midnight, and she's crazy enough to do it. If we don't act soon, they're dead."

"We don't have many options," Alex said. "We basically only have this one. The Huntsman knows her territory and our forces combined with his can keep her army busy while we save Lara and Riley."

Sera swallowed hard. "Fine. But I don't like this."

Then she said to Alex, "I'd say it's about time to signal the Huntsman. Are you ready to set the Golden Gate Bridge ablaze?"

17. Fortress

KAI AND LOGAN stood at the lookout point, their eyes trained on the Golden Gate Bridge. Night had descended on San Francisco, but none of the city lights were on. The buildings were as dark as the sky above. A blanket of thick fog had rolled in half an hour ago on the chilling Pacific wind, blacking out the stars.

Then, suddenly, magic fireworks exploded overhead. Streams of glistening, glittery magic poured down the beams and cables like liquid fire, lighting up the bridge. The tendrils of gold and pink magic crackled and hissed against the cool mist that saturated the air. Every few seconds, a magic flare surged up—then crashed down like an ocean wave.

The dark silhouettes of the sisters and their dragons flew across the sky, the heavy beat of their wings muted by the storm of magic brewing on the bridge. Kai and Logan stood at the edge of the lookout platform, waiting. The commandos were away, rallying the supernatural army, so it was just Kai and the assassin for the moment. Logan wasn't much of a conversationalist, but the look he was giving Kai was loaded with enough meaning to fill an encyclopedia volume.

"Ok, what is it?" Kai finally said.

"You've become calmer since you met Sera. You don't step on people nearly as often as you used to."

"Maybe I've just been too busy to step on people."

"No, your aura is calmer," said Logan. "You don't clench your jaw as much. You're different."

"You have no frame of reference. You and I met only once before I knew Sera."

"I am a careful observer of human behavior."

But not a big displayer of human behavior. "What's your point?"

"That you're content."

"And you? Are you content?" Kai asked him.

"For now."

Logan didn't say anything for a few minutes, and Kai didn't prompt him. The two of them barely tolerated each other at best. It was the assassin who broke the silence once more.

"I'm surprised you finally settled down," he told Kai. "You were always so fond of taking your shirt off for the cameras."

"First of all, that was *one* time. And, secondly, I only did that because I lost a bet."

"I don't take bets I cannot win."

"I'll bet."

Logan actually laughed at the joke. Maybe he wasn't such a stiff after all. At least not anymore.

Thanks to Alex, he'd changed too.

"Do you miss your old life?" Logan asked.

"No. My old life was shit. I was grumpy."

Logan's brows crept up. "As opposed to now?"

"The old me would have kicked your ass for asking these questions."

Logan looked utterly unconcerned.

"How about you?" Kai asked him. "Do you miss your old life?"

"My old life consisted entirely of killing people for large sums of money. What do you think?"

"I think that you like money."

"Says the man with his own airplane."

Kai chuckled.

"Yes, I like money," Logan said. "But I love Alex."

Strange as it sounded, Kai knew exactly how he felt. He loved Sera—so much, in fact, that the pain of losing her still tore at him, even though he'd gotten her back. He didn't ever want to go through that again. And yet here they were about to run into battle again.

Logan seemed to know what he was thinking. "They will always throw themselves into danger to save those they love. It's who they are. We can't change that about them. And I wouldn't change it about Alex."

"Neither would I," Kai decided. He'd fallen in love with Sera for who she was, and that included her selfless capacity to love.

"Only men change," Alex declared with a grin as she landed in front of them. Her dragon melted into streams of magic light that absorbed back into her.

Sera landed beside her sister. Her dragon faded, the magic swirling like golden glitter all around her, lighting her up in a halo. Kai wrapped his arms around her, hugging her to him.

"You are a survivor," he whispered into her ear. "No matter how many times you throw yourself on your sword to save the people you love, you always manage to come back from it."

She looked up, meeting his eyes with tentative hope. "So, you don't think I'm crazy."

"Oh, you're absolutely crazy, sweetheart." He kissed her forehead. "But crazy in the best way. And, come what may, I will stand with you to the end."

Sera rose to her tiptoes and kissed him softly. His hand curled around her neck, drawing her in closer. Her mouth parted, and he deepened the kiss, tasting the sweet depths of her mouth with a hunger that only she could incite.

Alex cleared her throat loudly. Sera pulled back, smiling against Kai's lips for one delicious second before she stepped away.

"Ok, love birds," Alex said. "We've summoned the Huntsman. Now we wait. And I have a feeling he won't keep us waiting long."

◆ ◇ ◆ ◇ ◆

Alex was right. They weren't kept waiting long at all. Within ten minutes, the Huntsman arrived with an army of two thousand hunters. He'd obviously been waiting nearby to move on their signal. Either he was optimistic or just downright desperate. Given his decidedly grim expression, Kai was going with desperate.

"I still don't like this," Sera muttered as they walked with the Huntsman's army under the light of the Golden Gate Bridge.

By now, the Witch Slayer must have seen the glowing bridge and realized that something big was about to go down. That was all part of the plan. They wanted her to send all her forces outside to meet their combined army of hunters and supernaturals. That would leave fewer to guard the castle's halls.

All but seven of the Huntsman's game-loving minions had gone on ahead to make a big show of attacking her castle. The mages, fairies, and vampires were there too.

"This way," the Huntsman said from behind his wall of seven bodyguards. In addition to being desperate, he was also paranoid.

Even though Kai and his companions were outnumbered two-to-one—and even though the Huntsman and his hunters were each carrying a magic-killing baton—Kai wasn't worried. The hunters were no match for the four of them. Kai didn't tell him that, though. Right now, getting inside the Witch Slayer's castle was more important than punishing the Huntsman for what he'd done to the people of this world. There would be more than enough time for ass-kicking later.

Kai looked at the thick curtain of interwoven climbing rose plants the Huntsman had indicated. The tunnel was completely overgrown with them. It looked like the sea of thorns from Sleeping Beauty. One of the hunters pulled out a large pair of garden shears and tried to snap off one of the black thorny branches. The blades of the shears snapped off instead. The next hunter unleashed a stream of fire from his flamethrower, but the flames puffed into smoke the moment they touched the black branches.

"She's created magical enchantments to protect every way in or out of her castle," the Huntsman said. "The front gate alone is warded by six layered rings of elemental magic."

"Do the batons work against those barriers?" Alex asked him.

"The barriers are large. It takes a hundred hunters armed with batons a whole day of hammering to break through a barrier—and there are six of them. Plus, she can recast the barriers faster than we can break them down."

"And these plants?" Sera asked.

"We don't really know what they are."

"Don't really know, or don't know at all?"

"At all," he admitted.

Kai stepped up to the plants and tapped one of the vines. It gave him a nip of electricity in response. "Friendly plants," he commented.

Sera repeated the motion, cringing when the magic zapped her. "That's a potent spell. The Witch Slayer is a real powerhouse."

"The plants are fire resilient, not fireproof," said Kai. "If we can get the flames hot enough, the branches will burn."

Sera glanced at Alex. "What do you say? Want to set the Witch Slayer's roses on fire?"

An eager smile spread across her face. "Oh, do I ever." Fire burst out of her hands. She turned them, directing the flaming stream into the web of thorns.

"Not hot enough," Sera said, and she added her own spell to her sister's.

The two streams danced together. Red and orange sparks flew as their magic drilled into the black plants. Their spell was shredding away the thorns. The broken pieces sprinkled down to the ground, but the branches themselves held. Kai stepped forward, pouring in his own magic. The fiery stream crashed against the plants like the burning rapids of a runaway river. Chunks of black wood shot in every direction.

"Still too slow. Sunrise will come and go long before you've broken through," Logan said, drawing a long dagger. The blade shimmered with an unearthly silver light.

"What is that?" Kai asked him.

"Just the weapon we need."

Logan raised the dagger to the plants, breaking the bonds the fire had weakened. This time, it was the branch that went up in smoke, not the fire. He struck again, sending more branches up into smoke. Alex watched him with feminine appreciation.

"Mmm," she said, giving the assassin a look Kai wished he hadn't seen.

"You can celebrate later," Sera told her.

"Oh, we will."

"TMI," Kai said through clenched teeth.

The three of them continued blasting the plants with everything they had, weakening the magic in them so Logan's special dagger could dissolve them. Burning and cutting, they made their way down the dank tunnel. Finally, they reached the door at the end, and by then, the tunnel wasn't wet or cold anymore. It was hot with burning ashes. The scent tickled Kai's senses, its delicious blend of magic and wood awakening the dragon in him. Sweat beaded up on his skin, and it wasn't even from the heat saturating the air in the tunnel. It was magic. He felt awake, alive, powerful—like he could fight all night. He found himself not only hoping that they'd run into the Witch Slayer's hunters, but *craving* it.

"Are you all right?" Sera asked as they waited for Logan to pick the lock on the door.

"Of course I'm fine. You're here."

She smiled at him. The look in her eyes made him want to kiss her, but they had a job to do. Kissing Sera would distract him too much. He might not have been able to sniff out magic right now, but that didn't mean magic couldn't affect him. The magic in the air had him so riled up that if the crimson hunters didn't attack soon, he was going to lose his mind. The essence the plants expelled was obviously the Witch Slayer's second line of defense in case someone was able to break their way through the black plants, but why would she choose magic that spiked her enemies' adrenaline and power?

"I would like to get away when we're done saving the world this time," Sera said. "You know, we still haven't decided where we're going on our honeymoon."

"I figured I'd take you monster hunting in the Amazon."

Her nose crinkled up with adorable skepticism. "You've got to be kidding."

"Only partially."

"A monster hunt in the Amazon?" Alex wrapped one arm around each of them. "Count me in. Hey, Logan you want to come too?"

"If I don't, you'll do something reckless," he replied, his eyes still fixed on the lock he was cracking.

Alex snickered. "Logan wants to come too. Hey, it could be like a double date." She wiggled her eyebrows at Sera. "And you know what they have in South America, don't you?"

"Chocolate."

"Exactly. We can go straight to the source."

"Do they always chat so much in the middle of an operation?" the Huntsman asked Kai.

"Of course."

"Those sisters love to chat," Logan said. "Especially about chocolate. And pizza."

"What's pizza?"

Dually horrified expressions crossed the sisters' faces.

"He comes from a world without pizza," Sera muttered.

"It must be hell."

Sera nodded in agreement.

"I was only kidding," the Huntsman said. "I know what pizza is."

"That wasn't funny," Alex told him.

"You don't joke about food," Sera added.

The lock clicked, and Logan pulled open the door. Another dark tunnel lay in wait before them.

"At least this one doesn't have thorns," Sera said, then looked at the Huntsman. "Which way to the dungeon?"

"According to the plans my spies drew of this castle, take a right and then go up the stairs."

"Spies masquerading as defectors?" Kai asked him.

"Yes."

Kai wasn't surprised the Huntsman had spies. Any good warlord had spies. What did surprise him was that the Huntsman's spies had managed to convince the Witch Slayer to allow them into her castle. She seemed like the competent, paranoid sort. Then again, she was also the crazy sort. Perhaps they'd used her madness to their advantage.

"Let's go," Sera told Alex. "I want to get Riley and Lara out of this creepy castle now."

Sera and Alex took the lead. Kai and Logan followed, keeping the Huntsman and his hunters in their sight.

"You don't trust me," the Huntsman said.

"You hunt supernaturals for sport. Of course we don't trust you," replied Kai.

The Huntsman laughed. "In your shoes, I wouldn't trust me either."

"Guys," Sera called out.

Kai pushed past the green hunters, turning the corner. Sera and Alex were standing outside a prison cell with iron bars, the choice material for keeping supernaturals in. Iron bounced magic. The only way to avoid the spectacular headache that resulted from being bombarded by your own magic was to invert your magic. That kept your head clear, but it also left you completely powerless to cast a single spell.

But it didn't prevent you from mixing potions.

Riley stood opposite Lara, stirring his finger through the green concoction bubbling inside her cupped hands. The potion burped black bubbles, and Lara pivoted sharply, hurling it at the bars. Magic hissed against metal, and like a silver waterfall, the bars melted to the floor. Lara and Riley stepped over the gurgling puddle. Sera and Alex nearly collided as they rushed forward to embrace their brother.

"Lara," Kai said, wrapping his arms around her. "Are you all right?"

"Sure. No problem."

She tried to sound nonchalant, but beyond her tough exterior, he could tell she was shaken. She had no reason to feel embarrassed about that. She'd been imprisoned by a mad mage who planned to execute her for fun. The anger in Kai simmered hotter again, drowning him in battle fever. Instinct was taking over. It was pushing out all rational thought. That's what the smoke of the burning black plants had been all about. Kai swallowed the boiling rage inside of him. This was a battle that would not be won by raw power alone. To defeat the Witch Slayer, they would have to be smart.

"How were you captured?" he asked Lara with a calmness he didn't feel.

"I don't know how it happened." She shook her head. "One moment we were in Rane's living room fighting the necromancer, and the next Riley and I just appeared in this cell."

"The necromancer works for the Witch Slayer, who is Merlin's sister."

"That explains her insanity."

"Her insanity is more complicated than that.

Merlin erased her from the real world, and in doing so, she lost her mind. She can't leave Merlin's domain or she'll disappear. He's spent the last seven hundred years trying to fix her, but I have to wonder if she can't be fixed."

"I'm glad my brother isn't a psychopath," Lara said, giving him a final tight squeeze. Then she walked over to Sera.

The rage in Kai slowly subsided as he watched the two most important women in his life embrace like sisters.

"Cutting this rescue a little close, aren't you?" Riley said, stopping beside Kai.

"I thought you were all-powerful now."

Riley extended his hands, showing him the cuffs on them. "Not at the moment. They've neutralized my shadow magic."

"How did they do that? Shadow magic is outside the laws of normal magic."

A dark look crossed Riley's face. "The Witch Slayer understands the magical sciences like no one I've ever known."

"She's better than you?"

"Yes."

"But you got out of that cell anyway," Kai said.

"Lara swiped a few things off the guards. Your sister is a master pickpocket. And we spent half the day scraping away at those bars to accumulate enough iron to mix into the potion."

Kai brushed his finger across Riley's handcuffs. They responded to his touch with a nasty zap. "These look a lot like the magic-neutralizing batons the Witch

Slayer's hunters carry around."

"I could maybe take them apart given enough time," Logan said.

"Time is one thing we don't have," replied Riley. "The Witch Slayer will be here soon to take us up to the highest turret in the castle. She's going to push us to our deaths."

"She is going to do no such thing," Alex told him, taking both of his hands.

"What a touching reunion," the Huntsman said, his dry tone cracking against the stone walls. "I've upheld my end of the bargain. Now it's your turn." Looking at Sera and Alex, he pointed at the closed door across the hallway.

A glowing blue curtain of magic covered the door from top to bottom. The word 'Armory' was written in thick black letters across the sign nailed to the wall. Alex frowned at the Huntsman, but she turned toward the door. Magic shot out of her hands, visible only through the ripples of distorted air. That invisible wave of magic-breaking power slammed against the door with a heavy crunch, then it ricochetted, throwing Alex back.

"Potent stuff," she groaned, standing slowly.

Sera took her hand. "Let's do it together."

The crunch of magic was harder this time—and so was the push-back. The sisters flew back, slamming against the wall. They rose stiffly to their feet.

"This sucks," Alex coughed.

"Something is blocking our Magic Breaker power," Sera said.

The Huntsman's eyes flashed with anger. "Dragon

Born deceptions."

"It's not a deception," Alex snapped back.

Laughter echoed down the hallway. An enormous glyph flared to life beneath their feet. Kai had never seen a glyph so large. It covered the entire ground. It was inescapable. Magic stirred, and the dark tunnel dissolved away. The next moment, they were all standing inside what looked like a throne room. And on the gold throne sat the Witch Slayer.

"How lovely to have guests," she purred, rising. "Though I must say you're late. I expected you to be here a good hour ago."

"You knew we were coming," Kai said.

Her lips drew into a wide smile. "Of course."

The Huntsman whispered to one of his hunters.

The Witch Slayer laughed. "Don't bother trying to get back to my armory. You can't open it." Her gaze slid across to Sera and Alex. "And Dragon Born magic doesn't work here in my castle. Not Sniffing and not Magic Breaker." She planted her hands on her hips, smiling victoriously.

"I will take what is mine by other means then," replied the Huntsman. "My forces are overrunning yours. You've lost."

She waved her hand at the window, and the curtain fell away. "You are mistaken."

Outside, beyond the window that covered the entire wall, a battle was playing out between the red and green hunters. Slowly but surely, the green hunters, the Huntsman's forces, were advancing toward the castle.

"It looks good from where I'm standing," the

Huntsman told her.

"Then allow me to change your perspective."

Glyphs appeared beneath the green hunters, swallowing them in sparkling swirls of blue light. And then they were just gone. The Huntsman's jaw dropped in shock.

"You didn't think I'd leave my territory unprotected, did you?" The Witch Slayer giggled. "It will all be over soon, and then this world will be mine. The victory will be mine." She twirled a lock of her black hair around her finger. "How does it feel to know you've lost a seven-hundred-year-old war?"

The Huntsman glared at her.

"Now, on to other business." Looking away from him as though he no longer mattered, she turned her pale eyes on Kai and his companions. "I can't have you here, threatening my glorious victory."

Six glyphs shot out of the ground like daisies, one for each of them. Before Kai could move a muscle, the spell snapped, flinging them out of the Witch Slayer's castle. And for the third time, Kai fell into the Beast's cavern.

18. Twin Souls

A SOULLESS HOWL echoed off the black walls, cutting across Sera's skin like the kiss of winter. It was a sound born in the bowels of hell, a song of unending misery and a hunger that unchecked would devour the whole world.

Blackness oozed across the walls like a river of burning oil. The overwhelming stench of decomposing plants saturated the air. Beside her, Kai was looking around the cavern like he expected something to fall on them at any moment. Alex, Riley, and Lara were also here. Logan stood off to the side, locked in a staring contest with the Witch Slayer.

"What are you doing here?" Sera demanded.

"I would like to know the same thing." The Witch Slayer glared at Logan. "Why did you drag me here?"

Wow, Logan moved fast. Sera hadn't even gotten in a breath between the time the glyph had appeared and pulled her in.

"Aggravating, isn't it?" Logan said drily. "Being thrown across the city without your permission."

The Witch Slayer folded her arms across her chest and intensified her glare. Another howl echoed in the chamber, and it sounded closer this time.

"Why do you keep sending me here?" Kai demanded of the Witch Slayer.

"This is your destiny."

The black walls shifted, casting a kaleidoscope of shattered shadows across everyone. A beast emerged from the mouth of the wide tunnel before them. Prowling with the gait of a large cat, the enormous monster looked like an attempt to stick together the parts of a dozen different creatures. Whoever had stuck the parts together hadn't done a very good job of it. Its body was shaped and scaled like a dragon, but it had the wings of a butterfly, the claws of a cat, and the tail of a scorpion. Irregular tufts of silver wolflike hair stuck up between a few of the black scales.

"I think I want a different fate," Sera said.

"Isn't that what this is all about?" the Witch Slayer laughed. "Changing your fate? But can you ever truly escape it?"

"Your brother seems to think so," Alex told her.

"Indeed." She snorted. She obviously wasn't surprised that they knew who she was. "He thinks himself a god, but even gods cannot change the world without consequences. There is always a price to that kind of magic. Someone must pay it."

"You," said Sera.

"No, I got off easy."

The beast growled softly. What was it waiting for?

Why hadn't it attacked?

The Witch Slayer gave the creature a curious look. "When someone changes reality, it throws everything off. You see, the world needs balance. My brother's spells require an enormous amount of magic to rearrange reality. What happens to the leftover magic, the waste? Where does it go?" She pointed at the Beast. "The leftover magic went into *it*. It is all the leftover stuff. That is my brother's legacy. His sin."

"The Original Sin," Sera muttered.

"Merlin pushed the beast down here. He trapped it, but he can never destroy it," said the Witch Slayer. "The creature feeds off the magic Merlin uses to create these shards of reality. And the more my brother weaves his spells—the more of these worlds he creates—the stronger the beast becomes. Soon, it will consume this world and those beyond it." Laughing, she stroked the Beast's scales. "I can feel its hunger. It feeds on magic, and it wants yours."

"That's why you keep sending me here," Kai said. "You want to feed me to the Beast."

"You are powerful indeed, shifter, but you are just the appetizer. It wants pure magic, raw magic. Dragon magic." She looked at Sera and Alex. "The magic of the Dragon Born. It craves it. Yearns for it."

The Beast brushed past her, prowling toward them. Hunger burned inside its red eyes, igniting the obsidian depths with fire. Magic dripped down its extended fangs. Tiny fires blazed to life everywhere its spittle splattered.

"How are you controlling it?" Sera asked the Witch Slayer.

"I'm not. It's drawn to the Dragon Born. It won't stop until it has drained the life and magic from you."

Her words were not a lie. Sera saw the truth in the beast's hungry, soulless eyes. Its gaze flickered from her to Alex, as if it couldn't decide which of them it wanted to eat first. Alex made the decision for it the moment she shot a firebomb in its face. The Beast charged at her, its roar shaking the walls.

"Not one of your better ideas!" Sera shouted at her from the other side of the creature. She drew her sword and struck the beast, but the blade bounced right off its scales.

"Wait for it!" replied Alex as the Beast lifted its foot to stomp her.

She sank a knife into the soft, unprotected flesh between two of its talons. The Beast reared, screaming in agony, trying to shake her knife from its foot. Alex rolled to avoid a heavy swipe, then rose into a squat to plant a knife in its other foot. Sera caught hold of the monster's swinging tail, running up to its back, where she found a patch of wolf hair to set on fire. The beast bucked so wildly that it threw her off. Kai caught her before she hit the ground.

"Thanks."

"I told you I'd be right here to catch you when you fall."

She grinned at him. "So you did."

"Hey, someone stop her!" Alex shouted out.

A glyph had blossomed up beneath the Witch Slayer. In a moment, she would teleport out of here. And Sera was too far away to stop her. Logan darted around the raging beast and quickly cuffed the Witch

Slayer's hands together. Her spell sizzled out. Sera looked from Riley's free hands to the Witch Slayer's cuffed ones. It seemed Logan had figured out a way to remove the anti-magic cuffs from him after all.

"Your boyfriend is efficient," Sera said to Alex as she ran up beside her.

Alex smirked at her. "Don't tell him that, or he'll think you're flirting with him."

Lara had summoned two dragons to keep the Beast busy. They circled around its head, flying so fast that they were nothing but a turning ring of red and blue magic. Like an agitated kitty, the Beast swiped its paws at the dragons.

"Our fate is your fate," Logan told the Witch Slayer.

She laughed. "I wouldn't have it any other way." She watched the Beast with detached amusement, as though she'd removed herself from the reality of the situation.

Riley blasted the Beast with a web of shadows. As the spell smacked against its leg, the limb exploded into smoke. That smoke thickened, quickly reforming into a new leg.

"The Beast was born from shadow magic. You cannot hurt it," the Witch Slayer told Riley.

The monster opened its mouth and unleashed a black cloud that tore apart the blue and red dragons. Lara expelled a gasp of shock. Kai was bombarding the Beast with enough elemental magic to level a building, and it didn't even flinch.

"We cannot overpower it," Sera told Alex. "We need to break the magic that holds it together."

Nodding, Alex shot a stream of magic-breaking power at the Beast as Sera did the same. It glared at them.

"We don't seem to be doing anything but annoying it," Alex commented. "We need more power."

"But how? We're already hitting it with everything we've got."

The Witch Slayer laughed.

"Something funny?" Alex asked, glaring at her.

"You aren't very good Dragon Born mages."

"We spent our whole lives hiding our magic so we wouldn't be murdered for what we are, so forgive us if our magic isn't up to snuff," Sera shot back.

"Your problem isn't one of power. It's one of technique."

"So you're an expert in Dragon Born magic, are you?" Alex asked her.

"I've been stuck here in this horrid realm for over seven hundred years with little to do but play games and explore my brother's extensive library. I'm an expert in a lot of things. "And since your lover has tied my fate to yours…" She sighed, jangling her cuffs. "You need to link to your other half."

"We've already linked to our dragons," Sera said.

"No, not your dragons," she replied impatiently. "You need to link to each other. Two souls born into one body, twins. Two sides to each soul, mage and dragon." She sounded like she was quoting a passage from a book.

"Where did you read that?" Sera asked her.

"In one of my brother's books. Now that you've

each joined with your dragon side, you can link with each other. That will give you the power you need to destroy the Beast."

"What do you think?" Sera asked Alex.

"That I don't trust her. But what can it hurt anyway? Nothing we're doing is working."

"How are we even supposed to link?" Sera looked at the Witch Slayer.

"Don't look at me. I'm not Dragon Born. I guess you're just going to have to wing it." The look on her face said she believed it would take a miracle for any of them to make it out of here alive, and yet she didn't seem to care. Maybe she thought she was low on the Beast's menu—and that by the time it got around to eating her, it would be so stuffed full of magic that she'd escape while it was napping off the caloric overdose.

"We excel at winging it," Alex declared.

"You bet we do." Sera pulled out the rock the mages had given her. She twirled it in the air, turning it into a pair of knitting needles.

"Going to knit the Beast a sweater?" the Witch Slayer said, her tone mocking.

"This isn't for the Beast," Sera told her. "It's for us."

She moved the needles, knitting a long band of magic. She tied one end around her wrist and the other around Alex's. As soon as the band linked them, Sera felt a surge of magic shoot up her arm. It rushed through her body, tickling her senses, bringing them to life. For the first time since she'd woken up in this world, she could feel magic. She shifted her magic, trying to match Alex's aura. It was the most natural thing she'd ever done. Her aura and Alex's were one and the same. Their souls were linked, their magic intertwined.

"Wow," Alex gasped. "This is so cool."

A blue halo twinkled around them like crushed sapphires. Sera lifted her free hand and blasted the Beast. A shock wave tore out of her, catapulting the monster across the cavern. She'd never felt so much power before in her life. She was drinking from a well twice as deep. Two mages, two dragons—all united. Sera was complete. She was whole.

The Beast charged at them, its magic flooding the chamber. Sera couldn't just feel Alex's magic now; she could feel everything. The hard and heavy thump of dragon wings that thundered inside of Kai. The warm scent of Lara's cinnamon roll magic. Riley's dual blend of light and creamy magic that frothed at the surface of the dark and dangerous shadows that lay within. Logan's crisp and steady aura, ticking like a metronome. Vampire, fairy, and mage magic hugged him like a suit of custom-fit armor. It was so different from the Beast's ugly magical mismatch.

Goosebumps broke out across Sera's skin as she drank in all the magic around her. Refreshed, revitalized, she and Alex blasted the Beast again. It hit the wall so hard that the black river of magic froze. The shadow spell shattered. Tiny obsidian tears rained down from the wall, melting against the ground. A sharp crack split across the chamber with resounding finality. Sera stood there, fearing the roof would come crashing down on them, but the avalanche never came.

The Witch Slayer stumbled forward, falling to her

knees. "What's happening?" The mad light left her eyes, and as she looked around the cavern, fear shook her shoulders.

The Beast snapped its head around, turning its hungry eyes on her. One after the other, the black gloss split from the walls. The shards shot toward the Beast, covering it in smoke. The monster thrashed and roared as the magic that bound it together dissolved. Even after the Beast was gone, the echo of its magic lingered on.

A golden glow shone from behind one of the walls, lighting it up. The rocks shifted and slid apart to reveal a door. Sera stepped forward, breathing in the sweet song humming off the rocks.

"It's so beautiful," the Witch Slayer said, stepping toward the wall. A magic barrier filled the doorway. "It's a passage."

"Where does it lead?" Sera asked her as the band of magic linking her to Alex dissolved.

"I don't know. I've never seen it before." The Witch Slayer reached out toward the barrier. "I see…paradise. It's bright and beautiful. So many shining lights!"

"I guess she's back to being crazy," Lara commented.

"No, I don't think so," Sera said.

The Witch Slayer's fingers brushed against the barrier, and the handcuffs popped off her hands. The wall of magic shattered.

"That's not possible," Alex gasped. "Only the Dragon Born can break magic like that."

"Yes, we can," a woman said, stepping out of the doorway. Her long dark braids swayed from side to side as she walked. "I am Vivienne, a Dragon Born mage like you," she told Sera and Alex. Her gaze shifted to the Witch Slayer. "And you are my twin sister."

19. Midnight Magic

THE MANIC FLICKER died in the Witch Slayer's eyes, revealing the woman beneath the madness. Arianna. A look of pure contentment slid across her face, and her turbulent, erratic magic settled into a low, steady hum that beat in time to Vivienne's. Sera knew Vivienne's words were true. She could feel it. Vivienne and Arianna were Dragon Born mages—sisters, twin souls linked by magic.

"We must move," Vivienne said. "Now that the Beast is gone, the tunnels are unprotected. The Huntsman's army is coming."

Surprise flashed in Arianna's eyes. "How do you know about the Huntsman?"

"I know a lot of things. We are linked. Our dragons have been talking all these years, even before we were trapped in Merlin's domain."

"So those were the voices in my head."

"Some of them anyway." Vivienne cupped her hands around her sister's cheeks, looking her in the eye. "Because of Merlin, you have suffered. I've suffered. But we will take care of him soon enough."

"He's my brother," Arianna protested.

"Not your brother by blood or magic."

"He loves me."

"Let's not fight, my sister." Vivienne smiled. "Let's just get out of here before the Huntsman finds us. He has returned with something more dangerous than mere hunters looking to play a game. He's brought Merlin's army this time."

She waved her hand. The barrier flared to life again, then turned to stone, sealing the doorway shut. The gateway between worlds looked no different than the surrounding rocks now.

"The others will be safe until we can free this world," Vivienne said.

"What others?" Sera asked.

"We have much to discuss," Vivienne told her. "Do you have someplace safe we can go?"

"Yes," said Riley.

Shadows slid across the floor, surrounding them. Sera felt a hiccup of magic ripple across her body, and then they were all standing in the middle of Rane's living room.

The demon looked up from her pink-and-white teacup. "Well, I see you found your lost sweetheart," she said to Kai. Her gaze jumped to Vivienne, flickering between her and Arianna. "And you found two Dragon Born mages. This one smells like Merlin, though." Her frost-kissed brows arched. "His little sister?"

"How could you possibly know that?" Sera asked

her.

"I might not be able to see into Merlin's domain, dearie, but I'm not stupid." She waved at Arianna and Vivienne. "I can feel their magic. And they are every bit as Dragon Born as you are."

"Dragon Born," Arianna said in a soft whisper. "I always felt there was something missing…even before." She gave them all a shy look. "Before Merlin's spell erased me from the real world, confining me to his domain."

"What happened to you? How did you end up trapped behind that wall?" Sera asked Vivienne.

Alex shot Arianna a suspicious look. "And why didn't you know you were Dragon Born?"

"I was adopted. My parents—Merlin's parents—told me that when I turned twelve."

"Merlin mentioned you. He loved you." Rane told her.

A tear slid down Arianna's cheek. "I know."

"Merlin did this to us," Vivienne declared, her body tensing up. "He's the reason I was stuck in that prison for centuries, guarded by a hellish Beast that could only be defeated by two united Dragon Born. And my other half didn't even know I existed."

As she spoke, magic fog rolled in around them. A flash of images played against the walls. Sera looked at Rane.

The demon shrugged. "I'm projecting her thoughts." She waved her hand. "Tell your story."

Vivienne nodded. "Arianna and I were born at a turning point, a crossroads. It was the time the supernatural world had just begun to turn against the

Dragon Born. Tensions were especially high in our village."

A flowering field surrounded them on all sides. Sunshine shone down from the sky, bathing the blossoming white flowers in golden light. Past the flowers and quivering blades of long grass lay a house made of wood. Time had taken its toll on the little house; the seasons had blackened and warped the wood.

"You know how Dragon Born magic works." Vivienne walked toward the house, her eyes wide. "You can never predict when all the conditions will be right for us to be born. On another day, Arianna and I might have been born some other kind of mage entirely."

"Tell me about our parents," Arianna said.

"Our mother was an ice mage and our father a mage summoner. His favorite summons were tigers and hawks." Vivienne paused on the doorstep, smiling with relish as she slid her hand across the wood. "It feels so real."

"Of course it does," Rane said smugly. It was an emotion the demon wore well.

"Our neighbors were all decidedly anti Dragon Born," Vivienne continued. "They'd already tried to convince Father to join their crusade deep into the mountains to kill a Dragon Born mage living there. Father refused, using our mother's approaching labor as an excuse. Little did he know that she would soon give birth to two Dragon Born mages."

Magic flashed, the scene shifting to the inside of the house. A man stood over the bed, his sweat-soaked hair plastered to his forehead. He knelt down beside his wife, pulling back a fold of fabric that concealed the face of the bundled baby in her arms. He looked into the baby girl's eyes. They glowed with an unearthly light, bouncing an infinite repeating circle of reflections.

"She is Dragon Born. No, not she. *They*," he gasped.

"Two souls born into one body," the mother quoted, holding the baby protectively to her chest. "We have to separate them. They will die if we don't."

"They will die if we do," her husband replied. "The neighbors will find out what they are."

"Then we' will have to make sure the neighbors don't find out."

Vivienne stood there, as still as a statue, as her father walked out of the house. "Father consulted our village's elder, a mage who had seen many Dragon Born mages born in his years. He was one of very few people who knew the spell that could separate us into our two bodies."

A man with young skin and old eyes stepped into the house. Vivienne's father followed, shutting the door right behind them. Her mother was waiting there, the baby in her arms.

The elder stared into the baby's eyes. "There is little time. We must work quickly."

"You will perform the spell?" Hope sparked in their mother's eyes.

"Yes, of course. I cannot allow these two innocents to die." He muttered a few words under his breath, and then suddenly there were two babies in her arms.

"How will we protect them?" their father asked. "The others will find out what they are."

"You must send one of the twins away," the elder told him. "Find her a good family who will love her."

Tears rolled down their mother's cheeks. "I won't give up one of my babies."

"You will if you love her." The elder's expression softened. "I know it's difficult, but these are hard times for the Dragon Born. Hate and fear are powerful, and they are turning the supernaturals against them."

"They say you can see the future," said the girls' father.

"Only glimpses of it."

"Then tell us. Will the world ever be safe for our daughters? Will the others ever embrace the Dragon Born?"

"Hard times are ahead, harder than any the Dragon Born have ever known," the elder replied. "Things will get worse before they get better."

Their mother's shoulders slouched over and her neck sagged, as though he'd just dropped a bus on her head.

"Such beautiful girls. Not identical but very close." The elder tapped his finger to their foreheads, and the matching star birthmarks there faded into their skin. "This will hide their true nature, but it is up to you to keep it a secret." He met their dour expressions with a smile. "Do not despair. Not all hope is lost. One day, centuries from now, the sun will rise on the Dragon Born once more. And your daughters will be at the forefront of the revolution."

Confusion crinkled their mother's brow. "I don't

understand. How can our mortal daughters live for centuries?"

"I do not know, but they will. If you have any faith in my magic, then trust me when I say this."

Their father nodded. "We trust you."

"Good. Now choose which girl will stay and which will leave. And have faith that they will be reunited someday."

The house dissolved, melting back into the walls of Rane's house.

"Our parents couldn't choose, so the elder chose for them," Vivienne said to her sister. "He told them that he believed your path led elsewhere."

"And he was right," Arianna replied. "Here we are seven centuries later, just as the elder said. But how did it come to this point?"

"Father brought you to old friends of the family. Merlin's parents. They adopted you as their own."

"Did they know what I was?"

"Yes, Father told them."

"And yet they never told me I was Dragon Born."

"Knowledge isn't always power, Arianna," said Vivienne. "I know that firsthand. Before Merlin's spell, I was already seeking you out. I knew a part of me was missing, but our parents wouldn't tell me where you were. They said it was for your protection. I'd done some suspicious magic, and our neighbors were keeping a close eye on me. Too close, as I soon learned. When I went looking for you, they followed. They cornered me in the woods and tried to force me to confess that I was Dragon Born."

"The people of my village did not hate the Dragon

Born," Arianna said. "We lived in peace with them."

"Then you were in a far better place than I was," Vivienne said darkly. "As the crusaders tortured me, I saw the storm coming. I felt things changing. The world was changing all around me. I could feel it, and yet I was powerless to stop it."

"That must have been horrible."

"As I said, knowledge isn't always power. Sometimes knowledge is merely torture." She drew in a deep breath. "As the storm approached, the crusaders ran, but I was tied to a tree. I was stuck. The fog swallowed me. And I wasn't the only one. When Merlin cast that spell, the fog claimed two hundred people from all over the world and dumped them into that broken world. Another few hundred followed in the days that followed. We were trapped there, with only one way out."

"A way blocked by the Beast," Sera said.

"Yes, I could feel it scratching at the door, trying to get to me. It craved my magic. It was born of that spell just like the broken world we were dumped into. For centuries we were trapped in there, stuck in the same, monotonous routine day in and day out. Until a few days ago."

"When Merlin's magic storm swept the world once more," said Alex. "People went missing in the fog."

"They started appearing in our world." Vivienne looked at Arianna. "We were apart for many years, but our bond is not one that can be broken so easily. There was something between us. I could see some of what you saw. I knew what Merlin was doing. I was trying to reach you through our dragons, to call you down to that door to free us."

"That's why you kept sending us down to that cave," Kai said to Arianna. "Part of you knew what was happening."

She rubbed her head. "Yes, I suppose you're right. Though at the time, I thought I was just losing my mind."

"Of course." Rane's eyes lit up.

They all looked at her.

"When Vivienne was sucked into the fog, Merlin's reality-shifting spell had to remake the world without her in it," she explained.

"The Dragon Born are two connected souls. Without Vivienne, Arianna could never have been born, and so she began to fade away," Sera realized.

"Merlin erased you," Alex told Arianna. "And no matter how many times he changed the world, he couldn't put you back as long as Vivienne was out of the equation, as long as she was trapped behind that door."

"But we are free now. Both of us," Vivienne said, taking her sister's hands. "Together, we can return to the real world. And this time, you won't disappear."

"Merlin has been trying to fix me all these years." Arianna looked at Sera and Alex. "But it was you two who saved me. You saved us." She smiled. "You reunited me with my sister, and I will be forever in your debt.

"We both are," Vivienne added.

"And I think I know just how I can help you. I'm going to talk to Merlin."

Sera and Kai lay at the edge of the pier, looking out at the sailboats on the bay. Their toes were naked, their skin cool, and their tummies full from the picnic dinner they'd just devoured. The full moon shone down on the boats, setting their sails alight.

This world—Vivienne's world—wasn't as bad as she'd made it out to be, but Sera supposed the real horror was in being trapped, cut off from her sister and everyone she loved.

But that didn't mean they couldn't transform hell into paradise. As soon as the Huntsman had left the Beast's cave in frustration, Sera and Alex led the game world's supernaturals through the doorway to Vivienne's world. Their mission as saviors had been fulfilled.

It was nearly midnight, the time the day reset. A new day meant a fresh start, a new chance—but right now, it also meant one day fewer to fix the world before Merlin's spell became permanent. Sera tried not to dwell on that right now. She and Kai needed a moment alone, a moment to breathe before the next storm came.

"Riley says the Huntsman is searching for Arianna. He thinks she's running around aimlessly between worlds," Sera said. "Apparently, her crazy side has done that before."

"Good. As long as Merlin's army is somewhere else, they aren't here."

"You don't trust the Huntsman," she said, eyeing the chocolate muffin peeking out the top of the picnic basket. Sure, she was full, but that was beside the point. There was always room for chocolate.

"No, I don't trust the Huntsman. And I don't trust Merlin."

"Arianna thinks she can convince Merlin to fix the world. Now that she's been reunited with her twin, she won't fade away. She thinks that's good enough to stop Merlin from tinkering with reality."

"Since when have things ever been that easy, sweetheart?"

She sighed. "I know."

"Merlin has been trying to change the world for too long. I doubt someone who's gone that far, who's done the things that he's done, can come back from that," Kai said. "This isn't over."

"No, it isn't. But for now, we should rejoice in reuniting two sisters." Sera rested her head on his chest. "I wonder how many more Dragon Born are out there."

"More than we can imagine."

"We saved all these people, Kai, and we're going to save the people of our world too." Hope bubbled inside of her. She couldn't stop the smile that spread across her lips—and she didn't want to. "We're going to put our world back, then we'll find a way to have peace between the Dragon Born and the other supernaturals."

"And it will start here." His hand curled around hers. "It starts with us."

"It's peaceful here. It would be so easy to stay here. To be happy. To not have to fight."

"You always have to right the wrongs of this world,

Sera. Giving up is not who you are."

"It's not who you are either. We are one and the same."

"That's why we found each other." The perfect confidence in his voice made her heart skip a beat.

"I'm glad we found each other," she told him.

Fireworks shot into the sky, lighting it up with magic.

"That's Alex's signal." Sera sighed. "She's summoning us to the party."

Kai's hand tightened around hers. "Not just yet, sweetheart. Tomorrow chaos will come calling, but right now, it's just the two of us."

They lay there, entwined in each other's arms, watching the moon, the water, the shadows. Sera drew in a deep breath and drank in this last perfect moment before the storm.

BOOK THREE
Magic Storm

1. The Castle

FROM HER PLACE behind the curtain that cloaked the balcony, Sera looked down on the grand hall. With its glossy hardwood floors and gold-accented walls, it looked like a picture-perfect scene out of a fairytale story. Too bad it belonged to a villain.

The majestic arched ceilings, painted in gold and midnight blue, resembled the night sky with its many stars and worlds. Six chandeliers hung down like enormous diamond flowers, each one sparkling with a distinctly different flavor of elemental magic: fire, ice, water, lightning, earth, wind. Their low, steady tune hummed against Sera's senses, tingling her skin.

Arianna had led them through the labyrinth of worlds that littered the Dump. There was a secret path to Merlin's castle known only to his inner circle. As his sister, Arianna was as inner circle as it got. Sera tried not to worry about the fact that their only hope of reversing Merlin's reality-altering spell lay in the hands of his little sister, a woman who had, just a few hours ago, been completely mad. Arianna's madness had lifted the moment she was reunited with the Dragon Born twin she'd never known she had. Her twin, Vivienne, had come along with them to Merlin's castle. She didn't look any more confident that their plan would work than Sera felt, but they had to try. The fate of the world depended upon their success.

The ballroom was full tonight. Roses and lavender saturated the room with a sweet aroma that almost drowned out the smell of sweat and greed. Those people down there, dressed in their perfectly-fitted tuxedos and ballgowns, belonged to Merlin: body, mind, and soul. This castle was his temple, and they had come to pay homage. Twirling, turning, sweeping —they danced to the acoustic flourish pouring out from the orchestra, consuming the hall like a river of lightning. Waiters glided across the room, carrying trays of wine, champagne, and bite-sized appetizers.

There were five other balconies that looked down on the ballroom, but none of them were occupied. Their thick velvet curtains were drawn back, revealing nothing but pristine empty boxes. The party was downstairs, not up here. But where was Merlin? According to Arianna, every lord and lady in his domain was here, and yet Merlin had still not made an appearance.

"Tonight is a celebration. He's clearly happy about something," Sera said, peering out between the two curtains. The soft material kissed her fingertips.

Alex frowned. "That doesn't bode well."

"Merlin's most loyal supporters only gather when

something big is about to go down," Arianna said.

"How did Merlin ever convince so many people to join him?" asked Lara.

"Loyalty is easily won, especially when power is on the table. Each of these lords and ladies rules over at least one of the worlds in the Dump. Some rule over many worlds. Merlin made them kings in their own right, and they would do anything to keep that power," Arianna explained.

"The Huntsman is here," Kai pointed out.

Arianna's former opponent stood beside the empty throne. He looked so different in a tuxedo instead of his green battle leather, but he was the same man under it all. He wore the same sword as he had back in the game world. His sharp eyes scanned the ballroom for threats.

A gust of magic shook the room, throwing open the large double doors. The music fizzled out in an instant. So did every conversation. Everyone stopped and stared as a man swept into the room. His gait was graceful, if not forced. He was tall and gaunt, but not from age. Stress had eaten away at his body, leaving little more than a shell of a man. That didn't detract from his undeniable charisma. It was a charisma won with sweat and blood. And magic.

Every cell in Merlin's body sang with magic. It permeated the room, snuffing out all other magic nearby. He was like a giant tree blocking the sun, keeping it from reaching all the smaller plants below. Every drop of sunlight they got was because he allowed it. That was Merlin in a nutshell. Sera had a sinking suspicion that every victory they'd won had come only because Merlin had allowed it.

But his power had come at a price. It hadn't just eaten away at his body. It had twisted his mind and marred his soul. Dark circles hung under his bloodshot eyes, like he hadn't had a good night's sleep in centuries. The rest of him was young, almost beautiful. Though he was centuries old, he didn't look a day over twenty.

Merlin's chestnut hair was slicked back. His tuxedo shimmered with shadow magic, oozing like hot ink, like the walls of the Beast's cavern. Despite his stressed, haggard appearance, he did not look weak. On the contrary, his aura was pulsing with magic, each thump like the strike of a blacksmith's hammer against Sera's magic. He lowered onto his throne, then waved his hand for the festivities to continue.

"The Huntsman is not leaving Merlin's side," Logan observed as the orchestra began to play once more.

Sera glanced down at Merlin's throne. The man of the hour sat with false calmness, his racing magic giving away the excitement he felt inside. The Huntsman was glued to his side, his hand on his sword.

"Is that going to be a problem?" Sera asked Logan.

He shrugged. "That depends on how things play out."

Sera looked at Arianna. "How do you want to do this?"

"I'd say it's high time we made our dramatic entrance."

Pushing back the curtain, Arianna swung her legs

over the edge of the balcony and jumped down. Magic cushioned her fall. As she set down in the middle of the dance floor, the music whimpered out. Everyone stopped dancing. The couples parted to clear her path to Merlin.

"Dear sister," he said, standing in surprise.

"Brother."

Arianna strode forward, her heels clicking against the wood floor, her cloak fluttering in the wind she'd cast. Sera and Alex landed on either side of her. Then came Kai and Logan, Riley with Lara and Vivienne, and the commandos brought up the rear. Merlin's people stood frozen, their eyes locked on their master, waiting for him to tell them what to do.

"What is the meaning of this?" Merlin demanded as their procession stopped at the base of the stairs that led up to his throne. "Why have you brought my enemies here, Arianna?"

"They are not your enemies. And they are my friends."

"This is madness."

"No." She stepped forward. "Look in my eyes and tell me what you see."

He looked her over. "The madness has left your eyes. But how? How have you accomplished this miracle?"

"They have cured me." Arianna waved to indicate her entourage. "I'm whole again. No, not again. I'm whole for the first time in my life. I can go back to the real world now."

"We've talked about this. You would die in an instant."

"No, I wouldn't," she insisted. "You've spent centuries trying to figure out why I was wiped from existence in the real world. Well, now I know." She waved Vivienne forward, and the two sisters joined hands. "This is Vivienne, my sister. My twin. When you cast the spell that changed this world, the fog swallowed her up and threw her into one of your waste worlds."

Merlin stroked his chin thoughtfully.

"But now that Vivienne and I are together, we can go back to the real world," Arianna said. "There is no need for any of this anymore, Merlin. We can all return to where we belong. You can put the world back. You can give Sera and her friends the world that they know. No one has to suffer anymore. Not them. Not us. We can break free of this so-called sanctuary."

"Is this world so bad?" he asked her.

"It's a dream. A bubble. It isn't real. But out there, we can experience the passage of time, the change of the seasons. We can *live*."

"We have that here."

"Not really. You stay here in your castle, laboring away in your lab, day after day, year after year. Nothing ever changes. Here, everyone is frozen, immortal."

"So you're bored, are you? Is that it?" he asked her.

"I'm dead, Merlin. Or at least I was. I have been reborn. You've kept me trapped in this crystal tower for centuries, trying to keep me amused with games, thinking that would make me happy."

"The real world is a hard, cruel place, and you are too fragile to survive it. You would waste away.

Literally. You do not exist out there."

"You aren't listening to me," said Arianna. "Things have changed. I've found my sister."

"Nothing has changed. These people are lying to you, dear sister. They think they can hurt me by tricking you into leaving my domain, by making you disappear, but pain doesn't cripple me. It only makes me fight harder." Merlin lifted his hand. Streams of shadows shot out of his fingers and wound around Arianna's body. He gave them a solid tug, pulling her toward him.

"What are you doing?" she demanded, struggling against his magic.

"Saving you."

Dark magic burst out of the floor, gushing vile smoke. It surrounded Sera and her companions. The air within their shadow prison dipped into darkness. In another minute, they wouldn't be able to see a thing. They wouldn't be able to breathe either. Merlin's spell was burning the air away.

They hadn't expected anything less of the shadow mage. Sera looked at Riley, and he nodded. Magic shot out of him, slamming against the wall of shadows. Merlin's spell shattered—and the smoke dissolved.

"You are far too much trouble," Merlin said in a bored voice. He waved his people forward.

Sera and Alex cast a wave of wind and lightning that pushed them back, trapping them at the far end of the ballroom. The lords' magic hit the barrier, over a hundred spells at once. It was like aiming a flamethrower at a piece of tissue paper. The barrier tore apart within seconds. The commandos were ready.

While Logan hurled knives, they hurled potions. The glass vials shattered at the lords' feet, splattering them with sleeping spells. Kai ignited the potions with magic.

Merlin's hands were in the air. He was readying another spell. Riley cast a ring of shadows around him, chaining him to his throne.

"I gave you your magic. It knows its master." Sneering, Merlin flipped Riley's spell inside out. The shadows turned on Riley, encasing him in his own magic. "And as for your friends, they are no match for me." Magic swirled over his head, roaring like a volcano about to erupt.

Arianna broke free of his spell. She planted herself directly in the path of his magic.

"Move." He flicked his hand to push her aside, but she didn't move a muscle.

"There's no need for us to fight," she said. "Put the world back, Merlin. Your experiments are over. I can go into the real world again."

"Lies told to confuse you," he hissed.

"No, they're not lies. I was there, and I didn't fade away."

Anger ignited in his eyes. "You risked yourself?"

"Nothing happened. I am free now."

"It's a trick. You were wiped from existence. Your sister's return shouldn't make you whole again. Unless..." His eyes flickered to Vivienne and back again. "You are Dragon Born," he said softly.

"Yes."

The storm cloud raging around him settled down to a gentle breeze. "Oh, that changes things. In fact, it changes everything."

"So you'll let us go?" Arianna said hopefully. "You'll fix the world?"

"Yes, dear sister. I'm going to fix the world."

Rage drowned out the manic flicker of obsession in his eyes. Sera realized what was going on, but she wasn't quick enough to stop it.

"Get Merlin!" she shouted at Logan. He was the only one of them who might be able to reach him in time.

"I'm going to give you a hell beyond all you ever dreamed of, you abominations of nature," Merlin promised them as Logan ran toward him. Every word dripped with pure hatred.

Logan never reached him. Magic burst out of Merlin, slamming Sera and the others to the floor. Sera felt like a mountain had fallen on top of her. No matter how much she pushed, neither her body nor her magic could break free. She was trapped. The ground was shaking, splitting. Merlin was opening up a portal. He was deporting them from his domain. The hopeless hymn of the Shadow World sang softly in the distance, but with every passing moment, it was growing louder.

"Why are you doing this?" Arianna demanded. "You wanted to save me."

"My experiments were never just about you, Arianna."

"This was about destroying the Dragon Born," Sera realized.

"Yes," he said with vicious satisfaction. "This is about the Dragon Born, that pestilence of unnatural magic that has plagued the world for far too long."

"*We* are unnatural? Just look at your magic," Alex shot back.

"And your actions," Sera added. "You put the whole world through hell—again and again—just so you could wipe out our kind."

"The Dragon Born cannot be destroyed. They cannot be wiped from existence, even by shadow magic. Your magic is too strong, too odd," said Merlin.

"So you changed the world to turn everyone against us, and then let that world kill us?" Sera said.

"You wouldn't die. No matter how many scenarios I tried, you always survived." His brows drew together in annoyance. "The Dump is littered with my failures. And then I thought I had it, a spell finally worth casting."

"The Shadow World didn't turn out as you'd expected, did it?" Alex said with a smirk.

"No, it didn't. Your magic is too unpredictable. It throws off my equations. But I was going about this all wrong, it seems. The world I create is irrelevant. It's the initial shockwave that matters. I must direct it at the Dragon Born. If one twin is swallowed by the abyss as the new world is forming, the other twin ceases to exist." His grimace curled up into a smile. "Thanks for that little tidbit."

"I am your sister," Arianna declared, tears staining her cheeks. "We grew up together."

"And I *loved* you with my whole heart," he growled. "We were not bonded by blood, but I loved you."

"And now? Were all our years together for

nothing?" Arianna swallowed hard. "You hate me. And all because of what I am. Nothing has changed about me, Merlin, not even my magic. It was always there, even if I never knew about it. I am still your sister." She reached out for him.

He slapped her hand away. "You're Dragon Born," he spat with disgust. "You are an abomination."

The hate in his eyes had been forged in pain. That pain was still there, buried beneath the venom.

"This is a personal vendetta," Sera realized. "What did the Dragon Born do to you?"

The ground crunched, as though a giant had just stomped down on it.

"Enough chitchat," Merlin said, anger swirling in his eyes. "Welcome to your new fate. I would have doomed you to remember the world you lost, but I'm afraid your memories make you too much of a nuisance."

Black lightning crashed down, splitting open the ground. Merlin's magic storm pushed them out of his domain. Sera dropped into nothingness, weightless, powerless. And then she hit the hard dirt of the Shadow World. She looked up to find herself completely surrounded by Blackbrooke's army.

2. Battle Dragon

A BATTLE WAS brewing all around Kai. He stood in front of the Dragon Born mages' San Francisco base. Its protective wall had been breached, and the Crusaders were streaming inside. Flames raged on the burning buildings, filling the air with a thick, noxious smoke. Streams of magic shot across the battlefield, a high-pitched whistle that mixed with the hard, heavy clang of clashing steel.

Kai walked toward the vampires, mages, and fairies dressed in synthetic black suits. They wore the emblem of the Magic Council on their chest, and right next to it the mark of the Western Territories. These were Kai's people.

"Stop! Stand down!" he shouted at them.

His voice, amplified by magic, penetrated the sounds of battle, but no one stopped. And no one stood down. They were ignoring Kai's commands. That annoyed him even more than the fact that they'd started shooting at him.

"I can take care of them for you," Logan offered.

"Fight to disable, not kill," Kai told his companions.

Logan landed a knife in a Crusader's leg. "Going soft, Drachenburg?"

"No, I'm just not going to waste perfectly good soldiers. Especially when they are mine." He blasted a pair of vampires at the wall.

"It doesn't look like they're yours anymore," Logan observed.

"I just need to get their attention."

The commandos looped around a large cluster of Crusaders, tossing sleeping potions into their midst. The great thing about Riley's potions was that they worked against any corporeal supernatural.

"Where is Riley?" Kai asked.

A quick count told him that Riley was the only one missing. Everyone else who'd gone on the mission to Merlin's castle was here.

"He's… I don't know," Sera said as she caught a fairy in her web of lightning. "I can feel he's somewhere in the city, but I'm having trouble tracking him down."

Alex shook her head. "Same here. Something is interfering with his magic, blocking it somehow."

The last Crusader had fallen, but more were on the way. Lara, Arianna, and Vivienne headed off the new group of soldiers who'd just arrived. The Crusaders weren't giving up.

"Is the interference on your end or on Riley's?" Logan asked.

Alex looked at Sera. "His."

"Yes," Sera agreed.

Kai felt the same thing. Merlin had separated them from Riley and found some way to keep them from tracking him. He'd taunted Riley for being weak, but his actions said otherwise. Perhaps he didn't fear Riley, but he must have thought his magic was a threat to him.

Naomi jumped down from one of the buildings, her glowing wings slowing her fall. Ghosts swirled around her like a brewing cauldron. Then the silvery figures shot up, swarming the group of Crusaders who were hot on Naomi's tail. The ghosts swallowed the soldiers midair and spat them across the battlefield. They landed at Makani's feet. He and his Dragon Born mages made sure they didn't get up.

But the Crusaders weren't giving up. They just kept coming. The numbers were in their favor, even if their magic was not. This was a battle doomed for heavy losses on both sides—unless Kai could make them stop and listen.

He ran straight at them all, shifting into a dragon as he moved. Magic flashed across his skin like a fever, the spell cast between one second and the next. Shifting spells were quick and clean if done right, slow and sloppy if done wrong. Most people were so wowed by the terrifying sight of an enormous dragon that they didn't understand the subtlety required to make the shift.

Kai stomped down hard, forcing the vampires back. That move cut them off from the mages. One of the mages hadn't jumped away fast enough and slammed into Kai's leg. The impact of soft flesh against hard scales knocked him out cold. Towering over everyone on the battlefield, Kai opened his jaws and let out a thunderous roar. Every single person froze. Even the Dragon Born mages stopped and stared.

As Kai shifted back into human form, the commandos fell into line beside him, backing him up.

"See, I told you I could get their attention," Kai told Logan.

"It's hard to ignore a dragon." Logan glanced at Alex, who winked in response.

Kai stared down the Crusaders. "Ok, now that I've got your attention, someone tell me where Blackbrooke is."

"Around back."

"You won't step on us, will you?" another soldier asked. He looked like he was going to be sick.

Sometimes it was good to have a reputation as a beast.

"That depends entirely upon you," Kai told him. "No one move a muscle until I get back. I've had it up to here with this nonsense. You are *my* army, and you will obey me, not Blackbrooke."

"Blackbrooke says you defected, that you're a traitor."

Kai gave the Crusader a hard look. "Does that sound like me?"

The man's mouth clicked shut.

Kai waved for the commandos to follow him. "Let's go get Blackbrooke before he causes any more trouble. I swear that man is a nuisance in any world." He glanced back at Logan. "If any of them so much as sneeze, shoot them."

Logan drew a gun that looked like it had been designed to shoot through dinosaurs. Holy shit, where the hell did the assassin get his weapons?

"They look even more scared of him than they are of you, Kai," Tony commented as they walked past the gawking Crusaders.

"The assassin has a reputation of his own. But he certainly isn't scarier than I am."

"It's that Mages Illustrated cover. Being a celebrity kind of makes you less frightening," Dal said.

"I am every bit as frightening as Slayer."

Callum's eyes twinkled. "If you say so, boss."

Kai clenched his jaw. Sometimes the guys had entirely too much fun egging him on.

Tony quickly changed the subject. "What are you going to do to Blackbrooke when we find him?"

"That depends on what he says."

"And how contrite he is about stealing your army?" Callum asked.

"He has a lot more than just that to be contrite about. In both this world and the World That Was."

They passed more Crusaders, but those soldiers just stepped aside and let him pass. Kai didn't even have to turn into a dragon this time. The look on his face was enough. Good. The shifting spell burned several thousand calories, and he still hadn't had any dinner. He was in dire need of a steak. Or two.

"The world knows no horror like a hungry dragon," Tony commented.

"I could use a snack myself. Too bad there's no Wizard House Pizza in this world," said Dal.

"That alone is reason enough to break Merlin's spell," Callum added. "What I wouldn't give for a salami pizza right now."

A wistful look slid across Dal's face. "With extra salami."

"And hot peppers," said Tony.

"Stop it. You're making me even hungrier," Kai told them.

There wasn't time for food fantasies anyway. They'd found Blackbrooke. The Crusaders' strategic director lay on the ground, surrounded by the Dragon Born mages' fairy allies. They wore the same badass leather as the rest of the Dragon Born forces. Kai looked down upon Blackbrooke. It seemed the Director's plan to take out the Dragon Born and their allies had backfired.

"We'll take it from here," Kai told the fairies.

A fairy with spiky silver hair turned his dark eyes on him. "Kai Drachenburg. You're Sera's friend."

"Her fiancé actually," Dal amended.

The fairy blinked in surprise. "That was fast."

"Long story. How's Blackbrooke?" Tony asked him.

A vicious smile curled the fairy's lips. "Napping."

The unconscious Blackbrooke was as still as a corpse. The glow of Fairy Dust still lingered on him, crackling across his body, hissing like a bug zapper.

Kai frowned. "Are you sure you didn't kill him?"

"Nah, he's all right. It takes more than Fairy Dust to kill a mage."

Dal knelt down beside Blackbrooke, feeling for a pulse. "He's alive." He looked up at the fairies. "How many times did you hit him?"

"Once for every insult he threw at us."

Callum let out a low, long whistle. "That must have been a lot of hits."

"It really was," said the silver-haired fairy, shaking out his hands. Blue Fairy Dust popped, sprinkling down. "I think I jammed my trigger finger." He snickered.

Kai nudged Blackbrooke with the toe of his boot. "Wake up."

Blackbrooke didn't move.

Kai crouched down and punched his fists against the Director, shocking him with lightning. A pained moan parted Blackbrooke's mouth. Kai shocked him again.

"And I thought I was mean," the silver fairy said, giving Kai a look of pure admiration.

Blackbrooke curled up into a tight ball. His eyelids fluttered open slowly, his gaze drifting up. The moment his eyes met Kai's, he shuddered.

"Good, you're awake," Kai said. "Now, Director, it's about time we had a little chat."

3. Allies and Enemies

KAI TOLD THE commandos to carry Blackbrooke back to Sera and the others. He let them decide which one of them was stuck with the honor of hauling the Magic Council's Strategic Director fireman-style. Tony drew the short straw.

"He's heavier than he looks," Tony said.

Callum grinned at him. "Or maybe you've just been slacking off at the gym lately. You've been spending an awful lot of time in that aerobics class instead."

"He fancies the instructor," Dal said.

"Oh? What's she look like?"

"Good enough to make Tony skip weight training."

"She has a nice smile," Tony said. "And, by the way, I can still lift more than either of you."

Callum and Dal chuckled.

"Your soldiers are engaging in frivolous smalltalk,

Drachenburg," Blackbrooke said.

"And?"

"It's unprofessional."

"You say that as though I give a shit what you think."

Drachenburg nearly choked on his tongue. "It is precisely this kind of rogue conduct that lost you your command."

"I didn't lose anything. You stole it from me." Kai flashed him a vicious grin. "And now I'm taking it back."

"You traitor, Drachenburg," Blackbrooke spluttered in protest. "My soldiers will—"

"Let's just get a few things straight," Kai cut in. "First of all, they are *my* soldiers. And second of all, I'm not a traitor for not wanting my people to drown in blood and hatred. This war is tearing the world apart. Can't you see that?"

"What's happened to you?" Blackbrooke looked at him with genuine confusion. He just didn't get it. Maybe he never would, but Kai had to try.

Kai motioned for Tony to put him down. "I woke up. It's time for you to do the same. Make peace, Duncan."

"The Dragon Born—"

"Are not our enemy."

"I never thought you of all people would betray us for a pretty face." Blackbrooke looked past him, his eyes narrowing in pure loathing as they fell upon Sera and Alex. "The dragons are sirens. They are beautiful, seductive, and pure evil."

"Does he even listen to himself speak?" Sera

commented.

"I think he speaks *just* to listen to himself," said Alex.

Sera extended her hand toward him. "There's no need for us to be enemies."

Blackbrooke spat at her feet. Kai resisted the temptation to set his hair on fire.

"Charming," Alex said. "The man truly is incurable."

"I don't want your cure. Whatever dark magic you're casting, whatever spell you've put Kai under, I want no part of it."

Alex smirked at Sera. "Maybe he just needs a great, big hug."

Horror washed across Blackbrooke's face. "Stay away from me." He backed up, bumping into Kai.

Alex rolled her eyes. "Geez, relax. I'm not going to touch you. You probably have cooties."

Sera made a face. "The highly contagious kind."

"When my army comes, you will feel the full might of the Magic Council."

Kai grabbed his arm. "Which forces have you summoned here? When will they arrive?"

Blackbrooke remained mum, but he was wearing smugness like a second skin. Fire erupted on Kai's hands, ignited by his complete and total unwillingness to put up with any bullshit.

Blackbrooke's smug face melted into fear. "This world will not fall to the Dragon Born. I will not allow it." His voice shook.

"He's nothing but hate and propaganda." Sera sighed. "We're never going to get anything useful out of him."

"I could torture him if you'd like," Logan offered, his voice casual.

Blackbrooke turned, his eyes widening as he realized who Logan was.

Torturing Blackbrooke might get them the information they needed to fend off the next attack, but what about all of the others after that? In this world and the one that was, the problem wasn't weapons or strategy or even magic. It was people wearing their hatred like it was their favorite color. They were so caught up in their hate that they didn't realize they were making the world worse, not better. If they could just see how much this hate was destroying the world, maybe people would stop fighting and start listening. But it was hard to see beyond your own world, hard to see how much worse things could be.

"Let's try something else," Kai decided.

But before he could say more, magic shook the ground. Kai looked at the base's buildings. They were no longer on fire, but they were still smoking. Somewhere past those houses, a few final skirmishes were playing out. Arianna and Vivienne had gone to help Makani and Naomi. Lara was with them. Every so often, one of her dragons shot above the rooftops before it dove again, breathing out fire and ice.

Alex glanced at the smoke rising from the buildings. "Blackbrooke is too much trouble."

"Yes, he is," Kai agreed. "But imagine how much trouble he would cause our enemies if we could turn him to our side."

"I would never—"

"No one asked you," Kai snapped. He looked at Sera. "Can you make him remember?"

Sera nodded, smiling. "Let's jog his memory," she told Alex.

The sisters stepped forward, their hands linked. Blackbrooke's eyes danced with panic. He tried to run, but the commandos held tightly to him. Sera slammed the heel of her hand against his chest. Alex slammed hers against his forehead. Magic sizzled in the air like static electricity—and then something popped. The force of the spell was so powerful that it ripped Blackbrooke from the commandos' iron grasp. He hit the ground.

"Did it work?" Kai asked. "Did you return his memories of our world?"

Rane had taught them how to use their Mind Breaker magic to return people's memories of the World That Was. It was a difficult spell that required a lot of power, so much power that the sisters had to link their magic to perform it.

Alex pulled Blackbrooke off the ground. "There's only one way to find out if it worked."

Sera snapped her fingers in front of his face. "Good morning, sunshine. Give us a smile."

Blackbrooke's eyes opened, blinking rapidly. "Serafina Dering," he croaked.

"Well, at least we didn't give him amnesia." Sera snapped her fingers again in front of Blackbrooke's dropping eyelids. "Tell me about the first time we met."

"It was on the battlefield... Wait, no..." He shook his head, as though he were trying to jostle his memories free. "It was at the Magic Games. No matter what challenges I threw at you, you didn't break." His frown crinkled his face. "Then and there, I should have known you were Dragon Born."

"It's slowly coming back to him," Sera said.

"Duncan, this world is not ours," Kai told the dazed Blackbrooke. "A powerful mage named Merlin changed it. Back in our world, you wanted to lead the supernaturals against the Dragon Born. Look around. This Shadow World is what happens when war tears us apart. The Dragon Born are not our enemy. They have done nothing to us. They just want to live, like we all do."

This time, Blackbrooke didn't reply with threats or insults. "I don't trust them," he said, glaring at Sera and Alex.

"And they don't trust you," replied Kai. "But they are willing to make peace with you. For the greater good."

Blackbrooke frowned. "They keep secrets." To him, that was a sin akin to treason. He believed only criminals kept secrets—and that it was his sworn duty to expose them.

"Yeah, you'd hide the truth of what you are too if everyone wanted to kill you," commented Alex, handing him off to the commandos.

"You know both worlds, Duncan," Kai said. "I think we can all agree that for all its faults, the World That Was was still better than this Shadow World."

"Yes." The word dropped like a stone into a calm lake.

Kai set his hand on Blackbrooke's shoulder. "We

can put the world back to the way it was, but we need your help. You must call off the attack. If we don't break the spell soon, the Shadow World will become permanent. We have to put aside our differences and work together if we want to fix this."

Blackbrooke's brows drew together. "I don't like it."

"I knew you wouldn't."

"But I will help you. For the greater good," he added.

Kai waved at the commandos. "Release him."

They did so with obvious reluctance. They'd always been professional. They would never dream of allowing their personal dislike of Blackbrooke to keep them from following Kai's orders—or from doing the thing they knew was right. They weren't just loyal soldiers. They were true friends.

Blackbrooke fished his phone out of his jacket and dialed. "Call off the attack. Don't move until you hear from me." With that said, he hung up and looked at Kai. "It's done. My forces outside the city are holding position."

"How close were they?"

"Close. In a few more minutes, we would have been having an entirely different conversation. One with you stuck behind iron bars."

Kai flashed him his teeth. "You underestimate our magic."

"And you underestimate our numbers. Numbers trump magic, Kai. That's a lesson you never allowed yourself to learn. You were too busy shifting into a dragon and stepping on your problems."

Sera snorted.

Kai kept his eyes locked on Blackbrooke. "And you were too busy hiding behind your army to understand how it really is on the front line—and what you have to do to win."

Blackbrooke stiffened.

"Let's not fight. We have more important things to discuss." Sera offered Blackbrooke a smile. "Thank you for calling off your forces. It was the right thing to do."

Blackbrooke repaid her kindness with scorn. "I don't want your thanks. We are *not* friends. I don't like the Dragon Born, nor do I trust you. I agreed to help you put things back to the way they were, but that is as far as I will go. This is a temporary truce, not a reason to join hands and sing songs around the bonfire."

Alex grinned at Sera. "I think he's starting to grow on me."

"It must be his endearing personality."

Magic boomed in the background, cutting off whatever sarcastic remark Alex had cooked up in response.

"What now?" Sera pointed at Blackbrooke. "Your soldiers are still attacking. You need to call them off."

"That's not my soldiers." His eyes drifted up, growing as wide as saucers.

Kai followed his gaze into the sky raging with swirling, storming purple clouds. He knew those clouds. Even if he'd been blind, he would have known them by their magic alone. They reeked of Merlin.

"He's changing the world again," Kai declared.

"No doubt he's making a world worse for the Dragon Born," Alex said.

Sera took their hands. "And when it hits us, it will all be over. We won't be able to undo the damage he's done because we won't remember a thing."

4. Magic Storm

THUNDER RUMBLED FROM deep within the heavens, but there was nothing heavenly about the magic storm. It was coming in fast. Pink clouds rolled out like a thick carpet, flashing with accents of purple-gold lightning. The storm consumed the light, blotting out the sun, the moon, everything. Block by block, the city was being swallowed by darkness.

Sera stood there, frozen. She didn't know what to do. Her powers were useless against this tsunami of shadow magic. She felt so tiny, so helpless standing before it. Even combined, she and Alex could not break it. They'd barely had enough magic to free Blackbrooke's memories of the World That Was—and this spell was a million times bigger.

Sera squeezed Kai's hand. "I love you. No matter what happens, no matter how much the world changes, that won't change."

"Sera…" Her name died in his throat. She'd never

seen him look so helpless. It broke her heart.

Tears rolled down her cheeks. "I *will* find you, Kai. No magic, no matter how powerful, can tear us apart." She gave Alex's hand a squeeze. "It can't tear any of us apart."

Alex squeezed back. "We're one. A family. Merlin might think he's found the way to end the Dragon Born, but he's wrong. Our bond is stronger than his magic. It will not fade." She took Logan's hand.

One-by-one they all linked hands—all except for Blackbrooke. He kept his distance, his prejudices fully intact.

"How touching," he said. "But if this Merlin has the power to change the world and make us forget everything we know, all the love and sappy speeches won't protect us."

What would it take to break him free of his hateful habit? Was it even possible? Despite what he'd done, Sera believed he was not beyond hope. In fact, she liked to think everyone could be saved. Except Merlin. He'd cast aside his sister, his love for her vanishing just like that. And all because he'd learned she was Dragon Born. His hatred knew no bounds.

"You know what your problem is, Blackbrooke?" Sera said. "You have no faith. No hope. No love. You're driven by your obsession to impose your order over everyone and everything. You only agreed to help us because you can't stand the thought that someone has more control over the world than you do. Well, Merlin does. He is more powerful than you. He's going to change the world. He's going to throw you into a hell you cannot escape from, and you won't be able to do a damn thing about it."

"I know what you're doing."

Sera arched her brows at him, an unspoken challenge to prove her wrong.

"You're trying to rile me up so I will stand with you and fight this spell," he grumbled. "You're a lot smarter than I'd thought."

"Alone we are weak. Alone he can pick us off," she told him. "But together we're strong. We're a force that will never fold, never break, never falter. That unity is more powerful than all of the magic in the world."

"Love conquers all?"

She smiled. "It's worked out for me so far."

Blackbrooke was clearly unimpressed. "You're naive." He joined hands with Kai anyway.

And so they stood there with linked hands, bracing for the magic storm, for that inevitable moment it would hit them and shatter their world. And, truth be told, Sera did feel stronger together, joined by love and a common purpose. It would be enough to weather the storm. It had to be.

Merlin's storm was so close now that she could feel the dewdrops of despair clinging to her skin, trying to wash away their bond. Magic exploded in her face, and when the sparks and flames fizzled out, Rane was standing in front of them. She grabbed Blackbrooke's arm with one hand. The other she extended up into the sky, up toward the storm.

The clouds froze in place. The carpet stopped unrolling. The thunder was silenced. Only the echo of the last roar still lingered on, purring against the wind.

Sera sighed in relief. "Thanks, Rane."

"Don't thank me yet," replied the demon. "I merely froze the spell in time for now. I wasn't sure I could do it, but whatever funny magic you have going on here…" She waved to indicate their line of linked hands. "It's powerful. I drew on it to cast my spell."

"That *funny* magic is called love," Sera said, smirking.

"Love, huh? I never had much use for it myself."

"Perhaps you will rethink that choice."

"Or perhaps not."

"Blackbrooke will marry a Dragon Born mage before Rane embraces the power of love," Alex muttered to her.

She was probably right, but Sera wasn't ready to give up on Rane. Even though she was a demon, her soul was purer than Merlin's.

"This is only a temporary fix," Rane said. "The storm will break through eventually if we don't do something."

"What can we do?" Sera asked.

"You need to find the person who cast the spell. Only then do we have any hope of stopping this storm before it changes the world—and all of you with it."

"The person who cast the spell? Merlin?"

"No. He wouldn't dare cast a spell like this. Seven hundred years ago, his first spell nearly killed him. Just like last time, he's using someone else to cast the spell for him by proxy."

"Riley?" Alex asked.

"No, I taught him enough to allow him to resist Merlin's control."

"Then where is our brother?" Alex demanded.

"Somewhere in this city."

Alex folded her arms across her chest. "Thanks. We already figured that out."

"Merlin sent him away so he couldn't help you. Find Riley. And find the spell caster. She has to be somewhere nearby."

"She?" Sera asked.

"Yes, she is clearly a woman. I can feel it in the streams of magic that hold the storm together. Just as I can feel she is in love with Merlin." Rane's expression hardened. "Which means she won't come with you willingly. This isn't a matter of breaking Merlin's hold over her. Love is a tougher spell to break than any magic."

Sera couldn't argue with that.

"Get Riley, get the spell caster. I will need them both to break this spell. And hurry. I can't keep the storm frozen forever."

"We'll hurry," Sera promised.

"Protect Rane while we're gone," Kai told the commandos.

Rane stiffened. "I am a demon. I do not require protection."

"All of your magic is going into holding back that storm." Alex held up her hand, preempting Rane's protest. "Don't even try to deny it. I can feel the flow of your magic. Take the help and be happy to have it."

Rane's eyes drank in the sight of the commandos standing before her. "I'll admit that the idea of accepting help from mortals has never been more appealing."

"Make sure Blackbrooke doesn't cause any trouble

while we're gone," Sera told the commandos as Rane continued to undress them with her eyes,

"Sure thing, Sera," Tony replied.

"We'll sit on him if need be," Dal added.

Callum shot Blackbrooke a crooked smile. "Or just freeze him inside of an iceberg."

"If you so much as lay a finger on me, you will come to regret your insubordination," Blackbrooke threatened them.

"Insubordination?" Amusement flashed in Callum's eyes. "No, we're only insubordinate if we don't kick your ass."

"So you take orders from that Dragon Born mage now?" Blackbrooke looked like he was going to be sick. Not that it was much different from his usual expression.

"Of course we do. Isn't that right, Mrs. Drachenburg?" Tony beamed at her.

Sera glared at him, which only made all of the commandos burst into laughter.

"You should see the look on your face, Sera," Dal said.

Callum nodded. "I've never seen a more perfect expression of complete terror."

"You guys are hilarious, you know. Try not to humor Blackbrooke to death."

Their triple grins bounced off her back as she, Alex, Kai, and Logan headed for the broken gate that had once protected the Dragon Born base.

"Be careful. The spell caster is a shadow mage. She'll have magic like Riley's," Rane warned them.

It had taken Sera, Alex, and Kai combined to

defeat Riley when he'd been controlled by Merlin, and they'd gotten lucky. Fighting Merlin's latest shadow mage wouldn't be easy.

Kai had a car parked inside a garage a few blocks over: a big, black SUV that was the love child of a race car and a tank. Kai's taste in cars seemed to be a constant in every world. The four of them piled into the car, and they followed the trail of shadow magic toward the piers. As they got closer to the water, Sera realized it wasn't just Merlin's lackey they were sensing. There were two signals. Riley's was weak, buried beneath the other shadow mage's noxious magic, but he was around here somewhere.

The piers lay inside the Forsaken District, which meant monster territory. Kai parked in front of the wall the Crusaders' telekinetics had thrown up hastily after the monsters had swallowed this shoreside neighborhood. Something had torn a sizable hole into the stone wall. A monster no doubt, and it had happened recently. There hadn't been a hole the last time Sera was here. No walls could hold back the beasts, at least not forever. Merlin was right. It wouldn't be long before the monsters consumed the earth.

A beautifully tragic song echoed across the water, stirring the strings of Sera's soul. Selkies. They'd come in close to the shore. Their eyes shone brightly through the fog, like a field of twin-towered lighthouses. Their voices floated along the cool, salty breeze. The wind was eerily calm at the moment, as though time had frozen still. That must have been a side effect of Rane holding off the storm.

"The magic is so weird here," Alex commented. "It feels like its echoing off the storm clouds."

Logan inhaled deeply. "The trails split here." He pointed toward the shore. "The spell caster is that way." He indicated a cluster of ugly, burnt buildings. "And Riley is in there."

"Alex and I will find Riley," Sera decided. "You two go after the spell caster."

The guys turned toward the water, and Sera and Alex moved into the cluster. As they walked through the maze of broken buildings, every house seemed to howl in agony, every pile creaked, as though the whole thing could come tumbling down at any moment. Monsters lurked in the shadows, their red eyes watching. With every step that Sera took, she could feel more of Riley's magic.

"He's close," Alex said softly, as though she were speaking over a grave.

A savage growl pierced the dew-dripped silence. The fog parted, revealing their brother. But he wasn't alone. A pack of Blight wolves had him surrounded. There were six of them, each one nearly as large as Kai's car. They snapped at Riley with mouths of jagged, dagger-like teeth, dripping drops of blood and venom. Shadows slid across Riley's arms, spinning into twin whips. He lashed out at the wolves, the pitch black whips cracking deliciously. Shadows poured out of the tips, twisting around the wolves' legs, pinning them to the ground. Riley moved quickly. Step, slash, step slash. His whips were quick and merciless. As the last wolf fell to its knees, he walked up to it.

"Go," Riley said, his voice pulsing with command

—and with magic.

The shadows squeezed the wolves, then burst into flames, setting their fur on fire. Yapping and yipping, the wolves scrambled to their feet. They ran in confused, zigzagging strides, banging off one another in their rush to run away. Riley watched them go, his face less satisfied than weary.

Sera rushed forward, embracing him. "Are you all right?"

"Fine. For now."

Alex joined in their hug. "For now?"

"They weren't the first monsters to attack me since Merlin dumped me here. I expect the next ones will be along shortly. It would appear he wants to keep me busy."

"Because he's trying to change the world again, and he knows you could threaten that plan," Alex said.

Riley looked up at the frozen storm clouds. "Rane's doing?"

"Yes," Sera replied. "But she can't hold off the spell for long. We have only minutes."

Thunder rippled through the clouds, and the magic storm stirred again.

"I don't think we have even that long," Riley said, paling.

5. Slayer

KAI LOOKED UP at the rumbling storm. It stirred and swirled, then froze again.

"We don't have much time. Rane is losing her hold over the storm," he commented.

Kai could feel the spell caster's magic nearby, but he couldn't seem to track her. The materials in this area were distorting her magic. The storm cloud of supercharged magic overhead wasn't helping either.

"This way," Logan said, following the shore. "She's not far away. I can smell her excitement. And her frustration. She's fighting Rane's magic, trying to push the spell through."

"And the spell wants to push through. Once cast, magic's natural state is to go forward and consume. Rane has the uphill battle. As do we," he added as two web-footed monsters leapt into their path. Giant frogs. Great.

Kai dodged a flaming spitball one of the giant

frogs had launched at him. He countered with ice, freezing the creature's amphibious toes to the asphalt ground. Kai cast a quake to swallow it up. The assassin threw a knife at the other frog. The blade sank into its fat belly, and the beast stumbled back, falling onto the frog trying to leap out of the hole Kai had made.

"So, why did you decide to become an assassin?" Kai asked, sealing the hole with a rocky ceiling.

Logan gave him an inscrutable look. "Sera put you up to this, didn't she?"

"She thinks we should start bonding."

"And from your delighted expression, you wholeheartedly agree."

"You're strangely sarcastic for an assassin," Kai slid another layer of rock across the former hole in the ground. He could hear the frogs bouncing down below, trying to get out.

"I spend a lot of time with Alex," replied Logan. "It's contagious. I can see you've caught it too."

"The Dering sisters," Kai said with a sigh.

Logan nodded. "Indeed."

Two gigantic magic dragonflies, each one as large as a house cat, dove out of the sky, their silken, fairylike wings shimmering in the unearthly glow of the magic storm clouds. Giant dragonflies were as beautiful as monsters came—and they were also as nasty as monsters came. Like their smaller, mundane counterparts, they were biters. But unlike those smaller, mundane counterparts, they had razor-sharp fangs the size of steak knives.

The monsters swayed and fluttered in graceful loops, each one of them as delicate and strong as a prima ballerina. The sweet, dark melody of their magic brushed across Kai's aura like crushed velvet, soft and lush. The dragonflies circled him and Logan, spinning so fast that they were only a blue-green streak. Kai couldn't tell where one beast began and the other ended. His gaze never leaving the dragonfly stream, Logan slid two knives from his wrists. Silver flashed, and then the two monsters were dead on the ground, a dagger through each eye.

"You are a good fighter," Kai said.

Logan's brows arched. "Careful, Drachenburg. I might mistake that for a compliment."

"It's merely an observation. You know I don't approve of your methods, especially when they involve stealing from me."

Logan recovered his slimy knives from the dead dragonflies. "I know. Your ego can't take the hit. No one steals from the *great* Kai Drachenburg. Well, no one except for me."

He didn't sound like he was gloating. He was just stating a fact—a cold, hard fact—so Kai could forgive his words, if not his actions.

"I must admit that you do get results," Kai said, continuing to walk along the pier. "I could use someone like you."

A slight smile touched the assassin's mouth. "You couldn't afford me."

"I don't know about that. I can afford a lot."

Logan chuckled.

"You haven't been taking a lot of jobs since you got together with Alex," Kai continued. "You've been saving the world for free."

"Not exactly for free."

"People are saying you've turned over a new leaf."

"Which people?" The look on Logan's face said he wanted nothing more than to find those people and prove them wrong.

"People."

"You?"

Kai snorted. "No. I know better. But I could still use you."

"I have no desire to ever be used again. My parents engineered me. They infused me with magic, turning me into a living weapon. Well, I got sick of being their weapon, so I left. I am my own man now, but I am still what they made me."

Kai knew how he felt. His magic had made him too, but he'd been the one to decide what he would do with it. As the heir to one of the greatest mage dynasties, it was his sworn duty to uphold the Magic Council's law. That included killing Dragon Born mages. Well, he refused to be a slave to obligations he didn't agree with.

"Have you ever tried to live a normal life?" Kai asked him.

"What is 'normal' for someone like me? I am neither human, nor do I fit into one of the neat categories the Magic Council has created to classify supernaturals. After I cut ties with my parents, I tried to fit into the humans' idea of normal, but it was no use. I am not normal, not even close. The world had the misfortune of learning that firsthand. You can't just go from being a killer to waiting tables. My mind couldn't stop working, assessing scenes, seeing threats everywhere. I decided I could drive myself insane trying to be what I wasn't, or I could embrace what I was on my terms. I became an assassin, but I chose the jobs. Killing bad people. A hit on an evil warlord pays quite well, you know. Whenever the world was short on warlords, I stole from the magical elite. Genuine magical artifacts are worth a lot."

That was the truth. A charred tennis ball that had been set on fire in a mage duel was worth two hundred dollars in an online auction. Objects that were legitimately magical were often worth millions.

"Magical artifacts are dangerous in the wrong hands," Kai told him.

"And the magical elite are the right hands?"

He had a point. Kai certainly didn't trust Blackbrooke with powerful artifacts. Once this was all over, given the chance, the Director would take out the Dragon Born.

"Don't worry. I didn't sell doomsday devices to teenagers," Logan told him. "When the magical object was really hot, really powerful, I just sold it back to their original owners. Through other channels, of course. I called it a recovery fee."

"I'd had my suspicions about those miraculous recoveries."

"I gave the owner a few days to panic and realize how much they needed that artifact, then one of my agents offered to sell it back to them. I didn't have to worry about finding a buyer for a hot item everyone was looking for, and the owner was happy to get it back. Win-win."

Kai frowned. "I wouldn't call that a win."

"No, neither would they, if they'd known the thief had been the one to sell it back to them. That's why this is going to be our little secret, Drachenburg. We wouldn't want to damage your colleagues' delicate egos."

"Fine. As long as you don't try to steal from *me* again."

"Those days have passed."

"Ah, so Alex truly has recruited you."

"I couldn't very well let her work alone. Have you seen how she runs into battle without plan or preparation? If I hadn't teamed up with her, sooner or later she would have gotten herself killed."

"She's pretty resilient," Kai said. "And her heart is in the right place."

"Yes, and Sera's too. Though I have to admit I'm surprised that you convinced her to come work for you."

"I offered Sera her own armory closet. How could she refuse?"

Logan laughed. "Clever."

"If you and Alex worked for me, you would have more resources at your disposal." Kai thought it was a reasonable argument.

But Logan obviously didn't agree. "More resources perhaps, but I don't work well on a leash."

"You can have your own armory closet too."

"I already have one. Multiple ones, in fact."

Of course he did.

Logan shot him a suspicious look. "Why do you want me to work for you anyway? You don't even like me."

"I want Sera to be happy. And it would make her happy if Alex came to work with us. Alex will only come if you come too."

"You've already talked to Alex?"

"Yes, and she misses her sister. Everyone will be happier working for me. Win-win." Kai flashed him a smile. "You should appreciate that."

"You don't play fair," Logan said cooly.

"You really think I got where I am by playing fair?"

"No, of course not." Logan spun around and launched a swarm of knives at a squid-like beast creeping out of the water. "You are a worthy opponent, Drachenburg." He pulled his blades out of the squid's eight legs and two lightning-tipped tentacles. The monster screeched and slid back into the ocean. "After we've put the world back to the way it was, we'll talk about this."

That was as good as an acceptance speech. Above all, Logan wanted to make Alex happy. The sisters missed each other terribly. Working together would make them both happy. With both Dering sisters and Slayer working for him, Kai would have to triple the size of the cleanup department, but it would be worth it. He would finally have his unbeatable team.

"The shadow mage is out there," Logan said, pointing to a lone sailboat bobbing on the bay.

Kai reached out with his magic—and met a wall of shadow magic. Logan was right. And it made sense that she'd be out there. Water magnified magic, so what better place to cast her world-shattering spell?

Kai cast his own magic. The shift hit him hard this time, the ripple of scales burning as they spread across his body, covering his skin. Wings cut through his back like daggers. Kai opened his mouth and roared.

"Easy there," Logan said, jogging up Kai's spiked back to sit behind his neck. "We'll find you a nice, fat flock of sheep to snack on later."

The assassin's ability to read body language, both in men and beasts, was uncanny. Kai kicked up into the air, pumping his massive wings to gain altitude. He flew Logan across the bay. As they came up on the sailboat, the assassin slid off Kai's back. He hit the deck, rolling his landing so that it was hardly louder than a whisper. At least Kai couldn't hear it from up here. The shadow mage didn't either. Logan snuck up on her, stalking like a cat.

She turned to gaze across the bay. Surprise flashed in her turquoise eyes when she saw the assassin. She recovered quickly, blasting Logan with magic born from shadows. The assassin was too fast, however. He evaded her smoke rings, dropping one hand to the deck. His other hand was already reaching for his knives. Silver streaked as he spun around. The shadow mage threw up a barrier. The moment Logan's knives touched it, they melted. Liquid steel dripped to the deck.

Kai dove low, breathing fire. Dragon fire was hotter than normal magic fire. It tore through the shadow wall, trapping her inside a ring of flames. Logan ran up the mast and dropped down beside her. Her hand shot up to her neck. She pulled out a dart, throwing it to the deck with a defiant clunk.

"I am the Shadow Queen," she declared haughtily. "It will take more than a mere potion to knock me out."

"That's more than just a mere potion," Logan told her.

She fell to her knees.

"It has enough sedative in it to knock out a dragon." Logan looked up at Kai. "No offense, but I don't trust you."

Kai snorted. Smoke puffed out of his nostrils, burning with delicious perfection.

The shadow mage's magic died on her hands, and her head hit the deck. Kai breathed ice onto the ring of flames. Logan jumped over the frozen ring and grabbed the shadow mage. Then, throwing her over his shoulder, he ran up Kai's back.

"You need to watch where you breathe that fire, dragon," Logan said as they took off. He slapped the anti-magic cuffs on the mage. They were sure coming in handy. "That was too close. You nearly burned my hair off."

Kai grunted.

"This isn't funny," Logan said coldly.

A bolt of lightning crashed down, nearly knocking him off Kai's back.

"That wasn't funny either."

But Kai hadn't cast the spell. It had come from the storm. It was once again swirling in the sky, preparing to unleash its dark rain on the world. Kai pumped his wings faster, pushing himself as fast as he could. They had to get the spell caster to Rane.

6. The Shadow Mage

SERA LOOKED UP at the great black dragon flying overhead. Kai. Two smaller figures sat on his back—from the feel of their magic, Logan and the shadow mage. The dragon wasn't the only thing cutting across the sky. The storm was moving again, and it was angry.

Sera, Alex, and Riley had run all the way back to Kai's car, but standing there now, the vehicle seemed so inadequate. And slow. The fog was closing in all around them, freckled with the red glowing eyes of monsters.

"We have to fly," Sera decided.

Amara split out of her the same moment Alex's dragon did the same. Sera didn't waste time. She cast a gust of wind to blow her and Riley onto her dragon's back.

"She's beautiful," Riley commented, patting Amara's shimmering scales as they followed behind Alex's dragon.

Tell him he's your favorite brother, Amara said.

He's my only brother.

That doesn't make it any less true.

"Amara says thank you," Sera said aloud.

"She's a very polite dragon," replied Riley.

Sera threw a smirk over her shoulder. "Well, she is part of me, after all. We share a myriad of excellent qualities."

Ahead of them, Alex and her dragon dropped and spun to avoid a patch of fog.

"That fog looks familiar." Sera's stomach clenched up.

"It's the byproduct of the shadow mage's spell. You can't let it touch you."

"I don't plan on it." Sera stroked Amara's jaw. "Follow Alex's lead, fly where she flies." If anyone could outmaneuver the fog, it was Alex and her daredevil dragon.

Amara dropped and spun, following the same narrow stream around the fog that Alex had taken. She did a double loop, coming up on Alex and her dragon. Alex winked, then they dove straight down.

This is madness, Amara protested, but she followed them.

The fog was rolling in. The narrow patch of clear sky Alex had taken was sealing shut.

"We're not going to make it," Sera said, gripping tightly to her dragon.

Riley stretched out his hand and blasted his shadow magic into the fog. The dark purple particles ruptured and split, dissolving. Amara zigzagged through the uneven gap. Sera glanced back. Behind them, the fog was reforming.

"Merlin is controlling it. He's trying to swallow us," Sera said. "Can you hold him off?"

Riley's face was hard, his expression determined. "The fog won't touch us."

Despite his confident declaration, his magic had little effect on the fog. He blasted it apart, only to find that it reformed almost as quickly as it had dissolved. But that didn't keep him from trying again. And again. And again. His stubborn refusal coupled with some fancy flying from the dragons got them back to Rane and the others. Sera landed just moments after Kai, her dragon returning to her body as Kai shifted back into his.

Rane stood over the shadow mage. She'd anchored the woman to the ground with ropes of sparkling black midnight magic. Rane's spell must have subdued her magic because the storm had frozen once more.

"Where's my car?" Kai asked Sera as Rane muttered a few rapid instructions to Riley. They were getting ready to take on the storm.

"Your car? Oh, I think the monsters got it. That or the fog."

"My cars have a bad history with you," he grumbled.

"What are you talking about? I've never lost any of your cars before."

"Not lost, but the last time you drove my car, monsters tore off one of the doors." He sighed. "I should have known better than to let a monster-hunter behind the wheel."

"Must I remind you that I saved your life that

night? I think that's more precious to you than your car door. And, besides, when we put the world back to the way it was, your cars will be just fine. It will be like none of this ever happened."

"Why do I get the feeling more of my cars will be sacrificed before this is over?"

Smiling, she leaned in and kissed him. "It's a small price to pay for the greater good."

"None of those cars has a small price, sweetheart."

"You will all pay the price for daring to defy the great Merlin," the shadow mage said, her grin viciously happy.

"I wouldn't celebrate yet, dearie," Rane said.

The shadow mage's smile faded.

"Do you know who I am?" Rane asked her.

"A demon," she spat, her beautiful face crinkling up in disgust.

"Yes, that's right. A demon. A hungry, cranky demon whose dinner was interrupted by your ridiculous attempt to muck up the world."

"It's you who will look ridiculous when your spell breaks," the woman shot back. "I can already see it cracking. You can't hold back the storm."

"You're looking rather cracked yourself, dearie, but that's what becomes of people who trust Merlin."

"I heard he cast you aside," she simpered. "How embarrassing."

Rane's smile could have flayed the skin off a cow. "I will make this easy for you. What's your name?"

"Kiara."

"Well, Kiara. I have something for you. A gift, if you will."

Sera had a feeling that Kiara wouldn't like Rane's gift.

So did Kiara. She turned up her nose and said, "I do not accept gifts from dirty demons."

"Dirty?" Rane's eyes boiled like liquid gold. "Dirty, you say?" She waved her hand, casting a silver circle in the air. "This is a magic mirror." She pushed Kiara's face against the glossy surface. "A very special mirror. It has the power to make nightmares come true. Now, I wonder what your greatest nightmare is."

Kiara tried to look away, but Rane held her there, forcing her to meet her reflection. In an instant, her bouncy, golden locks shriveled up. Half of her hair fell out. What remained looked like wet, soggy straw. Her smooth skin bubbled, sprouting pus-filled pustules and fat, hairy warts. The vain woman watched in wide-eyed horror as her youth and beauty melted away. She slammed her fists against the glass, trying to shatter it.

"Make it stop!" she howled.

"Only you can make it stop," Rane replied calmly.

"You!" she snarled. The look on her face was as ugly as the nightmare reflection in the mirror. "You crazy bitch! Put me back!" The nightmare had taken hold over her mind. She didn't even realize that her real face was untouched.

"Now, now, Merlin doesn't like ladies with such foul language."

A string of curses poured out of Kiara's mouth.

"It will be horrible when he casts you aside, leaving you without beauty or magic," Rane said, egging her on.

"Put me back!" Kiara pushed against her restraints,

but they were forged by demon magic and didn't break so easily.

"There will be no place for you on earth," Rane continued with relish. "People will flee in horror of your wretched appearance. You will beg me to kill you, but the torment won't end with your death. I'll throw you into the ninth circle of hell for a century or two. The demons there just *love* snacking on pain and self-loathing."

"I demand that you release me, you demon whore!"

Rane shrugged. "I've been called worse." She brushed her hand across Kiara's face. "These are cursed scars. Only a demon can cure them. Good luck finding another one to do that. But I'll cure you if you do as I say. It's your choice. Stop the spell or live the rest of your life like…this. A monster."

"I'll never help you!" she shrieked.

Sighing, Rane looked at Riley. "Shall we transport her into Merlin's domain now or wait for the pustules to fester?"

"You can't transport me there. Merlin blocked you!"

"Yes, he did. How rude of him, but then manners never were his strong suit." Rane smiled at her. "Merlin might have locked me out, but he didn't block Riley." She gave Riley a little wave. "Be a dear and send her off to Merlin."

"Wait," Kiara said quickly.

Rane braided her fingers together. "All right, I'm waiting. But I won't wait long." She pointed at Kiara's face. "Oh, look. One of the pustules is popping.

Mucus is oozing out."

Kiara snapped her fingers, and just like that, the storm disappeared. The clouds parted, letting in the sun. Trembling from top to bottom, the shadow mage collapsed to her knees.

"Fantastic," Rane said.

"Fix me." Kiara's cheeks were wet with tears. "Make me beautiful again."

"Of course, dearie." She tapped the mirror. "You're cured."

Kiara rose and grasped eagerly at the mirror. Expelling a long sigh of relief, she ran her hand down her smooth cheek.

"There's just one more order of business," Rane said.

She pulled out a knife and stabbed Kiara in the chest. The shadow mage coughed out a final breath, then dropped to the ground. And just like that, she was dead.

Sera looked down at the dead mage in horror. "Why did you do that?"

"She made her bed when she took Merlin's," replied Rane.

Sera met the demon's inhuman eyes. "You cursed her, threatened her. She did what you wanted, and you still killed her."

"She would have cast the spell again when she was safely away from me. Now she can't," Rane said. "She knew what she was doing, Sera. She knew she'd destroy lives when she cast that spell, and she did it anyway. She doesn't care about them. She doesn't care about anyone except herself. She would have let the world burn and the Dragon Born die. Your people, your family."

"I…" Sera didn't even know what to say.

"The only way you're going to win against Merlin is by being smarter, by being more cunning and vicious than your opponent," Rane told her. "Love won't see you through this, dearie. Not this time. There are darker forces at work here."

"But if we act like that, we're no better than they are," Sera protested.

"Of course I'm no better than they are. Have you forgotten what I am?"

"You're different."

"Not *that* different. I'm a demon, little girl. Demons don't have a conscience. And we eat people. It's in all the fairy tales, so it must be true. Stop seeing me as a good person. I'm an evil, vindictive, vengeful demon. I'm not helping you for the greater good. I don't give a shit about the greater good. I'm helping you because I need you so I can get back at Merlin. And you need me. It's a match made in hell, and I'm not lying just to make you feel better about it."

"And I'm not ok with that," Sera retorted.

"The world is at stake. Your world. You'd better get ok with it real fast. Sometimes you have to make the hard choices. Accept that or get out of the game."

"We've defeated evil before without embracing darkness."

Rane let out a low hiss. "The luck of fools never ceases to astound me."

"And yet somehow, the soullessness of demons doesn't surprise me at all."

Rane's eyes were hard and unfeeling. "Sarcasm suits you, but try not to pile it on too thick or it will cover that sweet, naive little scent the dragon shifter finds so delectable."

"Get to the point, demon," Alex snapped, wrapping her arm around Sera.

Sera squeezed her sister in silent thanks.

"I already have. The point is you have to be willing to do what it takes. And *whatever* it takes," Rane said. "If you aren't prepared to go all the way, then the spell will never be broken. This Shadow World will remain."

"How do we stop the spell that was already cast?" Alex asked. "Can Riley undo it? Kiara undid hers."

"No, once cast, a spell like this cannot be taken back. We were only able to shatter Kiara's spell because she was still in the middle of casting it."

"So you knew she could reverse it?" Sera asked.

"No, I didn't. But there was at least a fifty percent chance that she could."

"You cursed her for a fifty percent chance?" Sera gasped.

"Again, I'm a demon. D-E-M-O-N. I curse people for giggles. When are you people going to realize that?"

"Let's just concentrate on getting our world back. Do you have any ideas?" Kai asked Rane.

The demon nodded in approval. "I like you, shifter. You're pragmatic. You don't waste time weeping over collateral damage."

Sera wondered how much it would hurt to punch a demon.

"You need to know the spell's recipe," Rane said. "Once we know how Merlin designed it, we can reverse it."

"Riley cast it. Maybe he remembers," Alex suggested.

"Unfortunately not," replied Rane. "I've tried sifting through Riley's memories already, but Merlin just used him as a conduit. Your brother has no knowledge of the spell."

"You really don't know anything?" Sera asked him. She wasn't about to take a demon's word for it.

"No."

"Well, spells have loopholes, don't they? We need to find what it is and exploit it," Sera said.

Rane nodded. "You're smarter than you look, Dragon Born. And you're exactly right. I think I have just the thing to expose the spell's weakness."

7. Dinner in the Demon's Den

THEY RETURNED TO Rane's domain. While the demon and Riley prepared her mystery plan to learn the secret behind Merlin's spell, Sera and Kai had a long overdue dinner date in their apartment inside Rane's castle. Sera couldn't say which she'd been looking forward to more: the dinner or the date. On the one hand, she was famished. On the other, she and Kai hadn't had a quiet moment together since their world had been thrown into shadow.

"The food actually looks normal," Sera commented, poking the pizza on her plate. "In fact..." She took a bite from one of the slices. "It tastes a lot like the pizza from Wizard House Pizza." She took another bite. "No, scratch that. It tastes *exactly* like the pizza from Wizard House Pizza. But they don't exist in the Shadow World, and I'm pretty sure they don't have a restaurant in hell. What magic is this?"

"You're overthinking it," Kai said, taking a bite

from his steak. "Just eat and enjoy."

"You're right." Sera quickly ate four slices. But as her tummy grew content, her mind kicked into high gear. "It's demon magic. It must be. Do you think she's trying to drug us?"

"No." Kai was already on his second steak. Shifting into a dragon twice today had really taken its toll on him.

"Bewitch us?"

"No." He nudged the carrots with his fork, pushing them to the side of his plate to make more room for the meat.

"I just can't shake this feeling that Rane is up to—"

"You're doing that overthinking thing again," Kai told her.

"Oh." She picked up another slice of pizza. "Sorry."

"You need to relax, Sera. Seriously. Rane is no angel, but for the moment, our interests are aligned."

"Of course. I'm sorry."

"Don't be sorry. Just eat your pizza and be happy."

"Be happy, you say? That would be easier if I had some chocolate."

"I'll see what I can do."

Sera caught his hand as he rose. "No, wait. I was just kidding. I'd rather you stay here with me than go off on a chocolate hunt."

"As you wish." He lifted his wine glass to her.

"Does wine even go with pizza?" she asked, clinking glasses with him.

"According to you, pizza goes with everything."

"According to me, yes. But maybe—just maybe—

I'm not a culinary connoisseur. I also consider chocolate and pizza to be the two most important food groups, followed closely by smoothies, of course."

"As long as you don't try to tell me peanut butter is a food group too."

"Don't be silly. Peanut butter is an accessory."

"Like a sword?"

"No, a sword is a main dish. Peanut butter is like a...scabbard. Yeah, a scabbard. Peanut butter goes with everything. Crackers, toast, ice cream."

Kai made a face. "I think I'm going to be sick."

She frowned at him. "No, you're not. You can eat raw meat. You have an iron stomach."

He chuckled.

"Are you messing with me, Kai Drachenburg?"

"I'd never do such a thing."

"You *are* messing with me. Well, just you wait. When we're married, I'm going to fill our pantry with jars and jars of peanut butter. I'll put it into your pancakes, your pie, your bread."

"It's a good thing you can't make any of those things."

Sera continued, "I swear I will make a peanut butter lover out of you yet."

"Sera, I'll tell you what. I will try your strange nut butter if you try live goat."

"Yuck. That's not the same at all."

"You're right. It's not the same. You are a dragon. Dragons catch their dinner and eat it while it's still twitching. It's natural. On the other hand, there's nothing natural about eating pureed peanuts out of a jar."

"That's where we'll have to agree to disagree. In fact, I believe that's one of the cornerstones of a good marriage."

Kai sighed. "What have I gotten myself into?"

"I love you too, honey." She blew him a kiss. "But are you sure you can handle me and Alex?"

"What do you mean?"

"Alex told me you tried to hire her."

"I have a lot of monsters that need catching."

Sera grinned at him. "You know I want to have my sister working with me again. That's why you're doing this."

"Yes."

"I stand by what I just said. I'm not sure you can handle both me and Alex working for you. We're twice the fun together."

"I've tasked Tony with making sure you behave."

"You know that task is impossible. Poor Tony."

"You shouldn't feel too bad for him," Kai said. "I finally agreed to put in that swimming pool in the office that the commandos want. The guys have been nagging me about it for years."

"Wow. They must be happy."

"They know I'm doing it because of you. I think they love you even more now than they did before."

"It never hurts to earn extra brownie points with the commandos. You know, for when I need favors." She wiggled her eyebrows up and down.

"I know it was you who convinced them to replace the proper energy bars in my desk at work with lady bars."

"I would never…" Sera coughed. "…do such a

thing."

He gave her a hard look.

"I was doing you a favor," she told him.

"Oh, really?" He folded his arms across his chest. "And how is that?"

"Your energy bars taste like sawdust glued together with sludge. And you go through how many a day? Two? Three?"

"Six."

Sera gawked at him.

"I burn a lot of calories," he said with a slow, easy shrug of his shoulders. His muscles shifted deliciously under his shirt.

"Right," Sera said, licking her lips. "So, the bars. The 'lady' bars have all the same nutrients as your man bars, but they actually taste good."

"They have flowers on the wrapper."

"What if they had dragons or manly warriors on the wrapper?"

"Better."

Laughing, Sera took another bite of pizza. "Speaking of manly warriors, Alex also said you asked Logan to come work for you."

"She made it clear that she and her assassin are a package deal."

"My sister drives a hard bargain."

"It runs in the family."

"Oh, I don't know," said Sera. "I'm so relaxed and easygoing. You only needed to offer me an armory closet to convince me to come work for you. Plus you pay better than Simmons." She chewed on her lip. "Why didn't I come work for you earlier?"

"Because you were afraid of diving in."

"I'm not afraid now." She brushed her leg against his under the table. "If I'm doomed, at least I'll go down with you."

Fire flared up in Kai's eyes. He reached over and took her hand, stroking small, deep circles into her skin. That knocked her pulse up a gear. Her heart was thumping so hard that her body buzzed—or was that his magic?

His magic crashed hard against hers, drowning her in rapids of liquid fire. Her mind drifted back to the fairies' hideout, back to their battle against the desire raging between them, against that magnetic magic drawing them ever closer.

Sera stopped, sliding back into her chair. What had possessed her to climb onto the table?

She cleared her throat. Clearing her head proved far more difficult. She focused on the painting of hell hanging on the wall behind Kai. Anything to not look at him. If she did, she might not be able to control herself. Magic burned deep inside of her—magic and an unhealthy dose of lust. She had to focus on fixing the spell Merlin had made. They didn't have time for sex.

Sure you do. We're still waiting on Riley and Rane. You have plenty of time.

You're a bad influence, Sera told her dragon.

I'm not the one fantasizing about burning Kai's clothes off.

Shit. Sera cleared her throat again. "I'm glad you and Logan are getting along better," she said quickly. "A double date would be awkward if you're trying to kill each other, you know."

"I wouldn't say we're getting along," Kai replied.

"Maybe you two should go out drinking together. Or watch sports. Or work on cars. That's what men do, right?"

He gave her an amused look. "What do you actually know about men?"

"I know about you. And that's all that matters."

His tongue traced his lower lip with delicious slowness. "There's no one in the world like you."

"Is that a good thing?"

"A very good thing." His voice was dark, seductive.

"Yeah, I guess it means you can't replace me."

His hand closed around her wrist. "Never."

Sera rose, leading him to the sofa. There was no point it pretending they were going to finish their dinner. The food was already cold.

"So what do you really know about me?" he said.

"That you like meat. And you don't consider chocolate a food group. The fact that I love you in spite of that speaks droves about the quality of your character."

Kai lowered to the sofa, motioning her forward. "No more jokes, Sera."

"I know I love you." She lowered onto his lap, her thighs hugging his hips. "Besides, I know all about dragons."

Kai gave her a hard tug, pulling her in closer. His mouth dipped to her neck. "Do tell," he whispered against her skin.

She shuddered. "Dragons are hard and tough on the outside, but warm and soft on the inside."

"Yes." His hand caressed her thigh with maddening slowness. "You are."

"Thanks for trying to hire Alex," Sera said, trying to keep her voice steady as his hands slid beneath her top, plunging down her back. "I know you don't really have enough monsters to need both of us *and* Logan *and* the commandos."

It was just the two of them there, and no one else. Nothing else.

"Actually, I was thinking of a better use for you and Alex."

His lips came down hard on hers. Heat flashed through her veins, igniting her blood, making every inch of her body pulse with denied need. She clawed at his back, pulling him in with a desperation that bordered on madness. She let out a painful, wretched moan when he surfaced.

"Don't you want to know my grand plan?" he asked, mischief twinkling in his eyes.

"Unless your plan involves removing all your clothes, no, I'm not interested."

"Ever since the moment I saw you on Sunset Tower three days ago, I've wanted you. You can't imagine how many times I've thought about taking what I wanted."

His voice rumbled with a desire so dark, so deliciously primal, that she could scarcely resist the temptation to pin him to the sofa with her magic.

"I can wait a little longer," he said. "Can't you? This is important."

"Tell me," she said, her voice cracking.

"You and your sister will be the Magic Council's

new supernatural enforcers. You will of course catch monsters, but your second role is to track down misbehaving supernaturals."

"So basically what I did when I was working for Mayhem."

"Except the pay is better."

"And the boss is hotter."

Kai arched his brows. "I'll be sure to let Tony know you think he's hot."

His tone was casual, his aura wicked. Sera gasped as his magic trickled down her ribs, sliding between her thighs.

"Tony will be in charge? Not you?"

"Tony will report to me." The corner of his mouth quirked up. "Disappointed?"

"He is an excellent commando." She caught his lower lip between her teeth, tugging gently.

He groaned in approval. "Yes."

She shot him a sly smile. "You could have put me in charge."

Kai choked on the suggestion.

"Or would you prefer Alex?" she asked.

"The Black Plague in charge?"

"Logan?"

"No."

"Maybe we could take turns being in charge," she suggested. "That would be fun."

"Sweetheart, I don't think you understand how a hierarchy works."

"Then please educate me. I'm dying to know." She pulled off her shirt, tossing it over the back of the sofa. "Am I on top of you or under you?"

He surged forward, their bodies crashing together. "We can take turns," he whispered against her lips. "That would be fun."

8. Mirror, Mirror

KAI STEPPED OUT of the apartment with Sera, their hands linked. Every few steps, she looked up and shot him a grin that seemed to light up the dark corridor. Kai meant what he'd said before: there really was no one in the world like Sera.

A door opened, and Logan glided into the hallway. "Rane and Riley are about to perform a spell in the grand hall."

Alex slid into step beside Sera. "Hey, there."

"Hi."

Alex's eyes darted from Kai to her. "You had sex."

A rosy blush tinted Sera's cheeks.

"It's so cute that you still need to blush when we talk about this," Alex said with a smirk.

"Do we *need* to talk about this?" Logan asked her.

Alex threw a look over her shoulder. "No one is forcing you to listen."

"Supernatural senses, remember, darling? I can't

not listen. Much as I'd prefer not to hear the play-by-play of Drachenburg's bedroom activities."

Alex winked at him. Then, grabbing Sera's hand, she sped up to put some distance between them and the guys.

Kai and Logan walked side-by-side in silence. Ahead of them, the sisters were laughing about something. It was so good to see Sera like this. She and Alex were happiest when together. Logan was watching Alex closely, as though he'd come to the same conclusion. He was wearing something resembling an expression on his face. Maybe he was thinking about Kai's offer.

They all entered the grand hall of Rane's castle. Like everything else in the demon's domain, the central chamber of her castle changed to suit her mood. Today, it was a hall of mirrors. The shiny surfaces covered every wall, floor to ceiling, an infinite loop of reflections. At the center of the room, Rane waited with Riley, the demon and the apprentice.

"Come," Rane said, waving them forward.

Kai and the others crossed the black marble floor, following the gold rings to the demon parked at its core.

"Riley and I are going to tap into the memories of the past," she explained.

"Whose memories?" Sera asked.

"Merlin's."

"I thought he was blocking you," Alex said.

"I cannot enter his realm, nor can I look into it. But the memories we'll be looking at played out long ago, before he withdrew into his domain. They are not beyond my reach."

"The spell he designed to create the Shadow World didn't happen long ago. It happened just a few days ago," Kai pointed out.

"His first spell and this one aren't all that different. In fact, they're linked by Merlin's magic. I'm hoping we can hijack that magical link to catch a glimpse of his Shadow World spell."

"Hope is a human emotion," Sera commented.

"Yes, and a human failing. But right now, it's all we've got."

Rane waved at the closest mirror, and her reflections carried her spell across the room. Swirls of black and purple magic, interspersed with streams of gold glitter, twisted and twirled, coalescing into cyclones.

A memory not his own hit Kai. And then another. And another. They were flashing past so fast that one had barely arrived before the next one pushed it out.

He saw Riley casting the Shadow World spell. Merlin grabbed Riley, thrusting his hand against his chest, infusing him with shadow magic.

A moment later, it wasn't Riley before Merlin anymore; it was Arianna. Her body was fading, her mind fleeing. A tear between realities opened up, and Merlin pulled his sister through it.

Kai blinked, and Arianna was gone. Merlin stood alone, his hands raised in the air, a storm brewing overhead. The original spell, that which he'd cast seven hundred years ago to change the world. The memories were speeding by in reverse order.

And then the rush of images stopped, frozen at one

distinct moment in time. Kai stood inside a dark shed, a wood workbench in front of him. Glass beakers filled one end of the table, pots and scales the other. Pale gold smoke bubbled out of the biggest of them. Kai tried to move in for a closer look, but his body refused to obey. He felt himself lift his hand and scoop up a spoonful of dark powder from one of the metal canisters on the table. As he poured it into the gurgling potion, he caught a glimpse of himself in the mirror.

Kai wasn't watching Merlin. He *was* Merlin—a younger, happier version of the shadow mage who'd destroyed the world. This must be Merlin's past. After Kai broke free of this memory, he was going to have a little chat with Rane about sticking his mind into the body of a psychopath. The fact that he couldn't control his body was only half as disturbing as hearing Merlin's thoughts inside his mind.

The door to the shed creaked, and a teenage girl entered, a basket dangling from her arm. Her hair, braided on top of her head, was as red as the sunset, her eyes as green as a meadow in springtime.

"Bianca!" Merlin said, grinning. "You've come just in time."

Returning the grin, the girl joined him at the table. "What great magical discovery have you made today?"

Merlin held out his arm, showing her the nasty burn blistering his skin.

"What happened? How did you burn yourself? Are you all right?" she asked.

Merlin pulled a ladle out of the bubbling potion, dumping its contents across his arm.

"What on earth are you doing?" she shrieked.

"It's quite cool, I assure you." He took her hand and slid it across the hard shell of dried golden mud caking his arm. The shell cracked, revealing smooth skin underneath.

"Your wound has healed," she gasped. "But how is this possible? You're not a healer."

"No longer do we require healing spells to make us whole again." He held up a potion vial. "We need only the magical sciences."

"What else can you heal?"

"Poisons and plagues, bones and burns—the sky is the limit, Bianca."

She smiled proudly at him. When he saw that look in her eyes, he was happy beyond measure. They'd grown up side-by-side, best friends. If only she knew how desperately he loved her… He dropped his hand to the drawer beneath the table. Inside, beneath notebooks of potion recipes, lay the necklace he'd spent months crafting from the magic emeralds he'd grown in his lab. A sign of his affection, a token of his love. His hand closed around the drawer handle.

The door to the shed swung open once more, and a man paraded inside. The people of their village called him a hero. The Dragon Born mage Varius. Their special golden boy had long, gold hair and eyes that shone like sapphires. His tan was as dark as his hair was light, and his body was built like that of an ancient god. Some people even considered him a god.

"Bianca," Varius said silkily. "Your father told me I would find you here."

Bianca turned to look at him, and that's when

Merlin saw something in her eyes that froze his heart. The look she gave him put the one she'd given Merlin to shame. She didn't just adore Varius; she worshipped him.

"You don't mind if I take your friend for a walk, do you?" The Dragon Born mage winked at Merlin, like they were sharing some great secret.

Bianca was already putting on her shawl. "Farewell!" she called out to Merlin. Then, linking her arm with Varius's, she left the shed without so much as a backward glance.

Merlin cleaned up his experiments in silent solitude. There was nothing better than work to take your mind off of life, but this time even a busy body couldn't calm his tumultuous mind. It did, however, pass the hours. By the time he left his lab, the sun was setting on the day. Merlin set off down the lakeside path to Bianca's house. He had to tell her how he felt. Now, before it was too late.

But he was already too late.

He heard Bianca's voice further down the trail, drawing him in. He kicked off into a run—and then just stopped. She wasn't alone. Varius walked beside her, stroking her hand.

"Tell me, dearest, how you feel about me," said the Dragon Born mage.

"Why, I love you, of course," replied Bianca.

"And there's no one else?"

"Who else would there be?"

"Your friend, the mixer of potions."

"Merlin?" Bianca's laugh shattered Merlin's heart. "He is just a friend. I could never see him in *that* way."

"Good." Varius set his hands on her cheeks and leaned in to kiss her softly on the lips.

Merlin pivoted around and hurried back the way he'd come. He didn't stop running until he'd barged into his lab.

"What I need right now is a good love potion," he muttered, his hands shaking.

Except love potions didn't work. Even he had never been able to produce a viable one. Love was too powerful—too complex—to produce with magic. There had to be another way.

Bianca *did* love him. He knew she did. He just had to make her see it. But how could he hope to do that when Varius was around? How was he supposed to compete with a Dragon Born mage? Varius was so perfect. So charming. So handsome. So *powerful*. He was every girl's dream lover, and Merlin was so… ordinary. He looked in the mirror, and didn't like what he saw. Well, he was going to change that.

There was no power on earth that could compare to that of the Dragon Born, but perhaps in another realm… He'd read about a great and powerful demon named Rane. She had the power to change the world, to bend the very fabric of reality to her will. That was a power greater than any on earth or in hell. It was greater than even the Dragon Born possessed.

"And I'm going to convince her to teach me," Merlin muttered.

He set off into the mountains with only a bag of potions. It took an hour to get there—and twice that long to set up the magic to summon the demon to him. She stepped out of the mist, her silver hair fluttering majestically in the wind.

She looked down on him with icy blue eyes. "Do you not realize how foolish it is to summon a demon, mortal?"

"But you aren't like other demons," he replied.

"What do you know of me?"

"Only that you are the greatest, most powerful of all the demons."

"Go on."

"No one can come close to your power. But it is your grace that really sets you apart."

"You flatter well, dearie," she told him. "What is it that you want?"

"I wish to serve you. To be your loyal servant. And your student." He lifted his gaze to gauge her reaction.

"I have no need for servants or students."

"Isn't it lonely by yourself?"

"I enjoy my privacy in my castle."

"I know how you feel," he said. "I know how it feels to get caught up in your great work. You're always so close to your next revelation. You just have to finish it. And then when you do, another fantastic experiment calls to you. You are always working, always pouring everything you have into your work. There's no time for anyone else. Then, one day, you realize you are alone. But it's too late."

"Yes," she said quietly. "Exactly that. Perhaps you *do* understand. Who have you lost?"

"My friend Bianca. I've loved her since I can remember. I was so busy working that I didn't notice I was losing her, that she'd fallen for another." A tear rolled down his cheek.

"You'd best dry your face. There are no tears where we're going."

He looked up, hope filling him, chipping away at the hard icicle that had incased his heart. "You're taking me with you?"

"We will leave at once."

She waved her hand, opening a rift in reality, the shortcut to her realm. Merlin entered a dark and dreary domain. Scenes flashed past Kai's eyes.

The months passed. As Merlin and Rane worked together, her castle grew brighter. Even cheerful. His power was growing. He was transforming into something else, embarking upon a journey no mortal had ever taken.

The months stretched into years, but Merlin never forgot Bianca. And he never stopped loving her, even as his relationship with Rane turned intimate. Afterwards, in the minutes before the demon kicked him out of her bed, she shared many secrets. Merlin collected every drop of knowledge, every spell. And then one day while she was out, Merlin left. He'd finally gained the power to travel across realms, the final piece in the shadow magic puzzle.

He went to his village, surprising his parents and sister. But it was Bianca that his heart longed to see; it was Bianca he longed to hold. He would confess his love to her, and then they would live happily ever after, just as things had always meant to be.

"Merlin?" Bianca said, standing in surprise as he entered her house. She'd grown even more beautiful since he'd seen her last. "Where have you been all these years?"

"Studying with a great master of magic."

Bianca's gaze panned up his body. "You've changed."

Yes, he had. He'd spent three years challenging himself with daily exercises, and his body had reaped the benefits. The admiration in her eyes was reward enough. She saw him as a man now, not as the weak boy who'd wasted away inside of a dark shed.

"I've missed you, Bianca." He took her face in his hands, dipping his head to grace her lips with his kiss.

"Stop." She pushed against his hold.

"I have waited far too long for this moment," he said, holding her steady. "And I will wait no longer. Let us share a long-overdue kiss, my love."

A surge of lightning cut across his arms, and he pulled away. But it wasn't the physical pain that cut him deep. The magic of this realm could hurt him no longer. He had transcended it. No, he pulled away in confusion. Why had his love struck him?

"I love another," she told him.

"Let me guess. The town's hero. The great Dragon Born god," Merlin hissed.

"Varius is not a god. He's a man. A good man. And I love him. We're to be married next month."

"No." The word came out as a low snarl. "It wasn't supposed to happen this way. You were supposed to love me. I am more powerful than he is."

Merlin waved his hand. Smoke swallowed him. He reappeared a moment later on the other side of the room.

"It's not just about the power," Bianca said. "It's about the man beneath it. The man I love."

"I never should have left you here with him. He's a fraud. They're all frauds, every last one of them. The Dragon Born came down from their mighty mountain, claiming to be gods, but they are nothing but tricksters."

"You cannot blame Varius for the actions of a few bored Dragon Born mages who died long before he was born."

"Oh, that's not all I'm blaming him for," Merlin said, snatching her by the wrist. He opened a rift between realms. "You will see. Once you're free of him, your mind will clear."

He began to pull her toward the rift. The door to the house flew off its hinges, and Varius stomped inside, lit up with a flaming halo. Magic burst out of his hands, chomping down on the portal. Merlin's spell popped and fizzled out.

"You," Merlin growled.

"The lady does not wish to go with you. I suggest you unhand her at once."

"You are in no position to make demands."

Merlin shot a bundle of pitch-black magic at Varius. The Dragon Born rolled out of the way.

"I've never seen anything like it," Bianca gasped, watching the shadows dissolve.

"I have. It's shadow magic." Varius glared at Merlin. "You are a demon's thrall."

"I am no one's thrall," Merlin said, launching another attack.

Bianca jumped into its path. The shadows wrapped around her body, swallowing her in a black web. The dark threads covered every pore, every opening. She thrashed wildly on the ground, trying to suck in air that couldn't reach her. Merlin ran toward her, but Varius cut him off.

"You've done enough," the Dragon Born said, then threw him back with a magic-shattering punch.

Merlin jumped to his feet. Varius had already broken Bianca free from the shadow web. He knelt beside her, holding her hand, stroking her cheek. The sight of them together sent Merlin over the edge. He strode forward, shadows rising up around him. He was going to send that Dragon Born pest somewhere he'd never return from.

Varius's friend, the Spirit Warrior, charged into the house, opening up a doorway to hell.

"For the protection of everyone, we must send you away, Merlin," Varius declared.

A wind funnel sprouted from the ground. It struck out at Merlin, but he was faster. He evaded it easily. He didn't see the rope of spirit magic lying across the floor. It coiled around Merlin's ankle, hurling him into hell.

"We'll just see about that," he said as the portal snapped shut.

Purple storm clouds rolled overhead, swallowing the red skies of hell. Merlin opened a magic tunnel to earth and poured the storm through it. The Dragon Born were a menace, a plague on this world. Hate cut through him, boiling his blood as he wove the spell to change reality. He would create a world that despised them as much as he did. He followed the stream of fog gushing through the rift.

Kai slipped out of Merlin's body. As the memory

faded, a few final moments flashed before his eyes. He saw the world shift in an instant. Merlin stepped into Bianca's house, a bouquet of lilies in his hands. The bouquet slipped from his fingers when he saw her—with Varius. Even in this world, they'd found each other, just as Kai and Sera had found each other.

"How can you still love him in this world?" Merlin demanded.

But she wasn't moving. She lay still in Varius's arms as he wept over her dead body. The roof was torn off the building, and a squadron of mages jumped down. Varius picked up her body and ran off, blasting through the window.

"Stop the abomination!" one of the mages called out.

Merlin withdrew from the world he'd created, agony carrying him along to his own personal hell.

9. Spirit Magic

AS THE MEMORIES faded back into the mirrors, Sera turned to Kai. His magic was erratic, unsettled—as though what he'd seen had cut him deep.

"Are you all right?" she asked.

"I experienced the memories as if I were Merlin."

That explained his rocky aura. Sera had only seen the scene unfold from a distance, as though it were playing on a television screen.

Kai looked at Rane. "Why was it different than the other time you used the magic mirrors?"

"The memories don't always reveal themselves in the same way," replied the demon.

"I could feel his anger. That insatiable rage. That's what drove him to cast the first spell. That's what still lives on in him now."

"I felt something different from him: heartbreak. And agony at losing his love," Sera said. She hadn't been inside of Merlin's head, but she'd felt the emotional ups and downs of his magic surely enough.

"Not just pain. Also guilt," Alex added. "I think that's driving his actions too."

Sera nodded. "He thinks if he can just figure out how to change the world in the right way, that pain will go away. That's what led him to go after the Dragon Born."

"He turned the world against us because he couldn't stand to see us being the heroes."

Logan set his hand on Alex's shoulder. "Every Dragon Born mage he sees reminds him of the woman he lost."

"He's lost his mind," Alex said.

"Grief will do that to someone," Sera told her.

Alex's magic hiccuped with annoyance. "I hope you're not excusing him."

"No. I didn't excuse him when I thought this was about saving his sister, and I certainly won't excuse a vicious vendetta. He will pay for what he's done." Sera unclenched her fists. "We didn't see how he cast the second spell."

"No," Rane said, frowning. "I thought we could access it through its link to his first spell, but it would appear he's taken precautions to block that back door into the memory."

"That's why the memories got all jumpy at the end?" Sera asked.

"Yes."

"What happened after he fled Bianca's house?" Kai asked her.

"I confronted him in his domain. He threw an epic temper tantrum, and then performed the ritual to expel me from his realm. I didn't even know he knew that one. It's an obscure spell. He must have found it in my library. I gave him too much freedom."

"That's a rather short summary," commented Alex.

"Do you want a play-by-play of everywhere I stabbed him?" Rane asked, grinning.

Alex mirrored her grin. "Maybe you can draw a picture."

"We can color pictures later." Sera looked at Riley. "Are you sure you don't remember anything about the Shadow World spell Merlin made you cast?"

"No."

"His magic must have left a trace somewhere."

"Merlin was thorough at cleaning up," Riley said grimly.

"No breadcrumbs to follow?"

"Not a single crumb."

"So where does this leave us?" Alex asked.

"In order to break Merlin's spell, we need to know how he cast it. All the conditions, the fine print, and the escape clauses," Rane told them. "You have to get me the spell's recipe."

"Merlin must keep the spell book in his castle," said Logan.

"Yes, in his castle's museum no doubt," Rane agreed.

"How do you know he has a museum?" Sera asked her. "And that the spell book is in it?"

"Merlin came to me seeking power because he felt helpless. Even though he now possesses more power than any other mortal will ever have, deep down he is still that insecure boy. He flaunts his magic, making a big show of it. He has a grand castle. A throne. He is the emperor of many worlds in his domain. Where better than a museum to flaunt his greatest magic?"

"I'm impressed."

"Don't look so surprised. Just because I'm not human doesn't mean I don't understand your psychology."

Rane was indeed an usual demon. If only she could get her moral compass aligned, she would be a great ally.

"So it looks like we're headed off again to Merlin's castle," Alex said.

"Have you forgotten what happened the last time we infiltrated Merlin's fortress?" Logan asked her.

"You mean Merlin expelling us into the middle of a magic storm?" Alex scowled. "Yeah, kind of hard to forget that."

"This time we need to do it differently, not so directly. I'm going to do a little reconnaissance."

"Good idea. I'm coming with you."

"I need to be stealthy. And," Logan added. "You're not stealthy."

"Fine." She waved him off. "Go. I'll be waiting here blowing things up in my utterly non-stealthy way."

"Not in my house, you don't." Rane puffed out her chest in indignation. "Take your explosions outside."

Riley fell into step beside Logan. "I hope you're not going to take issue with me coming along."

"No."

"Does that mean you think I'm stealthy?"

"It means you are the only person who can transport me to Merlin's domain," Logan told him.

"We'll work on the stealthy part."

"Aww," Alex said to Sera as Riley and Logan left. "They're bonding."

"We're going to be one big, happy family."

Lara entered the room with the commandos.

"Looks like the rest of the family has arrived," Alex said.

"How is it you're so badass?" Lara asked the commandos as they stopped beside Sera and Alex.

"It's from hanging out with your brother," Dal declared, raising his voice.

Across the room, Kai's mouth twitched, but he continued his hushed conversation with Rane.

"Kiss ass," Callum muttered.

"I'd love to see how you work in action," Lara continued, shining a bright smile at the commandos. "First-hand."

"Kai told us not to bring you along when we go on missions. He says you're too reckless," said Tony.

"Well, if you don't come with me, I'll just have to go out alone. To where there are monsters. Lots and lots of monsters. Imagine how reckless that would be."

Tony looked at Dal and Callum. "You see what she's doing here, guys?"

Dal nodded. "Yes, and I have a feeling we're being manipulated."

Alex snickered. "If you guys won't bring Lara along, Sera and I will. She's cool."

Lara grinned at her.

"I have a feeling she's going to get us into a lot of trouble," Sera told her sister.

Alex shrugged. "No more trouble than I get us

into."

"True."

A sliver of glistening purple magic split open the air, and Riley and Logan tumbled out of the rift. Riley slashed his hand across the whistling opening, rolling it up like a sticky car window. The rift belched a sulfur snowflake, then vanished.

"That was fast," Sera commented.

"Guards are posted at all of the entrances to Merlin's castle," Logan said, wiping the blood from his knife.

"There's no way we can get in unnoticed," Riley added. "And we don't have enough power to take the castle in a direct assault."

"How about an indirect assault?" Sera suggested.

Logan shook his head. "As I said, all ways in and out of Merlin's castle are heavily guarded."

"Not *all* ways."

"Oh. Right. Great idea." Alex gave Sera's back an affectionate slap. "We need Naomi's help."

"How can Naomi help?" Lara asked.

"Because she's a Spirit Warrior. She can travel between earth and the spirit realm," Sera told her. "Merlin's domain isn't completely different from ours. It has two sides: the earth and the spirit realm. That means there must be a flow of magic between them. Naomi can find us a way in through the spirit realm. And I'm willing to bet that entrance to Merlin's castle is unguarded."

◆ ◇ ◆ ◇ ◆

Sera and Alex returned to the Dragon Born base. The fight was over, but the echoes of battle lingered on. The air had grown cold, even frosty. It was as though the world knew the end was near—that soon the Shadow World would either disappear or last forever. Smoke wafted up from the burning trees and buildings all across the base's grounds. Arianna and Vivienne were helping Makani's soldiers put out the fires. Streams of water magic shot out from them in every direction like a fountain, drowning the crackling flames. The fires hissed in protest, and then melted into smoke.

Wounded supernaturals who'd fought on either side were strewn across the battleground. Healing mages hurried from one fallen soldier to the next, bringing them back from the brink of death. The less dire cases were healed with the help of potions. How ironic that Merlin had invented the world's first healing potions. He'd certainly fallen a long way from there.

Sera walked with Alex past dead and dying soldiers, her eyes burning. So much death and destruction on both sides—and for what? Because of hate. That hate tainted the air, thick and heavy. It clogged her throat and choked her breath. It made her sick to her stomach.

"Sera?" a Dragon Guard fairy said. "Are you all right?"

"None of us are all right." She swept her hand through the air, indicating the world dying all around her. "Where's Naomi?"

"I'll go find her." The fairy bowed, then ran off.

Sera felt something burning a hole through the back of her head and turned around to find it was just Blackbrooke glaring at her.

"How can you still hate us?" she demanded, marching up to him. "Look around. Haven't you seen how hate has torn this world apart?"

"I see that this world has too many Dragon Born in it."

"I think the point is lost on him," Alex said.

"I fear you're right."

"What do you want?" Blackbrooke shot back. "For us to be best friends?"

"Sorry, no. We don't love haters," Alex told him.

"What we want is for you to see what's going on here," Sera said. "Merlin is destroying the world and everyone in it. And all because he cannot let go of his hate for the Dragon Born. Nothing is important to him except wiping us out. Nothing. He is the whole reason you and the other supernaturals hate us. Don't you see? He changed the world to make you hunt us."

"He doesn't care about anything or anyone. Just like *you*," Alex hissed at him.

"No, I don't think he's that far gone." Sera looked at Blackbrooke. "What matters to you?"

"Order. The world must have order. Without order, without rules, everything falls apart."

"You can have that without hurting anyone. Without hating," Sera told him.

"The Dragon Born do not fit inside any order. Your magic, your existence, defies definition. Twins who were born as one, each one with a mage and a dragon half. Two bodies, four minds, one soul. The math doesn't add up. And don't even get me started on your ability to break magic. You break down order. Your existence destroys it."

"Magic works in beautiful and unusual ways," replied Sera. "Our magic is different. So is shadow magic. That doesn't fit neatly into one of your boxes either. Just because you can't make sense of something, that doesn't mean it has no sense. Maybe you should realize that you cannot stuff things into boxes."

"Such are the words of an anarchist," he said, horrified.

Sera sighed.

"Don't bother with him," Alex told her. "He has no imagination. He can't make sense of anything that's not spelled out for him. I don't trust him. Not one bit."

"Don't trust me then. I don't care. I don't trust you either." Blackbrooke glowered at her. "Be that as it may, for the moment we're stuck with one another."

"You won't betray us?" Sera asked.

"I will make no move against you until this spell is broken or settled, one way or another."

Sera didn't fail to notice that he hadn't actually answered her question—at least not in full. Even so, even despite his wretched personality, he was too proud to go back on his word. Kai had an arrangement with him, a temporary truce. He wouldn't break it. It was what he would do after they defeated Merlin that they all needed to worry about.

"Sera!" the Dragon Guard fairy called out.

She turned, watching him cross the battlefield to her. But he was alone.

"Where's Naomi?" she asked him.

"I asked around. Apparently, she disappeared shortly after the battle. Some of the Crusaders got her. Makani went after them."

Alex pivoted around, steel singing. She pressed the edge of her blade to Blackbrooke's neck. "Your soldiers have my friend."

"Not by my orders."

"You are going to call them back here." She reached into his pocket, fishing out his phone. She tossed it at his face. "Now."

"I tried as soon as I heard they'd left. They aren't responding."

"They call me the Black Plague." Alex's eyes glowed with blue fire. "Want to find out why?"

"I'm not scared of you." His shaking hands said otherwise.

"We'll just see about that." Her smile was vicious. "Why did they take Naomi?"

"I can only imagine they're still following old orders."

Orders to kidnap Naomi and force her to open a gateway to send all of the Dragon Born to hell.

"I can assure you that they will pay dearly for ignoring my order to cease fighting," Blackbrooke said, his jaw clenched. He was obviously more irked about the soldiers' insubordination than their kidnapping of Naomi. People were only pawns to him.

"We have to find her before the Crusaders hurt her," Sera told Alex.

"Don't even think about going anywhere." Alex withdrew her sword, allowing the edge of the blade to nip Blackbrooke's skin as she moved. Ignoring his foul curses, she motioned for Sera to follow her. "Naomi's magic trail is fading."

"But Makani's is lit up like a Christmas tree," Sera replied. "It will lead us right to her."

◆ ◇ ◆ ◇ ◆

They found Makani outside an old building that had been a church in a former life. In this life, it was barely holding together. The roof had long since collapsed, and two of the four walls were missing. The rich, nutty scent of rotting wood and old forgotten forests permeated the air.

"The Crusaders are inside." Makani's face hardened with determination. "And so is Naomi."

"They've laid down magical defenses," Sera said.

"I could break them, but they're rigged to blow up in our faces as soon as I do. And they're packing quite a charge," he replied with a calmness that chilled Sera to her bones. If given the chance, he was going to tear apart every single Crusader in that building.

"You need to keep your wits about you. Don't go off on a killing spree. Our priority is to rescue Naomi, not paint the walls crimson with the Crusaders' blood," Sera told him.

Gold sparks lit up his eyes, swirling the fury in their depths. "I give the orders here."

They'd freed Makani's memories of the World That Was, but that didn't erase the Shadow World from his mind—and here he was in charge of the Dragon Born. Sera was pretty sure that was exactly how he wanted things to be. After all, he'd once been a prince.

"If I may, I have a suggestion, My Prince?" Alex smirked at him.

"Very well," he said. "But lose the attitude."

Alex's smirk only grew wider. "If we all three put our magic together, we might have enough power to overload the Crusaders' defenses, including their nasty little boobytrap."

"Let's do it," he said.

They moved in closer, slow and steady, sensing for smaller traps. The big, explosive one covered the outside of the building.

"I will not miss this wretched world," Sera muttered, stepping around a gigantic monster skull that looked like it had once belonged to a tyrannosaurus rex.

She could see Naomi now. Her friend was chained to a stone pillar. She was bleeding from a dozen different cuts on her body, including a really big gash on her forehead. Her head drooped limply to the side, her eyes closed in sleep. Four Crusaders in torn uniforms stood around her.

"Wake up, pretty fairy," one of them said.

Lightning shot out of his hands, slamming against Naomi. Her body convulsed. Blood dripped from her mouth.

Flames burst to life all across Makani's body. He was on fire. Sera gaped. She'd never seen anyone do that.

"Stop," she whispered to him. "We can't waste any magic. We'll need every drop to overload that barrier."

Makani's flames puffed out. Not a single hair on

his body was burnt. Amazing.

"We need you to do something for us," the lightning mage said to Naomi.

She blinked rapidly, trying to focus her eyes. One of those eyes was bruised black. Someone had punched her hard enough to leave a mark.

"We hear you can raise the dead," another Crusader said. He was a summoner of some sort. His aura was rather wolfish, so Sera was going to go with wolf.

"Sorry, you need to get your facts straight, boys." Naomi's cheerful smile didn't match the sorry state of her body. "I'm the wrong kind of fairy for raising zombies. I'm not a necromancer."

"You're a Spirit Warrior," said the third Crusader, a female telekinetic. "You can cross between earth and the spirit realm."

"Yes, I can." A wicked look flashed across her face. "Would you like me to send you to hell?"

The fourth, a fire mage, backed up. "This was a really bad idea."

"Stop worrying," the lightning mage told him. "She's just a little girl. Fairies are all soft."

"Oh, yes, so soft," Naomi said. She disappeared.

"Where is she?" the wolf summoner said, his eyes darting around wildly.

"I'm right here."

Naomi reappeared in front of them. Her hands were still chained, but she didn't let that hinder her. She twisted them around with fluid grace, blasting the soldiers with a stream of sparkling pink Fairy Dust. They scrambled to the far corners of the hollow building, taking cover behind a crumbling debris pile.

"Now," Makani told Sera and Alex.

Sera's magic tore out of her, slamming into the barrier. It merged with Alex's stream, then with Makani's. Piece by piece, they were eating away at the Crusaders' defenses. But then a wayward bolt of electricity from the lightning mage hit the barrier. The safeguard triggered. The whole thing was going to blow.

"Step back," Makani said, pushing them back.

The barrier overloaded. A wall of flames shot up. Makani wove his magic into a lasso, catching the fire. Spinning and twisting, he rolled the flames up into a ball of fire. Smiling grimly, he unleashed it on the Crusaders. It ignited the Fairy Dust in the air, knocking the four mages out through the missing back wall of the building.

An exploding light show of pink Fairy Dust shot out of the topless building like fireworks. Naomi stepped through the twinkling mist, the pink particles bouncing off of her. Fairies were immune to the nap-inducing qualities of Fairy Dust.

"Thanks for the rescue," she said with a crooked smile.

Blood dripped from her fingertips, splattering the rocky ground. Naomi's eyes rolled back. Makani ran forward, catching her as she fell.

10. Demon-touched

THE COMMANDOS WERE waiting for them when they got back to the Dragon Born base. Makani wouldn't let go of Naomi, so Dal had to heal her from between the Prince's arms.

"Getting protective, are you?" Alex said to Makani with a saucy smirk.

"Dragons are like that."

Alex glanced at Sera, who shrugged. "Men are like that."

"Their gruff, overbearing protectiveness is kind of romantic," Alex said.

"There's nothing sexier than a guy who can kick ass alongside me." Naomi's eyelashes fluttered open.

"You're looking better. The bruise has almost faded from around your eye," Alex told her as Makani set her down.

Naomi brushed her finger across her face. "Dal, you do great work."

"Stop it. You'll make him blush," Callum told her.

"And he's too pretty already," added Tony.

"Commandos don't blush."

"Sure we do. We're deep." Dal patted Naomi's shoulder. "All right. You're all set. I've healed your exterior injuries, but the soreness will take longer to fade. Try to refrain from rushing into danger for the next day or two."

"I guess you'll have to cancel your date with Makani tonight," Alex told her.

Naomi snorted.

"Dates with me rarely end in bloodshed," Makani said serenely. He looked much happier now that Naomi was conscious.

"I think I once saw that printed on a t-shirt," Sera quipped.

"Of course our dates don't always end in bloodshed, honey," Naomi said over Alex's cackles. "So, my dears." She turned her smile on the sisters. "Tell me how I can help you."

"She always knows," Alex said to Sera.

"That's because she's awesome."

"Aww, now I'm the one blushing."

"Don't fret. Pink is definitely your color," Sera told her.

Naomi brushed her hand through her hair, changing it from blonde to pink. "That's better. Now, let me have it."

"The clock is ticking," replied Sera. "The fog has all but faded away from San Francisco."

That was the only sign they had that the spell was settling. Once all the fog was gone, the Shadow World would be permanent.

"Merlin's fortress is sealed up tightly, every entrance heavily guarded," Alex said. "Save one."

"The way in from the spirit realm," Naomi said in a hushed whisper. "Say no more. I will help you."

"So much for not rushing into danger," Dal sighed.

"Sorry, doc, but my friends need me."

"Thanks," Sera said.

"No need for thanks. This world is mine too. When you gave us our memories back, it was a real eye-opener about how much better things could be." Her eyes flickered to Makani.

"Whatever you need, we're here," he said.

A rift opened, and Riley stepped out of the smoke, Kai and Logan on either side of him.

"Ready to go?" Sera asked them.

"Yes," Riley declared, his face set, his eyes burning with determination.

"We do have one *small* problem that came to light while you were tracking Naomi," Kai said.

"Apparently, word has gotten out about Blackbrooke stopping the invasion," Logan told them. "The Magic Council thinks he's been compromised and is sending in troops from the outside."

"How many?" Makani asked.

"Five thousand."

Makani's gaze panned across the smoking buildings and broken barriers.

"Go," Naomi told him.

"Are you sure?"

"Absolutely. Rally the troops. Our people need you to command them, to unite them. I'll be fine."

His eyes darted to Sera and Alex.

"We'll look out for her," Alex promised him.

"Hey, I'm a tough warrior. I can look out for myself," Naomi protested with smiling eyes.

"Of course you are." Makani kissed the top of her head. "But I'm a gruff, overbearing, overprotective dragon."

"You bet you are." She rose up to her tiptoes, giving him a long, leisurely kiss.

"Go with Makani," Kai told Tony. "You are in charge of my forces. And if Blackbrooke has something to say about that, stuff a sock in his mouth."

"Sure thing, boss."

"And keep an eye on my sister," Kai called out as the commandos walked away with Makani. "Don't let her get herself killed."

◆ ◇ ◆ ◇ ◆

"Lara will be fine, you know. She is a very powerful mage," Sera said to Kai as they trudged through the bowels of hell.

He hadn't unclenched his jaw since they'd departed the Dragon Born base, and her comment did nothing to relieve his tension. "She's powerful all right—not to mention overconfident, stubborn, and reckless."

"So, everything that defines a Drachenburg basically."

"Careful, sweetheart." His voice plunged to darker depths. "I might think you're trying to taunt me."

"Teasing, not taunting," she assured him.

"What's the difference?"

She smirked at him. "The difference is how much you enjoy it."

"I fear I can't enjoy anything here." He waved his hand to indicate everything around them.

Sera had been to hell and back—literally—but it wasn't exactly her idea of a relaxing vacation getaway. The trees were burning. The grass was burning. Even the sky was burning. It was thick with falling ash snowflakes. Every so often, some of those flakes burst into flames and puffed out. A volcano loomed high above them, expelling a steady stream of liquid fire and burning rocks. It was no wonder the trees were all black.

"How deep in hell are we?" Alex asked, coughing.

"The seventh level," Naomi told her. Unlike most of them, she wasn't walking like she had boulders in her boots. As a Spirit Warrior, she was immune to the magic-sapping effects of hell.

"The seventh level? So we might meet demons," Riley said.

Demons lived only in the three core circles of hell. They couldn't survive in the others.

"I've been trying to keep them away, but they are persistent," Naomi said. "They're drawn to the taste of earth magic."

Sera shuddered. "Let's just get through this place quickly."

She tried to tell herself that it was only natural to fear hell. And besides, the last time she'd visited a core level of this realm, she'd died.

"This is the fastest path," Naomi assured her. "It

will take us to the edge of the spirit realm in Merlin's domain. That's where my magic hits a brick wall. I'll need Riley to help me push us through."

The ground exploded in front of her, spraying gravel everywhere. A creature resembling a centaur mixed with a eagle shot out of the growing hole in the path. It landed with a thump on all four hooves. A demon.

"Sorry, there are so many of them. I can't keep them all out," Naomi said, priming her magic.

Golden threads of spirit magic shot out of her hands, weaving back and forth to seal the hole in the ground. She wiped her shaking hand across her face, drying the sweat trickling down from her forehead.

"Stand aside, mortal," the demon sneered at her. "You're blocking my snack." His eyes panned across Logan, moved past Riley to Kai, then settled on Sera and Alex. "Those two. They have enough magic to fill my belly for a long time." He smacked his lips loudly.

A stream of shadows burst out of Riley, taking the demon hard in the stomach. The shadows twisted around his ankles and wrists, then plunged so hard into the ground that the force of the impact shook the earth. The restraints hardened and settled, their hold so absolute that the demon couldn't move a muscle, wing, or hoof.

"Wow," Sera gasped. She'd seen her brother training his magic with Rane, but this was incredible progress—even for a quick study like Riley.

"I know that magic," the demon spoke in a low rumble. His black eyes found Riley. "Shadow mages are Rane's mages. You are Rane's. Are you sure you know what deal you made?"

"I didn't make any deal with her."

"Are you sure? Are you absolutely, positively sure?" A devilish smile spread across his mouth. "Demons always make deals, but at least most of us are straightforward about it. Rane isn't. You never know you're making a deal with her." His orange brows swept his hairline. "Which is worse: the enemy you can see or the one you believe to be your friend?"

Riley opened his mouth, but no words escaped.

The demon slid his tongue across his lips. "I can taste Rane all over you. You're not just any shadow mage. She's done something to you."

"What?"

The demon inhaled deeply. "You don't just have her magic. You have her essence."

Naomi sighed. "Riley, don't tell me you slept with a demon."

"No, of course not. She's just teaching me to use my magic. Nothing more."

Naomi reached out to touch his shoulder—then quickly withdrew her hand, as though she'd been burned. "You and Rane synched magic."

"Yes, so she could guide my magic."

"You shouldn't have done that." Naomi shook her head slowly. "It means you're demon-touched. Who knows what she did to your mind. Or to your magic."

The shadow chains binding the demon turned to dust.

"My work here is done," he said, brushing the ashes from his hands. Then he disappeared, his wide white grin fading last.

"I was so stupid." Riley looked like he had to throw up. "I should never have trusted a demon. Her *essence*?" He turned to Naomi. "That means Rane can control me?"

Naomi gave him a pitying look. "Yes. It means part of her flows through you. She could use that to take control of you."

Riley slouched. "Like Merlin did."

"No. Merlin was controlling your mind. Rane is in deeper. She's gone all the way to your core. She is in your soul."

"So there's no resisting her." The look of wretched despair on his face broke Sera's heart.

"I'm afraid not," said Naomi.

Riley shot a blast of pitch black magic at a nearby tree. It crumbled to ashes.

"There is a way we can fix this," Naomi told him cautiously.

"Yes?" Desperation poured off of him like a waterfall in springtime.

"Sera and Alex can break the demon magic within you."

"You bet we will," Sera said, wrapping her arm around Riley.

Alex hammered her fist against the palm of her other hand. "We'll kick that demon out of you."

The spark of hope in his eyes fizzled out, melting into resignation. "No."

"No?" Sera asked.

"At least not yet. If you break my magic, I can't bring you into Merlin's fortress. And you will need all my power in the fight against Merlin."

Sera opened her mouth to protest, but he cut in, "You know I'm right. We have to break Merlin's spell before it's too late. And for that, you need me. You need my magic, demon and all."

"He's right, you know," Alex told Sera.

"I know." She frowned. "But as soon as we've taken care of Merlin and cleaned up his mess, we're going to fix this, Riley. I promise you."

Riley nodded, but his heart clearly wasn't in it. His magic was a miasma of fear, anger, and self-loathing. He rushed forward, falling into step beside Naomi.

"I don't know how to comfort him," Sera whispered to Alex.

"You can't. None of us can." At the moment, Alex's magic was more monotone than their brother's, and it was anger that crashed across it like a raging hurricane. "He knows he's a ticking time bomb. Sooner or later, Rane will grab control of him, and then he'll go off."

"I knew something was off about her."

"Well, she *is* a demon. Usurping free will and using mortals as puppets is kind of their thing."

"Don't defend her. Not ever," Sera hissed.

"Oh, I'm not. In fact, the next time I see her, I'm going to introduce her to the consequences of messing with my little brother."

The path had dead-ended in a brick wall—literally. Riley pressed his hand to the wall, and the bricks tumbled to the ground, revealing a forest lit up by a blood moon. A low, eerie howl sang on the wind, rustling through the trees' naked branches. A flock of black butterflies fluttered across the sky, their wings moving in sharp, mechanical flaps.

"Where are we?" Sera asked as they entered the forest. It smelled like sulfur and sunscreen.

"Merlin's version of hell," Naomi said. "Pretty, isn't it?"

Alex's nose scrunched up. "Positively charming."

"Don't worry. We're not going far. The entrance to his castle is just over there."

Naomi pointed at an old tree—no, make that beanstalk.

It was as black as all the other plants in the forest. Smoke puffed out of its purple flowers, spreading the stench of rotting leaves and overripe fruit.

"I never thought I'd actually miss normal hell," Alex muttered.

Sera craned her neck back, her eyes panning up the beanstalk. "Don't tell me we have to climb to the top of that thing." It seemed to go on forever. She couldn't even see the top.

"No, nothing so dramatic," Naomi said, yanking one of the fruits from the beanstalk.

She threw it against the black stalk, and the shell split open, oozing blood-red goo down the canals etched into the bark. The beanstalk shook violently. The largest of its violet flowers dropped from the branches, opening its fanged mouth to scream out the loudest, shrillest shriek that had ever pierced Sera's eardrums.

"Uh, Naomi," she said, watching uneasily as the violet continued to dive. It was growing larger and louder with every passing second. "Are you sure you know what you're doing?"

"Positive."

The house-sized flower chomped down its mighty maw, swallowing them whole. Magic flared up, burning Sera's eyes. And then they were standing at the entrance to a long corridor. A sleek, glossy layer of marble covered the floor, and there wasn't a shrieking violet or black beanstalk in sight.

"That is not like traversing realms in our world," Sera said, expelling a deep breath.

Naomi laughed uneasily. "The book I read said it was intense, but I guess there's really no preparing for being swallowed by a giant flower."

A horrible, high-pitched noise burst to life, trilling against the walls, flooding the corridor.

"It's even worse than that damn flower," Logan growled, covering his ears.

"Where's it coming from?" Alex's eyes darted up and down the hall.

"Everywhere." Sera cringed. "Apparently, this entrance into Merlin's castle wasn't unprotected after all."

"No," Riley said. "It's me. Merlin has set up wards against Rane's magic. I must have enough of her magic in me to set off the alarms, but not enough to trigger the defenses."

"Rane gave you her magic for a reason." Alex frowned. "Demons never do anything without a reason."

"We can't worry about this now. We have to keep moving," Sera said.

Soldiers streamed down the hallway, their footsteps masked beneath the wretched shriek of the alarm.

"You three go," Kai told her. "You and Alex are the

best magic-trackers, our best bet for finding the spell book. And when you do find it, you'll need Riley to perform the counter spell."

"He's right," Logan said.

"Well, if you two can agree on a plan, then how can I say no to it?" Sera teased them.

Kai cast a wall of fire between them and Merlin's soldiers. "I thought you'd long ago given up on saying no to me."

"Old habits die hard," she said, smirking.

Alex grabbed her arm. "Hey, you two can smooch after we're done storming the castle."

"That's how it goes in all the stories: first you storm the castle, and then you kiss the princess," Naomi agreed, blasting Fairy Dust at a soldier who'd tried to fly over Kai's barrier.

"All right then," Sera said to Alex and Riley. "Let's go visit Merlin's museum."

11. The Chamber of Wonders

IT DIDN'T TAKE long to find Merlin's museum. Signs were posted in every hallway, room, and closet, pointing the way to the Chamber of Wonders.

"You think he wants people to find it?" Alex quipped as they entered the museum.

Rane was right about Merlin. He definitely loved to display his possessions, magic, and power. This room was a testament to his legacy. Every accomplishment was catalogued, every spell saved and stored. It must be where he went whenever he wanted to feel big and mighty.

The walls were gilded in gold, the ceiling enchanted to sparkle like the night sky. There were treasure boxes everywhere, each and every one of them set up with meticulous precision. Merlin obviously didn't want anyone who visited his museum to miss a single moment of his greatness. He'd lined up every trinket, weapon, and tapestry with a single purpose in mind: to be seen. Well, that would certainly make it easier to find the spell book. It must have been the masterpiece of the museum, the crown jewel of his collection.

Sera soon found it wasn't that simple. The objects didn't appear to have been sorted in any order—or at least not any order she could see. They'd have to browse the whole museum.

"There's a library through that door," Riley said. "I'm going to look in there. You two stay here and try to track down the object Merlin used to ward his domain against Rane."

"How do you know he used an object?" Alex asked.

"Because that's how the spell is performed. If we can find the object he used, we can break the spell keeping her out."

"And why would we want to do that?" Sera said, planting her hands on her hips. "We should be setting up our own wards against that demon, not inviting her wherever she wants to go."

"I don't trust her either. But with her on our side, we'll have a better chance of defeating Merlin."

"Assuming she doesn't stab us in the back," Alex said.

"We're just going to have to hope that her need for revenge against Merlin is more important to her than whatever scheme she's brewing up to hijack my free will."

"You are putting a lot of faith in a demon," Sera told him.

"No, I'm putting my faith in my big sisters.

They've never let me down before."

Chuckling, Alex shooed him toward the library doorway. "Go on, you charmer."

Riley shot them a wicked smile, then stepped into the library. Sera turned her attention to the orderly chaos before her, reaching out with her magic. She sensed for anything that felt like either Rane, demon, or shadow magic. Unfortunately, every object in the room seemed to satisfy at least one of the three criteria. Merlin was a shadow mage, he'd stolen objects of power from Rane, and hell was probably his favorite playground. This was like searching for a needle in a room full of very tall haystacks.

"Are you able to sense anything?" Sera asked Alex.

"I sense too much. It's like walking into a perfume shop. After a minute or so, you can't differentiate the different scents. They all just bleed together."

"Let's concentrate on Rane," Sera suggested, pointing at the first in a long row of display cabinets. "Sense for anything that feels like her magic."

"Like our brother next door? He feels like her magic." Alex frowned at the pair of boots she'd plucked from the shelves, then discarded them over her shoulder. "I don't trust that demon."

"Neither do I, but Riley is right. Before this is over, we will need her help." Sera stopped in front of a pink-patterned teacup that looked like it had come straight out of Rane's tea set. She stared at it for a moment, then moved on. "Even with the extra magic she's given Riley, he's not powerful enough to defeat Merlin alone."

"I know. I just don't like it. I'd rather be hunting

demons than helping them."

They looked through bowls and pans, paintings and chairs. Merlin even had a complete set of enchanted blue diamond jewelry that felt like it had once been owned by a fairy queen. Silverware, tools, platters, scissors—every object in the room was humming with power. Every object had some great purpose.

"Merlin has been alive too long. He's collected so much stuff." Alex held up an old-fashioned male wig.

But Sera wasn't giving up. Amidst all the other things, she could feel something...different. It was singing to her.

"Do you hear that?" she asked.

"Yes." Alex walked toward the large luggage crate in the corner. "The song is so beautiful. So forlorn."

They shifted boxes and chairs aside, clearing a path to the plain green crate. The song was growing louder, stronger. It slithered across Sera's magic like liquid silk, as soft and sweet as fruit cake—a seductive but oh-so-bad-for-you treat that you had to eat, even knowing it would leave you with a huge stomach ache.

Sera threw back the crate's lid. There, swimming in a sea of crinkled old newspapers, she found a knife. A huge, blood-red ruby was set into its hilt. The gemstone swirled with magic, wailing out its painful song. It was a song of hell's burning branches and sulfur skies. But it was more than that. There was a fiercely intelligent beauty buried beneath that magic, calling out for freedom.

"It's demon blood trapped inside that stone," Sera said. "Rane's blood."

"So that's what Merlin used to block Rane out of his domain."

Alex grabbed the knife, sliding her fingertip across the red stone. Her magic hammered against the ruby. The force of the blow would have shattered most spells in an instant, but this one didn't even quiver.

"How are we supposed to break the spell on his knife?" she asked, handing it back to Sera.

"I don't know. Perhaps only shadow magic can break it." She tucked it into her belt. "Let's see if Riley's found anything."

As they headed toward the library, Alex sighed. "When this is over, all of us need to get together and do something fun."

"Like what?"

"Anything but saving the world. I'd settle for just a good, old, dirty monster fight. It's monster breeding season in San Francisco. The giant caterpillars will be out in full force." A wistful gleam lit up Alex's eyes.

"Or we could just throw a party like normal people do. A party with lots and lots of pizza."

Alex shot her a devilish smirk. "Oh, you're talking about your wedding."

"Can you imagine the scandal that would rock the supernatural community if the heir to one of their greatest dynasties served pizza at his wedding reception?" Sera couldn't hold back her grin.

"Their reaction would be almost as delicious as the pizza. You absolutely must do it, Sera."

"Lara has been talking about serving mini pizzas as appetizers."

Alex wet her lips. "Not a bad idea."

"Kai wants to serve steak as the main course. That's the one thing he's putting his foot down about."

"Well, you know what happens when Kai puts his foot down."

"It is a frightening sight indeed."

"So what do you think about the steak?"

Sera shrugged. "That I'll trade him my steak for his cheesecake."

Alex giggled.

"It's really a win-win," Sera told her. "Kai says he doesn't care about the rest of the wedding stuff besides marrying me."

"How romantic."

"He's so direct that it's sometimes easy to overlook how sentimental he really is."

"You can be pretty direct yourself." Alex lowered her voice to a whisper. "Lara told me about the red dress."

"I thought you'd approve."

"And I do. Wholeheartedly. Well, just as long as what's underneath is red too."

But their discussion of red underwear would have to wait for another time. They'd entered the library. Books neatly arranged on walnut wood shelves covered every wall, extending over fifty feet high. Massive crystal chandeliers dripped from the ceiling like icicles glistening in the moonlight. There were a few books showcased at central spots on the floor, set atop podiums. Riley was standing beside one of these podiums, a spell book in his hands. The cover was the color of midnight, but there were no stars on that canvas. It was a night without hope, without anything to light your way. Drenched in darkness, it hummed, vibrating with the thunderous power of hell. That was demon magic. Shadow magic.

"That's it," Sera said. "The Shadow World spell lies within those pages."

Riley turned toward her and Alex, looking at them with wide eyes.

"What's wrong?" Alex asked him.

"Nothing," he said. But there was a hard gleam to those eyes, a sharp edge. His jaw was clenched like he'd bitten down on scrap metal.

"Riley, is the counter spell inside that book?" Sera said softly.

"Yes." His breath froze in the air.

"Ok, then. What do we have to do?" Alex asked.

"In order to return the world to the one we know, the person who cast the spell has to die." Riley swallowed hard. "*I* have to die."

12. Sacrifice

SERA STARED AT Riley, her heart clenching, twisting up inside of her chest. Determination shone in his eyes. It defined the hard set of his jaw. She could feel it in his magic, in every pulsing beat. The thick stench of his fear was overshadowed only by the uplifting symphony of his courage. And his stubbornness. He was ready to sacrifice himself to save their world.

Alex's magic was just as stubborn. It galloped like a race horse hellbent to reach the finish line before him, determined to stop him. "You are *not* dying."

"It's the only way," he said. "The spell is tied to the life of he who cast it. That's why Merlin uses others to cast his spells. We thought he was afraid that casting the spell will kill him, and maybe he is. But it's not just about that. It's about what happens when someone tries to break the spell. Merlin didn't pick me by chance."

"He knew we might recover our memories and then go after him to break the spell," Sera said.

"The Dragon Born are resilient to magic. If anyone would realize the world had changed, we would," Alex agreed. "He could have chosen almost any mage to be the vessel of his spell, but he chose the brother of two Dragon Born."

"He chose me." Riley gripped the spell book tightly. "So that the Dragon Born suffer either way, whether the spell is broken or not."

"The spell's loophole is as bad as the spell itself," Alex said.

"No." Sera shook her head, refusing to allow it to sink in. "We're not going to let you kill yourself, Riley."

"You don't understand," he said sadly and set the book down on its podium. "Merlin designed this spell very carefully. I can't just kill myself. Someone who loves me has to kill me."

Sera's magic plunged, crashing against Alex's. She could feel her own despair mixing with her twin's, magnifying, building to the breaking point—her heart's breaking point. It was more than she could bear.

"No," Sera said, her eyes heavy with unshed tears.

"We won't," Alex added. "We haven't kept you safe all these years to lose you now. You are our brother, and we love you. There must be another way. There's always another way."

"Not this time," he said sadly.

Sera threw her arms around him, drowning his tears in her own. Alex joined in, her body quaking with every sob. Riley gave them a final squeeze, then backed away.

"What is my life compared to the fate of the whole world?" He wiped his arm across his wet eyes.

"*Everything*. You are everything to us." Sera set her hands on his cheeks. "Do you hear me?"

"You looked out for me for so many years, but now it's time to let me go."

"We don't let go of each other," Alex said. "Not ever."

A lonely tear slid down his cheek. "This time you have to." He drew the knife from his belt, handing it to Alex.

She knocked it out of his hand. "No. Not now. Not ever," she hissed.

"Sera?" he asked, his gaze sliding over to her.

"No."

"You are being stubborn!" he shouted at them.

"That's what we do: stubbornly protect our family," Sera told him.

"We don't kill the people we love."

"We don't have time for this," Riley said, thrusting his hands forward.

Ribbons of shadow magic shot out of them, slashing across Sera's body, burning her with darkness. He waved his hands again, and a second bundle of ribbons burst out of the ground and coiled around Alex's wrists and ankles. A horrible, hellish magic crackled across the shadow tendrils, but the pain of its icy bite was nothing compared to the pain inside—to the pain shredding Sera apart.

"Fight back!" Riley shouted at them, his voice a

beacon beyond the wall of agony. "Are you just going to sit back and let me kill you?"

"We know what you're trying to do," Sera choked out.

Alex coughed. "And we're not playing along. We will not kill you."

The shadows dissolved, but Riley hadn't given up. One look at his face was enough to convince Sera of that—and to scare her shitless. He snatched the knife from the ground. In one, quick movement, he slashed it across his wrist.

"What do you think you're doing?" Sera demanded, rushing forward.

He lifted his bleeding arm and cast a wall of shadows in her path. "If you won't kill me to save our world, then I will kill myself. I will die either way, but you can choose whether our world survives. And whether my death ultimately had meaning."

"That's not a choice!" Alex bellowed.

"Wait." Sera lifted her hand to the barrier. The shadows stirred, forming into a set of jaws that snapped at her, forcing her back. "We will figure this out, Riley. Together."

"There is no time. I can feel the spell settling. It's almost over." He slashed the blade across his other wrist. "What will it be?"

Shadows rolled up the walls, covering the windows, clotting the doorways. Something flashed across Sera's eyes, blinding her. When she could see again, Merlin was standing opposite her.

"Family drama?" he asked, his lips pulling back into a vicious sneer.

"This is all your doing," Alex spat at him, drawing her sword.

She swung it at Merlin, putting enough power behind the swing to take off his head. But he was too fast. Magic crackled like lightning as his shadow whip met her blade. The whip moved like it had a mind of its own, coiling around Alex's sword. He gave it a rough tug, and the sword slipped from her grasp. It landed at Sera's feet.

"Dragon Born," Merlin said with disgust. "You always think you're the heroes. But you're all frauds. A true hero would not allow the world to suffer to spare themselves personal discomfort."

"Discomfort?" Sera repeated in disbelief. "We're not talking about a rash, you psychopath. We're talking about killing our own brother."

"Yes, that *is* a dilemma." He yawned loudly. "What if I were to tell you that there is another way?"

"Your words are poison." Alex's voice cracked as sharply as his whip.

"If only it were so, I'd have poisoned you all already." A smile twisted his lips. "But you're too stubborn for my poisons."

"That's us. Stubborn," replied Sera.

"The world is suffering because of you. Because of that stubbornness. If you would just all lie down and die, none of this would have happened."

"That is the logic of a sociopath," Alex declared.

"I am not completely heartless." His cruel smile was screaming otherwise. "There is one way to save your world and your little brother too." Merlin glanced at Riley, then back again. "Odd that he didn't tell you.

It's right there in that spell book. In large print, in fact." The words rolled off his tongue with pure pleasure—and that's what had Sera worried.

"Riley?" Alex asked.

He said nothing.

"Your brother told you the first part. The loophole to this spell—the way to break it—is to kill the caster before the spell becomes permanent. More importantly, someone who loves him has to kill him. Nice twist, isn't it?"

"No, it's not," Alex growled. "It's sadistic. Just like you."

"It's not my twist. That's just how this kind of spell works. The classic escape clause, if you will. Apparently, the magic of love is indeed powerful enough to break any curse. Just not in the way you want." He laughed.

"Can we just skip to the part where we kill him?" Alex asked Sera.

"But there is a happy little loophole to this loophole," Merlin continued. "I wove my own personal twist into this particular spell."

"And you're going to tell us how to break the spell?" Sera asked.

"Yes."

"Out of the goodness of your heart?"

"Of course not," he sneered. "There is no goodness left in my heart. There's only pain. And rage. But I'm going to tell you my little secret anyway." He motioned them forward. "The Shadow World spell was bound in Dragon Born magic, specifically your magic. Love will set you free."

"What does that even mean?" Sera demanded.

"What it means, little Dragon Born mage, is that there are two ways to break this spell, and you get to pick your cure. Your brother." He pointed at Riley. "Or your sister." His hand turned toward Alex. "Choose, Serafina Dering. If you want to end this curse, decide which one will live and which one will die."

13. Love and Poison

SERA CLUTCHED THE sword in her hand. "I don't understand."

"Don't you see? I turned the strength of the Dragon Born into a weakness, using your connection—your bond of love to your siblings—to weave this spell. When I took control over Riley's mind, I was able to hijack your precious bond just enough to build this delightful loophole into the spell. It's ingenious, if I do say so myself."

"Stop talking," Sera said, her voice scraping across her throat.

"Your precious love has turned against you," he taunted. "I bet you never thought you'd see the day when love hurt you. But love hurts. It hurts horribly. It kills you slowly, as opposed to the swift, merciful strike of hate."

"Stop talking."

"Spells cast in blood must be broken in blood," he

laughed. "That's the way of shadow magic—and the only way you're going to win this. If you can even call it a win to kill someone you love."

"Shut up!" she snarled.

"Temper, temper, you're supposed to be the sweet sister." Merlin clucked his tongue. "Rane tried to break the spell last time, you know, but she couldn't stomach the consequences. I tied that spell to her life. So either she had to kill me, or I had to kill her. She wasn't happy with either option, so she did nothing. And I think you're just the same. Just as weak. Just as pitiful."

His laughter made a mockery of her pain. She'd sworn to return the world to the way it had been, and she would have sacrificed herself to do it too. But she could not kill someone she loved. And there was no way on earth that she could possibly choose between Alex and Riley.

"This is beyond cruelty," Sera said to Merlin. "The cure is worse than the poison."

"You have to kill me," Alex told her.

Riley grabbed her hand, pulling her toward him. "No, me."

"You are my other half, my twin soul," Sera told Alex. "And Riley, you're my little brother, the one I swore to protect. I love you both. I can't kill either one of you."

"Are you going to let everyone in the world suffer because of your selfishness?" Merlin taunted her.

"How black your soul must be to rejoice at the suffering of others," she shot back.

"You think there's another way to end this, to somehow sacrifice yourself," Merlin said. "You're looking for a way to satisfy the martyr in you, the part of you that wants to die."

"I don't want to die."

"Oh, really? Then why are you always jumping at any opportunity to kill yourself? I'll tell you what. I'm feeling magnanimous today. After you've picked which one of your siblings to kill, I will grant you a quick death. I will end your suffering."

Sera glowered at him. "We've faced worse than you before and won, Merlin."

"There isn't a way out, little girl. I designed this loophole very carefully."

Sera looked at the sword in her hand—at the sword at her feet.

"The clock is ticking," Merlin said. "You have mere minutes before this spell becomes permanent. I can feel it solidifying. Choose now. Your brother. Or your sister. Or you could just leave the world as it is. It is such a lovely place, isn't it? How long do you think it will be before the Dragon Born and the Crusaders annihilate one another? Or will the monsters get to them first? They have all but taken over San Francisco already, and the rest of the world is not far behind."

"You have to put the world back, Sera," Alex told her. "People are dying. The Crusaders are mounting an attack even as we speak."

"Merlin will just cast another spell."

"Why, yes. I will. But this will give you a few days to stop me." He laughed as though he knew that was impossible.

"I will not kill those I love." Sera lifted the bloodfire ruby knife.

Merlin's eyes darted to the weapon. Fear flashed across his face. "Where did you get that?"

"You shouldn't leave things out on display that you don't want people to find," Sera told him.

He backed up.

"You're afraid of it."

"Don't be ridiculous. I fear nothing."

"You are afraid—afraid of what will happen if Rane gets here." Sera drew on Alex's magic. Fueled by their combined strength, she whittled away at the spell bound to the knife.

"Rane cannot help you," he said.

Sera could feel the spell on the knife unraveling. "If she is no threat to you, then why did you keep her out?"

"Because demons have abhorrent table manners," Merlin said casually.

"You forget that I can sense emotions. You *are* afraid, and for good reason. Rane is coming." She snapped her fingers together.

Merlin's gaze jerked up to her hand. Sera didn't wait for an invitation. She launched the knife at him. It plunged into his chest, right below his heart. Blood poured down his front. The ruby shattered, and the enchantment on the knife popped.

Merlin let out an enraged roar. Shadow magic crashed into Sera like a wrecking ball, hurling her across the room. Her back slammed against the wall. She stuck there like a fly caught in a spider's web, watching in disbelief as he tore the knife from his chest and tossed it aside.

"It takes a lot more than that to kill me, especially

here in my domain."

The shadow magic uncurled from around Sera's body, and she dropped like a stone to the floor.

"Enough of this foolishness," Merlin said. "Two minutes, Serafina Dering. You have two minutes to choose their fate. Which one will you kill to save the world? And which one will live to fight another day?"

14. The Laws of Magic

TO SAVE THE world, would you kill the person you loved? It was a question no one should ever have to answer.

Magic split through the room, igniting the dust in the air. And then Rane was in front of Sera, helping her to her feet. "What is going on here?" she said. Her eyes flickered to the book on the podium. "You've found the spell book."

"Yes."

"I'm afraid the spell's loophole isn't to her liking," Merlin said, yawning.

Rane pointed at him. "You shut up." She looked at Sera. "You start talking."

"In order to break the spell, I have to kill either Alex or Riley."

Rane said nothing.

"You *knew*," Riley growled at her.

"I knew about you, Riley. But not about Alex.

That was a cruel twist."

Merlin shot her a savage smile. "I learned from a demon."

"And you still have a lot to learn, junior." She set her hands on his wrists, healing his wounds.

His tense jaw loosened, his expression going blank. He grabbed the bloodfire knife off the ground and began walking toward Merlin.

"What are you doing?" Sera asked him.

"Ending this."

Merlin laughed. "By killing me? It doesn't work that way."

"You're clever student, but you still don't understand how magic works." Fire flashed in Rane's eyes. "Magic is just as much about *intent* as it is about the wording. You should have figured that out by now."

Riley lifted his hand to touch the barrier Merlin had cast in front of himself. The smoke dissolved instantly.

"You were the intent behind the Shadow World spell, not Riley," Rane told him. "Your death will end the spell, not his."

Merlin waved his hand at Riley, encasing him in shadows. Riley pushed right through them.

"That's impossible." Surprise flashed in Merlin's eyes. "I gave you your magic. I can control it."

"He is beyond your control now," Rane said.

Merlin glared at her. "You did something to him."

"I gave him the power he needed."

"To kill me?" He laughed. "I put a spell on myself long ago. Anyone who kills me will die himself."

"I know."

Riley kept walking, the knife raised. There wasn't a single emotion on his face.

"She's controlling him," Alex said to Sera.

The black marble floor gurgled, turning liquid. Like a pool of tar, it washed over the sisters' feet, hardening. Rane had glued them to the floor.

"You will not interfere," she told them.

Sera hammered her magic against the demon-warped stones, but it didn't budge. She reached out, taking Alex's hand, linking her magic with her sister's. But even combined, their magic wasn't strong enough to break the demon's spell.

"You knew this would happen!" Sera shouted at Rane, hitting the marble again. "That's why you infused Riley with your magic."

"To defeat evil, you have to be willing to do what it takes."

"You are a monster," Alex snarled, her magic pulsing in hard, heavy beats. The rocks around her feet shook. Black marble slivers erupted, sprinkling the ground. She wasn't chipping away at the spell fast enough, though.

"I am a demon," Rane replied coolly. "Being a monster comes with the territory."

Riley kept moving toward Merlin, caught in the demon's trance.

"Riley!" Sera screamed at him, her eyes wet. Her little brother was walking to his death, and there wasn't a damn thing she could do about it. Even combined, she and Alex weren't strong enough to break the demon's magic.

Merlin watched nervously as Riley and Rane closed in on him. "You are a coward, just as you were back then," he growled at Rane. "You're letting someone sacrifice himself for you."

"Says he who has others cast his spells so he can hide from the consequences. Well, you can't hide from these consequences. And you can't trick the magic. It knows who was really behind the spell." She clapped her hands together, and the shadows snapped shut behind him, sealing his retreat. "For all your tinkering, you still don't understand the fundamentals of your own magic."

"Stay away." Fear had taken hold of him—and it wasn't letting go.

Rane gave him a sad smile. "You brought this upon yourself, Merlin. I could have saved you. But instead of accepting my help, you locked yourself away in here for centuries. You kept going, drowning in your obsession. Where is the young man who came to me so many years ago with stars in his eyes?"

"Gone."

"Then there is no saving you. It's a shame. Once, you were a good student."

Merlin's twitching eyes flicked to Riley. "It looks like you've found a replacement. And I see you're taking a different approach this time, depriving him of free will. What is it you always used to say?" He snapped his fingers. "Ah, that's right. Free will is overrated."

"You would have done well to listen to me. Just look at what you did with your free will."

Merlin lifted his hands in the air. "All hail the

demon queen!" He shot the sisters a loathing smile. "Demons devour free will. It's an addiction. Now that she's had a taste, she won't be able to stop. Rane isn't like other demons. She can move freely between the earth and the spirit realm. She can bend reality to suit her will—and to crush yours. You thought the Shadow World was bad. Just wait until you're living in a world ruled by demons."

A silver spark flashed in Rane's eyes. Merlin was right. She was getting high off of controlling Riley.

"What have we done?" Sera said to Alex. "We've handed her the world."

Alex slammed her fist against the magic holding them. A fissure formed, but it quickly sealed. She tried a dozen different times in a dozen different ways. She couldn't break through. True to its nature, the shadow magic was malleable. It adapted.

"Stop that," Rane snapped at Alex. "You're making it hard to concentrate."

"We're never going to stop fighting!" Alex promised her.

"Riley! Riley!" Sera called out to their brother. "Stop. You have to fight her control!"

He didn't even acknowledge her.

"It's too late," Merlin told her. "She has him. That's what you get for trusting a demon. They know only power and hunger. She is no different."

"Wrong again. I am a lot different," Rane snapped at him.

Snatching the knife from Riley's hand, she ran at Merlin and stabbed him through the heart. He expelled a surprised gasp, then fell over. Blood spread out from Rane's chest, drizzling to the floor. The spell around Sera and Alex faded away.

The light returned to Riley's eyes. He gaped at Rane. "What have you done?"

"Merlin's spell was too strong. And your magic was not enough." She coughed out blood. "It takes something more powerful than shadow magic—or even demon magic—to break a spell like that."

"Love," Sera said. "It takes love. Only someone who loves Merlin can kill him."

"You love him?" Alex gasped.

"I have loved him for seven hundred years."

"You knew it would come to this. You knew you would have to die."

"Yes." There was no sadness in Rane's eyes, no regret. A moment ago, Sera would have said a demon wasn't capable of such emotions, but that was before a demon had sacrificed herself to save the world.

"You could have let us die instead, but you didn't," Alex said.

Rane coughed. "What would have been the fun in that?"

"I was wrong about you. You're not like other demons," Sera told her.

"Don't you dare spread such lies," she snarled. "I am *exactly* like other demons."

Riley set her hands on Rane's arms. "There must be a way to save you. You're immortal."

"There is no other way than this. As I told Merlin, you cannot trick or cheat the laws of magic. Only when my life goes out will Merlin die. Only then will the spell be broken."

Merlin looked into her eyes, fear shaking them. "I don't want to die." His voice was quiet, almost childlike.

Sighing, Rane set her hand on his forehead. "None of us do, dearie. But sometimes it's just our time." Her fingers traced down his face.

"I don't understand," Riley said. "Why did you give me your power if not to sacrifice me? Why give it to me if you were just going to do…this?"

"You will need my magic. Without it, you can't go there."

The walls began to shake. Merlin's life was leaving him—and taking his whole domain with him.

"Go where?" Riley asked.

She reached up and touched his face. A golden light shone in his eyes, then faded out. He gasped.

"What is she talking about?" Sera asked Riley. "Where are we going?"

"Out of here," he said as Rane and Merlin let out a final staggered breath. "The rest you'll just have to see for yourself."

The roof shook and split—and then collapsed onto them.

15. The Gift

SOLDIERS STREAMED DOWN the corridor, brandishing steel and magic. The lightning barrier Kai had put up absorbed their magic, and it shot a nasty shock up their swords. But every strike weakened it. This was already the tenth barrier he'd had to cast.

"They've been gone a while," Kai commented.

"Yes," agreed Logan. He looked like he was considering going after them.

Truth be told, Kai was considering it himself. "Hiding behind a barrier is not my style."

"You don't say." Something akin to amusement twinkled in the assassin's eyes. "You are not a subtle man. In fact, I'm surprised that you asked Sera to marry you."

A firebomb exploded against the barrier. "Oh, really? And why is that?"

"Because you are a notorious bachelor, Drachenburg."

"Says who?"

"Says the Supernatural Times. So it must be true."

Naomi was laughing so hard that her whole body shook.

"Did you just try to make a joke?" Kai asked him.

"No, of course not. I am perfectly serious." His mouth twitched with amusement.

"All right then. Since we're being perfectly serious, when are you going to ask Alex to marry you?"

Logan's silence drowned out the low hum of lightning. A chair collided with the barrier, and the spell sizzled out. Logan burst through the falling sparks of the exploding barrier, launching a barrage of knives at the incoming soldiers. Kai slammed his magic against the ground, and the earth shook. A wall of rocks burst out of the floor, splitting through the marble, trapping the soldiers inside a stony prison. Naomi shot Fairy Dust against the marble. It bounced off the smooth walls and hit the soldiers.

"Are you scared of diving in?" Kai asked Logan as the soldiers fell unconscious to the floor.

"No."

More soldiers poured around the corner, blasting the rocks aside with no concern for their comrades sleeping beneath them. Kai cast a wall of fire, blocking the storm of spells raging down the hall. A telekinetic lifted her hands in the air, slamming a block of broken marble at the barrier. The flames hissed and melted the rock to ash. The telekinetic wasn't giving up, though. She tried again and again, hitting the barrier with anything and everything in sight. A chair the fire mage had set on fire. A chandelier. Swarms of stone that hit the barrier like raindrops on a rooftop. The dead bodies of their companions.

The other mages added their own spells to the attack, and soon the barrier overloaded. Before Kai could cast barrier number twelve, the telekinetic launched an attack squad of vampires and fairies. They shot over the growing debris piles, landing right in front of Kai and Logan. Naomi disappeared, popping up again behind the vampires. She blasted them to dreamland with a rainbow of Fairy Dust.

One of the fairies pivoted around and shot his own blend of Dust into her. Naomi stumbled to the side, barely staying on her feet.

"Half breed," the fairy taunted.

Spirit magic swallowed him, encasing him in a translucent bubble. Four vampires jumped over the bubble at Naomi, their fangs fully extended. Logan dashed around them, snapping their necks one after the other with brutal efficiency

"Fear does not hinder my actions," Logan said to Kai, landing a knife square in the forehead of the last vampire standing.

"War is one thing. Life is another."

"He has a point," Naomi said.

"I was not asking for a psychoanalysis."

Naomi grinned at him. "Just observing."

"I performed a blood magic ritual with Alex that linked us in blood and magic," replied Logan. "I am most certainly not afraid of 'diving in'."

Kai met the assassin's granite stare. "You know what? I believe you. I think you aren't afraid of doing anything to keep Alex safe and happy."

Logan dipped his chin.

"Which is why you're going to come work for me. So Alex can work with her sister again."

Naomi snorted. Logan gave Kai a hard look, but there was a hint of reflection in his eyes, as though he'd finally made his decision.

The whole castle shook like the ground had ruptured beneath it. Dust snowed down from the ceiling. The banners hanging from the walls quivered. The rods holding them broke off the walls.

"Merlin's spell," Kai said. "They've done it. They've broken it." Kai could feel the threads of Merlin's magic unraveling, dissolving back into shadow.

Soldiers streamed down the hall, but they weren't attacking. They were fleeing toward the exits. Sera, Alex, and Riley ran behind them. Sera stopped when she saw Kai.

"I take it from the collapsing castle that you defeated Merlin and broke his spell," Naomi said.

"Actually, Rane did," Sera replied. "She killed him."

"And where is Rane?"

"She's gone," Alex said.

"Killing Merlin cost her her life. She sacrificed herself that to save us. But not before she gave me a gift." Strange magic glowed in Riley's eyes. It burned like the fiery pits of hell. And his magic—it felt so much like Rane's. "Merlin's domain is collapsing. We have to get out of here."

"What about the worlds in the Dump? All those people? What will happen to them?" Sera asked.

"The worlds will crumble. They're tied to Merlin's

magic. But we can still save the people. *I* can save them."

"How?" Alex asked.

"By using the power Rane gave me."

Fog rolled in, swallowing them. Kai felt the familiar jolt of teleportation. When the fog cleared, they were all standing in a meadow surrounded by forests on all sides. Nothing was shaking. And they weren't alone. Makani, Lara, the commandos, Arianna, and Vivienne—they were all there.

"Where are we?" Kai asked.

"In another world," Riley replied.

Sera looked around. "This isn't one of Merlin's worlds. It feels different."

"No, it isn't one of Merlin's. It's one of Rane's. She made it long ago."

"How do you know?" Alex asked.

"Rane didn't just transfer magic to me. She transferred memories. We'll be safe here. Think of this place like a honeycomb—infinite isolated chambers but only one way in or out. And only Rane can use that door."

Or someone with Rane's magic. Riley was teeming with demon magic. It burned the air around him, snuffing out all other magic, including his own.

"This place is where she brings people and things for safekeeping," Riley continued. "I've transported everyone from Merlin's worlds here."

"Everyone? All at once?" Sera gasped.

"Yes." Obsidian slid over Riley's eyes, drowning his natural green color. "I put each group into a different empty chamber of the honeycomb."

"Some of them aren't empty? What's in them? Monsters?" Alex asked him.

"Some of them hold monsters you can't even imagine. But there are other things too."

He pointed at the rustling trees. People were marching out of them, dozens of people. No, hundreds. They just kept coming. Their magic sang out to Kai, its familiar song igniting the dragon in him.

"They are Dragon Born," he said.

"All of them?" Naomi asked.

The Dragon Born continued to come. There were thousands by now.

"Yes," Sera said, her eyes shaking. "Every single one."

16. Dragon Born Legacy

SEVEN HUNDRED YEARS ago, thanks to Merlin's magic, the world had turned on the Dragon Born and hunted them to near extinction. Those that lived today had survived by hiding what they were. Sera and Alex had been the only two Kai had ever met. Then Naomi had rescued Makani from the spirit realm, and they'd all rescued Arianna and Vivienne from Merlin's domain. And now this. In a single moment, the world's Dragon Born population had gone from five to thousands.

One of those thousands stepped forward. She wore a black leather suit that consisted of a bone-crunching corset and a pair of leather leggings with knee-high boots. The soles were flat. She didn't need the height boost. She was as tall as anyone in that meadow. Her stance was confident, commanding. The metal band across her forehead made her look like a princess. A warrior princess, Kai decided, his eyes dipping to the twin daggers strapped to her thighs.

"Cordelia?" Makani said, stepping forward. "I thought you were dead." His gold eyes slid across the others. "I thought you were all dead."

"It is a long story." She looked into his eyes, as though she were trying to read something in them. "I thought *you* were dead."

"That, too, is a long story."

Magic swirled around her, singing of forgotten ages and warmer days. Riley stirred the shadows, sprinkling silver drops into it. He was casting Rane's memory spell.

A dark forest took shape. Makani trekked through it, passing black trunks and bleeding flowers. A low, tormented cry howled on the wind. Makani broke into a run, crossing the forest in long, powerful strides. Something ran ahead of him, fleeing in terror. The shrieks and sobs were growing louder. Makani cornered it against a wall of rocks. The creature looked up—except it wasn't a creature at all. Well, not exactly. Shaped like a man, his spiky hair was midnight blue, contrasting with his bright red skin. His magic sang of earth and hell; it was like a devilish dark chocolate ice cream with rainbow-colored sprinkles on top.

A half-demon. And Kai knew this particular half-demon. His name was Onyx, and he was at least fifty percent crazy.

"W-who are you?" Onyx asked, shaking against the rocky wall.

"Stay." Makani lifted up an amulet.

The spirit magic inside of it slithered toward the half-demon and froze his naked feet to the ground.

Onyx thrashed his hands around, trying to get free. The spell held.

"What do you want with me?" he said, panic shrieking in his voice.

"With you? Nothing," Makani replied. "I merely require you to bring me to the person I need. Or should I say, the demon."

"You want me to bring you to a demon?" he whimpered. "That is madness. Why must you mortals always make deals with demons?"

Makani stepped forward, his long shadow blocking out the light. "Do I look like someone who would make a deal with a demon?"

The half-demon looked him up and down. "No. Then why—"

"That's between me and Rane."

Onyx's lower lip quivered at the mention of her name. "No, not her. She's the worst of them all. I can't go near her."

The look Makani gave him sent him into a panic.

"Ok. I'll bring you to her realm. But then I'm leaving."

"Lead the way." Makani extended his hand, and the silver strands of spirit magic melted off the half-demon's body.

His hands shaking, Onyx drew a circle in the air. A portal opened between realms. Makani grabbed his hand and pulled them both through.

A great house waited on the other side, as large as a castle. Onyx took one look at the Loch Ness Monster living in the moat, then spun around and disappeared.

Makani approached the castle. The monster swam

toward him, spiky jaws snapping. Makani glared at it with dragon fire burning in his eyes. It dove under the water and swam back the other way.

Inside of the castle, Makani found Rane. She was sitting in her throne room, weaving. She looked up at him as he entered.

"I do not recall inviting you here, Dragon Born."

"I need your help."

"Is that so?" She laughed. It was a sweet, superficial laugh, the kind a silly schoolgirl would have. But there was nothing silly about her. A dark, fierce intelligence shone in her eyes.

"My people are being hunted." Makani stepped forward. "The rest of the supernaturals have turned against us. You have the power to help us, to change the world."

"You are too late. It has already changed."

He frowned. "How?"

She gave her hand a dismissive wave. "That isn't important."

"They say you have great magic. That you can bend reality to your will."

"That's kind of the deal with demons," she said with a smug smile. "And you wish to make a deal with me?"

"What I want is for you to make the Magic Council remember that we are friends."

She giggled. "Sorry, but you can't convince fools to not be fools."

"Surely there is something you can do. Or is the great demon Rane not so great after all?"

She stood, her magic flaring up behind her. The

loom continued to weave the threads without her. "I'd be more careful with my words if I were you, mage."

"You are afraid," he said. "But of what? What can make a demon shake in her boots?"

She lifted her hand. A sword appeared in it, summoned forth by magic. Makani thrust up his sword to meet hers. Both blades shattered.

"How is this possible?" she said, watching the shards of steel sprinkle to the ground.

"Never met a Dragon Born mage before? We break magic."

Makani moved in, striking out with his power. His magic slammed into her nose, breaking it. Blood poured out of it, staining her white dress.

"That was a mistake," she said in a savage growl.

Twin streams of shadow magic shot out of Rane. They tore through the air, hitting Makani with so much force that they hurled him out of her realm.

"I landed in the great battle between the Dragon Born and the Magic Council," said the Makani of today. "But before I could fight, my Spirit Warrior partner shoved me into hell. She said she was saving me, but I didn't want to be saved. I wanted to fight. She left me trapped there and went to save the others. She never came back. She died." Makani looked at Cordelia. "You all died. And I spent seven centuries stuck in hell."

The landscape rippled like a watery reflection. The battlefield washed away, replaced by Rane's castle. She was pacing across her throne room, her loom still weaving away without her.

"You should have helped him."

Rane looked at her cat. "Merlin's spell has settled. It's too late to break it."

"Cast a spell of your own," the cat said. "Reform the world as it was."

"No. I could try to change the world, but it would never end up exactly like the old one. Besides, this isn't any of my business."

"Merlin is your business. This happened because you gave him his power," the cat reminded her.

"Fine." She waved her hand. "It's done. I've hidden the Dragon Born away in my honeycomb. They can make their own world there."

"It's not the same."

"Tough. They will have to make do. And they should be happy they're not dead. Dragon Born," she growled, cradling her arm. "What a nuisance. No one should be able to break my magic."

"Stuffing them away inside the honeycomb won't allay your guilty conscience," the cat warned her.

"I'm a demon. I don't have a conscience." She picked up her cat, stroking its black fur." And you shouldn't either. It's not fitting for a feline of hell to go around caring about people."

The car purred against her chest. "What about Makani? Are you going to send him to the others?"

"No, I'm going to leave him in hell for a while. That will give him plenty of time to think about why he shouldn't attack me. I'll let the others stay in their safe bubble. I'm sure they will be grateful. Maybe they'll even come to worship me."

"Demons," Alex muttered.

"She did the right thing in the end," Sera said.

"So, you were here all along?" Makani asked Cordelia as Rane's castle faded away. "There weren't so many of us before."

"This is truly an enchanted place," she replied. "Here, we have peace. Here, we are immortal. And every child who is born here is Dragon Born."

Dragon Born magic was a truly rare magic, touching only one mage in thousands. No one truly understood how it worked. Except, apparently, Rane. And now she was dead.

"This is amazing," Sera said. "All our lives, Alex and I thought we were alone. But you've been here all along."

"You are welcome to stay," Cordelia said. "But only the Dragon Born among you."

"Why only Dragon Born?" Alex asked.

"It is human nature to hate what you do not understand. Magic does not make you immune to that hate."

"They love us," Sera said.

Cordelia sighed sadly. "The spark of hate lives in each of them, just waiting to go off. When the Magic Council declared us abominations, I watched as my neighbors turned against me. So did my friends. And even my family. I will not allow that to happen here. I will not allow our sanctuary to be destroyed. They must leave."

"We were hoping that some of you might come with us," Sera said.

Cordelia's brows lifted. "Leave our heaven to burn in hell?"

"It's not hell," Naomi said. "Technically."

"A Spirit Warrior?" Cordelia gave her an assessing look. "Makani, she is a good match for you. You always did enjoy charging head-first into the jaws of hell. I guess that means you won't be joining us here."

"No." He took Naomi's hand. "It is not my world."

"But it *is* ours." Cordelia smiled at Sera. "I hope you understand why we can't leave it."

"We need you. We have so many questions," Alex told her.

"We will always be here for you. To teach you. Come whenever you like." She glanced at Riley. "He knows the way."

Cordelia turned, leading the Dragon Born back into the forest.

"We're staying," Arianna said, giving Sera's hand a squeeze.

Vivienne hugged Alex. "We had a wonderful adventure with you, and we'll always be grateful to you for reuniting us. But we need this. They can help make us whole again."

"We understand," Alex said. "And we'll miss you."

"Thank you for everything," Arianna said.

Then, linking hands, she and Vivienne followed the Dragon Born procession. Sera watched them all leave, happiness and sadness crashing inside of her. There were Dragon Born again in the world—just not in her world. But somehow, just knowing they were there, knowing she wasn't as alone as she'd believed, filled her with hope.

"Ready to go?" Riley asked.

"Yes," she replied, taking his hand. "Let's all go home."

17. A New Beginning

SERA STOOD IN front of the mirror at the Fairy Queen dress shop, trying on wedding veils. Alex and Lara were on either side of her, quick to offer their opinion—or to make snarky comments at her expense. One of the veils even had little Hello Kitty heads dangling from the bottom. As soon as Alex handed her that one, Sera was sure they were giving her things just to get a few laughs.

"I like it," Alex said, her shoulders quaking with suppressed laughter.

Sera glared at her. "Shouldn't you be picking out your bridesmaid dress?"

"Already done. We had that sorted *hours* ago. Some of us aren't as picky as you. Bridezilla," she added with a snort.

"Cute, Alex. Real cute. Now stop messing around, or I'll wear that Hello Kitty veil just to spite you."

"Oh, please do." A look of pure rapture lit up her face. "I will be enjoying those wedding pictures for years to come."

Sera glanced to the other side of the shop, where Kai and Logan stood in dutiful silence as Nelly tossed tuxedo jackets into the growing piles of clothing in their arms.

The tiny silver bells over the shop door jingled, and a woman in a large sunhat walked in. She tilted up her face, her mouth twisting into a sinful smile as she met Sera's eyes.

"Rane," Sera gasped.

Alex's jaw dropped. "What the hell are you doing here?"

"Blunt as always, Ms. Dering," the demon replied, her voice as smooth as whipped cream. She sounded pretty good for a dead woman. She looked good too. There wasn't a single wrinkle in her daisy-print sundress. "Nice to see you too."

"But you're...dead," Sera said. "We saw you die."

"Yes, well, it's not that easy to kill a demon, dearie. You forget that I infused Riley with my magic."

"So that's why you did it."

"Well, it wasn't the *only* reason. Riley had to bring you to your present. How did you like it, by the way? Unfortunately, I didn't have time to gift wrap all those little mages."

A perplexed crinkle formed between Alex's eyes. "You are really bizarre."

"Thanks for noticing," the demon replied with a courtly curtsy.

Riley stepped out of the changing area. "Something is happening to me..." His voice trailed off when he saw Rane. "You're dead. You had to die to kill Merlin."

"Not dead anymore," she said brightly. "That's the power of magic. There's always a little loophole. And you are my loophole." She tapped her finger against his chest. "Thanks for holding onto my magic, by the way."

His shoulders slouched. "You're taking it all back."

"Of course I am. I need it, you know."

Riley's mouth thinned into a hard line. He looked so lost, so young.

Rane watched him with interest. "I never took you for the power-hungry sort." Her eyes flickered to Lara. "Oh, I see, You need to keep up with the dragon."

"What I need is control over my magic. Having your power allowed me to keep it in check."

"Oh, did you think I was just going to let you loose on the world with all that magic? No, dearie, you're going to train with me until you're in control. I couldn't have you destroying this lovely place." She smoothed out the wrinkles in her dress.

"How long will that take?"

"Years." She wiggled her finger at him. "Don't give me that look, young man. Mastering this kind of magic takes hard work."

"I'm not upset. I'm relieved. Hard work I can do."

She cackled with glee. "I'm going to redefine your idea of hard work. And I can be very motivating. If you fail to control your power, I'll lock you up in my honeycomb."

Alex stepped forward.

"Hold your dragons there, girl. You know I'm right. Just look at what happened with Merlin. I will not unleash another out-of-control shadow mage on the world. It's a bitch to clean up after their messes." Rane clapped her manicured hands together. "Now, for more happy news. As if my resurrection weren't fantastic enough."

Alex rolled her eyes.

"I've brought you a present, dearies."

Rane waved her hand. The door opened, and Blackbrooke walked into the shop. Ok, maybe not walked. He was bound in shadow magic. It nudged and poked and pulled at his body, moving him as though he were nothing but a puppet.

"I did manage to gift wrap this present," Rane said with delight.

"Get your foul magic off of me, demon. I told you I was coming."

Rane let out a dainty little yawn behind her hand. "You weren't moving fast enough."

Kai stepped up behind Sera, wrapping his arm around her waist. "What is he doing here?"

"Probably came to deliver his declaration of war," Alex muttered.

"No, he's too much of a coward to do that in person," said Sera.

"Oh, I think you will be pleasantly surprised," Rane told them. "Blackbrooke and I had a little chat. I showed him a few choice scenes of where this world is headed if he continues with his hate campaign. Some of those possible futures end quite tragically in his death." She tittered. "I also promised to torture him when he ended up in hell. He *really* appreciated that one."

Blackbrooke growled at her.

"Tell them what you told me," Rane said with a sunshine smile.

"I will not allow the world to fall into chaos." Blackbrooke looked at Kai. "I wish to discuss how we can prevent that from happening."

"You want to work with me?" Kai had his professional face on.

"Working with you is preferable to the alternative."

"You will work with Sera too?"

Blackbrooke looked like he'd just bitten down on a lemon. "If need be."

Alex smirked at him. "So it seems you were wrong about us Dragon Born. We're not the problem. We're the solution."

"No, I still don't like you," Blackbrooke snapped. "But our world is headed for civil war, just like the Shadow World."

Anyone who had been on earth when Merlin's spell broke should have forgotten all about the Shadow World. It seemed Rane had jogged his memories. That demon sure was helping them a lot. Sera wasn't sure how she felt about that.

◈ ◇ ◈ ◇ ◈

"Thus begins the shaky alliance," Alex commented later in the changing room as she helped Sera into her wedding dress.

"Blackbrooke. Wow." Sera sucked in a deep breath—and it wasn't just because the dress's corset was crushing her ribs. "If you'd told me a week ago that he would be joining forces with us, I'd never have believed it."

"A lot has changed these past few days," said Alex. "Biggest of all, there are Dragon Born in the world. Thousands of Dragon Born, Sera." Alex could hardly contain her excitement. She was bouncing on her tiptoes. "There's so much we can learn from them."

"Maybe we can convince them to unite together with us, to start a new world where Dragon Born and the other supernaturals live in peace."

Someone knocked on the door.

Alex opened it a crack, peeking outside. "Don't worry. It's just Riley, not your groom-to-be." She opened the door just wide enough for Riley to squeeze inside the small room of mirrors.

"I'm not worried," Sera said.

"Lara will sick her dragons on you if you let Kai see the dress before the big day," Alex said with a melodramatic gasp.

Sera chuckled. "Lara is taking this very seriously." She patted Riley's arm. "So, when do the shadow magic lessons begin?"

"Tomorrow morning. Rane will be training me for two hours every day before work."

"But not before breakfast," Sera said. "Magic burns even more calories than running. Make sure you eat before you go play demon with Rane."

"Yes, mother."

"Careful, junior," Alex said, mussing up his hair. "Show some respect to your elders. Just like we taught you."

"Actually, you taught me to talk back."

"Oops."

"The dress looks good," Riley told Sera. "Kai will like it."

Sera waved her hand. "Go on. Shower me with compliments. I'm sure it will make me more amenable to whatever you're going to say next."

"How did you know?"

"You always fiddle with the bottom of your shirt when you want something from us," Alex told him. "Ever since you were a kid."

Riley pressed his hands to his sides. "I'd best watch out for that habit then."

Sera laughed. "Ok, spill it. What can we do for you?"

"You two are always helping people. I can't even count the number of times you've saved the world."

"Twenty-three," Alex said.

They gaped at her.

She winked at them. "Not that I'm keeping score."

"Well, I'd like to help you," Riley said. "Not just in the lab but in battle too. You've seen what I can do. Take me with you. Let me fight beside you."

"I think he's proven himself," Alex said.

Riley squeezed her hand, then turned his eyes on Sera. He looked worried, as though he were sure she'd protest like all the times before. She probably should have told him no. The word was right on the tip of her tongue, begging to be spoken. She'd always made it her mission in life to protect her little brother—but the thing was, he wasn't little anymore. Riley was all grown up, and he'd proven himself more than once, even before he'd gained shadow magic.

"Yes," Sera said. "We'd love to have you with us."

"As long as it's clear that I'm in charge," Alex said quickly.

A crisp, professional knock thumped over their laughter. Alex opened the door again.

"We couldn't help but overhear," Callum said.

"Because you had your ear pressed to the door," Tony added as the commandos entered the changing room.

"We are very pleased that Riley will be joining us in Kai's new squad of enforcers," Dal said.

"Kai's really forming his squad?" Sera asked.

"Yes, we just finished hammering out the details with Blackbrooke. The enforcers will be reporting to Kai," Tony told her.

"Kai let Blackbrooke have the desk job. They both decided that would be best for everyone," Callum said, lightning crackling across his eyes.

"And you're getting your pool," Sera said.

Dal flashed her a grin. "Yes. Thank you."

"Now we just have to convince Alex and Logan to join us," Sera said.

"That would be *epic*," replied Alex. "We have some messes to clean up back in Europe first. After that, I think I can convince Logan. It turns out he and Kai were bonding."

"Oh, really?"

"Well, kind of. This mission was good for them. Awful as things were at times, it was great to be all together again. But now I think the love birds need to be alone."

Alex shooed them all toward the door. Kai was

waiting on the other side. He cast a long, leisurely look down Sera before his eyes slid up to meet hers.

"I like the dress," he said as the others hurried out.

"I thought you would."

He stepped into the room, closing the door behind him. Sera looked up at him. The room felt smaller now than it had when Alex, Riley, and the commandos had been inside. That was Kai. His presence filled up any space, no matter how large.

"I heard you're getting your supernatural enforcer squad," she said.

"Yes, Blackbrooke has convinced his allies that peace with the Dragon Born is the best course of action."

"I guess they figured if the biggest cheerleader of burning the Dragon Born has changed his stance, then maybe there's a good reason."

"Yes. They all know we supernaturals have other things to worry about right now. Humans are turning against us. If we don't make peace with them, this world could end up like Merlin's game world, where we are *all* hunted and hated."

"And if the supernaturals don't make peace with one another, it will tear the world apart like in the Shadow World."

Kai nodded. "Merlin's worlds showed us many horrible possibilities. I can only hope that together, united, we can prevent any of that from happening here. For now at least, the civil war has been averted. We can get married without worrying about people like Blackbrooke crashing the wedding to kill us. This is the beginning of something new. Something great.

Dragon Born and other supernaturals will work together on my squad."

She smiled. "It will be awesome."

"Just wait until you see your uniforms."

"Is mine red?"

His expression hardened. "That color attracts monsters. You don't need any help in that department, sweetheart. You attract them all too well on your own."

"You know, red isn't only good for attracting monsters," she said, tracing her hand up the slit in her skirt. "I hear it's good for attracting dragons too."

Kai's eyes followed her hand. "You are trouble," he said in a silky voice.

Sera draped her arms over his shoulders. "You knew that when you asked me to marry you."

"I knew it the moment I met you," he whispered against her lips.

"And? Any regrets?"

"No, regrets are for fools who can only look back. I prefer to look forward."

"And what do you see?"

He stroked his hand down her face. "You. I see you."

Author's Note

If you want to be notified when I have a new release, head on over to my website to sign up for my mailing list at http://www.ellasummers.com/newsletter. Your e-mail address will never be shared, and you can unsubscribe at any time.

If you enjoyed *Shadow World*, I'd really appreciate if you could spread the word. One of the best ways of doing that is by leaving a review wherever you purchased this book. Thank you for your invaluable support!

Did you know that Sera has another series? You can learn about *Dragon Born Serafina* and the other books in the *Dragon Born* world by visiting http://www.ellasummers.com/dragon-born.

About the Author

Ella Summers has been writing stories for as long as she could read; she's been coming up with tall tales even longer than that. One of her early year masterpieces was a story about a pigtailed princess and her dragon sidekick. Nowadays, she still writes fantasy. She likes books with lots of action, adventure, and romance. When she is not busy writing or spending time with her two young children, she makes the world safe by fighting robots.

Ella is the international bestselling author of the paranormal and fantasy series *Legion of Angels*, *Dragon Born*, and *Sorcery and Science*.

www.ellasummers.com

Made in the USA
Middletown, DE
02 July 2017